CHALKTOWN

Also by Melinda Haynes

Mother of Pearl

CHALKTOWN

MELINDA HAYNES

A NOVEL

An Imprint of Hyperion
NEW YORK

Chalktown is a work of fiction. Names, characters, places, and incidents are either products of the author's imagination, or are used fictitiously. Any resemblance to actual events or locales or persons, living or dead, is entirely coincidental.

Library of Congress Cataloging-in-Publication Data

Haynes, Melinda.
    Chalktown : a novel / Melinda Haynes.—1st ed.
      p. cm
    ISBN: 0-7868-6656-X
    1. Teenage boys—Fiction. 2. Mentally handicapped children—Fiction. 3. Sharecroppers—Fiction. 4. Fatherless families—Fiction. 5. George County (Miss.)—Fiction. I. Title.
  PS3558.A862 C48 2001
  813'.54—dc21   00-063217

FIRST EDITION

10 9 8 7 6 5 4 3 2 1

For daughters Kristin, Spring, and Shiloh, each a sweet mystery,
and in memory of my grandfather, Opie Braswell, who painted a river on a
living room wall.

I fled Him, down the nights and down the days;
I fled Him, down the arches of the years;
I fled Him, down the labyrinthine ways
Of my own mind; and in the mist of tears
I hid from Him...

—FRANCIS THOMPSON, *The Hound of Heaven*

CHALKTOWN

BOOK ONE

1961

Ask any man what the only good thing about George County is and he will likely tell you this: the only good thing about George County Mississippi is that it's so full of flat nothingness that nobody, not even Jesus, can sneak up on a body.

CHAPTER
1

By the old pump shed, near where the holy yokes leaned, the late winter grass was worn down as old brown velvet. Slick and near napless, the path seemed straight and narrow as any good preacher might preach, for behind the trail sat his mother's house, spread out and pieced together, misshapen as sin. If ever there was a clear picture of salvation in Hezekiah Sheehand's mind, the worn-down strip of dirt stood to paint it. His brother strapped to his back, he reached around and patted the five-year-old's leg and wished Yellababy could smell the warmish winter air and appreciate it, or even notice the odor of goose shit muddying up the ground and make a face at that, but smells were beyond Yellababy's realm of understanding, as were most things the rest of the God-fearing world took for granted. Hezekiah knew this and kept on walking, his eyes down to the brown velvet path of salvation the whole while.

Behind him, the house squatted low beside a cherty road that wound through George County, Mississippi. Hot as hell in the summertime, with a wet steamy heat that soaked the skin and soured the clothes, the place seemed a final haven for mosquitoes and candle moths and cicadas 'til late at night, when finally—around ten or eleven o'clock—even the bugs tired out. Winters were better. Damp, but nicer. No bugs then. Just hoarfrost that crunched underfoot and icicles that pointed down to the porch where the guts of sewing machines and boxes of carburetors were stacked next to dead car batteries and bent buckets and glass-globed lanterns empty of oil.

Inside the house his mother was up and stirring, tagging clothes for resale, for the winter season was almost over and even dirt-road women were growing anxious for spring. Earlier, while still undecided about whether or not to go for a walk, Hezekiah had shared the doorway with her, their hip bones touching at uneasy points of contact. Wind had brushed through the opening and there'd been a flutter and out the corner of his eye he'd seen a tag pinned to the neck of the dress she was wearing. Twenty-five cents, he read. He'd decided he would go then, realizing she was modeling her goods and that as soon as he stepped off the porch, she'd find herself digging through the cardboard boxes of shoes in search of a pair that came close to matching the faded shade of the dress, and still this wouldn't suit her.

"The bus has come and gone," she had said to him while they stood inside the doorway, her arms crossing her stomach, his arms matching hers. Hezekiah had grown taller through the winter months, equaled out in portions of healthy weight and broader shoulders and larger hands and feet. The playing field was level now, he stood nose to nose with her, and knew it.

"And I werent on it," he had answered, matter-of-factly. Neither had his sister, Arena, but this had not been mentioned.

He glanced to the side, in avoidance of those blue eyes trying to stare a hole through him, and saw the corner table housing religious statues. Marys and Josephs and one or two Queen Elizabeths were huddled there, price tags fastened around their plaster necks with pale rubber bands. Hezekiah saw the craggy pink plaster face of Saint Joseph, one eye cast lower than the other as if the human hand painting it had slipped or misjudged the application, or, perhaps, grown lazy. That solemn orb seemed dead as a button, waylaid by false expectations and disappointments, more than a little sad, and Hezekiah could not help wondering why folks with religion always looked so bitter when all they had to put up with was thievery of the Sunday School money, or possibly the devil.

"Where you think you're goin to?" his mother had said, quietly. Her bare feet planted on the damp wooden floor.

"Maybe Chalktown, I was thinkin," he had answered, hoping for an instant that Virgin Mary might be murmuring a prayer from a point he couldn't see.

"No sir, you aint," she said.

"It's spring almost and I don't see why not."

"Because of school's why not. I thought Mr. Calhoun told you about that county car out here lookin for you."

He had. But Hezekiah had been marking his days of truancy with a red crayon he kept hid underneath his bed. Upon waking, he'd counted them up and done the math and come to the belief that he had three—or was it two?—days left. While he stood in the doorway and felt the uncommon warmish air, he drew inside his mind a map of George County. The small towns inside that map: Lucedale, Agricola, and Basin and the river that ran within spitting distance of all of them: the Pascagoula. The roads that ran alongside, and the houses situated on those roads. All the people inside those houses. The map became bigger and bigger inside its grid. And once it stretched beyond his mental margins he tried to imagine somebody at the county seat suddenly taking notice of one dirt-road boy skipping school, making a game of the system, but he couldn't. It would be like looking for one fly amid thousands buzzing the fat carcass of a cow.

"George County aint got the money to waste lookin for me," he said.

"Well," she said. "I think you're wrong there. The man in that car yesterday werent out here shoppin. He was pretendin was all. Studied that holy yoke for a minute." She pointed to THE EYES OF THE LORD ARE IN EVERY PLACE, BEHOLDING THE EVIL AND THE GOOD. POVERBS 15:3. His father, Fairy, had left the r out of *Proverbs*, and no one had bothered to repaint it. The ox yoke leaned against the pump house, marked down by fifty percent. "He stayed for most of an hour and never parted with a dime."

"I'm goin anyhow," Hezekiah had said, looking at her, noticing the slack skin around her mouth and the brittle sheen that lit across her forehead and the almost transparent covering of skin at her temples. Blue veins traced upward into her blond hair, where one shank had worked loose from its pin and settled over her ear. He felt a momentary pity for her that shifted something inside his lower gut. She was a formidable woman who was unraveling at her seams and it was this thing that made him want to walk away and never look back. There had been a sound then, a low troubled moan, and he had glanced down to his brother, stretched out on the floor atop his blanket. "I think I'll take him, too," he said.

"Suit your own self, then. I think you're askin for it, though. And I aint one to grieve when a person gits what they got comin."

Susan-Blair had walked away from the doorway then, and the dress tag quit its fluttering and Hezekiah went about the business of getting ready.

The kitchen was an unsightly mess. Stacks of dishes, all different makes and models, filled the counter space. Paper plates wearing leftover food, stacked by the sink. Three metal coffeepots set to the stove. She'd dirty one and go on to the next, he figured. What with her present occupation, there seemed no likely end to the supply, either. The milk had gone over so he filled a fruit jar with water, another with apple juice, and shoved four cans of Vienna sausage in the front pocket of the old haversack. Leg holes had been cut into the drab olive green and once his brother had been fitted into it, he would be carried out of the place. High time, too. Hez had gone to his back room and fetched up three clean diapers, stood looking at them for a long moment before picking up two more. No way a shitty bottom would set a curfew to his day.

On his way to the front room, he had stooped and turned off the gas heater in the hall and then gone to the kitchen stove and checked the registers. As much as he hated them, he'd not wish her, or his sister, to be a victim of leaking propane. He glanced around. Unless a messy house could suddenly acquire the ability to turn lethal, no one was likely to die before he made it back home that evening. Hezekiah left the room.

Yellababy had seemed tuned to some advent of change, for he stiffened once and pulled his arms to his chest and rolled his eyes and tried to speak. It was wasted effort and Hezekiah knew it, but he was stopped in his tracks by the color of his brother's eyes: the clearest blue he'd ever seen. And large and thickly lashed in hair so white they seemed dusted with gold. He unfolded the haversack and spread it on the floor and folded a blanket and set it to the seat of it. Through the maze of dresses and past the table full of somebody's cracked china and the naked dolls Hezekiah used to think looked like the real thing, until he saw the real thing and realized the dolls, even busted up, looked better, he saw his mother standing inside the wall of clothes. He bent and with careful hands worked his brother's body into the pouch, seeing the shafts of his mother's legs, stubborn and fixed inside a sea of handed-down dresses suspended from the ceiling. *I guess even as a baby I seen her legs before I seen her face*, he thought and then he whispered into his brother's ear in a quiet and determined voice, "And now here you are bound to do the same . . ."

The path led to his nearest neighbor's house, a place smaller, but ordered and clean, heaven-like, even though a colored lived there. A drift of vapor lifted out the stovepipe in the man's tar-paper roof and Hezekiah smelled bacon and biscuits and coffee and eggs, a potent blend that made his mouth water. He had not figured breakfast into the beginning of his day, but wished that he had.

The Calhoun place had rambly roses winding around the front fence posts and while no cows grazed beyond the wire, the colored man cultivated the acreage as though God Almighty might be planning on dropping two or three of them down from heaven at any given moment. Field hay had been mown and cubed and bound in silvery twine. Four bales were stacked near a gate, graying in increments that brought to mind things old and of little use, yet held on to for reasons sentimental. A ladle was there, as well as a tin bucket, and Hezekiah knew the man had made himself a recliner of the hay and had sat there during the day previous, staring at the road.

The geese were outside honking in the sunshine. Hezekiah watched as their long necks dug in under their wings and chucked up feathers to shapes resembling vertical white spears. When they raised their heads their feathers smoothed down slick as ice while their webbed feet steadied them in the mud next to Marion Calhoun's truck. Warm air rushed across Hezekiah's face again and he judged the day to be glorious and warm, and the geese seemed in agreement, for in one unified movement, like dancers on a stage, their necks accordioned out and they broke into a brilliant honking chorus.

"Well, there you go. Anybody with half a brain knows geese don't stir when there's to be a freeze."

His brother bucked behind him, afraid, and Hezekiah reached around and soothed him with one large hand to his leg and listened to Yellababy's *blaablaablaa* and felt his brother's damp hair along the backside of his shirt.

"It's okay. Shush now. It's just them geese," he said. Thinking the whole while: I guess folks with more brain power than his would rightfully be afraid of all that damn noise.

The geese had begun to bother Hezekiah, too, the way they appeared as wild as renegade dogs, and just as mean. The way they took pleasure in cornering snakes, or mice, or anything smaller and weaker, to a point of no extrication and making a party of bringing on death. Two of them were roosting on a greasy tire shaft underneath his neighbor's truck, their dirty heads still as statues, their black eyes glittery and narrow and in perverse contrast to the sky, which had turned up a notch to full-blown light. Bright blue slashed through the trees and across the yard pointing pearly streams of light in the direction of his colored neighbor. There's the way, Hez. Ignore them geese and head for it, the light seemed to be saying.

Walking the path burdened, but not overly so, he felt his brother settle behind him, lulled by the rhythm of movement. Yellababy's back was to Hezekiah's. What's he looking at, I wonder—the mud? the low pond? the path winding behind us now? Any of those things will do. Just as long as he aint looking at the house where we come from where Ma's eyes are peering out through curtains that aint even hers. That used to belong to somebody else.

Hezekiah Sheehand could see his nearest neighbor leaning on the gray-white fence post, his dark brown face still as a rusted-over weather vane, his arm stretched out along the top of the wire they'd both worked hard to stretch.

His mother said poor judgment had froze the nigger up, put a stop to his dreaming, and it was just as well, but Hezekiah held his heart against that reasoning. The colored man was simply a colored man, stalled and waiting, as most were inside the year 1961. And in Hezekiah's opinion this was cause enough to be constrained and careful and quiet as a mouse.

*   *   *

Now Marion Calhoun knew this for a fact: the Sheehand place was pure white trash and looked it. A shameful blight for all of Agricola, Mississippi, had not Agricola with its wandering dirt roads and switchbacks not been full of exact replicas that poxed the county. Looking across, seeing those mean geese and the leaning holy yokes and the upside-down bicycles and the towers of tires, was not the half of it, either. The house itself, if one could even call it a house, was an abomination to the senses. Made up of the strewn guts of other busted-up houses, it sat in a slut-like pose, multi-colored in hues no painter would be likely to claim. His place was no more than a hundred yards away, settled on a spot of land surrounded by a beautiful field full of easy-waving Jap grass. A field with its shoes off, Marion liked to believe. A field just sitting there minding its own business. He looked across and blinked and searched out the line of trees in the distance where the river ran. They were covered in morning mist and shrouded in gray. He looked to the east and then the west for a plume of dust that signaled travelers coming his way from the corner store, and didn't see any. All he could see was the Sheehand place sprawling beside him like a fast-eating cancer.

Now, Marion Calhoun knew this as well: he had a gift of acting stupid while actually being world-class smart. The weight of his knowing this thing chafed him, and stuck in his craw sharp as a fish bone, seeing how the world was just plain full of stupid people who didn't, or couldn't, know the difference. So when Hez wandered across a yard that used to be Marion's and yelled out, "How you doin, you sad ole man!" he just balled up his hands inside his pockets and let him be, thinking, Now this here Hezekiah has the gift of acting stupid as well as being stupid and me knowin this thing is enough to let the insult ride.

A dark man, with age on him, Marion peered across brown-eyed and quiet, thinking about things, his shoulders humped inside his faded blue shirt, his hands twitching once against a pocket of pennies. He finally looked at Hezekiah, who was nearing the halfway point between the two properties.

Hezekiah walked the path taller these days, but in much the same way he'd done since he was a three-year-old, just out of diapers. He had toddled then, dirty and snot-nosed. Sixteen years old now, Hez swaggered beneath a burden these days, cleaner around the face and ears, but weighed down by the cripple. Marion watched him reach around and pat his brother's leg while he walked and the way the boy's hand stayed there even after the child had stilled. The tenderness was not lost on him, and Marion wondered over it.

He saw the bruise to the little brother's arm, but didn't wonder too much over that one. Marion studied the two boys for a long minute before bending his head to spit.

"Christsakes, Mayurn," Hezekiah said. "Susan-Blair's got her busy eyes on me. And I tell you what." He pointed his finger for emphasis. "There's not a day goes by that I aint more and more convinced I'm not born to those two. If I could ever find the durn birth certificate, I bet I could prove it, too." Hez tugged at chest straps with bulging upper arms and hands that looked too rough and conscious of humanity to not be middle-aged.

"I see you aint learned to listen worth a lick."

"I listened." Hezekiah grinned.

"In one ear and out the other."

"I listened, though."

"You gonna get caught goin truant and then what? What you planning on doin once they pick up your scrawny ass and take you to county lockup? I bet you aint thought that far down the row yet, neither."

"True. I aint." Hez smiled and his blue eyes crinkled, happy and worry-free.

"How's Yellababy?" Marion reached around and played with stiff fingers that seemed oblivious to touch. The bruise to his arm was ugly yellow. The color of a vegetable gone bad.

"Same as yesterday and the day before that and last year and the year before that." Hez turned around so the man could judge for himself and then at the silence, turned back around again. The five-year-old made strangled, gurgly sounds. Hiccupped once.

"How'd he bruise up?"

"Ma says he rolled into the anvil." Hezekiah's eyes were sweetwideblue and trusting. "I swear to Jesus, Mayurn. There are times if I could get my hands on that durn Billy Reuben I would surely clean his clock."

"You would, would you?" Marion realizing the boy's heart was good as gold, but upstairs he was barely brighter than white flour.

"You bet your black ass, I would."

They both glanced upward to the sky, Hezekiah judging the sky to be inordinately blue for February. A few soft luminous clouds done up in pink and white swirled near the horizon.

"Looks like one a them big-ass suckers you buy once a year at the fair, and then don't dare eat because the durn thing's so pretty," he said.

"You gonna end up a hunchback for sure toting him round like that. He's full-blown five now, and too heavy."

Hez shrugged. "You don't seem to mind me luggin your load of feed into the barn ever time you come back from Lucedale. You don't worry much then."

Marion spit across the fence, the boy's logic reasonable.

"So I guess worryin depends on what you need doin at the time. Or maybe what you don't need doin. Folks tend to worry when they don't need you to be their own personal nigger-boy, but don't give a rat's ass about it when they need somebody to do their liftin." Hez studied the sky again and Marion's eyes followed to keep from looking at what was riding on Hezekiah Sheehand's back.

"That sounds true enough to make a holy yoke of." Marion's voice was low and thoughtful. "There aint been a new one painted in a while." He looked over at the one leaning against Susan-Blair's porch: HE THAT PAS-SETH BY AND MEDDLETH WITH STRIFE NOT HIS OWN IS LIKE A MAN WHO TAKES A DOG UP BY THE EARS. PROVERBS 26:17.

"Holy yokes is Ma's business, Mayurn. Not mine." Hez was looking up again. "I figure by the drift of the clouds and the color of blue that it ought to be good walkin. No rain in sight."

"Was a red sky this morning," Marion said, cutting himself a fresh chaw, his pocket knife flashing in the sun like a silvered fish.

"More pink than red, I'd say. Five miles to Chalktown. Then five miles back. Shapes up proper. Easy enough, even with my brother." Hezekiah shifted the haversack higher on his back.

Marion saw the lump that was Yellababy and then looked away, uneasy. There was a crippled pecan tree out in the front of his yard and he stared at it thinking, Seems like everthing within four hundred yards of me is afflicted somehow.

The pecan tree got itself sheared by a storm ten years back, its lower arms were jagged now. No pecans for the past four years for want of a good liming. But for occasional goose shit there'd been no attempt at fertilizing. That tree out there needs attention, near about as bad as Hezekiah, he figured.

Marion looked at those blue eyes again, thinking, This one's harnessed with a burden not of his makin. And it don't seem right. Not with sixteen as fresh as it is, and boys runnin round gettin some all up and down the river. And this one here with his yellow hair and big arms and fresh face not likely to anytime this decade.

"Chalktown's no good. You got no business goin there," Marion said.

"I'm goin anyhow."

"You ort leave them folks be. Go somewheres else."

"I made up my mind on it."

There was silence then, and the sound of field thrush and warbler drifted up from the thick border of the woods. Marion cleared his throat. "Seein how you aint learned to listen worth a lick, it'd be no trouble for me to sit the boy if you want to go on by yourself," he said. "I'd watch him good." Marion had suddenly remembered the gal near Basin who never wore underpants. Not even on Sunday. He supposed he could spread a blanket out in the sun, and place the five-year-old there while he trimmed up the old pecan and laid down a lime drip. "I'd make sure she stayed clear of him . . ." He gave one furtive look at the little boy's yellowing bruise.

Just like an open door, it was there between them. Marion's knowing and Hezekiah's knowing that he knew, and then the door shut again. Hez, his face placid and unconcerned, looked at the man. "Yellababy aint ever seen much of anything other than the lower half of life, and I feel that's a shame, don't you?"

"If that's what you think."

"Yep, that's what I think."

"Caint say I believe he'll remember much of what he sees, though." Unless maybe he were to see that gal who don't wear her underpants. I reckon that female would make a blind man swear to sight, quick as Bartemaeous.

Yellababy *blablabla*ed, singsong and idiot-like, while a goose waddled over and stood by the pump shed. In Marion Calhoun's opinion it was too still for a goose, even a good one.

"He knows more'n we think, I'd just bet." Hez hitched up the straps of his brother's harness again.

Marion spit brown tobacco juice over the fence and watched it disappear into the baked dirt path.

"Anyhow, I don't worry so much when he's with me."

"That's a way to look at it, I reckon," Marion said.

"Yessir, it is. The only way I got right now."

His arm stretched along the top of the fence, the man stood still as a tree while Hezekiah walked toward the graveled road. Yellababy's face peered out from his pack, those stiffened-up arms swinging like somebody's broken puppet.

Four geese waddled with outstretched necks to the road, and then stopped as though a hand were there, pinning them back, penning them in. Marion Calhoun watched the two Sheehand boys until they were two indistinguishable specks shrinking on the horizon. Looking up and down the long stretch of dirt road, those sweet mornings when it was just the birds and the quiet wind and Marion Calhoun seemed as far away as the Carolina mountains.

"Well, I guess it's true what folks say." Marion watched the geese stranded near the road, their feet glued to the earth. "Nobody ever really leaves this place. They just fool themselves into thinkin they do."

CHAPTER 2

Sixteen years back, inside a sweet season of magnolia blooms and clover bees, Marion Calhoun had harbored a thought on leaving. Folks would not have believed it, not even if they'd heard the words from the man himself, but it was true that he went so far as to pack his trunk and cut off the propane at the tank. He even took down a back section of good fence to carry along with the two of them. He was thinking hogs and good cattle and that things were looking up and the world was his for the asking. He let these thoughts pull him ahead by the nose, he had been that keen on leaving. He was forty-eight years old now with barely five acres left of his original twenty-five, but a paid-for tractor that ran good as gold, and the thought of that near departure seemed a vague dream put away in his pocket.

The geese were standing by the road, watching for something, anything. Dust blew up and powdered their necks in red while their bodies shimmered in the light.

"She's somewhere else, though, aint she? Somewhere else, other than here. Only sold one thing of herself to get there, too."

He had spoken the words out loud without realizing it and was embarrassed by them and looked around, wondering if Susan-Blair had heard.

Even after his personal business got whispered up and down the road, clean up to Lucedale, folks still had not believed it. He had the ring in a drawer, tucked down inside an old sock; shut away from sight. But the one who'd sold him the ring (hesitantly, and with great skepticism) had made inquiries and found out the truth of it: how she'd left with somebody else. A gospel singer schooled in Chicago. From the stockyard to the feed store, the news traveled. And still folks could not believe it. Marion would not have believed it himself, except for the pain of it. People said each to the other: "Him? Old Marion Calhoun? That land-holdin nigger sold the best of his acreage to the Sheehands? Why, I don't believe a word of it. Not in a million years!" "Yeah, he's the one. Got hisself a hardon for that half-Negro gal who run the singing school down in Hurley. That gal the color of creamed-up coffee." These were the kind comments.

Marion walked stiff as starched wood toward his barn. All he was thinking was that if he had a horse, he would whip it. Or if he had a dog, he would kick it hard.

Going down another baked path, he pulled open the heavy door to his barn and saw yellow first off, and it soothed him. The warm color, the dust motes drifting through the light from the loft, made a sanctuary of hay bales and rough lumber and old farm equipment growing webs in the corners. There in the center, at the altar of it all, sat his tractor. Pulling up an overturned bucket so he could watch the yard of his nearest neighbor while he worked, he saw out the broad barn door a blue so high it hurt. Every single thing outside its hue, even the evergreens along the far plats of bor-derland, seemed stunned by the sky, reduced and reconfigured to shades of shimmery beige. The only incongruity to this painting of peace was his neighbor's messed-up yard, full of salvaged relics hoarded since the folks moved in, one piece of trash at a time.

It lent a reasonableness to the way he tolerated the Sheehands' hatred of coloreds that not one single thing in all that overspilling yard was one-piece and working, while he sat next to a diligent tractor that had never given him a minute's worth of grief in close to fifteen years.

"They aint even got a truck. And they for sure aint got a tractor. And even if they did have one, they'd not know what to do with it."

He was working at the tractor's plugs, lulled by the periodic clang of wind on sheet metal next door, and missed the plume of dust that began along the western dirt road and then turned north, Calhoun's way, once the corner store was made. The county car was up near his neighbor's leaning mailbox before Marion knew it, and in a habit born in the year of Hezekiah, he looked around for the boy in an effort to warn. "Christ, he aint even here," he said.

But the girl was. The girl, Arena Sheehand.

Marion watched the car ease up slowly, until it was hiding behind a large azalea that had grown in overspilling plumes beyond the ridge of the yard. The Plymouth sat there in the swirling dust, scattering the geese from their stationary stance near the road while Arena Sheehand disembarked, smoothing down a skirt and tucking in a blouse and running a hand over her shiny blond hair. The man, dressed in a way that was not country, hopped out and ran around the car, appearing anxious to catch her before she broke the cover of the azalea. Putting a hand to her elbow, he looked around in all directions.

"You promised," Marion heard Arena say. She jerked her elbow free. Then, "The hell you lookin at? There aint nobody over there but a nigger."

Marion snorted and leaned back against a big ridged tire shaking his head, glad for Mr. Sheehand's sake the man had found peace away from his kinfolks, but wishing, in spite of it, that he were around to see his eighteen-year-old daughter climb out of something she didn't have no business being in in the first place, pulling down a skirt that didn't have no business being up, as well.

The man bent and said something low to her ear and put his hands on her shoulders, smoothing the blond hair that fell down her back.

Arena looked in Marion's direction once and the black man pulled his legs to himself, wondering if she'd seen him sitting in the shadow. He stuck them out again, ashamed that he was still, for the biggest part, a coward.

Moving away from the man, who was wearing sunglasses of the type the county sheriffs wore, Arena slipped sideways, climbed up over the ditch and sauntered toward her house. Susan-Blair met her halfway, near the center of the yard, grabbing her shoulders and shaking her violently before the girl slipped free and ran around the side, toward the back. In the middle of all this activity Marion watched the man move backward to his car, his hands palm upward toward the woman as though trying to appease a belly-to-ground dog. Failing at nonchalance, he turned and ran fast for the car.

Throwing gravel and dust all the way to the milk cans, the car left, fantailing only once because Susan-Blair Sheehand had picked up a rock and thrown it hard. Marion watched it bounce off the rear of the car while the woman stood breathing hard from the spot where the geese had paced. When she finally went inside, she threw open the front door to the house so hard a pot fell off the ledge.

Marion squat-walked his bucket into deeper shadows where he could listen to the noise coming out the house while he held an old grease rag and worked the plugs. Inside their fight, the female voices rose and fell, mimicking sounds similar to breaking glass. Old leather harnesses touched his shoulder, drooped down limp and weathered, their leather fingers placed in resting restraint. Sad and uneasy for a reason he couldn't fathom, Marion wished he had never opened the door to the barn in the first place, or turned over the bucket to sit, or later, slid that very bucket into a purple shadow in an effort at eavesdropping. I aint got no business listenin to this. No business atall. Now, if I were to hear a gunshot, I guess I'd have a reason, 'cause then there might be a need to git up and do something. But they aint no guns over there I know of according to Hez, who had looked for one a while back. And even if there were guns over there at some time previous, Fairy's gone and took 'em by now. Standing suddenly, hating the whole business, Marion moved to shut the barn door just as Arena came flying out the back of her house, catching him staring like a damned pointed setter. Sneering and ugly, she gave him the dirty finger before running off down the road.

Next-door's sudden storm was just as suddenly over. All noise gone; turned off neatly as a radio, swallowed up by the whitesound of birds and sheets flapping on the line. They'd been left there since the day before yesterday. The dew-heavy bottoms waved up slow, then seemed to shudder with a burdened snap. Susan-Blair Sheehand's threadbare sheets gone dirty, same as usual.

With his hand to the barn door, he reasoned the quiet to be too quiet and stood there wondering what to make of it. Nobody would know a thing, judging by the yard's normal look, those dirty sheets waving and all. Nobody would ever guess a thing. Same as everybody in Agricola went on about their business last year when that couple got et up in the gravel pit. Folks just went about their fishing at the quarry same as before, and those two trapped in their truck but fifty feet away. J. P. McCreel helping folks load their gravel same as always, maybe saying one or two words to the man who was buying that gravel while wondering quiet-like where that son a his had got off to. Marion leaned against the door frame thinking, I helped dig that couple out, too. Tied a rag round my face and worked that shovel. Dug them out like so much rotted cordwood, but I'd not do it again. I'd surely not do it again.

The girl was walking so fast she seemed halfway to wherever it was she was heading. Traveling at such a brazen pace, Marion himself would be hard-pressed to catch her. He watched Arena's legs work up and down like pearl pistons in some prize motor; they caught the light and gleamed and he looked away, tired. The female heart is not a heart at all, but something else, he reasoned. Putting the grease rag down and pulling the barn door shut on his most reliable asset, Marion Calhoun walked the path to his house, hands deep in his pockets while he listened to Susan-Blair Sheehand's sheets groaning in the wind.

CHAPTER 3

She had wondered what to wear when asking a man for a favor and
then remembered the one she was seeking out was a colored man and
fashion didn't matter. Susan-Blair knocked on his door a few minutes later,
a sweater thrown over her wrinkled dress, stained tennis shoes on her feet.
Her hand hit on the wood of the colored man's door and she reckoned it to
be around eleven o'clock in the morning, a bare hour before noon. Hezekiah
had left, her younger son strapped to his back, around nine and Arena had
stomped off shortly after. Susan-Blair had spent the rest of the morning
putting price tags to a stack of old work shirts and marking down the statues
on her religious artifact table.

Hesitant, and more than a little phobic, she looked overhead for spider-
webs or a wasp nest and didn't see any. She straightened slightly and
knocked one more time, scratching an itchy place on the shin of her left leg
with the slippered heel of her right foot.

Marion Calhoun opened the door a bare four inches, his fingers cautious to
the door frame, his face so dark there seemed nothing to the man but his eyes.

"Arena's run off," she said, looking away from him and to the field at the side of his house, noticing it was fenced in with rusted wire that sagged. She thought the stand of trees at its far perimeter so distant those large oaks seemed tiny as potted redbuds.

"Yessim."

His voice was deep. Susan-Blair always forgot this fact, the same way she always forgot that Fairy's was high and tenor and almost good enough for a barbershop quartet.

"Fairy's down fishing at the Leaf," she said while picking at lint balls on her sweater, looking up and down, everywhere but at his face. Susan-Blair judged the man's property as clean-swept as a hospital floor. What little there was to stack—buckets, pots, yellowing lumber—was organized neatly to the side of his house. She let out a low breath, thinking, There is no randomness to this colored man. Not one single thing outside its gate and this aint right.

Fairy was different. When they had crossed the Leaf River while hauling in the second portion of house, he had watched the ceramic toilet break loose and go tumbling off the truck and into the water. It was a random act the man took personally. A chance to test his skill as fisherman. She knew he'd been fishing for the thing for fifteen years now. Throwing out good rope weighted with heavy grappling hooks that never brought up more than one or two rotted logs. She also knew the whole Agricola community thought her husband a pure-d fool and undeserving of a peaceful existence and that more than a few honked at him when they went by in their trucks.

"Arena's run off," she said again.

"Yessim, I seen that."

"If you could go get Fairy in your truck, I'd be obliged." She felt him studying her with his tiny flickering eyes and before she could catch herself, she pulled her sweater over her breasts and stepped back to where the sunshine washed over the roof line, noticing that the man's mouth had tightened in a hard line for some strange reason.

He said, "Miz Sheehand, I . . ." and she could tell he wanted to say something else, but didn't. After a pause, he put his hands to his pockets and turned his face away from her and said, "I got work to do."

"Arena's run off."

He stepped out onto his porch, and she backed away automatically. She couldn't stop herself. "Fairy's at the bridge," she said. "Fishin, I think."

Marion Calhoun looked away and scratched at his head.

"Arena's run off," she said again.

"You got fifteen acres out back you aint been usin." Marion Calhoun nodded toward the back quarter.

"I aint sellin it back to you. I already told you that."

"I aint askin to buy it. All I'm askin is to work it. Put in some cotton. Now's the time to do it, too. Cut in the field before the rain comes." He crossed his arms over his chest and looked toward the road.

"I come over here askin for your help—"

"Work it my own self. Maybe give Hezekiah a reason to git up off his rear and busy. Split it with you seventy-thirty. Caint nobody git hurt over this. 'Specially you."

He stood in front of her, unimpeded by her nervousness, waiting, and she weighed it, clutching her sweater to her chest, evaluating her percentage. It would mean a sum of money with no effort from her. Just the signing away of something that sat there, day in and day out: a breedery for the rats.

"I'll go get the mister for you one way or the other," he said. "Just thought I'd ask about the land while you was out and about."

"You go get Fairy for me and you can work the land. Long as Hez helps you and watches out over what's comin to me." She stepped off the porch and looked back just once, hurrying along as if he were back there, sniffing after her.

"You aint gonna regret this!" he shouted, his voice sounding almost optimistic.

While Susan-Blair hurried to her house a goose fluttered upward to the low limb of a pecan tree and managed to balance there, its wings spread open and catching the wind. The image seemed as odd as a mule sitting upright behind the steering wheel of a car and Susan-Blair crossed herself against the evil eye and all oddities that harbor strangeness and perversion.

Marion Calhoun saw the goose perched to a low limb and it seemed an omen of sorts. A goodish one.

CHAPTER

4

Hezekiah was clear to Bexley before he realized it was Thursday, caught up as he was with thoughts on algebra and Teresa Beth Pierce and Banks County, Georgia, where his daddy was born. Of the three, Teresa Beth was the one thing worth pondering, sitting as she did in front of him in algebra class at the George County High School. What led him to think on her while he walked toward Chalktown was that the light coming across the fields to the west had shaped up similar to what he saw every clear day during second period. Second period being the designated time to sit, leaning over his inkwell while he sniffed hard at all that thick black hair, loose and shiny as Chinese silk.

Fairy had told him more than once that her folks were Eyetalians and to stay away because they all had the head lice, and if Mayurn Calhoun had told him this thing he might have hesitated more than a minute. But since the warning came from a fool born in Banks County, Georgia, who'd spent his youth plowing for niggers, Hez had kept on sniffing, thinking, Well, if she's got the bugs, she can sure share them with me 'cause this is the sweetest-smelling hair I ever had the opportunity to sniff. Teresa Beth had told Hezekiah she was from someplace in north Georgia and he was willing to believe her.

"Don't you wonder how come most folks stuck in the ass end of George County pine for the mountains of north Georgia?"

He had whispered this to the back of her head during an exam while he coiled her black hair around his finger. Making the whole business up, knowing full well that he, and most like him, were destinationless in their pining, but thinking to say he was pining for a place she'd come from might be a nice preamble into a proper conversation.

"I got no idea," she had whispered right back, pleased. "There aint a place further than it could be from the mountains of Georgia than this place is."

"That's the God's truth, girl." His nose was low to his inkwell. He continued: "My daddy was born at the end of a dirt road in Banks County and he said just bein born with Georgia dirt between his toes was enough to make a man rich." She leaned back into him, settled herself, offered up a little more of her hair.

Hezekiah plaited it between his large fingers, braiding a weave that was heavy and slippery. "Musta been true 'cause he always had a dollar or two in his pocket plowin as he did for the niggers for ten cents a hour. Him and the mule."

She was sitting there still as a scared colt. She could go either way, he reasoned. Either bolt or back straight into me, ready and willing.

He had leaned around and seen the teacher standing in good clothes up near the blackboard. There were chalk puzzles up there just waiting, and Hez thought the usefulness of knowing x plus y equaled something about as beneficial as knowing that his sister, Arena, by day's end, would be polishing up her shoes as well as her story and getting herself ready to head home to their mother. The reality of both equations worthless and something he didn't choose to think on.

"Daddy says he remembers one old black woman bein so impressed with his straight rows, she cooked him up a country-fried steak. He had to be back by dark, so she plowed the mule while he sat at her table and ate."

"Hezekiah, you got yourself a nice voice," Teresa Beth had said, and he had bent down and sniffed her hair and rubbed one cheek across a silky rope of black; then, hard as a fist inside a righteous dream, the ruler had come down on his shoulders and he'd been sent outside to the hall where he was told to stand, his nose to the wall, which suited him just fine, school being about as worthwhile an endeavor as church attendance.

While he walked on down the county road he remembered her hair and how it always smelled of beeswax, and it made him wonder if Teresa Beth robbed the hives, somehow, as part of her daily routine. And if that was the case, if the treatment was sticky or attracted ants or flies. He remembered her pink arms and the partial side of one pink cheek that he always saw and he wondered how so many of the county girls could be so sweet and delicious-looking and come from such obese, roller-haired women. He'd seen Teresa Beth's mother in the hardware store and judged her to be a bench-assed woman—meaning her broad rear end was too large to be contained in a standard-sized chair. He had been thinking on all these things instead of the particular day of the week while he walked down County Road 614 headed for Chalktown.

"Shit Yellababy, it's Thursday aint it?"

Yellababy was silent. Oblivious. Peaceful. Hez felt his brother's hiccups against his shoulders.

Thursdays were special for two reasons: it was the day of the week that Teresa Beth wore her pink dress with purple flowers and he got to sit behind her and feel its folds, and Thursday was also the day that Fairy met up with his first wife, Silva, and the two of them fucked down by the river. He had never had the good luck to catch his father doing it, always managing to come up when they were done. But he could tell by the way they sat close, their shoulders touching and their clothes too loose to be anything other than recently thrown on, that they had just been laying together, tangled as bones in the bushes.

"I bet I could a seen it too. Caught 'em this time."

He reached around and patted a leg. Felt the cold. Knew he needed to stop and free his brother from his harness so the blood could catch up from all that dangling. While he walked, scanning the roadside for a spot where they could rest, he wondered what Teresa Beth might be doing on this fine day. If she were at school. If her hair were freshly washed. Overhead a crow called out, nasal and ugly, a small black streak of mean in the morning sky and Hezekiah remembered Marion Calhoun shaming him two months back. Telling him it wasn't proper to spy on his blood father, saying, "You got no cause to run off and watch Fairy lay that woman." The man had finished his sermon with, "You aint got no business seein things before their rightful time, and it aint ever gonna be a rightful time to watch your daddy do that." He pointed to the side of the pump house, where the biggest of the holy yokes leaned: HE THAT DIGGETH A PIT SHALL FALL INTO IT. ECCLES. 10:8.

"Yeah, well it's a soft pink pit, if ever there was one," Hezekiah said softly.

Yellababy was hiccupping steady while the sun beat down on both their heads. The small community of Bexley had come and gone while Hez thought on these things. He saw the flat landscape that marked his corner of Mississippi, as even and unbroken as a sheet of brown glass, but for the occasional silo and rusted-out barn. Like a slumbering, knocked-down drunk, it just lay there. Immobile. Near worthless. Cows, mostly black-and-white mottled ones, stood scattered and dumb as cardboard cutouts, their four dirty legs slabbed into the ground. Behind them, scrub oak and trash trees jockeyed for space, edged themselves in forward encroachments alongside low green pastures and fields that seemed to stretch forever. Seeing all these things, and judging them inordinately glorious, Hezekiah found himself a good enough spot to sit across from a cut-open field. While he took his brother off his back he said out loud to the birds and the wind and anything else wanting to listen, "Lord God, You may be after me for watchin my blood father fuck. And that county car might just be wantin me for skippin school one too many times, but I swear to sweet Jesus, it sure seems to be headin out to be a near perfect day, in spite of it."

                              *   *   *

"Well, Susan-Blair Sheehand might a thought he was here fishing—but he aint."

Marion Calhoun saw the long span of the old bridge stretched empty as a hallway, clean to the other side of the Leaf River. Twin magnolias leaned heavy over the concrete slab like well-acquainted friends, their outward limbs entangled green fingers. The girders overhead were rusted and rained down a red powder that coated his arms and lightened him up, giving him an imagined look of Choctaw or maybe Suwanee. Something other than Negro. The temporary mask disappeared with the next gust of wind and he looked over at the new bridge, a hundred feet away, where cars crossed over every few minutes, their tires humming a one-note boring song.

"This is where he'd be at, though. Right here on this old trestle. Cars don't drive over no more, and even a idiot can fish for a toilet in peace."

Marion looked across the way at the lazy traffic. The not-so-new bridge scarred at its cusp. One long angry green streak where half a house had swiped it and shit its commode.

"Fairy!"

This through his cupped hands.

He heard the deep echo and jumped at the sound of his own voice washing back on wind tide waves. Wide open as the sky, the Leaf had a broad berth of sand fragged with stranded logs. Upriver loggers, he reasoned, hating those men in company hard hats who worshipped the greenback. Those big paper mills were bad as locust set to a full harvest, in Marion Calhoun's opinion. While he walked he looked to the water and watched a log break free and bump shoulders with the rocks, flushing birds, while his shoes, and the sound they made on lonely pavement, echoed as if soled in lead.

Marion looked broadspan, left to right, before his eyes settled on something queer drifting up from the bend. The camp smoke was as telling as a gossipy woman, the way it drifted up and floated midways through the trees, pinpointing clear as a road sign to a spot down river where the man was laying up.

Marion leaned over, wondering how Fairy got down there in the first place, judging the drop too much for one with such scrawny bones and weak initiative. He calculated the grade, did the math in his head while looking for footholds and roots to grab on to. He couldn't find any. So he had slid down on his ass, then. Got hisself dirty. Her too, probably.

And then Marion began to wonder what type of woman would be willing to go sliding down a dried-up riverbank just to have herself a man and if there were a special breed of females willing to get themselves all dirtied up just to sit by a ground slug who didn't have sense enough to keep himself at home. That being the case, he wondered where that special breed of females might keep themselves. How they might look. What type a face went along with a woman willing to carry on that way over old turkey-neck Fairy? Marion shook his head while he watched red dirt sift down like rain onto his arms.

"Fairy! Eulis Farris Sheehand. You needed at home!"

The words came back at him jumbled and confused as the man he was yelling for.

I guess that's fittin, too, what with the way he don't lay his head in the same place twice in a row. So aimless he sleeps out in an old bus, or down by the tracks, everwhere but home where he ought. Lord! What a sorry bunch.

He yelled out one more time. Just the man's name, sharp and quick, and then he put his hands to his pockets and headed to his truck, done with them, determined to turn a deaf ear the next time he heard that knock sound on his rickety front door.

"I don't owe these folks nothin. Not a durn thing in this world." A breeze caught in the tops of the magnolias and it seemed those green limbs shook hands in brief agreement.

Fairy Sheehand sat leaning against a tree wondering at the small quarters of his life; all those parceled-out pieces that had started out strong and fully intact now seemed so pathetically reduced, and it was a comfort. Brilliant light fell through the dark of the trees and bathed his lower legs, his worn-down boots and faded jeans, his pack of cigarettes resting on a stump. Through the wall of sumac and cattail he could see the Leaf River, swollen from recent rain and he could hear the rush of it, the way it pitched low and guttural with a sound like that of a drowning man. The cypress knees along the near bank barely broke the surface today and he looked over at the nearest group, saw tangled fishing line and floating bottles, careless trash. Yesterday they had been hidden entirely. Without having to see proof, he knew clots of yellow foam had gathered around the spires. He looked at his ex-wife, who was speaking,

"You owe it to them to git yourself home."

His life was small now. Inconsequential. The size of a diorama made by a child. He just looked at her, knowing she wasn't aware of this and would speak again.

"You owe it to your own self, then," she said after a moment of silence.
"Seems to me I aint lackin," he said.

They sat at the edge of the river, around a barbecue built of rocks, on a spot that had grown familiar. Silva had brought the meat. Fresh deer sausage from Shoemaker's over in Lucedale. Venison must be cheaper than pork, he figured when he first saw her pull it out of the crumpled brown bag, disappointed she hadn't sprung for a steak. But once it was set to a hot grill, its smell belied its cheapness. He watched it bubble and swell while potatoes and corn cooked inside aluminum foil next to the coals. Happy as a dying man could be, he leaned back and stretched out his legs while the woman speared things with a meat fork.

"I used to think you just didn't care enough about them to go home. That you were lazy. I don't know anymore. About anything."

His life was so small now, so contained, he could practically hold it in his hand. He looked over at Silva, noticing her mouth barely moved when she talked. Air was sucked in and then let out with ghost-like lip movements and words would follow, seemingly out of nowhere. Like one of those ventriloquists down on the streets of New Orleans who caught tossed nickels in a cup. He strained to listen, same as he'd been doing for close to twenty years, only he understood it now: why her words always seemed to shift and disappear on him and leave him with the worry he was a man going deaf. She was still talking and he tried to concentrate but was left with the cold realization that even in those faded jeans, and even with all those years between them, even with that gray hair of hers that he loved piled up high, she was still too truthful to tolerate.

"That's just one of my problems, you mean. I got me a whole list, don't forget," he said, hoping he had caught the gist of her speech.

"True."

She smiled easy enough at him and he relaxed and grew expansive.

"Silva, I wish I'd knowed you'd turn out so sweet." He blew smoke rings that floated up above his head, drifted momentarily into low gray tree limbs wearing Spanish moss, and then vanished inside the hot, white light of the sun. She studied him.

"I never was sweet and you know it. I was too honest, was all. Seems you wanted somethin other than that." A speared potato let out its steam.

"I wanted some things. That's true enough." A truthful woman (especially a wife) was hard to deal with in his opinion. You couldn't fuck with honesty, or with a practical nature. Silva had both those things. Susan-Blair, on the other hand, was hot and loose as a lie; easy to laze around with. "You could a pretended I had a little sense. That wouldn't a kilt you."

"You had sense. You just lost it where that one was concerned. And the sad thing is, you knocked her up and got *caught* losin it." Silva wiped at her forehead with the back of her hand.

"Arena's a sweet girl. My daughter aint never been a problem."

"The hell would you know? You're not ever there long enough to see if she's trouble or not."

"I'm there enough." He looked up at the trees. Wondered where his life had gone. The sun sat midways in the sky, making patterns that hurt his eyes: a kaleidoscope of yellows and greens and blues that seemed to ridicule him. "I been there enough to know I caint live with them, I don't care how sweet she is. Or how much trouble she might be into. Any of those things."

"Farris, there's a selfishness in the way you're planning to die. It aint right."

"So?"

"What'd that doctor say?"

"Not much more than he said the last time. Give me some more pills, and I shook his hand and said, 'Much obliged.' "

"You tell her yet?"

"There's nothin to tell," he said.

"Fuck's the matter with you?"

"I spent the last ten or so years living mostly on my own. I reckon that's as good a way to die as any other. And I reckon you bein the only one to know the state of things is as good a thing as a man could wish for."

The meat was done and she laid out the plates and he picked up a knife and sliced his sausage way down to little slivers and mixed it with potato. He had choked the last time and become frightened of something other than the cancer killing him.

"You should a left her, instead a givin her one more baby," she said.

It was the first time she had ever expressed anything resembling regret, and this did not go unnoticed.

"I guess a man keeps thinkin things will improve." He worked at his food, smearing the potatoes around without taking a bite, aware of the plastic salt shaker near his foot and the plastic fork in his hand and the soggy paper plate sitting on his lap—implements temporary and disposable. Silva prepared food the same way she prepared for life, with the expectation that everything ends sooner or later, and once done, the easier to toss it away, the better. So different from Susan-Blair, who felt it her duty to hold on to every goddamn thing under the sun. His life was small now, quiescent finally (a diorama), he could reach inside and take someone out and they would be gone. Silva was speaking again, her words as quiet as the tree frogs were loud.

"... say twenty years is too long to wait. First time she bought somebody's used shoes and decided to set up shop you should a took a stick to her."

"I aint never hit a woman."

"That's not what I heard."

"I shoved her, is all. 'Cause she hit Hez. I never laid a hand to her otherwise." He swallowed his meat with great effort. "She never laid a hand to my boy again."

"Your boy. Now that's a good joke." Silva snorted out her nose. "You live out of a bus, Fairy. How many times you been around him since he was out of diapers?"

"More than you know."

"That nigger next door's done more to raise him than you have."

"Shut up, Silva."

She ate silently, eyes and mouth focused downward on the paper plate.

Setting his plate to the side, he watched her, wondering how the woman could count him a durn fool one second and attack those potatoes of hers the next, argumenting being hardset against his nature and having a way of provoking indigestion almost as bad as the cancer.

She finished her plate and eyed his. "You need to eat," she said, as if all her other comments were nothing.

"You want it? You act like you aint et since Christmas." The sun was leaning a little toward the one o'clock mark carrying with it a haze, thick-shading and deceptive. Making a body foolishly think they could look the sun straight on and not burn out their eyes. Same as a man can think he knows a woman and not wind up gettin themselves kilt. He studied her long neck, the way her gray hair was held fast by hairpins, remembering her body, how it had always been a challenge for him to come inside her before she opened her mouth about the next day, or the next week, or the next four decades. It was a race he very seldom won.

"Don't you wonder how they're gettin on without you around? How the baby is? He's five years old now, in case you forgot."

"I aint forgot." He watched her hands and then her face, remembering how the two of them had danced at the co-op four hundred years back. How all he'd wanted at the time was a farm of his own and a good-enough plow to work it with. Maybe a job on the railroad. Remembering that once they were married, he didn't want any of those things anymore.

"Truth told, the only thing I wonder over is what you ever saw in me in the first place." Tired and worn slap out from talking, he put his hands behind his head as a prop.

"A way out a Washington County is what."

"I got you out, too, didn't I, sister?" He lit a cigarette for them both. Putting hers to the right side of her mouth the way she liked it. Silva leaned against a tree and smoked and looked up to the sky every once in a while. It would be a fierce summer what with the way the heat had swallowed up February. A bead of sweat was forming underneath her neck, dampening the collar of her shirt.

"You got Susan-Blair out, you mean," she said. "You left me there watchin the whole bunch of you pack it up. I found my own way out three months after you left."

"I married you first. You could a gone instead a her, had you not divorced me."

"We were married for fifteen months and Susan-Blair was pregnant for four of those. I think that cancer a yours is goin to your brain, Fairy."

"I told you I got a whole list of faults. I have never in all my born days lied to an individual about my nature. Especially you." He looked at her and the look was genuine and relaxed, void of expectation or hope.

"You keep hunchin over like that, they gonna bury you with a hump. No way you're gonna lay flat inside that coffin." Her voice broke and she looked away, feeling foolish.

"Hez walks just like me. He's but sixteen and already stooped." Fairy flicked his cigarette, leaned forward to wrap his arms around his knees, his shirt sweatfaded blue and overly thin at the elbows.

"That one's stooped from carryin everbody else's load. You and Susan-Blair ought to be ashamed." Silva stirred at the charcoal and glanced once at her watch.

"I already told you, I caint live with her."

"You've not tried lately."

"Why in hell are you going at me? If I go back that'd be the end of me. The end of us."

"Watchin you die is too much of a thing. I caint spend every waking minute worryin over whether folks are taking care of you, or if you're able to eat or not, or if you're suffering slow. Besides . . . I got my own life now. I met somebody."

He appeared to have heard and yet not heard, as if he'd been deaf a huge score of years and suddenly gone to hearing again, only to lose it the very next second.

"Who?" he said.

"None a your damn business."

"Do I know him?"

"No."

"Well, that's good then, 'cause I'd hate to kill somebody I knowed first-hand."

"You're too weak to kill a soul." She flipped her cigarette into the fire. "You act like it's years back and there's still somethin ahead for us."

"You mean I've pissed my life away."

"I mean I met me somebody and high time I did, too, what with you wastin away and not carin whether or not you set things right before you go."

"We aint laid together in three months. Is this why?"

He watched her look at her hands, turning them over until they rested in her lap, palm upward as if in appeasement. "We've not been together since you found out you were sick. I would have early on, but not now."

"This is how come when I called you last week, you wouldn't talk to me on the telephone."

"Yes."

"He was there."

Silva looked at him, evenly, calmly, and her calmness surprised him, told him this thing was serious.

"Fairy, there's nothin between us," she said, her lips barely moving. "There's not been for a long, long time. If there had been we would have left everthing we had to go after it. It's never been that way with us. I thought it was, but it wasn't. We just used each other to run away is all."

"I never used you."

"Yes you did and you know it. I did my own thinkin back and found out that what we are to each other is as tired and weak and stupid as a thing can be."

He sat up, trembling, suddenly hating the smallness of his life, while he ran his hands down the front of his pants as if they were dirtied up from food. He didn't know whether to cry or scream or take a rock and bash in her head.

As unexpected as thunder, the sound of his name came up from the road and his first thought was that Susan-Blair had sent somebody to spy him out. His second thought was that he would kill her because of it, too. His third thought was that he hadn't the strength to kill a mosquito should it pause on his hand.

"Somebody's callin you."

"I may be dyin, but I sure aint deaf."

"There . . . listen." She stood to her feet as if he needed convincing, walking out a bit closer to where the trees broke open to water, giving way to cattails growing up out of dirty wet sand. While her back was to him, she looked at her watch again.

Fairy heard the words "home" and "Susan-Blair." "I'll have to kill her, I guess. Try and pick up that two-dollar anvil and cave in that big woman's skull."

Silva looked at him and then sat down, leaning back against the blue-and-white cooler holding bread and bottles of bootlegged beer. "You want me to drive you down? Sounds important."

"I got my bike set in the weeds. I can manage."

"It might be Yellababy. Or Arena." Silva slathered up bread with mayonnaise for a second sandwich; she gave him one quick glance and then sucked mayonnaise off her finger. Piled high with sauerkraut, the sandwich made his mouth water and he began to wish he had the stomach for it. Wished he could still eat food just for food's sake and because he was hungry and not worry about choking it all back up.

"I guess you're gonna stay here and finish eatin without me." He picked up his cap and put it to his head, his fingers brushing lightly over the new knob behind his right ear. There were three more under his right armpit and one hatching beneath his collarbone. Nuisance things that didn't pain him much, but made him worry about his eventual appearance when laid out for the whole world to see.

"I must say, Silva, I'm surely glad to see your appetite aint been squelched by me dyin slow and this new man of yours." *His life was so small he could climb inside it and disappear.*

"I paid for the meat, didn't I?" She gave him a hot, hateful look and then went at her sandwich, eating as daintily as one could a Polish sandwich the size of a cinder brick.

"Well, I reckon you surely did. I reckon you did at that," he chuckled while he walked up the grade in the direction of the bridge where he'd hidden his bicycle, the handholds along the way familiar enough to grab on to in the dark.

CHAPTER 6

Hezekiah tilted the jug and drank from it, propping a diaper under his brother's bottle of milk while peering down at a calm, untroubled face. Education was important, even for a retard, and he scrambled around for new topics of enlightenment.

I could tell him all about life, Hez reasoned. About our father and how he fucks his old wife down by the river; and Teresa Beth Pierce and how I'd like to go and fuck her one day soon. I could sure tell him about how we're headed to a place where folks aint talked in over five years. A place where the only ones talkin are the ghosts who kick up dust in the street. I could tell this one here about all these things but it'd be about as worthwhile as me taking up a course on sewin.

His brother coughed and he looked down at him, wondering, of all the silly things, who it was going to be to help him lose his baby teeth.

"You caint pull them yourself, I sure know that," he said. "Susan-Blair's about worthless too, when it comes to takin care of anything besides those used clothes of hers."

Hezekiah put a finger in his brother's mouth and felt around the teeth and gums. Firm. Good. He hoped they would stay that way for a while, yet. Worried over what his brother might think of having a slipknot tied around a tooth and feeling it jerked out courtesy of a slammed door.

"That there's a cotton house," Hez finally said to get his mind off his brother's teeth. He pointed to the almost square building set in the center of a brown ribbed field.

"The reason it aint got a hall like a barn, is 'cause it aint a barn. It's a cotton house."

He heard the sucking sounds and the noise was remedial, similar in memory to the sound of steady water feeding through a trough.

"When they bring in the cotton, folks stack it there, because it takes more'n a day to do the work and with so much money ridin on it, they don't want what they just tore their hands up over, gettin ruint."

A rust-colored tractor sat mired deep in muck near the road, one rear tire lower than its mate, but other than that, the vista was unmarred but for the squat building in the center of the field. "I reckon he got rained out before he started cuttin in." Hez rubbed Yellababy's stomach and felt his little-boy ribs. "Might be if we sit here long enough, we'll get to see him come back and get it goin again."

The sky was beautiful. Deep ocean blue up near its center drifted to pale, pale grayish pink down near the horizon. The wind seemed warm enough to stand naked in, even after a bath.

"Things sure got tangled up, though, didn't they?" he said, missing Teresa Beth and halfway wishing he'd gone to school in spite of the weather. Picking up the edge of his brother's blanket—the worn satin part—he rubbed it between his fingers, shutting his eyes while he imagined how similar to that polished cotton of Teresa Beth's dress it might be. He sat there, his head back on his neck, in the hot sun for an uncounted lazy time, his eyes shut while he listened to his brother drain his bottle.

"I guess sometimes things get tangled up before they make themselves right again—"

"How come you're sittin there like a dummy talkin to the air?"

The girl had come up from the other side of the cotton house, apparently. Hez opened his eyes to see her leaning on her arms on the other side of the fence post, chewing on a piece of hay. She rolled it from one side of her small mouth to the other with a speed he found amazing. Her eyes were wide apart and warmly colored. She was grinning, too.

"I aint talkin to the air. I'm talkin to my brother. It aint none a your business, anyhow."

"How come he's so big and suckin on a bottle like a baby?" She spit over the rail like a boy and he judged the range admirable.

" 'Cause he's retarded is why, and that's the only way he can drink."

The girl's hair was pulled back into a ponytail and she was wearing too-big gray coveralls; coveralls of the type railroad folks, or the state prisoners doing road work, wore. They looped at her feet like beat-up gray buckets. Even with the belt cinching at the waist they looked like they were not hers, had never been hers, and never would be hers.

"Why aint you in school instead of standin out here askin me all sorts a nosy questions?" he said.

"I live with my aunt and uncle and they don't make me go, so I don't." She shrugged her shoulders and looked away for an instant, down toward the cotton house where a shadowy movement traveled across an opening. It could have been her uncle, or it could have been the sun. He wasn't sure.

"We gotta plow today, anyhow." Hopping the fence, boy-like, one hand to the top rail and her legs vaulting over, she crossed the road and squatted to the ground. The smell of hay and sweetfeed and fertilizer traveled with her and something underneath, similar to lotion, or shampoo. Hardworking, but clean, in Hezekiah's opinion.

"How often you skip school?" he said.

She looked up at the sky as if the answer were written on a cloud, then counted on her fingers. "Maybe six days a month. Don't rightly know, though."

"Does a man in a county car ever drive out here lookin for you?"

"Nope."

"What grade're you in?"

"Seventh."

"And nobody's come lookin?" He couldn't believe it. Either she was too dumb to qualify as a true student, or the school board paid more attention to the boys.

"We got a letter once and my uncle went down and cussed them out, and we aint got no more letters concernin it." She paused and scratched her nose before grinning at him. "I aint even sure I'm registered anymore."

Hez was not sure what being registered meant. He knew he had a birth certificate somewhere that just might prove he was no blood kin to Fairy Sheehand, but that had nothing to do with school, or a county car, or whether or not he had three (or was it two?) truant days left.

"What's his name?" she said, looking down.

"Yellababy." Before she could spit out the question he explained, "And before you go and ask, that aint his given name. His given name is Levi Sheehand, but it got changed to the other when he was about a week old."

"How come?"

" 'Cause he turned yellow as a squash all of a sudden and had to go to the hospital."

"How come him to turn yellow?"

"How come you're sittin here askin me all these questions? I thought you had to plow."

"My uncle aint here yet. He's down at the cotton house cleanin the rig. It got mucked up late yesterday evenin and we lost a bolt. Made me dig around out near that fence until after dark for it, too. He's down there now searchin for another to fix the thing. I told him yesterday he'd do better to get up off his ass and go down to the hardware store instead of making me get all dirty lookin for somethin that don't cost but twenty-five cents. He says I can crank it up and drive it down for him when he whistles."

"You lie like a snake." Hez saw that she had freckles across the bridge of her nose and that her teeth were slightly misaligned, forcing her mouth open in a false state of wonderment, even when she was done talking. His eyes slid downward to nothing up front. Eleven or twelve, then, seeing how her chest was flat as a flitter. Stupid, too. There was no way anybody with half a brain would let her drive farm machinery. "You look too little to drive that thing."

"Well, you just sit here and watch. You'll see soon enough." She grinned at him, her eyes crinkling up like raisins, her confidence impenetrable.

Yellababy stiffened, his arms pulling into his chest.

"I aint ever seen a real retarded person before. My aunt told me about them, 'cause she used to work over in Alabama. At Searcy. Retarded folks over there plant gardens and build birdhouses and drool a lot. But I aint ever seen one." She stretched out a hand to touch Yellababy's knee and Hez pushed it away.

"Yellababy don't like strangers."

"My name's Cathy, so I guess I aint a stranger." She put her hand to Yellababy and smoothed out his pants, pulling them down to the tops of his tennis shoes, regarding him as one might interesting roadkill. "How come you're out this way?"

"We're headed to Chalktown."

Her hand froze, suspended over Yellababy's torso. In a quiet voice she said, "You know somebody there? Is that why you're goin?"

"No, but I just heard about it, is all. Heard it's interestin, and I want him to see the place. He don't get out much."

"The houses are all different colors. One's brown, another yellow. The blue house man died recent, and his place is gone vacant. My uncle says he wishes he could go live there for a while and rid himself of female talkin." Cathy looked away, "But he aint ever gonna do it. He's too scared." She crossed herself the way she'd seen a man on television do it, shivering a little. With an old maternal movement she tucked Yellababy's diaper closer to his face, away from dried grass, and Hezekiah wondered if all females were born knowing this thing: how to tend to somebody smaller.

"Uncle Jimmy said he heard the blue house man was dead for two days before the rest of the folks knew it. He never was one to communicate daily. Last message he wrote out on his chalkboard was a recipe for currant bread. And it werent even the time of year for such a thing, neither."

Hez watched her, thinking the point to her chin might be considered cute by some but not by him. Now that she was up close he could see her eyes were more green than brown, and in the olive orb of her right one, a tiny gold speck rested. "Did the man draw buzzards?" he said.

Cathy looked at him, wide-eyed, as if she wished she had considered the possibility. "Nobody said a thing about that. He was dead two days, though. So, maybe."

"A man and his girlfriend got caught with their pants down in the gravel pit over in Agricola, near where I live. They was missin two weeks, though. Durn birds knew it before we did. Drew more'n a dozen at final count. I guess if it'd been cold weather we might not a known the truth of it 'til summer time, or maybe even spring. Old man McCreel went to chase them birds off when folks started making fun a those black things sitting there atop his gravel like they owned the place, and thought he smelled something. Once he dug in about a foot, the stink got too large for him and he called in the niggers to finish the job—"

"How come their pants to be down?" She looked at him, her eyes stretched wide as twin moons.

He knew her age then. That she had not even come close to wondering about things down there, or how they worked. Had probably not even pulled up her shirt and touched herself at night when everbody else was sleeping.

"Their pants were down because they were foolin around. They was both married."

"Then how come they was out foolin around and werent home where they belonged?" She came down off her haunches and sat, her legs crossed Indian-style.

"They was married to *other* folks, not each other."

Cathy's eyes went back and forth looking at his hands first, and then at his feet, and then while he watched, she straightened up her mouth. Why, she's trying to act like she knows what the hell I'm talkin about, he reasoned.

Hez said, patiently, "You don't have any idea what I'm talkin about, do you?"

"I aint stupid. I know some things."

"Not too many, though. Seein how you've missed my point."

Which had been the keen-smelling buzzards that led to old man McCreel pulling out the shovel and then having to call in the blacks.

Hezekiah said, "Like I was sayin, J. P. McCreel smelled them first."

"I think now my uncle did say the blue house man carried stink."

Yellababy's bottle was empty. Preoccupied, Cathy took it from his mouth and casually inverted the rubber nipple with a not-too-clean finger.

Hez watched, disgusted. "McCreel's own son was the one buried under the rocks. Under the very gravel he sold to folks. I caint believe you've not heard about this." He leaned forward to peer into her eyes.

"Seems to me a man ought to know where his son is for two weeks. Seems to me, if somebody's flesh and blood was to disappear for that long a time, if they were a proper father, they'd know somethin was up."

So, she's not as dumb as she looks. He'd had the same exact thought. "True. Seems that way, don't it?" He reached for his smokes. Struck a match to the hard leather of his shoe.

"Seems to me that old man probably had himself an idea, 'cause there's not much that you can keep from folks," she said. "You might can for a while, but sooner or later, whatever it is you're tryin to hide, shows itself. Lordy, anybody with a grain of sense ought to know that."

Hez pointed a finger at her. "That's exactly what Mayurn said." He shook out a cigarette for her while she sent one furtive alltelling look down to the cotton house before licking her finger and picking one out.

"Thanks," she said while she smoked it quick. Like she'd done it before out behind a barn or maybe squatted down in a ditch where that Uncle Jimmy of hers couldn't see what was going on.

"Mayurn, he's my colored neighbor, dug them out and I went down to watch. Him and four other big Negroes did it. But I tell you what, there's not enough money in the world for me to do that. Nosiree. I had to tie my shirt around my head after a while. Only things around that seemed happy about it were the buzzards."

"How come them to end up buried?"

"They was married to other folks and sneakin around. J. P. McCreel Junior—and it's a shame about that one, too, because he was the only boy old man McCreel had—but anyhow," Hez drew long on his cigarette. "Seems like he thought parkin down behind the biggest gravel pile his daddy owned was a surefire way to keep folks from knowin where he was at."

A man had come out of the cotton house and Hez reached over and took Cathy's cigarette out of her mouth and felt the damp end with his fingers.

"The hell you doin?"

He nodded in the direction of the field while she sat across from him, quiet as a mouse.

"Your uncle just come out," he said, and that seemed to be enough.

She folded her arms into herself and waited. He watched, knowing that a part of her was already older than the man out in the field, in spite of no boobs, and it was this part of her that was listening and smoking and sitting down on her ass while he told her about the dead folks that drew carrion birds.

"Finish the story," she said.

"Well, a train come by barely fifty feet away and shook loose a load and it covered the truck and kilt them."

"Lordy."

"Amen." Hez looked at her, the way her teeth didn't quite meet, at her scaly work-worn hands and long, white, slender neck. Thinking during that covert stare, I bet this one would risk death to get herself kissed. Maybe not now at this very moment in time, but soon.

The tall man stood midfield, his hands on his hips, irritation spread out all over his being. His height was just about right for the coveralls the girl was wearing, but there was something to the rigid set of his jaw that made Hez think he had once been a prisoner, and not a railroad man. A whistle cut through the air and she jumped to her feet, pointing a finger.

"You watch now. You're gonna eat your words about me bein too small to crank up a tractor." When she walked across the road, she left clumps of mud behind like the cows do when they come up out of a low pond. While he watched, she climbed up on the bogged-down tractor, let the glow-plug warm, and then cranked it up, right as rain.

"What's your name?" She yelled this over the noise of it while blue smoke poured out the top, making diesel haloes around her head.

"Hezekiah Sheehand. I live over Agricola way, and I'll be coming back this evening."

"My name's Cathleen Purvis, and I'm older than you think, too!"

While he sat there wondering what in the world she might mean by that, the girl rocked the tractor back and forth between gears, her ponytail swinging while black ridged tires slung mud all the way to the center of the road. Those big tires were finally free and he watched her head for the cotton house. When she threw up a hand in a wave, Hezekiah saw down her sleeve to the underside of a curve and could not help but be impressed.

CHAPTER 7

Susan-Blair was sitting in deep porch shade when her sister pulled up in the pickup truck. The Ford's tires scattered pea gravel and dirt as far as the first step of the house and Susan-Blair's feet. Climbing out, Julia stomped at the geese saying, "Shoo! Shoo! Hell now! Git!" while she kicked sand at their heads with her boot. The geese took three steps back and stood there staring, unimpressed. Their heads cocked, they appeared to be measuring the cooling tick of the engine and its duration.

"They're not harmful. Just curious, is all. If you stand still they lose interest soon enough," Susan-Blair said in a cautious voice.

"I'll not bow down to a goose. You know that. And their curiosity will get you sued once they attack the propane man. I'd not have them on my land. Not a one of them."

Susan-Blair looked around her yard for something to clean up, or straighten up, but abandoned the effort just as suddenly. She noticed Julia was wearing a heavy yellow cotton shirt the color of good stiff butter with silver studs riding up the front and perching on its cuffs. A rodeo look.

Slick and starched, the shirt went well-behaved into the jeans, just like the woman. Susan-Blair caught her cheap cloth dress between her fingers and rolled the fabric against her thumb while she sat there feeling old and spread-out and large-thighed.

Julia stood in the sun watching her sister.

"Arena passed me, walkin fast," she said. "I was down to the feed store and there she was. Like she was headed somewhere other than school." Julia looked past Susan-Blair to the porch of the house. It bothered her. The smell of old, the least of it.

"She didn't come home last night. Some man in a county car brought her back this mornin, big as you please, too. Tried to hide his Plymouth behind that azalea bush there, of all things. Acted like I werent nowhere around."

Through the opened front door Julia saw the tiny passageway that led through the living room. Clothes were suspended from the ceiling and there were boxes and crates full of shoes and old purses and beat-up lampshades and plastic hula girls missing their skirts.

"Saw the dust from the window, though. Plain as day. Who could miss a big car on this dirt road, anyhow?"

Julia kicked at the dirt. "She's old enough to be out on her own, I guess. Why not let her go?"

" 'Cause I caint, is why."

Julia sat down on the front steps, her legs stretched out, her boot heels making circles in the dirt. Her blue-jeaned legs threw off good heat and Susan-Blair saw where cow manure had dried across the toes of her sister's boots and turned the worn leather two-toned like those fancy oxfords the college girls wore.

"She's run off three times already. Since October," Julia said, leaning on her hand.

"Time enough to get her fill of it then."

"There are other things to tend to around here besides Arena." Julia looked over at the Calhoun place. "Where'd he go to?" She had passed him, too, about a mile back. "Don't tell me—"

"Down to get Fairy off the bridge." Susan-Blair rubbed at a smudge on her shoe.

"Fairy's not on the bridge. I just rode over it, and he's not there."

"He's there. The man always could hide well enough from kinfolks. Takes a stranger to find a good-for-nothin husband."

Susan-Blair finally looked her sister in the eyes. Julia's hair was shiny and swinging, the exact color of a shimmery snake Hez had killed during summer. She continued to sit quietly while studying the busy yard and the geese. Two were trying to mate next to the rain barrel.

"I don't see why you had to go and involve Calhoun in this. Seems to me the county knows more than enough of our business, as it is—"

"You sound like Ma. Ma would a said a similar thing."

"I'm just saying Arena's gone off before, and she'll be back."

"I know she'll be back. It's what she'll be back with that's got me worried."

"Lockin her in the house wont stop it," Julia said.

"No?"

Julia looked at her again. "It sure as hell didn't stop you."

A truck had turned onto the road down at the corner store, a half-mile away. They both heard those grinding gears cutting through the warm February air and sat up straighter, in anticipation; a habit of old, when visitors on a stretch of road usually meant something good.

"I had my reasons. You know them well enough." Susan-Blair rocked a little, her arms a cradle for her stomach. "Arena's not had any of those reasons."

Julia rubbed at her knees and looked around, afraid to ask the question. "Where's the youngest, Susie?"

"Hez took him with him for a walk. Headed to Chalktown, is what he said."

Chalktown. Julia studied her sister's face. Those pale, pale eyes, the blond hair sitting on her shoulders.

"I just wish you'd called me instead of Marion Calhoun," Julia said in a quiet voice. "Now everybody will know."

"Including Fairy. Maybe this time, he'll see fast enough with his own two eyes what his daughter's turned into."

The truck passed, dusty red and loud as thunder, sending pebbles from the road's far embankment down across the way like a minuscule landslide.

"What are you doin out here, Julia? Why aint you runnin all over the county tendin things? Taking care of the cows?" Susan-Blair watched the geese going at a leftover puddle. They would bury their heads in muck and come up dirty as hogs.

"I told you, I saw Arena storm past. I tried to phone but the line's been cut off. I thought you might need help is all."

"Well, you can leave now. I've told you everthing there is to tell and what trouble there is, is mine. It aint yours."

"Ma believed kin should look out for one another."

"Ma's dead. I think you can go back to your business now."

"I made a promise."

"Ma made us both promise a lot of things. Remember the plate?"

"The plate?"

"Yeah, that plastic melamine plate. When Daddy died, Ma had that picture of him put on it. Daddy was sittin on his mule."

"I remember."

"I've still got it somewhere. She couldn't have a good-lookin plate. Couldn't settle on one with FDR or the White House on it. She had to have Daddy and his great big mule—"

"I said I remember, Susie."

"The fact that the mule tossed him into the ravine and broke his hip and eventually killed him didn't matter in the least. Daddy sure loved that mule." Susan-Blair rubbed her eyes. "The day that plate come in the mail you'd a thought it was a thousand dollars worth a somethin the way she tore into that package. And there it was. Daddy. His hands crossed over that rope harness. The dumb mule with its broad white nose and long ears. You remember what she did with it?"

Julia didn't.

"She fed the dog off it. Put it out on the back porch step and fed the durn dog off it."

"How's the baby, Susie?"

"Folks used to come over and laugh about it, too. Gossiped up and down the county line about how we fed the dog off Ma's prize plate—"

"Susie, how's the baby?"

Susan-Blair looked at her sister, at the still, quiet brown of her eyes.

And then she peered out into the yard, "Julie, I caint tend him anymore." Her words came out like bullets shot at a tin target. "Levi's too big to tend ...he's gone and grown too big."

"You're bein foolish now."

"Well, you asked me about the baby. Asked me more than once, too. And here I am givin you your answer. I guess a person shouldn't open their mouth when they don't really mean it." The largest goose charged at the smaller, weaker one. Long necks tangled while both women watched.

"Ma did her Christian duty with daddy. With all of us. He was laid up a long time and she tended him. And it werent easy to do, either. Not with him bein as large and mean as he was. Bathed him. Kept him shaved ..."

Susan-Blair shuddered though the day was warm. Tiptoeing away from what scared her, she said, "Remember how Ma used to say Jesus was everwhere at once?"

A smell like that of asphalt was in the back of her nose and she knew there would be a migraine, a fierce one; some days she imagined the headache as a billowing miasmal cloud drawn toward her, orange in color, a shade she found terrifying for some strange reason. "She used to see Christ everwhere—bathroom, bedroom, watchin while she hung out clothes, driftin along the ceiling like a smelly old peepin Tom."

"Ma was raised country."

"Hell, Julia, what do you think we are? City?"

"No, but she was old-time Pentecostal. You know that."

"She quit the marriage bed with Daddy 'cause Christ was up there watchin. Even though Daddy begged her for it, she wouldn't. Never cut her hair because Christ was watchin. Never left a dirty dish to soak because Christ was up there watchin. Never used the bathroom in full light because—"

"What's your point, Susie?"

"It just seems strange that all her business about Jesus watchin didn't stop Daddy from screwin every gal in the county willin to drop their drawers."

Julia laughed a nervous laugh.

"The thought a Jesus bein everwhere used to scare the shit out a me, though. I never could get away from the possibility of it. That it might be true."

"So Jesus is watchin? What's the big deal?" Julia popped her knuckles and stood up suddenly, as if she had grown afraid.

"Yellababy . . . I mean, Levi . . . he's grown so big I caint . . ." Susan-Blair shut her eyes because on certain days he seemed large as a baby cow. Or a large dog. His manhood dangled now.

"There are things we have to do, Susie. This is just one of them. Lord, he's just a five-year-old."

"You never had a hard day in your life. You breeze down here for the first time in a month and stay what? Five long minutes? Ask me about somethin you don't want to know about?"

Julia, her stance locked somewhere between retreat and advance, folded her arms over her yellow shirt and looked straight at her sister. She knew how to settle a horse, but this was different. This was crazy.

"Remember how we used to play down by the creek?" Julia made her voice to be low and soothing, the way she talked to her mare. "Take our dolls down there with all those baby clothes and those bottles? We'd spend hours down there hidin from our chores."

Susan-Blair nodded. With a dry mouth she mumbled, "We used to set the bottles by the rock in the stream; down in the cool water. And we'd pull off our socks and dangle our feet."

"Bathe our babies. Comb out their hair." Julia looked through the front window at the table of naked dolls, their tangled rubber limbs, and then she looked back at Susan-Blair. "That was a sweet time, Susie. A good time. Maybe you could think about that. The way you were so sweet to your dolls."

Susan-Blair remembered those days: the blasting breath-sounds of the cows; how they smelled awful and wonderful at the same time; the ivory-yellow salt blocks sitting in the sun, crawling with flies; the weed wall they'd lean back against, having pressed down the goldenrod while they sneezed; the way they'd talk for hours while they chewed straw, their legs crossed and swinging. She looked up at her sister and pulled her face together, quick-like. Bored by the story, the largest goose darted toward Julia's leg and got a kick in the face for it.

"Christ! These geese are mean as hell! I was barely out of the truck when one ran up to me," Julia said, her voice tired.

"I told you, they're not that mean. They've just turned curious all of a sudden."

"And like I told you, one day one's gonna take a bite out of somebody and you're gonna end up gettin sued."

With that she walked to her truck, climbed in and left. Susan-Blair looked up once, halfway hoping for a wave or something sisterly, but not really expecting it. All she saw was one yellow arm resting on the door frame while the truck stirred up dust on its way back to Agricola.

"If you'd stayed a little longer," she muttered, "I'd a told you one already had. I didn't get sued over it, though. I guess I could a gone to jail if I hadn't stopped. But I surely didn't get sued."

She blinked and saw it: that fast yellow beak to Yellababy's skin. Him outside for just a little bit, too. Just long enough for me to go back in the house for a pack of cigarettes. Him out there stiff in the sun on his blanket. Those arms straight out like he thinks he's a damn airplane. The goose then. And way too much cryin. Too much even for a four-year-old. Loud, like the early morning train. Loud enough for people to hear all the way down to Beachum's Corner. I picked him up and brought him inside and slung him down hard in his bed. I threw him hard just like before, and I put my hand to the noise to stop it. I put my hand there and want to leave it, but I know He's up there *watchin*, so I don't. I want to, but I don't. Christ is up there *watchin*. Just like Ma says, hoverin near the rain-stained ceiling, *watchin* me ... *watchin* me ... *watchin* me.

CHAPTER 8

Hez kicked at an empty pork-and-bean can while he studied the train tracks running parallel to the road. The rail, in his opinion, cut into the trees perversely and with an unnatural splendor for something involving a bulldozer and human sweat. There were miles and miles of tracks. Stretching long as the eye goes looking. Hezekiah hoped a train would come by soon, thinking he'd surely like to see it out in the open, running against the deep green trees. At Susan-Blair's it lumbered past things colored in a dull brown, echoing against wrecked and rusted automobiles and the trash cans burning slow and foul. Against the green, he bet a train would be something grand. Those tracks would sing, he bet. On the other side of the road was one more slice of pastureland, marked with a black-and-white cow patiently chewing its cud. He knew that he'd gone the better part of the distance now. Up ahead was the rickety white church that stood as a marker.

"Chalktown," he said out loud. Liking the feel of it to his tongue. "They talk that way, and not any other," he told his brother. Yellababy was to the front now, the haversack cradled under Hezekiah's arm, his brother leaning back and watching the sky. As one absent from the earth, but still conscious of its obligations, Hez rubbed at his brother's legs, reworked the circulation while he fished a piece of chewed-up sausage out of his mouth and placed it on his brother's tongue. Rubbing gently, as though baiting a timid fish, Hez watched him catch the taste of it and try to chew. Arena always gagged when she saw him do it. Gagged. Like his sister had a better idea on how to feed a little boy who couldn't feed himself. Baby food would be good if Susan-Blair would spring for it, which she had done for a while before those pennies became too precious.

"I hate all women, Yellababy. I think all women should be strung up naked and shot. You do, too, don't you?"

He played with his brother's tennis shoe while looking again at the long stretch of rail, wondering who did the planning of it and how many Negroes had to be hired to do the actual work. Yellababy gurgled old-sounding, his eyes wide-shiny as new mirrors. If Hez had glanced down he would have seen twin crows poised there, swimming across innocent blue.

Walking farther down the road, he found the shade of a sycamore noisy with wren and thrush and made a rest stop of the blanket, fanning the flies away from his brother while he listened to the bird chatter.

"Somethin bad happened on that street, but I don't care."

Hezekiah masticated another bite; smaller pieces this time because he had already fished out one or two chunks that had refused to go down Yellababy's throat. The two boys seemed at peace, each lost in thoughts with no bearing on the other's, and at different levels of understanding, but still at peace. Hez tried to recall what Mayurn had told him about the Chalktown business, but it all seemed muddy. There was a death. Some gal died, he thought he remembered. The story rode the papers for a while. Made the front page of the *Hattiesburg American*. But details were right up there with a math equation: scribblings that meant nothing in the long run.

"I bet there was a reason for the death, though. Some mystery behind the doin of it." He poured water from his jar into the bottle, sucked the nipple clean and put it in his brother's mouth. "There's no mystery concernin you, though, is there? Not one single cloudy thing."

He kissed his brother's mustard-smelling hair, then looked around to see if anybody had seen him do it. The cow stood broadfaced in the sun, her shadow spread out underneath her, a low blue, cast down on green. Other than the bovine, the place was empty.

He was born in the middle of an April thunderstorm that most in George County thought would be the death of them, and upon his exiting from his mother, the name Levi had been proudly placed on the latest Sheehand by Susan-Blair, who had been nine and a half months from the whiskey bottle. She had thought the name priestly and providential. A name an oracle might wear.

Hezekiah was young when his mother took on the Holy Book and got herself saved, and he'd seen her both ways: unredeemed and sweet-drunk, and redeemed and mean as a snake. He preferred unredeemed and drunk and used to pray God would give her a yearning for the taste of whiskey again, but then Yellababy got himself poleaxed by Billy Reuben, and Hez repented and changed the method of his supplication. But in spite of his adjustment to his prayers, Hezekiah could not help remembering how his mother used to talk soft to him and laugh, playing peekaboo through the clothes hanging from the ceiling. And how she used to hold him and rock him when he was way too big for it, singing a lunatic lullaby the whole while. Back in those drunken unredeemed days Hez would smell her brittle breath and count it as one more strange side effect in a house as far from normal as a house could be.

For two days after he was born, Yellababy was still Levi Sheehand, growing oracle and country preacher in the making. The time felt good and sweet, almost happy. On the third day his brother woke up yellow as a squash and everything changed.

Providence was handy, but late as usual, having appeared in the form of a Negro midwife who had happened along looking for a replacement for the Blue Willow platter her son-in-law had thrown at her and smashed. People as far away as Leakesville had heard about the strange woman in Agricola who hoarded cast-off pieces of everything under the sun, and even a Negro who normally would never set foot inside a white woman's domain could be tempted to try it. This one had wandered slow past the table holding shoes and found herself next to the wicker bassinet in the corner. Looking down, she shouted, "Lord have mercy! We got to get this youngun out to the sunshine quick!" Susan-Blair, still fresh enough saved in Christ Jesus to make a show of being kind to coloreds, let the woman have her way with the baby. Levi was lifted up out of the bassinet and placed on a soft blanket out in the yard, where he squinted and blinked and mewed like a cat.

Marion Calhoun had wandered over and commented on his fresh pumpkin color and come to his own conclusion, saying I'd git that baby off the grass and call a doctor. Any doctor. And right soon, too. He'd been jumped by the midwife, who saw the black man as a threat to her healing skills, and said as much right up in his face. "You the man who got jilted by that gal. You hush up! We all know about you. Whole wide world knows about you!"

Hezekiah remembered sitting on the wooden porch next to a box of gears, thinking the whole business seemed like a clown act at a second-rate circus, put on and gaudy, while underneath nobody really cared a tit's shadow about the heart of it, least of all Levi, who was squalling and intermittently sucking at his tiny fists while he squinted and kicked his legs up in the air. The baby got yellower and yellower throughout the day, the whites of his eyes finally turning the ominous color of a late summer thunderhead.

Once the sun had set and done its fullest remedial work, and the colored midwife had left holding a replacement platter, they rushed him off to the same place he'd been born two days earlier. Two days later, on a Thursday it was, Fairy drove up in his bus, crying and sobbing while he stumbled across the front yard, his hands down at his sides.

"Damned bilirubin's stole my baby's brains, son!"

He clung to Hez in a way he'd never done before, and for a second or two, or however long it took him to smell his father's breath, Hez thought the man so affectionate he'd taken up drinking.

"Who's this durn Billy Reuben fella?" Hez had asked. Crying by that time because he'd grown attached to the baby, what with his smallish head and big blue eyes shining out like two bright cornflowers.

"A killer is what . . . That's what bilirubin is!"

"You want me to kill him for you?" Hezekiah was serious, constraining his father by the arms, oversized for his age, almost as big as Marion Calhoun. That one was leaning on the fence, watching the whole business while he shook his head.

"Where's the sonofabitch at, 'cause I swear to Jesus, I'll do it! This fella's dead as a knob or my name aint Hezekiah Sheehand!"

To his amazement, Fairy had started to laugh. Long swells of it that started gut level and moved outward 'til he shook all over, knocked loose Hezekiah's concerned, constraining arms.

Later, after all was said and done Hez attributed Fairy's actions to fatigue and grief and suffering, not noticing, or not remembering that he had noticed, Marion Calhoun walking off in the middle of it with a disgusted set to his broad colored shoulders and not one single back-looking glance.

"We'll be going, soon," Hez said, straightening his brother's pants, looking down into his blue eyes. "You'll see somethin new today, and maybe you'll even remember it."

The sixteen-year-old shut his eyes and leaned back his head. The place was sweet and calm and beautiful, and the air was amazingly warm for February. The forlorn train tracks, the feathery trees wearing their deep green cloaks, the one lonely cow—all seemed anointed and predestined for an austere life, yet soft and cozy as a cocoon. I could sit here for hours, he thought. Sit here and wait for a train, and then when it comes, if it's going slow enough, I might could run and run and run and jump on board. With you, of course. No way in hell I'd leave you behind. You may have worn your Holy Scripture name for only a day or two, but it was a true name, an important name. And if there's a God hidin somewhere in the middle of this shit-kickin county, there has to be a reason for it. There has to be.

CHAPTER 9

In the bright sunlight, Cathy stood like a lost bookend, misplaced and impractical, leaning against the hubcap stand set to the side of the road. It had been a place for selling fruits and vegetables before it was a hubcap stand; she could see faded chipped paint announcing tomatoes and pears and Chilton County peaches decorating its dirty-white front. An old colored woman had set up housekeeping in a large droopy tent behind the stand, near a thicket of honeysuckle and bracken and smothery kudzu. Underneath a green flap Cathy could see a metal folding chair and various crates and tiny blinking lights of unknown origin. An old spotted dog, with every rib showing, was crouched in the dirt near the woman's feet, licking up and down her legs. The woman was a large one, all shifted weight and as low to the ground as a stump. She sat on a board placed between two overturned buckets, her heavy tits, overcome by gravity, resting along her waist. Yellow socks were on her feet and the skin between dress and sock was pink in quarter-size patches, like her pigment had grown tired of being Negro and chosen something easier to live with: perhaps white.

"How come you aint got no fruit?" Cathy asked the woman, whose eyes were jet black and rheumy and sunken in her lined face.

The woman was silent for a moment, her gums moving sideways, and then she spoke. "What month is it?"

"February," Cathy said.

"What fruit you know growin in Febery?"

Cathy grinned and shook her head, swinging her ponytail. "Then how come you to set up shop out here when there aint no fruit to sell?"

The woman reached down and scratched the head of the skin-and-bones dog and looked away. Her whitish hair was kinked and held close to her skull by a flowery scarf and Cathy could see that the dress she was wearing was undone in the back. To accommodate those tits, she figured.

"I find 'em by the side of the road and take 'em. Folks lose hubcaps and need anothern. Even in Mississippi." The hubcaps were hanging on nails, some bent and rusted, others brilliantly shiny.

"And you sit out here all day long and wait for folks to look you up for a spare hubcap?"

The woman glanced at her, her fingers linked together, her thumbs working against each other in a private game of thumb war. The dog became more frenzied in its licking, hungry for attention. "Them shore is green shorts," she said.

Cathy looked down, embarrassed. She had pulled off her coveralls and scrubbed off her knees and then rummaged through a box in her closet for the nearest thing she owned to casual wear. She felt the woman saw through her, saw those thoughts she was beginning to have. She pulled at the left leg of her shorts, tried to make it longer. "You sit here all day and wait for folks to come lookin for a hubcap?"

"They's some days folks come. And some days they don't. Aint no never mind to me either way."

"Seems a lonely way to spend time."

"Never had no use for folks. I like my dawg, though." She bent and rubbed the dog's head and he ceased his licking and swooned up at her with lovesick eyes. "I seen you cut 'cross that field there." The woman pointed to the ribbed brown that stretched out in front of her. The road cut through it, with a newness that seemed irreparably wrong. Paved for twenty years at least, County Road 614 still seemed a fresh stranger. "Thought you was a dawg at first. Then I seen you werent nothin but a gal."

Cathy wondered at the comparison and why a dog was considered more valuable. She looked around the woman's site, tried to peer inside the tent. What she saw lent a permanance to the woman's situation. There was a tiny woodstove and a palette of faded quilts, even a lantern half full of oil.

"You live here, don't you? You aint got no house."

"I don't need no house."

"I thought everbody needed a house to live in."

"I aint complainin."

Cathy found it charming, now that she thought on it. Gypsyish. Pack up and leave soon as folks disappoint you, or meddle where they got no business meddling.

"You got dirt to yer elbow," the woman said and the dog seemed to understand the criticism, and stared at her.

"Uncle Jimmy had to cut in the field and I had to help," Cathy said, spitting in her palm and rubbing at the offending spot of skin.

"You run away from work, did you?"

"I worked enough. The reason I was runnin is because I wanted to git here before somebody else did." She brushed at the fine hairs of her arms. "I guess I did, too," she said to the bright air, "beat him here, that is."

The woman leaned to her elbows and her breasts leaned with her. Reaching into one yellow sock, she pulled out a packet of chewing tobacco and worked a dark damp wad in her fingers before stuffing it in her mouth. Cathy could smell the sweet of it all the way over to where she stood.

"Aint you curious about who I'm meetin?"

"I aint yer kin."

Cathy stared at her. "True. They aint curious about me either, now that I think about it. Anyhow, the one I'm waitin for is goin to Chalktown and he's totin his retarded little brother on his back." Cathy brushed her hands together, and then ran them down her lime-green shorts.

"You ort stay away from there. Them folks is touched."

Cathy shrugged. Everybody was touched, in some way or the other, especially this one here getting her bath by way of a licking dog.

"Got their speech stolt from 'em."

"Uncle Jimmy thinks they're foolin."

"Some says they got their tongues cut out—"

"Uncle Jimmy says that's a lie."

"This uncle of yourn sounds like a man full of opinions."

"That and nothin else. They aint a thing to him other than what he thinks about somebody else." She leaned into the stand and the hubcaps bonged together with a sound like no other.

"Well, I'd shore like to know what that uncle'd say 'bout you hangin round waitin for a boy." The woman grinned at her and laughed a deep wet laugh. When she spit her juice, the dog bent to it and sniffed, and then licked at the dirt.

Cathy wondered a little bit about that, too. She looked past the woman, into the dark of the tent, at the strange blinking lights. It was sunlight catching on glass. It seemed this woman was a collector of bottles. All sizes and shapes stood upright along the back flap of the tent. Some were full of liquid, others half full, others barely held an inch. The liquid was shaded in different colors, too. An amber brew in one of them, something the color of chokeberries in another. A backwoods apothecary came to Cathy's mind. Either that, or the woman was into homebrew and hadn't yet learned the art of it.

Cathy looked over at the black woman, who was shaking her head. The woman had said something as a form of reproof, but the words were lost. Something about the green shorts and how she'd tear up the legs of one of her younguns should they skip school and cut across a field, chasing after a boy. Cathy thought it an empty boast seeing how the younguns she was so proud of had seen fit to leave her living by the side of the road in a tent.

"Kilt a gal deader 'n Moses. Got away with it too. Theys be Negro you'd find 'em hangin from a tree. They hainted down there."

"You don't know that."

"I know anuff," the black woman said. "You aint got no call goin down that road." She reached down and scratched the side of her wide, cracked foot and the look she gave Cathy seemed knowledgeable and concerned.

"I aint afraid."

"You mighty big for them bright-green britches—"

"I said, I aint afraid."

"Hear them folks don't take to visitors," the black woman said in a quiet voice.

The dog was done with her and lolled about on the ground, his pink tongue falling like a curtain out his mouth. Cathy looked at the tent. Imagined fleas and ticks jumping like gangbusters over bedding and skin. Fought the urge to scratch hard at her socked ankle.

"We aint gonna bother nobody," she said.

"No mor'n you botherin me, I s'pose. Need me some blinders, I do. You and them bright-green shorts take the prize—"

"You can hush up cause I aint listenin."

"You steppin in shit that aint yourn," the Negro said.

Ignoring her, moving out into the hot noon sunlight, Cathy put a hand to her eyes and strained to see up the road. A spot was growing bigger in the east and she knew it was Hezekiah. She squinted to get a better look, studied the blond hair and weighted shoulders and gangly arms swinging into focus and thought, Lord have mercy, aint he a sight!

CHAPTER 10

Fairy pedaled slower once he passed Beachum's Corner, worn slap out by the heat. The place seemed blasted and empty but for a few bleak-knobbed crows sitting near some limb's limit, rocking in hot wind and not bothering to stir, just eyeing Fairy's dust as he pedaled under, then past. For a reason he couldn't determine, he felt more kin to the crows than he did the woman waiting for him. Maybe it was the size of his life now: its new immediacy and quaintness, the way it seemed small enough to balance on his shoulder. He tipped his cap toward a pair of blue-black wings and pedaled on. *I could put my hand round a crow and place it in my small life, and should the mood strike me, take it out and set it free again. No one would be the wiser.* For February, the wind was a hot one, and carried on it the odor of moldy earth laid open in neighboring fields, and the rich piney smell of torn greening vines, as well as brackish water. He took pride in this new cognizance concerning nature and marveled that death seemed a rich teacher these days: spilling secrets previously clutched in the palm of a selfish hand. He was nearing Susan-Blair's house. The overflow from her crowded yard was already in view: the rusted tubs of used-to-be washing machines, the cast-iron bed frames forming prison bars for kudzu and honeysuckle, the ox yokes bearing red-painted proverbs. Coasting, he fought the sun's glare and tried to search for her feet stuck back under a chair, the blond head leaning back against the wall of the house while she surveyed her kingdom, but the porch seemed empty. Empty but for the gutless things and the rusted things and the busted things.

"You Susie! I'm here now! Where in blazes are you?"

He leaned his bike on the porch and stood still for a minute to catch his breath and said aloud, "I'll not fight with her this time. I'll be good and it won't take a toll on me." His ribs felt rubbery to the touch, inflamed, and when he put his hand to his face and wiped away the sweat, he was alarmed by the amount of wet he slung to the ground.

"Susan-Blair!" he yelled, mounting the steps and going through the door, meeting a wall of clothes that he pushed aside before wandering through the front part of the house.

"Susan!"

"In here, Fairy."

He found her in the dark, stretched out on her bed, a thin coverlet spread over her legs, her face lit by a sick, greenish sheen. Damp blond hair fanned out across the pillow and he could see that her eyelids, paper-thin and grained with tiny blue capillaries, were pulsing. Another headache. Bad one, too, by the looks of it. They had come early-on in the marriage and he'd grown accustomed to them, but their intensity never failed to alarm him. Fairy wondered for the hundredth time if some type of brain hemorrhage might be happening. She had put an army blanket over the window to block the light and when he first came through the door the woman seemed dead and void of features and then she'd spoken and he settled, almost laughed at her ability to play possum.

"How come you to send for me?" He studied her. Even stretched out on her bed, hindered by severe pain, she seemed tall as a church pillar. Way too big for him. While he watched, she clutched at her printed dress with oversized hands.

She was whispering and he bent down to listen and got hit in the face with a thick smell radiating off her. The headaches carried the stench of vinegar that seemed to emanate from the female juncture of her body and he stood back up again. "I aint got all day," he said, running a hand across his eyes.

"Arena's gone." Her blue eyelids were quivering.

"The hell you mean she's gone?"

"She aint here. She run off."

A galvanized pail was by her bed and he watched her fling out one hand and touch its cool rim, heard the click of her fingernails tapping on the metal side.

"Run off where? How?"

"You want the where or the how? Answer's the same for both. I aint got a clue."

"You don't seem too broke up over it."

"I'm sick. Too sick to think about it."

So am I, he thought, wishing he could take a stick to her, drive her up off the bed and out into the yard where there was sunshine and sense.

"How can somebody who don't never leave the house not keep track of her only daughter?" he said.

"Same as you can disappear for months then ride up and act like it means somethin."

He was confused by the comparison and studied her for a long moment. "Did you see her leave?" he said.

"She was out all night. Climbed out the window, I guess. Man brought her back this morning and then she left again, walkin—"

"What in blazes are you talking about? What man?" Fairy walked over to her dresser and looked into the mirror and worked his neck from side to side. His wife's reflection floated in the air over his shoulder, framed by cheap mahogany but still accusatory. He could see her eyes studying him, waiting. Fairy looked down. The one and only barren space in the overcrowded house was this scarred surface of veneer, shiny with lemon wax; superficial. He put his hands to it, smudged it with his palm prints. Her stretchy-band Timex was there, facedown, ticking away. Her wedding band was next to it throwing a green-gold orb. "Tell me," he said.

"I don't know who he is."

"Tell me what you do know, then."

"She was out all night but come back this mornin."

The last time Fairy had seen Arena she'd been slumped in a pout, haggling with Hezekiah over a box of movie magazines. "If she'd been up to somethin ugly, she'd a picked the dark to come home in. She come home in broad daylight. That has to mean somethin."

"A full-grown man dumped her in the yard, Fairy. I guess you think she was out pickin blackberries all night long and just hitched a ride home to get herself ready for school?"

"Who is he?" Fairy felt as though he were entering a dark woods, a place of uncommon foliage done-up in colors contrary to nature. The grass was black here, leaves hot orange and shaped like flames, insults whispered from the hearts of trees, but in the middle of all this queerness, his voice was low, almost calm, and it surprised him.

"I don't know his name," she said. "He drives a county car is all I know. Does somethin for George County."

"Does somethin for George County."

"How come you're repeatin me?"

"How'd you come to know he does somethin for George County?"

"I just know."

"Oh, I bet you do." He didn't doubt it for a minute.

There were things she couldn't admit to, not even to God. The county seat was one of them. And how this man had first set eyes on Arena while Susan-Blair talked to the lady about the baby and how to get rid of him. That horrible, opinionated lady who'd said they should count their blessings and not consider putting the child away in the State Institute for the Infirm. Told them there were folks who could train them to take care of him; help them build braces and ramps and show them where to find child-sized crutches, and nurses who could train their hands to massage those spindly legs dead set on pigeon-toeing, and so on and so forth, *blahdeeblahdeeblah*. Eventually, if they played their cards right, there might even be a tiny wheelchair. Susan-Blair knew that during the discourse the man in the suit had sat across from Miss Social Opinions. There at his cluttered desk with its oscillating fan and chewed-up pencils he had watched Arena preen and reapply her lipstick and cross and recross her legs. Susan-Blair couldn't admit these things, though. Not and have Fairy get wind of her wanting to dump the baby.

She reached for a wet washcloth and put it over her eyes so she wouldn't have to see him.

"You think real hard now and tell me if you've seen him anywhere else, 'cause I'm goin after him. Goin to the law if I have to. And once I'm done goin, once I've found my daughter, she won't step out again. I tell you that."

He looked out the window at Calhoun's truck and wondered what it would cost him to use it. He thought of his big cumbersome bus and the way it would look prowling through the streets of Lucedale, pots swinging, lawn chairs bouncing and then he remembered Silva's truck back at the fish camp and how she had offered him use of it and then he buried all these thoughts as not worth the effort of thinking.

"I think he might work with the school board. Maybe." Susan-Blair turned her rag to a cooler side, bit down on her lip, reached for the bucket. The metal felt cool as water. It sat inside a palm like a lifeline. "Julia says maybe that's where he works. That he was checkin for truants a while back."

Fairy said, "Hezekiah bein one of them?"

"Yes."

"Out babysittin somebody that ought to be to your lap this very second?"

"Or yours."

Fairy noticed her breasts were fuller than Silva's. Always had been. Where Silva was as lean as a weathered fence post, this one here spilled out like a field full of weeds. Susan-Blair leaned to the side and he watched her left tit slide into her armpit. "You're his mama," he said, pressing his hand to the surface of the dresser once more, leaning down to check the standard of his life crease. It was shorter than the day before, he would almost swear to it, and now this. "Mamas tend their young. Most mamas, that is."

"I know you, Fairy. How you feel about him. God knows it, too. So shut the hell up." She peeled up the corner of the wet cloth and looked at him.

For a minute all there was between them was truth, and he found it unbearably bald and ugly. "I aint here to talk about Yellababy. I'm here to talk about my daughter."

"Well, talk then."

"How long you known about this, sister?"

"Don't call me sister. I hate it when you call me that."

He mended it. "How long you known about this, Susan-Blair?"

"Not long," she said. "Probably long enough, though. I bet you anythin
it was long enough."

Five minutes was long enough for you, he thought. And if Silva had
been able to keep from plannin my whole life and eternity, I would a never
given you a second of my time. He wondered about women and their sticky
flaws and why he felt the need for extrication whenever he was with one
of them.

Fairy left her, walked through the hallway shoving a rack of clothes out
of his way. There used to be a couch where the boxes of shoes sat. A
goodish chair, too, plaid was it? Somewhere in that corner there. Disgusted,
he pulled open the door and went out onto the porch. He could see Calhoun
putting a drip ring around the crippled pecan near the road. The black man
looked up and then went on about his business. Jerking the bicycle upright
and straddling it, Fairy caught his breath. The lumps were acting up. Apparently the ride over had given them a new song all done up in sharps.

"Well, you just hold on now, boys. You caint have me 'til I'm done
here. When I'm done rescuing the only one I ever cared about, the only one
who aint ruint, I'll go peaceful."

Susan-Blair listened to him leave. Tracked his progress by the squawking
of the geese. In two minutes she heard the jingle of the bicycle bell when
he turned off at Beachum's Corner. Reaching for the bucket, feeling its cool
comfort rim, she realized it took him longer to get there than it had the last
time he'd pedaled over, but she didn't stop to wonder why.

CHAPTER 11

Arena walked up his long sandy drive pulling at her dress and wishing
she'd carried the good sense to wear clean socks. Every time she
glanced down she saw the dust of the walk clamoring up from her ankles
and catching around her knees, threatening the hem of her rose-print dress.
The dust had started back near Beachum's Store with just a low benevolent
powder that turned her socks red as a cock's comb. A mile out, the dirt
found her shins and by the time she got to his road, she looked as though
she'd been waist-dipped in red chalk pigment. There was a plan to her life,
and this wasn't in it.

"I should a cleaned myself up a little," she said, spitting into her hand
and brushing at a printed rose capping her knee. The sun was directly
overhead and she was circled by her shadow. Trees and low shrubs and
azaleas yet to bloom formed neat borders that framed her and locked her into
the hot, still landscape and from a bird's perspective she appeared ant-like,
slow-moving and dusty, but determined.

The man had manicured boxwoods bracketing his driveway. Yards and yards and yards of them and she knew the cost of every shovel-turn, because he had told her. Attentive as a two-year-old, she had listened to him brag while she looked out his dark car window, believing the dark humps they were passing had turned to bowing dwarfs from a yet-to-be-written fairy tale. Arena had not been overly taken by his worship of greenery, but hitched herself up at the news it had cost seventy-five dollars. Later on that night she stood outside a ring of camellias, wiping her hands on leathery leaves, and tried to calculate the sort of things seventy-five dollars might buy, completely overcome by the sheer mass of possibilities.

Remembering that night and what she had done, she reached out and stripped the tiny leaves from off the nearest shrub. When she dropped them to the ground, movement caught her eye. The strap was flopping on her left shoe. The one she'd fixed two months back with embroidery thread. The one she had busted her thumb over. Now it was broke.

"I guess I should a worn some other shoes. As well as clean socks," she said with a shrug while she walked, holding up a hand, marveling that her nail polish matched the color of those curled cups of camellias.

Folks who threw away their shoes were all clodhoppers, as far as she could tell. Big-boned with wide flat feet that sat at the end of their legs like blocks of wood. The smallest she'd ever found in the resale box was a size eight, a full size too big for her. Sometimes she would stuff toilet paper in the toes and this worked fine, at least for school. Not for a long walk, though. For a long walk a body needed something that would fit proper and not tear up halfway there. She had been roaming the footprint of the county since she was ten years old and felt she knew the ins and outs.

In the early days, when she was five or six and just discovering it, she would travel it with her father, Fairy, tucked safely inside the wire basket on the front of his bicycle. Down to the stockyard they would go, and then over to the one malt shop on Magnolia Avenue and finally to the Lucedale Restaurant with its huge white scratching post on the sidewalk.

The restaurant was the best place in all of George County as far as she was concerned. The padded red benches felt good to her bottom and for only a nickel she could play a song from the small jukebox that sat one each to a table. The surefooted waitresses in their white uniforms, all of them large-breasted women with big netted hair, were quick and confident and keen-eyed with a smell to them of good things: fried chicken, okra, butter beans flavored in pork. While Arena would sit, her hands curled around the chrome-edged table, she watched them handle the men at the counter with straight-backed confidence and bawdy humor. Arena thought that to be a waitress in the town of Luce-dale, or any town for that matter, would be a high achievement for any woman. For a female who could handle a man as well as she handled a piece of meat, could handle anything at all.

The county's footprint felt huge then, limitless. The creeks and rivers. The winding dirt roads. The courthouse square, where Fairy liked to sit and watch folks wandering in and out the door, speculating the whole while on the nature of business that brought them there. The feed store that smelled of sweet corn, and the five-and-dime, where she could look long and hard through the window at the hats and the smart, city umbrellas that nobody in George County would dare be seen with. Fairy bought her a pennywhistle once and she blew it until she was red in the face. It made the baby cry, though, and Susan-Blair took it away from her and put it high on a shelf behind the blue dish with the windmill. Arena felt the footprint begin to close in on her that year, but she still tolerated it. By the time she was ten, she was roaming on her own, her bottom too big for a basket on a bicycle.

She could see his house set back off the road. He called it a cottage and spit would collect in the corner of his lip when he bragged on the shutters. Cottage shutters don't come cheap, he said. Had to send all the way over to Vicksburg for them. His method of putting on airs, sophisticated at first, appeared simply stupid and prissy a week later. The house was white with a wide screen porch that shielded the swing and the potted geraniums and the blue-satin dog bed. She hadn't seen the porch swing or the blue dog bed, or the flowers, but he had told her about them and how much they cost and how the dog would curl up and go to sleep at eight o'clock on the dot each and every night. While the two of them sat inside the dark car bracketed by boxwoods and she worked on him with her hands, he explained the complexities of the canine.

In her opinion the dog, a French poodle for Christsakes, was wasteful of time and energy. He said it had an irritating habit of waking at three in the morning and yapping the rest of the night away, and during bad weather, it chewed on the legs of the furniture, sometimes vomiting on the Oriental rug, and this confirmed her estimation.

How come you don't kill it? she had asked and seen, by the light of the moon, his horrified face and quickly put her hand to his arm and said, I was makin a joke, is all.

His eyes said he didn't believe one word of it was a joke, but his hands weren't paying attention to his eyes, and she was glad. She had sat still in the dark, musing and making plans. As soon as I'm honestly married to him, and not just taking his money, the dog is a goner. She'd not have any animal, or child for that matter, chewing on furniture and keeping her up all night. One retarded little brother had worn out the motherly side to her early on and she had no intention of recultivating it. So the dog was living on the outside edge of the lap of luxury. One yap away from scrapping under the house and licking pork drippings out of a tin pan, like all the other dogs she'd ever seen.

The man loved his porch. He said he had painted the planked floor blue and that, come the summer, he was enclosing it to make a brand-new room. He loved his house, too, and spent way too much time talking about it, in Arena's opinion. But the porch was nice enough and the house was pretty, too, what with the way it looked more like a picture-book house than the real thing.

The screen porch was in front of her now, fifty feet away, plain as day.

This was the second time she had made the walk to his house, and this time, like the last, she made a game of counting the boxwoods along the drive. Passing the twentieth one, with just a little ways to go, she licked her lips, thirsty as all get out.

"At least he buys me a co-cola after I do it. A drink and peanuts would be good on a hot day like this."

Wiping her face with the side of her arm, she sniffed, saying, "Lord, I stink like a driven horse. Nobody would want me like this. Not even him."

Arena tried the screen door and realized it was latched. She pulled on the black iron fleur-de-lis grillwork, but couldn't make it jump the hook. Leaning back, she gauged the strength of the hinges against her fingernails, freshly painted in pearly pink, and decided no. Hezekiah had showed her how to break into Susan-Blair's jewelry box with a penknife, and she wished she had paid more attention to her brother's lesson on thievery.

"If I had me somethin sharp I could split the screen and reach in and free it. Finally see the actual porch and the actual front door and all that other stuff he talks on and on about. I would do it in a second, too."

She knelt on the top step and pressed her face to the screen. The dog was on the other side, a fluff of Frenchy white curled comfortably on its blue pillow. Yellow-brown stains ran down from its eyes and she wondered what in the world the damn dog had to cry over. While she watched, the animal opened one lid and stared at her for a minute and then tucked his head under a leg, so unimpressed he didn't bother to bark.

CHAPTER 12

Susan-Blair lifted down her one valuable piece of glassware, taking precaution against jiggling her head. The plate shimmered in the dull afternoon light and she shut her eyes for a second or two against the glare because the headache was not fully over, not completely done.

Blue and white, the plate had a windmill to its center, glazed and fired beyond movement. Tulips were frozen along its borders and in her opinion what she held in her hand was a precious piece of Holland trapped on a dirt road in George County, Mississippi. She couldn't remember the face of the previous owner, or how much she'd paid for it, those years too far back now, having played out before awareness. Before Fairy's first time of leaving and before Levi turned to Yellababy. Before she began to feel empty and hungry and needful of clutter and woke one day as famished as a great lumbering beast that refuses satisfaction. Her heart felt empty as a hollow leg, which each and all knew could never be filled up. That sense of awesome hunger a thing that lasts forever in the South.

"Awesome hunger," she said out loud in a deep false voice and thought it sounded like a mating call of a zoo beast. She spoke it again and was sure of it. She wiped the plate clean and set it back in its plate holder, moving Arena's old pennywhistle out of the way in the process. Her left eye was twitching as persistently as a clock's tick, a sign the headache was truly easing. A flask, tarnished and empty, was still hiding behind a ceramic cornucopia full of glass corn and plastic leaves and out-of-season rubber grapes. Susan-Blair picked it up and rubbed at it with the hem of her dress and saw a brow first, and then a nose. Her face came back to her concaved and metal-eyed and near-green and while she held the container in her hand her fingers trembled and marked it with moisture prints up and down its slender side. It had been years since she'd last seen it. So long in the past she'd almost forgotten it existed and who had touched it and what he had said that made her stop drinking.

There was a road that led down to the river that seemed to have her name written on it. At first, in those early drunk days, she would wander down it to do her thinking and to have a covert drink or two. The path was not a well-traveled road, but near enough to home should she get so drunk she'd not be hard-pressed to remember the way back.

The actual name of the road was County Something or Other. County 451, or 452, maybe. Picked on and shot at, its marker fell to tall grass every few years and folks forgot it. Took to calling the road by its more definitive and hopeful name: Sweet River Road. Almost a sweet place, the dirt road had a sharp curve that butted into a view of moving brown water and when she would walk down in late evening, while the sun was spreading fiery fingers behind the trees, it appeared as though the road dropped off to a heavy gold liquid and she would imagine it that way. Maybe not a pot at the end of a rainbow, but a cool river bath for sore feet, at least. There, on a rock jutting out over a shallow pool like the hand of a giant, Susan-Blair would sing, or drink, or sleep, should she feel the need to. The time it had happened, it had happened there, near the rock that felt like a hand, back in a year that, for a few months at least, had seemed brighter than the years before.

Weeks earlier the man had parked his black car at Beachum's Corner and set up the bullhorn in the middle of the summer harvest and while peas, pink-eyed and purple-hulled, as well as butter beans and corn needed tending, those black-boxed speakers blared atop a Plymouth all day long and into the night. John 3:16. "For God so Loved." The words prodded them. Goaded the country women away from *The Secret Storm*, where they'd more than likely be sitting shelling a basin of legumes while watching golden-haired women flirt with men they ought not to.

Hez was almost ten years old and into everything at once. Arena was eleven and not into enough of anything. Just staticky radio music and scratched Nat King Cole selections on the secondhand walnut turntable. *First the tide rushes in . . .* over and over, hanging up and skipping fourteen words before jumping to *Mona Lisa, Mona Lisa, Mona Lisa. . . .* Fairy more gone than not. Susan-Blair overly dependent on Wild Turkey and Jim Beam to help her get through the mornings and their basins of peas and silty corn and "What's My Line?" with Kitty Carlisle and Bennett Cerf and then through the afternoons where, with the help of a drink, daytime would slink into eventual night again.

She had finally gone to the meetings and sat on a wooden chair same as all the others, and been hypnotized by those hands. Slender and well-defined, long fingered as sweet ivory bones, they tore with divine purpose through fragile gold-dusted pages of the Good Book. He had a black Bible the color of good leather shoes, its cover pebbled and limp as old, loose skin that had lived good.

"God sees into the heart of man," he had said that first day at Beachum's Corner.

She'd frozen then, heat stealing up from her gut to her head where it felt like it met up with gunpowder and exploded. She had never thought of God as having prying eyes, just his son, for some dumb reason. Just the Only Begotten always nosy and waiting to tattle.

"God knows your thoughts before you do."

It filled her throat. Gushered up. She looked down at her shoes and saw purses scattered in the sawdust. One woman had brought a bag of corn as a donation for his offering basket.

Clutching her funeral fan she ran out to where the others couldn't see, all the way out to a yulaberry bush where she puked and spewed, pock-marking the dust.

"I should not a come here," she told herself, looking at those speakers on top of the car. Checking out her shoes to see how bad she'd splattered.

"You got no business bein here either," she told the speakers, wiping a hand across her mouth, seeing their square shadows stretching outward to the tent tie-downs.

Feeling such a load of glaring anger in her deep stomach she felt like screaming, she looked over her shoulder at the six others hanging on to his words, their feet in wood chips, their peas and beans waiting back home on a sticky table, same as hers. She caught his eye and wished for a gun. Him standing there with that Good Book open and loose over his hand. Like a hunk of dead flesh, broken open and exposed. No longer good.

"I got what you need, sister." He had called this out, and his words seemed to echo in the damp summer heat. "I got just what you need." He shut the book and held it up for her to see. Twelve eyes followed his to catch her standing by a bush in drippy shoes.

"You got nothin I aint seen before," she said aloud to all of them before walking off toward home, familiar with Christ and his words and how he liked to suffer them down on her head from a hovering presence in her kitchen. Dealt cards tossed from a low cloud, was how it felt to her. A constant raining down of bad-draw judgment.

Foolish and soiled, she walked home to her clutter.

Arena had lazed through most of the beans, run a rag over the kitchen table and then left to go somewhere involving less work.

Susan-Blair looked out the kitchen window and saw Hezekiah over at the colored neighbor's back porch picking through a Mason jar holding nuts and bolts. A yellow cat was curled by his side.

"You got what I need?" she said to the cabinet over the fridge. "I think you just might."

Julia would be at home. She could go over to her sister's. And then Susan-Blair shuddered, the idea sickening. Or maybe to the Sweet River Road, where the warm palm of a rock sat quietly waiting in a place that seemed sequestered. And that thought soothed her. Reaching to the cabinet she took the flask Fairy had given her the Christmas before and slipped it into a pocket. Not bothering to leave a note—they'd think she was still down at Beachum's Corner at Bible study anyhow—she headed off to the only peaceful place she knew of.

He came up behind her while she was sitting on the low rock singing like a drunk. She wasn't drunk. She had just felt like singing, was all. When she heard someone walking through the brush ten paces back, instead of hushing up, she sang louder. She had not yet taken a drink. She was going to, but for now, it was inside her front pocket, waiting.

"I thought I might have offended you."

He said it like two words: off ended.

"I had no business bein there," she said and then began singing the second verse of her song, ignoring him and his Good Book. There would have been room on the rock if she were to slide over, but she didn't. At that point she didn't want anything to do with him. Just wanted him to leave so she could sing in peace. Her singing made her feel like two people: one wild and darkly vagrant, the other scared and huddled in her pocket. The wild one was singing while the other peeped over clutched fabric, scared of everything in general.

"I told the Lord that I would preach his word to all the nations—" he began.

"You need a new map then," she said, interrupting him. "We aint a nation. Just a dirt road goin nowhere, is all. Mostly Methodist, too. Or Hard Shell Baptist. Caint think of a single person keen on that Holy Ghost of yours."

"There is a truth here that's wider than any road you can imagine."

"I doubt it."

He laughed then and it gave her the first chance to really study him. His nose was overly long and he seemed housed in an awkward slenderness that appeared fragile. Tall, too, with well-pressed clothes that made her wonder who in town had offered to do his washboard work. She had no idea how he'd found her on the trail. The trail was hers. Nobody knew it, or what she thought while she was walking down it. She had no idea how he'd found his way and she wondered if he'd followed her, maybe waiting out near the road while she stood in the kitchen considering. Hell, I don't even know his name.

"I don't even know your name," she said.

"Brother Mills," he said.

She waved a hand in the air, "Don't bother then."

He recovered somewhat grudgingly. "Mitch. My given name is Mitchell."

"Well, Mitch, what do you want with me? I aint goin back to that study group, so you might as well leave."

He reached for her, his hand brushing lightly across her stomach, and caught the neck of the flask and lifted it out of her pocket. Weighed it. Rocked it back and forth like a square silver ship. She could almost see the liquid hurling itself in waves against metal walls. Without saying a word, he handed it to her, his eyes gray-quiet and softly sad, as if he'd walked all that way full of great expectations and then found himself face to face with a waxwork.

"You know the Shepherd will leave everthing he owns, the ninety and the nine, to find that one lost sheep." There was a moment's pause and from some distant glade a whippoorwill sounded. Then: "Them is not my words, but His."

She sat there, quiet as a dead mouse, her hands in her pockets fingering that other self, that shivering, scared, dying one. The boisterous one, the one who had done all the foolish singing was long gone, cutting through the woods like a shot-at deer.

"He'll leave everthing he's got and go lookin," Mitch said and then he got up and walked away from her, his eyes to the ground. He headed ghost-like through the woods, leaving her the frail image of an icy back.

"He found me a long time ago," Susan-Blair had whispered, frightened. "Found me a long time ago, I'd say."

She quit drinking that very night. Put the flask behind the ceramic cornucopia with the plastic leaves. And try as she might, she could not make herself stay away from the Bible study. She'd gone everyday solid for a week, her dress clean and starched, but her hands shaky, the bottle too freshly behind her for steadiness. Everybody knowing everybody else. Everybody knowing everybody there had better things to do, too. Washing. Canning. Plowing. All those chores waiting for them while their menfolks were out in the fields, or on the boats, or down to Mobile at the shipyards. All their women sitting huddled under a tent, wanting a fresh word, or a not-so-fresh word, wanting those slender hands put to their heads more than they wanted any-thing else. All of them knowing what those others wanted, too.

　The man explained the workings of Saint Paul's Galatians to them: *I am crucified with Christ, nevertheless I live; yet not I but Christ liveth in me....*

Susan-Blair, bored to tears, skimmed on down to the next chapter; played with the first verse: *O Foolish George Countyians, who hath bewitched you ...*

Day two was spent covering chapter twenty-seven of Deuteronomy, those blazing sins of the flesh that caused spit to fly out of Mitch's mouth and land on a tent post:

Cursed be he that lieth with any manner of beast ...

(Susan-Blair nodded her head. She'd heard about men who did that sort of thing.)

Cursed be he that lieth with his father's wife because he uncovereth his father's skirt.

(She was momentarily bewildered. She'd not ever seen a man in a skirt.)

Cursed be he that lieth with his sister ...

(She was thankful Hezekiah seemed to hate Arena with a passion.)

Susan-Blair looked down at the bags of tomatoes and butter beans leaning against chair legs and decided to rewrite verse eighteen, *Cursed be he that maketh poor ignorant country people lose their way and wander out of sight and suddenly inherit the belief that a tomato is currency.*

The women sat in a semicircle, blushing, trying to pay attention, their men's tractors humming too far off to be of any consequence. They eyeballed scriptures while old man Beachum refilled his coke machine, or swept off his dusty porch for the hundredth time. Doing these things while he shook his head in disgust before walking back into his store.

Throughout the week Mitch taught them the books of the Bible. Sang holy songs. Spent forty-five minutes in sermonizing, then forty-five minutes, at least, of individual prayer. When he put his hands to her head that sixth day, he whispered into her ear.

"I know you've quit the bottle. The Lord is mighty proud of you, Susan-Blair."

She kept remembering the sound of him coming up behind her while she sat singing on the rock, and she wished he'd said something a little more personal. Something other than how proud God was of her. She had never called him Mitch to his face; never let on to anybody that she knew his given name, but right before he walked away to pray for somebody else, she reached up and hooked his arm with her hand and said, "Thank you, Mitch."

Standing, embarrassed, her palms to the front of her unfamiliar freshly starched dress that just by touching, made her feel guilty (she'd never starched a thing for Fairy), she walked away fast.

A singular thought was with her, prodding her forward with hammering persistence: come late evening during that creeping, longing time between the sun's going down and the river's mist coming up, she would walk down Sweet River Road. She knew that he'd be there, too. The strange thing was that a part of her believed God just might be behind it all. That maybe God had sent this man named Mitch to sit beside her on a rock and make her feel special; that it was God's peace offering for all that spying His Son had been doing while floating along the ceiling of her kitchen. God the Father's way of saying "Sorry my son made a regular ass of Himself, Susan-Blair—"

That evening she left Hez sitting squat inside a makeshift tent between the two yards, as hunched down as a dog wary of a storm coming. It was his season of camping out in headgear resembling an Indian's, of lighting small fires that fizzled and popped, of sleeping outdoors, his eyes closing on the stars. The night before she had watched his flickering campfire from her bedroom window. The geese had been wandering near it, curious as ever over the flame, and there he was: neck deep in summertime. Marion Calhoun had left his back porch light on and the combined light from bulb and fire came through her bedroom window and formed patterns on top of her bed like dolphins leaping up out of water, bewildered by air. The dolphins danced and danced across her buried feet, hidden beneath a knobby coverlet, and to Susan-Blair's way of thinking, it seemed the sea creatures were living life on an incoming tide, bearing on their backs the bounty of the Lord.

Walking down the drive, she was remembering these things. Hez called out to her, "Watch out for snakes, Ma! They come out to the road and warm themselves at night." She thought about his low level of curiosity concerning her walking away at dusk. The way he called out a warning as if a female relative headed off into night bare-legged and sweaterless was an everyday occurrence, and his good-hearted warning seemed an irritant. Proof of her negligence. It fought hard with things she was just beginning to feel and want and dream on. Things she didn't have any business feeling or wanting or dreaming about.

"I know the color of hell."

Mitch had whispered this strange sentence into her ear, first thing. She'd been quiet this time. Her singing voice gone. She had been visualizing him cutting through low brush, stumbling on roots in dirt-speckled shoes, his head down with purpose. She imagined him pushing through the thick weeds and seeing her on the rock, her back to the world. And then she saw his hands to her shoulders and his bony chest to her fleshy one. She imagined him moved by the fact that she was sweaterless, and therefore, vulnerable to those hands that looked like precious ivory bones. Her breathing was hard and ragged and she heard him walking toward her for a long time while fantasizing. And during that time of waiting, she discovered something: those minutes of him coming toward her were better than when he finally appeared, and she was disappointed.

"You got any family?" she said, finally.

He seemed a stuck record as far as communication was concerned, and she squirmed while he skimmed over her question, going immediately into Corinthians, the love chapter, instead. She fidgeted while he talked on and on about clanging cymbals and sounding brass and how like the absence of love they were.

He's using scripture just like a shoehorn, she thought, amazed. A thing to help something else go in. Same as Fairy used to come wandering into the bedroom with a bottle of Jergens and the offer to rub her feet. Lotion. Scripture. It was all pretty much the same. Foreplay.

"Clanging cymbals and soundin brass, that's all life is without love," Mitch said, patting his pockets as if searching for a smoke.

Susan-Blair looked up at him. "You got any family left?"

"How come you to keep askin about family?"

"You said earlier you knew the color of hell. I just figured you had kinfolk somewhere as livin proof."

He laughed for a good long time over her words.

Her wit had surprised her. She felt bland and pasty most times, as though her brain were in neutral somewhere resting for an uphill climb. This new humor had set Susan-Blair spinning, made her feel young and careless, almost drunk.

"I got leftover relatives scattered back in Texas. I aint got much to talk with them about so I aint seen them in a while. I guess they're still there." He looked at her, "Tell me about yourself," he said, reaching over and touching her wedding ring. His finger left it spotted and dulled with moist proof of commitment. "Why're you doin this?" he said, leaning back and looking at her mouth.

"I'm not doin a thing."

"Yes, sister, I think you are."

"What am I doin, then?"

"Showin me the color a hell. And if not hell, then sin."

She stood up, remembering for one split second Hezekiah's advice concerning snakes, before ignoring it, amazed by her inner calm. She heard the sound of crickets and July flies; the creak of cooling trees and limbs and the shuffling, shuffling, shuffling of the leaves. She watched a mimosa tree sweep the ground with feathery concentration, its fuzzed branches doing urgent work while the mist from the river settled all around.

She breathed in the deep smell of damprot and spice weed while night fog rolled in, caught at her ankles, covered her feet. He stood and moved away from her toward a low grove of poplars, his white starched shirt shimmery as ice. His thinness and humped shoulders were exposed by moonlight and it made him smaller than true reality. While she watched, he whispered, "Help me, Jesus," low and under his breath before he pulled out a cigarette and lit it up with shaky hands. Smoke was everywhere at once. The ground. Above their heads. Drifting midways around their waists. The tip of his cigarette glowed red, brilliant as a star, then flew meteoric to the side where it hissed behind the rock.

If this is the color of sin, it is a genuine surprise, she told herself while she walked toward the shimmering frailty of him. Because it is not color at all. Just non-color vapor that builds from the ground up until it swallows us whole. No warnin color at all.

Nine months later, in Susan-Blair's due season, a son was born. Levi Mitchell Sheehand. Three days later his skin turned to pumpkin yellow and she became fully aware of the color of sin.

Hezekiah found himself at a crossroads not of his making.

"Nobody asked you to chase after me," he said to the girl, irritated as hell, eyeing the loopy old tent stationed on the side of the road, wondering over the faded boat oars supporting it and the haphazard lean to the whole contraption. There was a wrinkly old black woman crouched on a makeshift bench fanning herself with a funeral home fan in front of it, listening in that nonlistening way those folks had about them. He wished for a piece of fruit, like the faded stand promised, imagined it would be hard to gain nourishment from a hubcap belonging on a tire. He looked at the girl, at the brilliant swatch of green that rode high above the knee, at the juncture of her legs, the small mound where cloth met, and then he looked away, swallowing hard.

"Them shorts is blindin, aint they?"

The old Negro said this, elbowing her way into his afternoon. She chuckled and then reached for the dog lying in the dirt, panting in the heat. "Fruit ort to be left on a tree, though. You pick too soon you git a bellyache."

She slapped her knee, disturbing the dog from whatever dog-thoughts he might be having, laughing 'til she choked.

Cathy had seen Hezekiah look at her legs before he could catch himself, and she was glad she had scrubbed off her dirty knees and put on a clean shirt.

"I never said you could come," he said in a low voice, watching the road and the dirt beyond it, his composure a lie.

"I reckon I didn't feel the need to ask," Cathy said. While they talked she hit at the grass with a long privet switch, all its leaves ripped off, but for a handful cluster near its end.

"What's that Uncle Jimmy of yours gonna say once he finds out you left off the plowin? Once he sees that muddy tractor stuck out in the field?"

"I'd like to know that, too, I sure would." The old woman again. The dog rolled to its back, its legs splayed wide, its privates saluting the world.

Yellababy was sleepy and growing heavy. Hezekiah grunted while he sat, spreading the blanket with one hand, tucking his little brother down to it gently with the other. The boy went instantly to sleep. They all listened while he snored in and out like a young rhino.

"Your uncle's gonna shoot me and you both," Hezekiah said, looking up at her.

"No he aint."

"She's as green as them shorts she's wearin." The old woman took off her scarf and scratched hard at her head while Cathy glared at her, tried to stare her down and failed at it.

Hezekiah watched the exchange, hazy on what to do next. Instinct drove him to the next level of confrontation: the insult.

"You're witless, you know. Don't know a shit's worth of anything."

I know where them Chalktown folks put that dead baby, was Cathy's thought, but she shelved it, held it close to her chest like a "thump" card, as her aunt liked to say to her friends when they sat around the kitchen table playing cards. Cathy sliced through the air with her switch. Conducted the wind. "I know enough," she said.

Yellababy was drooling in his sleep. Hez leaned over and wiped at his chin, picked a crawling gnat off his lip.

"What's struck that youngun?" the old woman said, pointing with her fan.

Hezekiah sighed, wondering whether to pay attention to her because she was motherly and old and was sitting out beside the road in a pitiful tent, or ignore her because she was Negro. Before he could decide, Cathy spoke up: "He's retarded is what. He don't like strangers, neither."

Hez wanted to slap her.

"And when he wakes up we're gonna put some a them hubcaps you aint sold down on the ground and let him watch them. I think he might like that." She smiled confidently at Hez, as though he'd just been sitting there waiting for her to plan his day.

"Shut up," he said.

"Why?"

"This is my day, it aint yours."

The black woman was laughing so hard the board bounced underneath her ass. "I say they aint no harm in that fruit bein picked anytime soon. Nosiree. No harm at all. Girl, you go on and wear them green shorts. Won't be nothin crawlin over you but a grasshopper."

Cathy spit across the stretch of grass like a full-grown boy, unfazed. Let the day do what it will, she thought, and it was an adult thought, full of half-grown awareness nudging up from a small part of her she was just then meeting.

Cathy was right. Yellababy loved the hubcaps.

They lifted four of them off their nails, promising the woman to put them right back, of course, and set them on the ground in front of the little boy like shiny pies. Yellababy watched his reflection, as well as one or two birds flying high up, his arms stiff-out in mirrored joining, still able to dream. He'd done this for about ten minutes before a hushed audience, all of them judging his movements a preamble of sorts. To what, Hez had no idea. It could mean anything, or nothing at all. The woman fanned herself slowly, one arm down to her dog, her black eyes buried so deeply inside her face they seemed a mere myth of eyes, nothing more. Cathy could barely contain herself, her face glowing at the discovery. They were only metal tirecaps placed on the ground in a semicircle, but she was the one who had the idea, and Hezekiah knew it; knew he'd never hear the end of it, either. How she fished those hubcaps off the stand and placed them on the ground and ushered in sky and birds and God only knows what other glories for his brother. Hez sighed, conflicted over the duplicity of emotion: that strange union of hatred and appreciation. Yellababy finally went facedown on the grass and relieved them all, the little boy's nose snuffling in the dirt, worn out by the shine, Hez supposed.

The woman stirred herself, shook herself all over, sending the dog skittering into the tent in alarm. Apparently the woman seldom moved and when she did it set in motion some canine warning based on experience. "Yall aint got no reason to go there," she said, her hands squarely to her knees.

Hezekiah looked at her, wondering how she saw life out those buried little eyes.

"She knows where we're headed," Cathy said as explanation.

"The hell else does she know?"

"That's all." Cathy switched the privet at her tennis shoes.

"Those people struck dumb for a reason," the woman said, shifting until she was backlit by the sun, her body's placement granting urgency to her words.

"Here we go—"

"Shut up, Cathy."

"She's tryin to scare us, Hez. Don't listen to her—"

"Two people's dead, there. The dirt's been soured over what they done. You two aint got no reason to go meddlin where you aint wanted."

"All that is is talk," Hez mumbled.

"You right there. Talk is talk."

"Rumors don't scare me."

"Boy, sometimes talk is bigger than the deed. And sometimes talk aint near big enough."

"I'm goin and you're stayin," Hezekiah said, pointing to Cathy. Let her think he was being protective, he didn't care. "I never asked you to follow me anyhow."

"I didn't follow you. I cut through that field there. That aint followin a person. That's beatin a person to a place. Now who's witless?"

Hez hauled his brother up and harnessed him in, fitting his arms through the straps and positioning him for comfort.

"I'm goin," Cathy said.

"You aint, either." There was no way a gal was going to ruin his day, especially a smart-ass gal with keen ideas about hubcaps. He didn't care how tan her legs were.

"You caint stop me. I reckon this is a free road."

The black woman sat still as a stump, and then she stood. The crippled child winked with eyes slow as a camera's stuck shutter, those blue orbs drawn to her as if magnetized by some hidden commonality.

"You two git on from here. I'm closin up shop." She swayed from side to side while she walked, pulling a hand-printed Closed sign from underneath the counter and letting it swing in the breeze. With her back to them, she entered her tent and disappeared into the darkness.

*   *   *

A church was down the way. Hez could see the hand-painted sign: Apostolic Church of God Pentecostal, Inc. Before he could speak, Cathy said, "How come you reckon God needs to incorporate himself?"

Hez figured without guesswork that even God, in spite of His success as creator, must be leery of the Internal Revenue. He didn't want to talk to Cathy about it though, even though hers was a righteous and well-thought-out question, so he said, "I got me a girlfriend," thinking on Teresa Beth and her beautiful hair.

"Most boys want one of those, I guess." Cathy rubbed her hand across her freckled nose. Unaffected. "You kissed her yet?"

"She aint like that."

"Then how come you think she's your girlfriend? I mean, you aint kissed her or nothin."

Another good question.

There was a path to the right that led to the river. A path that had its beginning near his place and then wandered all over creation, one stop along the way, being the river. Sweet River Road, folks called it, for a reason Hez was yet to figure out. He smelled Yellababy's shit and was thinking ahead, knowing he'd need water (real soon) for a proper cleanup.

"We talk a lot. She lets me feel her hair in algebra class. She's got real long hair. Beautiful black hair," he said.

Cathy froze. Stopped her walking as sure as being shot. Hezekiah went on six paces before turning, "What in the cryin out loud is wrong with you?"

She ran forward, her hands held up in disbelief. "This gal lets you feel her hair. That's how come you to think she's your girlfriend? You aint even kissed her yet?"

He looked for the approaching path. Calculated. Estimated his ability to endure the smell for the remaining miles. Once decided, he turned off the county road and cut through the brush with a strong arm, leaving Cathy standing with her arms up.

"Hey. Where're you goin?"

"I got to get some water. He needs cleanin." He could hear her crashing through stiff palmetto behind him. "I aint talkin about my girlfriend anymore either. So you can hush about it. I've said all I'm goin to."

"If you ask me, she aint your girlfriend."

"Well, I aint askin you, am I?"

"I been kissed." She smiled. Smug.

"Liar."

"I have!"

"How old are you, anyhow?" The sound of the water was to his right, vague yet promising, cutting up through the pines. Yellababy seemed to sense it and began a low bellow, a moaning sound Hezekiah found eerie and disturbing.

"I'm old enough."

"Yeah, that's what you said about drivin the tractor. You're old enough. Sounds to me like you got somethin to hide. I've ask you your age twice and you've yet to give me a righteous answer." He looked at her, saw her frown. That smug look washed clean away.

"I been kissed, though. More'n once, too."

If his brother hadn't been in such dire need of having his ass wiped, Hez would've stopped in his tracks and demanded proof. A boy could tell if a gal had been kissed before, same as he could tell if she'd done the other. The dirt had turned to sand beneath his feet and when he pushed aside cutty brush he saw the water stretching and shallow and brown, its center trough rushing. Down a drop-off, though. Which meant sliding down and then climbing back up. Impossible to do while holding a load. Idiot, he thought. I'm a durn idiot for not bringin along a simple roll of toilet paper. Well, shit then.

"You caint get him down there."

"I aint a moron. I got eyes."

"I could, though. Climb down easy as pie. Just you watch—"

He looked at her. Studied her arms and muscular legs. She just might could. But what if she slipped and broke something, forcing him to get her back up? "Hold it. Wait a minute. Help me here."

He turned his back to her, indicated with his hands what he wanted her to do. She put her arms under Yellababy while Hez squatted, leaving the little boy dangling and free of the pouch.

"Shit! Hurry up, he's heavy." She had both arms around him, his left eyeball to where her right tit was sprouting. There was a vague smell of mustard to his hair.

"Here, I got him now." Hez held him up like it was nothing, and then laid him to the ground in cool shade. "I'm goin' down there. You watch him. Don't let bugs get on him, either."

"I aint ever watched a real droolin idiot before—"

Hez rushed her, grabbed the front of her white shirt in a tight fist, lifted her to her toes. "You bitch! I ever hear you say anythin like that again, I'll kill you!" He was nose to nose with her freckles, so close he could smell the girl-smell coming off her hair, or from some deeper place hidden behind clothing. " 'Til I'm convinced otherwise, I think my brother hears ever word said. Understands it, too."

"You said yourself he was retar—afflicted. What the hell do you want me to call him then?" She was near the point of crying, grabbing at his fist, trying to free her shirt. They were both shouting; echoes rambled in all directions and then washed back.

Hez released her and backed down, tried to smooth the front of her blouse and then stopped his hand midcaress. "Shit, Cathy," he said. "Shit," he said again, in a softer voice.

A huge tear welled up in the corner of her eye and spilled down her cheek and hung on the rib of her chin. Hezekiah watched it thinking, By God, a snail trail, then, No, that drop of salt is sweeter than that. He patted her arm, embarrassed. "Just say you aint ever sat somebody who caint walk, okay? I didn't mean to yell at you." Yellababy seemed contented. His sweet-wideblue eyes traveled from one face to the other and then to a tree and then to a cloud, maybe seeing things, maybe not, concern as vacant from his heart as the moon is free of human sweat.

"I said I'd climb down and go for you." She ran a hand over her eyes.

Hez dug a cleaning rag out of the pack. "He's my brother. I guess that means I ought to be the one tendin to it."

Like a monkey was how Hez looked to her and she wondered if she should have told him she was almost fifteen years old just in case he fell and bashed his brains out and went to his death not believing she'd ever been kissed. The trees along the far banks of the river were getting their buds; the limish yellow and pale green leaves were beginning to speak from the outermost spriggy limbs. Cathy watched for a while and wondered at the temporary season, how it made its appearance year after year impeded only slightly by fire and rain and wind and death. The spring of the year was her favorite time and she wondered how she could forget it so suddenly once summer swallowed the land. She felt a tug and looked down at the little boy. Yellababy had a hold on her socks and was trying to pull himself forward through the grass.

"For Christsakes! Look at you, little boy! You aint so helpless after all, are you?" She put a hand over her eyes and watched Hez make it down with just a meager pebble-slide of surface clay.

"Well, look at you!"

"What's goin on? He all right up there?" Hezekiah's voice sounded distant and small, of little consequence.

"We're just fine! Your little brother's smilin at me, is all! A great big shiny smile, too!" There was a pause and then a brutal string of swears washed up from the water while Yellababy went *bleebableebaaa*, and kicked at her, blowing bubbles with his spit. All this because of her sock. Well, I be damned. Out the corner of her eye she could see Hez pulling himself up and over, red-faced and dirty. The river-wet rag slung over his shoulder had soaked his shirt to a deep cobalt blue.

"What's the matter with you?" she said.

He jerked at the rag and water droplets splattered to her cheek.

"Nothin."

"Somethin sure is. You're mad as hell and I aint done a thing but sit here."

"I've been waitin years for a smile and you're the sorry one who gets to see it, is what." He pulled a ratty blanket out of the backpack; unsnapped his brother's pants and worked them down along his legs. Cathy could see big safety pins through the plastic. "Been totin him around and playin with him. Constant! All the time, you hear me? And you had to go and be the one—"

He looked at his brother, then back at Cathy and pointed his finger. "You turn yourself around. Don't look now. It aint right."

"He's a baby, Hez. You said so yourself. I aint turnin around."

He took her by the shoulders and turned her himself. "If I was afflicted, I wouldn't want folks lookin at my . . . lookin at things. Just look at the water. And I damn well mean it!"

"I'm sorry he smiled at me. I werent tryin to make him or anything. He was just holdin on to my sock and I guess he thought it was funny."

Hez was quiet for a moment and Cathy could hear the busy work of hands to cloth and skin. Then, "I just wish I could a seen it, is all. You sure he smiled?"

She turned without hesitation, her eyes seeing Yellababy's privates, in spite of trying not to. "Holy God," she said.

"Turn back around!" Hez finished up the diapering. Careful of those pins.

"Shit, Hez, I didn't mean—"

"Just shut up. Just shut your fuckin mouth." He was tired.

"How come he's so lar—"

"I mean what I said. Hush about it." He wadded up Yellababy's green pants and pulled out a fresh pair: blue corduroy snap-togethers with brown cowboy fringe up and down the sides, twenty-five cents in last week's pile until he lifted them when Susan-Blair wasn't looking. He didn't know what he was going to do once Yellababy outgrew all these things. Nobody that he knew of made grown-up-sized pants with snaps at the crotch.

Cathy was leaning her chin to her knees, wondering over things. The wind off the water had suddenly turned chilly and she felt goosebumps springing up on her arms. She looked to the west, rested her cheek on her knee and watched the pale green of the trees move away from her until the horizon grayed like a fog. All she had of spring was right in front of her, within distance of a loud yell, and this seemed important.

"I'm fourteen years old," she said, softly. "Be fifteen next month." It was the truth, an embarrassing truth. It was also a peace offering for her eyes trespassing where they ought not to.

"How come you're still in the seventh grade?"

" 'Cause I'm dumb as a rock, I guess. Aint that what you said? That I didn't know nothin about nothin?"

He was quiet for a few seconds, then shrugged. "You know my brother smiled at you. I guess that's somethin."

"Why's smilin such a big deal?"

Hez looked at her, the way her chin was resting on her knees. Across the way was a chimney that leaned old and crumbly; it stood on the far bank of the river, a middle finger thrown up in the face of God. He wondered if she thought the same thing.

"They said for us to watch for it because it was a way to tell."

"Tell what?"

"Fairy said the doctors down to Singing River said if he don't smile before a certain age, then he's for sure . . ."

Yellababy was reaching for Cathy's back. Hez pulled his hand away from her and rubbed his fingers.

"Said he's for certain gonna stay the way he is. Afflicted. Billy Reuben worked him over sure as shootin. He aint been the same since." Hezekiah put a hand to his brother's stomach, felt those tiny muscles that spasmed over and over. He tried to straighten his small arm and couldn't. "I been waitin on that smile is all. You sure he smiled at you?"

"I aint ever been more sure of a thing in my life." She wiped at her nose again. "Billy Reuben the name a somebody you know?"

"That's who done this thing to him."

"How do you know?"

" 'Cause my father come back from the hospital and said so."

"What'd he say, exactly?"

Hez thought about it. "He came runnin up to the porch and said 'Billy Reuben's a killer, son. A hateful killer.' Or something like that. I guess my brother got attacked at the hospital. Don't know if they ever did catch the fella either."

Cathy looked over her shoulder and watched his large, old man hands fixing Yellababy's clothes and running across frazzled hair. Such tender hands for a boy, she thought. As far as her recall traveled, she'd not seen such a one as Hezekiah Sheehand. "Let's hope they find the guy and put him away, once for all," she said in a soft voice.

Hez nodded, his eyes straying to her green shorts bunched around her upper thighs before his hands went to work retying Yellababy's shoes.

"Where'd you get your name from?" Cathy said, watching the river again, studying the leaning chimney across the way and how it stood like one abandoned. While watching, she breathed in the fragrance of sassafras and cedar as well as clusters of spice weed that tumbled down the embankment.

"Fairy named me."

"The hell's this Fairy person?"

"I thought I told you. He's my father. Got married once a long time ago before gettin a divorce and marryin my mother, Susan-Blair. I guess he had a change a heart, 'cause him and that first one he married still meet once a week, too. Still friendly. Real friendly. I seen them." He cut his eyes to her to see if she'd ask for a deeper explanation. She was staring at the water across the way, missing the point again. He thought her neck was pretty, now that he noticed it, at least the backside of the neck. It was long and slender, with tiny fine hairs coming loose from her ponytail and settling in the cords that ran to her narrow shoulders.

"I never heard nobody call their daddy by their given name. Who the hell named him Fairy?" Yellababy had managed to grab her shirt. She turned around and leaned on a hand to allow him more cloth.

"His real name is Eulis Farris Sheehand. Everbody's always called him Fairy."

He looked away from her, tired of talking about relatives. Over her shoulder he could see the river running true and brown. "I seen a real river once," he said. The phrase *Now there's the river, and then there's The River* swimming up, unexpectedly. The truth of the comparative words nearly knocking him senseless with longing. The Leaf River out in front of them spread itself like dirty blood. Dark. Its center trough deadly, as most everybody in Mississippi would swear, since most everybody in Mississippi had lost a drunk relative to it at one time or the other. He studied it again, thinking: all that brown but for a slender golden margin that stirs the border sand in a way that is false. The river is like my mother, he thought, breathless with fear: deep and dark and deadly. "The real River is beautiful."

"What aint real about that one there?" Cathy was knocking dirt off her tennis shoes.

"I went with my nigger neighbor once, over to Mobile, and seen the real one." The two of them had stolen discarded railroad cross ties. Hid out in the bushes while the hand trucks sped up the tracks and away. Spent hours loading them. Mayurn saying the whole while, "Money from Heaven, Hezekiah Sheehand! Sho is money from Heaven." The next day they made a run for the rich folks up near Bellingrath Gardens and the Dog River region. Women in hats, their gardeners standing aside like slaves, paid good money, even for the ruint split ones. There was a quality to that slender run of water that set it aside, gave it a meaning all its own, regardless of size or source.

"Everthing there is blue and white. Even their boats." He had caught sight of the river while sitting on the truck's tailgate. Seen crisp sails and powder-blue boats. Seen houses with gardens that cascaded down into the water. Seen ducks and swans and small boys with clean hands. *Now there's the river and then there's The River.*

"There's this river and then there's The River," he said. "A clean river. Square sails and triangles of white and golden birds listenin. Heavenly. No brown to it at all. No mud. Just squared up bulkheads looped with heavy clean rope. A whole school of sailboats bobbing."

"Seems to me to see somethin like that might be hurtful," Cathy said, remembering her cold calves pressed to a slab down in New Orleans. Aunt yelling at her while sugar powder dusted her hairy chin. The woman had held fast to a plate of fried doughnuts to make the seeing of her mother's grave easier, Cathy figured. Eat while you talk on death and just like sugar to cod-liver oil, it makes the viewing of a mother's tombstone easier.

The stone chimney across the way seemed proof of what they were both feeling. A hearth had been built facing brown water and set to the side of it were four boards nailed across two tall pines. Catfish cleaning, probably. Nail their heads clean through and then peel off the skin. All the Mississippi men she knew liked to skin them alive, watch their whiskers shiver in death throes.

"You aint dumb, Cathy," Hez said finally, looking over at her. Those tiny bumps along her back where it curved with her body seemed so girl-like. Through her shirt he saw a band's blue shadow, which equaled a bra. "You aint been kissed, though. I know that for sure."

"How come you think that?"

He grinned, patted his brother's stomach. Yellababy cut a sharp eye to him and recognition flashed and swam a moment before it disappeared. " 'Cause you'd see the opportunity to kiss a expert spread out in front of you and make a beeline over here."

"You're full a shit, and you know it. You got a girlfriend, besides." She was still under the spell of the sad chimney across the way, spring and all its new-green almost forgotten.

"Teresa Beth aint here, is she?"

"The fact that you're willin to kiss me just because she aint here says a large thing, you know. Besides, a kiss has to mean somethin."

"Did all those other kisses mean somethin?"

"Nope."

"How come?"

"He werent seein nothin but my lips. That's how come."

Hez knew what she meant, sure as shootin. Those big senior gals had given him a dollar just to pull out his dick. He did it behind the cafeteria next to a garbage can full of tuna-fish empties. Once they paid, and touched it, they laughed. Proud for about two seconds, he watched their group-huddled backs move away from him. Not one of the three had glanced up at his eyes.

The mood passed and he began to bundle up his brother. "You ready for Chalktown, or not?"

"I'm ready."

The sun was over the noon mark when they broke through the palmetto and hit the steamy black asphalt of the county road again. "Chalktown inside an hour," Hez said. Cathy followed along beside him, her shoulder bumping into his every now and again.

CHAPTER 14

Rosie stood out on the front porch of her Chalktown house remembering the dream. Remembering how she had stumbled across the floor in bare feet, pulling into her abundant chest dark velvet air, so overcome by the angels she'd nearly wet herself. She had seen a minor light at first up near some forgotten corner of the sky, and it was as if a timbrel had been struck in a call for attention, or a small bell had been rung beside the altar of a church. Watch this, it seemed to say. Watch now, because this is important. The light paused and pulsed and then it twisted out of its chrysalis and became two. Up over the trees—catalpa and mimosa and loblolly pine—this translucent body of light grew larger and more expansive, transmigrating among dead stars, resurrecting light, by light. Angels, they were. Angels turning and spinning in approaching circles. The smaller one was crippled, barely able to complete an orb, his shape was overly thin and he was crying in soft snuffling sounds that moved clean through the woman in the dream. Rosie felt tears well up from her closed-off heart, the tightening on her throat real enough to cause her to stumble again, this time in panic. Don't you

worry now, Rosie had shouted up to him from the distant corner of her
bedroom, her voice rusted-over, even inside night's cover. Hush your cryin!
Come on down from there and don't you worry one little bit, Rosie'll take
care of you. Help you out. In the way of flowing water they funneled
through the sky and bobbed alongside the moon, the older angel, his glowing
fingers pressed against the frailer one's back, leading the way. Down from
the treetops where onyx night made cutouts of their wings. Down from the
winking stars, they came. Close enough to touch finally, they hovered inside
her meager kitchen, near the old icebox that hitched and rolled its rollicking
cycle. He needs cleaning, ma'am, the older one had said, embarrassed. And
Rosie had cocked her head and then bent at the waist and reached out a
hand to the smallest form, her fingers trailing across a golden gown so marvelous in texture it seemed all heavenly water, or magic air, or some other
indescribable material. I'll do it fer ye, she said. Hush now. It'll only take a
minute. Taking that small fragile hand she led him to her bathroom, where
she wiped his angel bottom, rearranged his angel gown. Not at all perplexed
over the strangeness of an angelic bowel movement. Bent over and lame, he
seemed to glide beneath her fingertips while he undulated with gratitude,
beamed up at her a smile sure to melt a cast-iron heart. Just like his brother,
who was grinning from a spot near her yellow table.

There inside her kitchen they had pardoned her. Blessed her with great
drops of grace while levitating over her canisters. And then they were gone.
Out through the window with its decade-old dotted-Swiss curtains. Out over
canted chalkboards leaning against the fences. Out and still deeper out to
where Rosie had never been, or if she had been once, she had long since
forgotten. Following, feeling her feet lift up off the cracked linoleum floor,
Rosie flew out the window and up over her winter turnip greens, noticing
they would need watering come morning. The chalkboard was below her
now, a square the size of a postage stamp. The message already forgotten.
All was behind her now. Her arms were up to the sky, embracing the dark,
while her heart chased the angels; her gift of grace and forgiveness, this
apparent dream of flying. She soared over yesterday and the day before and
six years before that. Soared over Chalktown with wings pearlescent and
strong. Cool wind against graveled floppy skin padded with surplus. Thighs.
Arms. Wallowing middle untethered. Sweet night breathing a kiss over all

her blunderings. Ah, Sweet Jesus! Who would a thought it? All I did was clean an arse! she said, reaching for the angel trail. Spilt salt shining like diamonds was how it looked to her. It fell across her palm and glimmered with a precious afterburn. She looked up from her hand to the spiraling angels and watched them blow twin kisses while in broad descendant loops Rosie drifted down to her tar-capped house.

The sunlight was up and brilliant, washing the yards as well as the narrow dirty road, when the two men watched her make her way to the chalkboard set up in her front yard. As geared to routine as Pavlov's dog to the bell, the men took a step forward and waited. Rosie was first in line to write now that Henry Prox was dead, his blue house empty for close to two years. Not that the man ever wrote more than a few simple words. He'd just stand there tossing chalk, grinning at them all like they were blooming idiots while he conversed with the wind. But that was Henry. Rosie Gentle was different. Waddling, her weight like a dragged anchor in a shallow bay, she erased yesterday's message, her eyes casting upward through the magnolia limbs as if something were hidden there. A thought, maybe. Or at least the beginning of a thought. Her back was to them as she wrote her message with a trembly hand, and when she walked away from the words, her steps were faster and lighter than either of them could ever remember.

Aaron Class and Johnny Roper drifted to their porches and stood like statues, wondering what to make of it, what sad meanness the woman had unleashed this time, what preamble to calamity might be lowering itself upon them. Tree limbs and sun conspired, pocked the ground with palm-sized openings of light while the men stood looking at the words with cracked-open mouths.

The Worm has Turned,

Rosie Gentle had written.

The worm has turned.

CHAPTER 15

There had not been enough rain for the season and it worried Aaron Class, a man who noticed the phases of the moon and the maneuvering tides, and took into account how the face of his world was being treated. Not enough rain. Not near enough, he thought, his eyes glancing up the road to the far mimosa that was so big now, its thick limbs swagged down as low as a broken arm.

The chalkboard was across from him and the words seemed seared into his brain, as hot as an electrified street sign. Rosie had not ever been one to carry thoughts much deeper than an occasional creative recipe and Aaron knew this and was alarmed by her cryptic message. True, she had inquired that time about her dog. A one-eyed mutt that howled all night long. Who shot my dog? she had wanted to know, leaving the message on her board for most of a month. Hell, Rosie, we all did, he wanted to answer, but hadn't, because it wasn't true. He didn't know what had become of the bitch. Heat probably. Not seasonal, atmospheric heat, but the other kind. The animal kind. The irresistible kind. He sighed, unsure of his hesitation. The old Aaron

Class would know what to make of it and he wished he could call him up on the phone and talk to him a while, maybe shoot the shit over nonsense matters that never would amount to a hill of beans. He folded his handkerchief and then stretched out his leg to gain access to his back pocket and slid the cloth home. His face was tingling and he wished he'd grown a little extra aloe to carry him through the summer months. Never thought spring would be so unseasonably warm, he mused. Never thought I'd find myself poleaxed by scribbling on a board, neither. The day had started out normal enough. There were things he had wanted to do. Small items on a small list he intended to check off throughout the day. And now here he was, trapped and hunkered down inside a place where a woman named Rosie had stopped him dead in his tracks. It was hard to believe, too, seeing how he had lived such a tall life before the scars took him.

Shrimping out of Pascagoula too young to be doing it legally, he'd fallen overboard in the middle of the Mississippi Sound when he was fifteen years old and been given up for dead. A pair of bootleggers, running their load in a beat-up johnboat, found him ten days later washed up on a barrier island, sunburned and tired, munching on a raw flounder and drinking rainwater he'd collected in a shell. Folks had talked about it for months, gone on and on about the life-and-death ratios along the Gulf Coast and how the skinny boy from George County had beaten the odds, and Aaron liked it (then). His mama put her new funeral dress up in the closet, believing this to be the end of his adventures—for that was what he called them: adventures—but she was wrong. Aaron went straight back down to Gulfport, climbed aboard the *Bayou Belle*, and worked his ass off until he was twenty-two years old, making the money to prove that pride in one's vocation came after a fall and not before. True, he drank a large sum of it, but the bulk he placed in a bank in Jackson County, the dream of owning his own boat his largest motivation.

The summers were fierce and Aaron turned brown as a Mexican doing coon-ass labor most soft-bellied farmers would never consider. When he would walk the streets of Bay St. Louis, folks would stop and stare, such was his weathering, and he stood a little taller when they did this, turned his face a little more in their direction because he liked it (then). Let 'em see what workin hard out under a bitch sun will do to a man, was his thought, and it was a proud rumination, one that carried a certain ring of arrogance in it. It was ball-busting work. Bigger men than he had gone on to tame papermills and shipyards, turned their backs on the boats with a curse for wasted time, taken up with beige-natured women who only wanted one thing out of life: a yard full of miniature versions of domesticity. Aaron wanted folks to know what he was willing to pay, how eager he was to throw himself in the arms of unreliable Nature. It didn't hurt that the seasons suited him, either. Working those three to four months and then laying off, packing up his duffel, thumbing his way west, or north, with nothing to do but chase whores and see the country. He would disappear for months at a time. His buddies along the low coast expected it and sat around bars sucking foam off their beers, speculating on what he might be seeing, what those women out west, or north, or east, might look like. Aaron knew that they did this, and was glad. He wanted to see the country and he wanted people to know he was seeing the country. He went to Yuma, Arizona, once, sat out in the middle of obese nowhere staring up at the Gila Mountains. He bought a cowboy hat with a snakeskin band from a one-eyed goat-roper before turning around and thumbing his way back to the boats of Mississippi.

During what turned out to be his last season of shrimping—an unbearably humid period—he holed up with a redheaded whore in Biloxi and took a strange fever that he tried to drink off. It wouldn't leave. "Come here, Daddy. Let Clovine tend you," the redhead whispered, sleepy-eyed and bed-creased, running a hand up his chest to the base of his neck, which hurt like hell. "Shit! You're hot as a roasted rock," she said, jumping up off the bed and sidling along a bedroom wall like a frantic bug. Aaron was on fire and he knew it. "Go down the hall and git me some cold water and I'll be okay," he said in a croaky voice, and she did, but he wasn't. He had the chicken pox. A full-blown adult case of it, an ailment more than a few died of, and twenty-four hours later, Aaron Class, destined to be a survivor, began to wish he had. By day three, he imagined it an invasion. Tiny pus-capped battalions marched down his throat, up his penis and ass, through his lungs and lower intestines. The internal eruptions were life threatening, and he came perilously close to dying (a lot closer than he realized), but the explosions on his face were what brought him down. Regurgitated veal was how it looked to him. Either that or the splattered pulp of a thrown tomato. It took him a month to recover and try as he might not to scratch, he couldn't help it. The day hours were tolerable, gifted as he was with enough self-control to keep his hands clutched in his lap or crammed in some lint-flecked pocket, but at night there was a time of helpless dreaming that sent him vaulting through a world of demon insects seeking nourishment from his face. He clawed and dug and scraped and moaned. He woke, day after day, to find his sheets drenched in yellow and red.

A small girl screamed when she saw him, shrieked with that decibel level honesty gives to children, and Aaron's life began to shrink in worrisome installments. A moment here. An embarrassment there. An insane aversion to visibility taking its place. The tilt came when he went out on the boat late in the season, those keloid scars blazing like storm banners, worked as hard as he had always worked, and watched in astonishment the nets turn contrary, bringing up tires and tree trunks and worthless crabs, everything except what they were supposed to produce. His buddies didn't blame him, at least to his face, but they didn't slap him on the back and offer to buy him a beer, either, and that mattered. Aaron figured his scarred face had set Nature against them. There was only one thing to do. He took his money out of the bank and bought a small house on a buried back road in George County, Mississippi, and determined to live his life there, hidden and low-key, a safe distance from people who stared and children who screamed. The move had the vulgarity of last-minute penance, but Aaron did it anyway, hoping time would heal his face, and that he would be able to live out his life inside the purple shade of anonymity.

He sat out on his porch in Chalktown, dazed by the heat. His eyes, brown as mimosa seeds, peered out with the look of one both perpetually longing for, yet stunned by life. He still remembered the Gila Mountains and the way they stove into early night with rose-colored shoulders. He still believed the sun in the west was a thing of wonder and that the word "traveler" was carved for all eternity into some long bone in his body. He also believed those days had disappeared because he no longer had the face to support them. He looked down at his hand, and where it leaned.

Symbols decorated the steps to his porch, laid there himself before his hands shook and the facial neuralgia drove him out of harsh light and indoors to quiet blue shade. A bronze crescent moon. A sword. A camel. Bits of cobalt-blue and aqua-green tile against burnt brown grass and terra-cotta planters. He sat next to the moon and ran his hand across the strange surfaces of his steps while he studied Rosie's message on the board. He wondered what worm had turned and how come.

Them scarves she made me. I be durn.

Because he was remembering years back. The kindness of cloth brushing his chin. How he'd been there on that country road an over-long time and was yet to show his face to Rosie, to any of them. How the neuralgia had driven him to hats, the shade easing the sting of damaged nerves, each brim a little wider than its worn-out predecessor's. How he used to cringe at hearing her out and about and would hightail it around the corner of his house to avoid speaking. How, finally, he outdistanced his luck and had to face her, one hand to the brim of his hat, his head dipped a little in her direction: a pathetic attempt at reluctant courtesy. How he resented the obligation while at the same time hoped it was acceptable.

That bitch sun. I be durn.

Because it was summer then. And the heat and humidity, imbued with dazzling August light, turned bully on him, herded him along a tight course toward shabby shade. A scrubby sycamore. A leaning shed. But she'd had her fill of it, Rosie had. Walking across the dirt strip road with a stride that said Fed Up and Enough of This Shit, she pursued Aaron, who was in a head-lowered retreat, into the yard of his neighbor, into the blue-bulbed hydrangeas belonging to that neighbor, before she caught him and reached out to lift the hat clean off his head, surprising him with her thievery. He turned to her with a slowness that was deceptively calm.

"It's fer ye hat," she said, snapping open a square of cloth she'd been holding in her hand, fitting the hat through a hole cut in its middle, settling it all around with mother-fingers. "I seen ye and figgered this might help. Take a turn with it and see if ye aint relieved some."

Aaron had watched her face, the way her eyes peered into his without blinking, and then he felt his face fire up with a blush. He wondered if she was remembering her schooling, the spinning of a globe set atop a desk, a teacher's lesson on geography, those foreign places no one in Mississippi ever expected to see. He wondered if she would notice his purple scars had done their busywork, transforming his face to a mixed-up map of the world. South America slashed down the entirety of his left cheek; Italy melted down his nose, and above his brows spread the warped United States of America. (He was sure if he were to shave his head he'd find Africa or maybe Greece.) Those faded eyes watched him steadily. She hadn't put a hand to him or seemed to expect words or exchanges of any kind. In fact, she seemed in a strange way indifferent to his appearance. She finally turned and walked away, her girth already destined toward the mighty side, and Aaron could breathe again. He spent the rest of the summer viewing life through a curtain of flour-sack ticking, fighting a sneeze, wondering how long he had to wear the durn cloth before he could shove it in a drawer and enjoy air again.

Two summers it took.

And then there came the news that stole the triviality of what to wear on one's head clean away: that deep nasal radio voice telling of the Threat, and then the Harbor, and then the War. George County boys, their ears tuned to the same news, spilled off their tractors and out from the hayricks, to do their part. Aaron tried, but was turned away because of bad eyesight, or so the man said. Aaron knew better.

It was like losin them shrimp, he thought while he walked down the street, his face away from pedestrians, angled inward toward whatever store-front he was passing. My durn face will guarantee defeat.

Another neighbor, Johnny Roper, a diminutive man with a jut to his lower jaw like that of a bulldog, was turned away because he was too short. He stood barely five foot in his best Sunday shoes.

The last man on the road, Henry Prox, whose wife was already sick with the cancer, stood out on his sun-drenched porch and announced to the trees and the dirt paths and any human willing to listen, "I am old. And so is the wife. And what we got to fight is older than any of us. Tell Uncle Sam I am bivou-acked here on a dirt road in George County, Mississippi, and I aint leavin." And then he turned and went back inside and tended his wife.

So there they were, the five adults and one child, growing used to each other in the hapless way of country people: with attitudes docile and slow and measured with ambivalence. A sweet-enough time, too. For a while there . . .

*   *   *

But now this worrisome worm.

Aaron put his hand in his pocket and felt the chalk and wondered if he might write an inquiry as to Rosie's strange message. Then he felt the curiosity dissipate in a way that old, weathered men must feel usefulness loosen its hold on their day-to-day living: it just drifted away, leaving him weak and hot and tired, all at once.

He looked around. His house was back aways from the others, set apart as though shamed but not so far away that the others were not themselves indicted. Painted the color of an eggplant, a color he concocted by mixing barn red, sea blue and brown, it held the heat like a tar-covered doghouse. He could feel it radiating into his back and along the shafts of his arms.

The blue house next door to his, Henry Prox's old place, was in disrepair, in desperate need of a new door and Aaron was ashamed. He owed the man more than that. Trash blew in and out the opening and squirrels roamed freely and disrespectfully through the hallway. Aaron could hear a tin can rattling in the living room while a clotted, abandoned nest skated across the porch. He made a mental note to see to the business of a door once Johnny Roper got through spelling out his thoughts on that damn board of his. If he ever put something down, that is. Aaron eyeballed those words again.

Johnny Roper was out on the porch, scratching at his neck with supreme concentration while he studied the yard. Wondering over the weather, probably. This unseasonable warmth. Wondering whether or not it might mean a hurricane was in the cards come late summer. I could tell him about storms, I sure could. Tell him how it feels to go head first over the side of a smelly boat at the hands of one. I could tell him about rubbery moments of time that stretch near to eternity while water makes a claim for the lungs. How the sun seen shinin through that depth of blue-green gulf makes near-drownin seem gift-oriented: a kiss from God. Roper, short-limbed as a near-midget, looked up and nodded in Aaron's direction as though he had read Aaron's mind, and Aaron returned the nod, tired enough to be civil, finally.

The wind was up and the weeds along the fences seemed a sepia tide of bristle and sedge. Late winter grasses were sloughing off their drying husks, spring was almost here, and out in some distant backfield an anonymous cow was bellowing for a bull. Aaron looked over his yard. There was work to be done. Weeding. Clipping. Pruning. His hands itched to do it, and he wished he held inside his being some celestial power to move the sun to its zenith so it would begin to ease away, bringing on evening and cool air and softer light. He studied Johnny Roper, the man's stalled appearance, and it seemed the bitch sun and near-midget were related in their reluctance to move.

Aaron took out his handkerchief again and carefully wiped at his face. He checked the cloth and then folded it and put it back to his pocket. Johnny Roper's jaw was unhinging and Aaron wondered if the man might be about to speak. Come on then. Talk, he thought, while he kept his head and hands still. Say you done it and git it over with. Say you let them shine my hideous face over ever newspaper in the South the whole while knowin it was you who kilt that gal, not me. Aaron watched the man reach into a front shirt pocket, dig out a matchstick and go to work on his bicuspids instead.

Aaron's hand played against the bronze camel set into his steps and then his fingers caressed the crescent moon and finally the sword. Near his feet, the mums clustered in orange and bright yellow and white and on down the path toward his gate, lilies were just now cutting through the turf, reaching upward for the sun. While he watched Johnny Roper across the way and Rosie's strange message on the chalkboard, Aaron wished irrational things. He wished for a job inside a large hotel garden down in Florida: a weeder's place alongside the roses and begonia. He wished he'd seen more of the country—especially the West—before being felled by a disease named after poultry.

Thinking one action might spur another, Aaron stood, pulled his hat lower on his head and walked to his chalkboard, set leaning near the fence. Fed up with Johnny Roper and his cowardice, he picked his chalk out of his pocket, put his hand up to the board and began to write.

What worm?
What the hell you talking about Rosie?

He figured the woman must have made a peep-through hiding place of her white gauzy curtains and then stood there, waiting to spring, like a cat on a mouse. As soon as Aaron had put the chalk back to his pocket and turned to walk back to his steps, Rosie had slung open the door to her house and hurried off the porch and gone to her blackboard again. Scratches in the form of beat-up butterflies appeared first, then came the words printed with care and deliberation. Aaron noticed her legs and all their surplus were shaking from her effort at art.

Last night I had two visitors in a dream that heeled me.
These.
That's howcome the worm has turned

She drew a long arrow to the beat-up butterflies at the top of her board and then turned around and smiled at the men on the porch. Neither of them smiled back.

Johnny Roper grimaced and then walked to his board and pulled out
his chalk:

You are crazy again Rose

Aaron Class looked away from the words on the board to Johnny's
modified porch. It never ceased to amaze him. The man had done just about
everything he could to make things appear normal and he thought it a poor
testament to hope and delusion, to the lengths a person would go to feel big
in their world. No way to get around it, or ignore the obvious, the man was
as close to being a midget as a man could be. Leave it to Johnny to try,
though. The chair legs had been cut down so that his feet could touch proper.
The door frame had been lowered and boxed in, and inside, Aaron knew
the cabinets had been reconstructed to accommodate his size. And now this,
he thought. Not one single thing he's done is gonna matter once some strange
mailman notices things are stirrin again. Takes a look-see and realizes we're
slingin more than insults and recipes on the goddamn blackboards and then
heads back to town and folks grow curious about us again.

Aaron scratched his head, sure now that Rosie Gentle had gone over
and he wanted to kick her in the ass because of it. A mother couldn't lose
a daughter to a slit throat and not be transfixed by it and he knew it. A
fever held her in its grip, some low-grade hovering thing just waiting for an
opportune time to poke up its head again. Waited just long enough to catch
all of us off guard, he thought. Well, I be damned—

Johnny Roper stood out in the sun, rubbed at his eyes, then added a
notation:

Go in and let it pass

Rosie watched the two of them and then pulled out her chalk again

Sometimes a dream is the onliest real thing

With that she brushed her hands together and headed back to the house.

Aaron followed her movements as she walked back inside, the set of her shoulders was too familiar and told him she was pleased as punch over those beat-up butterflies of hers. Well, good then, Rosie. Maybe you can catch a bus over to Hollywood and get yourself a job at Captain Kangaroo's Magic Drawing Board. Aaron turned eastward, listening.

Through the wind and the trees there seemed to come the sound of distant wailing that was high-pitched and childlike. Something similar to a storm sweeping their way. He could still remember the sound, even after all the years spent away from the boats. Aaron watched Johnny Roper sit down in his small-sized chair. The man's hands were to his lap as one accustomed to non-movement and Aaron looked away in irritation, and then he cocked his head, listening past the wind to what had to be an honest to God child screaming its lungs out from a direction beyond the trees and the break in the road. And while listening, he felt the hair stand up on his arm. Bewildered, he cleared his throat and the sound of his own vocals startled him. He noticed Johnny Roper staring across at the sound, his pale eyes still and cautious. After a moment of intense eye contact, Johnny pointed to Rosie's board and shrugged his shoulders, good-naturedly.

Aaron ignored him, embarrassed by the man's attempt at communication. There were still those things he had needed to get done. Work to do. He had woke with an urge to garden, a talent he'd not realized he had during those early days of shrimping, or those later days spent with a bag on his back, pavement under his feet. New Mexico, he thought. That was where it hit him, this strange attraction. Adobe cubes bordered with yellow roses. Those queer combinations of geometry and nature that seemed to speak to him and promise him things. He almost forgot it, too. And then that damn bearded iris he found sprouting out the side of a red ditch in Mississippi reminded him all over again. Walking along the crusty bank of a dried-up creek just to get away from it all, not expecting to find anything of interest and finding more than enough laid aside like a bride's forgotten gift. Then those ferns. Shit. I must a walked the whole county. *Thelypteris kunthii. Dryopteris marginalis.* More gifts stolen while the sun dredged downward through the sky. The air cool. The shade deep enough to shrug into. Those emerald spires, coiled and fuzzed, worth it all.

But to garden, he needed certain implements, his smallest spade being most primary. He had tulip bulbs waiting in a sack on his porch. He looked over at the evening primrose, realizing he would need to trim off the low limb of the sycamore to provide more light. The spade. Where in blazes was it?

Debris blew across the porch of Henry Prox's blue house and he turned to watch. A rolling pinecone. A skittering thatch of brown holly. Magnolia leaves.

I brung Prox out that very house, there, Aaron thought, looking past the weeds growing tall around the man's porch. The poor fool already beyond rigor, thank Christ and thank a cool March that kept him chilled. I don't think I could a stood to tote him over my shoulder like a board. Not that one. Not after all he done for me. Aaron rubbed at his face absentmindedly, remembering how Henry Prox had seemed a representative of what was best in life, even from the beginning, and he wished he had the ability to intersect with time past and tell him that. I carried him out a the house, though. I guess he would a wanted it that way. He was still old Henry. Just a little swole-up and tired-lookin, was all. And blue. Lord was he blue.

Someone had kicked Henry's old paint cans across the yard. One large smear of color had bathed the base of the centurian oak a shade of cobalt hydrangea. Aaron studied the mess, frowning.

Pint-sized Johnny Roper moved down his steps to his board, where he took his chalk out of his pocket.

You wuz sleepwalkin again. Round 2 in the a.m.

Aaron shucked up his shoulders and held to his elbows, embarrassed, realizing he must have kicked the durn paint cans himself in his sleep. Probably tossed the spade to who-knows-where, too.

Nobody seen it but me

Johnny Roper turned to make sure Aaron had read it and then he erased it with the palm of his hand.

Aaron appreciated that. Good as gold manners for a near-midget who was a murderer. He nodded but it was too late. Johnny had picked up his short chair from off the porch and headed back inside.

Somnambulist since spilling overboard out in the Gulf of Mexico, Aaron had woke countless times in strange terrain, bewildered and disoriented. The Allentown cemetery. A dog pen. A ditch by the side of Sweet River Road. Aaron rubbed at his wrist, wondering if it might pay to lash himself to the bedpost at night to keep from wandering.

The light seemed distilled and Aaron peered up at it through the waving trees, the pure blue shining through gnarled oak and sycamore. That final frenzy of speech still clung to him on days like this. Residue of old conversations stood up to greet him again. Aaron pulled his hat down lower on his head, but he could still hear them, the yammering of panic and opinion. Rosie's daughter, Annie, was there, and Rosie, and the baby that never stood a chance. And there, whining beside a camellia bush, stood Johnny Roper, wringing his hands, and off on his own porch stood Henry Prox, waving his paintbrushes and shouting. Remembered noise became a symphony of chaos that time seemed intent on refining, a song played over and over again, for a group deaf to it.

Aaron kicked aside a pile of leaves and saw the handle of his spade. Bending, he picked it up and turned it in his hands; the steel tossed back the reflection of his face. Dirt blended with his scars, and he thought it an improvement.

Johnny Roper came out his house with a bang. The door slammed so hard the back tail of his screen door peacock vibrated like a hen in heat, and two doors down, Rosie appeared, dusty with flour, confident, her arms opened wide as she walked across her yard and through the gate and onto the road.

The fuck is this—

Like Father, Tomboy and crippled Holy Ghost, they appeared as trinity near the hem of the street. A small child was screaming bloody murder from a pack on the boy's back. When Rosie got to within hugging distance she dropped to her knees and her arms flew up in the air as if Jesus stood there, or the new Catholic President of these United States, or maybe some other troublemaker. Her mouth working like a fish, she moaned, was all. Just low moans that built with the child's crying to a conjoined sound like that of an approaching train.

Well, here we go again, Aaron thought.

Here we go again.

BOOK TWO

1955

*In the beginning was the Word and the Word was
with God and the Word was God.*

CHAPTER 17

Annie counted the rows while she walked the field, the sun hot to the top of her head and along her broad shoulders.

Fourteen rows.

Why, I guess we stood over there underneath the shade of that very tree, she thought, pointing with her eyes, but not her fingers, her hands tucked away inside her faded cloth dress patterned in flowers. The thought seemed to resonate against her belly, thump it as a finger might test out a watermelon at market.

She looked down to her stomach and spoke softly, "You're so out to the front now, I caint even see my durn shoes, or lack, thereof."

Dry from too little rain, the rows ran crunchy beneath her feet and she stood still as a scarecrow in the middle of them. Just like before.

I stood here first, and he come later, and then we both stood out under the moon that hid a little, but not too much, and then we didn't stand atall.

She smoothed back a strand of thick blond hair and wondered when the last time might have been that she felt good about herself. Felt wrapped up tight and warm and important. She had not invited the thought, but it was there anyway, as unbidden as a gnat crawling up the ivory shaft of her arm.

" 'Bout midways down row fourteen, I'd say."

Two dark-winged birds lifted off a far tree limb and flew straight at the sun. Annie blinked, her hand up, shielding her eyes while she watched the wings dip and pull, dip and pull.

Her mama, Rosie, was back in the kitchen doing those things mothers did in the kitchen. Cooking again. Planning tomorrow. Mixing things up. A pot called to her. The peculiar clang of it announced it as a bean pot and said that it was going on the flame along with a ham hock and that it would stay put and send bubbles around that ham bone for nearly an hour. Annie looked to the west and saw the strange dust-covered car sitting out in front of the house, the tree limbs spreading liquid shadows across the long black hood, and knew there would be company. The car belonged to the preacher, who was tall and skinny as a post and carried a black Bible in his hand while he talked about Jesus and the will of God to anybody who would listen. So, another body around the table tonight. Again.

Annie walked down three more rows, her head up and attentive in case there was a silhouette to be seen in the evening sun. Wondering over it, she moved midways down to where the tiny green shapes were coming up out of brown. Curved and humped. Looped as bright green buttonholes. Soybeans this year. Next year, cotton. Just like last year. She put a hand to her stomach and felt the lurch. Felt one with this season of change.

"Maybe things'll be okay, once everybody quits looking for normal," she told the baby.

She didn't believe it, though.

Not one word of it.

The rows were baked-dirt hard, so she stepped carefully across the brittle brown shards, her eyes downward and then upward to the empty horizon with shy hope. She tiptoed across furrows as though the very dirt were precious; as if memories, or memories of memories, might live inside the very crunch under her feet. She looked to the distant field break where the grass surrounding the large magnolia was littered with boat-shaped leaves; the tree's lower limbs left to drag the dark earth, as was proper.

He brung me flowers once from the side of the road, too. Flowers he found low to the ground.

Low to the ground.

Same as me and him was when he looked at me and I saw myself and not nobody else. Me just seeing me and that blue dress I wore, shining inside a brown orb of a eye.

"You Annie! Come on in here and help me with supper!"

She looked over her shoulder.

"I'm a comin!" she yelled.

Slipping back into her shoes she headed toward the small yellow house while evening sun fell closer to the earth. Red now and deepening to purple. The shade she'd wish for a dress of exotic velvet, should it be feasible.

The rear side of the house always seemed the prettiest to her. The way the door trim was painted white. The concrete steps that felt so smooth and cool to her feet. The hand pump still sitting where it'd sat for more years than she could remember. Water ran down to a concrete trough where she knew horses drank once. Hot horses tired from running. Or plowing.

He drank from that pump, too. Washed dirt off his hands. White skin ran like clean rivers to his elbows while he grinned at me and made me see myself.

Once more, she looked over her shoulder, down the rows, looking for a shadow.

He'd be taller now, I bet. A taller shadow now, I reckon.

Once more she remembered eight months back and that night's moon and the emerald trees and the blue-black sky that had hid enough, but not too much. Once again, staring back at her in the here and now, there was nothing to see but dirt, and more dirt, and still more dirt.

In anticipation of the prayer meeting, Rosie's small house was lit up like a Christmas tree. The two men stood midyard, their feet frozen by dissimilar emotions.

"You feel any different?" Aaron said quickly, a careful note to his voice.

"Nah." But Johnny Roper did. Just a little.

The two of them stood turning their hats in their hands like steering wheels while they watched the porch. Light from Rosie's small living room filtered out and across and down the tilted steps and then across again, nearly to the road. A streak of illumination, almost to their feet had they not been standing back aways, inside the dark. Their standing was nervous, with a color to it resembling apprehension. Night wind blew up all of a sudden, catching at the dead leaves in Rosie's yard, resurrecting them with ghost movements as they danced across the road.

"Always thought the Holy Ghost would make one feel different," Aaron said.

"Caint say about different. Thought it would make one feel calm at least."

Johnny Roper looked over his shoulder to his house across the road. His windows were all opened and the night breeze was still blowing and he watched his kitchen bulb swinging in the wind. Back and forth and back and forth. Hidden behind the cabinets one minute. Exposed the next.

His truck was almost hidden as well, tucked behind the willow tree. Roper Salvage in red on white. He turned his hat in his hands. Felt the damp brow band underneath his fingers, realizing he was nervous because he did feel different. Almost hopeful. Free of burdens from that point way down inside where burdens usually took root and multiplied. Free, was how he felt. Just like the man said he would feel. But there was also the worry that a bill needed paying. Something costly yet to be tallied up.

"By its very name, it seems to fight calmness," Aaron said, matter of factly.

"How so?"

"Ghost. Holy Ghost. Who'd expect a haint to bring a measure of comfort?"

"You got me there."

But he or she or it or whatever, had. At least momentarily.

"What'd he do to your leg?" Aaron looked at the man, the way the top of his head barely measured to the level of Aaron's shoulders, the way he was tilted now. "You asked to grow taller. Didn't hear you ask nobody to make you lean."

"He set me in that chair..." Johnny tried to remember the sequence: those bony fingers working their way up his thigh while the other hand cupped his socked heel; the embarrassing stink of dirty feet (the man insisted he take off his shoes); the prayer; the pull. "He said if two or more agree on anything, it shall be done—"

"Agreement's hard to come by in these parts, I guess."

Johnny Roper tried to make his body stand tall and straight and failed at it, stumbling a little into Aaron, who caught his arm, steadied him. "I swear Aaron, I'm wearin the proof this leg growed out a little."

Two inches too much in my opinion, but Aaron was quiet about it, more worried over the excited sheen to Johnny Roper's face than clarification of a chiropractic trick. Nobody could grow out a leg. Nobody. But who was he to steal a toy away from a child, especially a child who had lived his entire life never expecting one. "How'd it feel?"

Johnny thought on it, looked over at Aaron where the falling light lit on his scarred face. "Like a sort a tinglin. Up near the hip, I reckon. I didn't ask for it, neither. Don't nobody better say I did."

"Now wait. You said you wanted to grow taller."

"That's true. I did say that." Johnny leaned down, tried to calculate the amount of thickness required to build up his other shoe. "Didn't ask to lean, though."

"No. I don't figure leanin would be a desire most would carry."

"Shit, Aaron."

Aaron patted his arm. "It'll wear off, Johnny. You'll be back tomorrow wandering around here, same as ever." There was movement inside Rosie's house, a buildup of motion where bodies previously spread-out came together and seemed to join in some upright mating practice. They were only holding hands and singing, some with arms upraised, others with their heads thrown back, but it carried with it exclusivity, an intercourse of sorts.

"Annie seemed moved by it," Johnny said. God's truth, that was the only reason he wanted to grow. It stung when she turned up her nose at his advances. He wouldn't lie to nobody on that account. Especially with her belly big out to the front of her and nobody walking up the road to help her out of her predicament, neither.

"I seen it." She aint ever gonna love you over it, though. But Aaron kept quiet on it, glancing once and looking away again. The man seemed struck with a permanent lean, which was a hard thing to see.

". . . . just wanted a prayer, was all. I aint never complained about what's been handed to me. You know that."

"I know it. You aint got to explain."

Next to him the man was talking nonstop into the breeze. Bothered, it seemed, by his brand-new unequal height.

". . . never had no truck with God no how. Rule for me was this: I don't bother him and he don't bother me. You seen I didn't go in there feelin sorry for myself over nothin." He rubbed a rough hand over his eyes.

There were moments of the prayer meeting that rang true; that seemed untouched by the trick of a man's hand. The strange language was one of them. "I heard you talk in the tongues. Inside that room there," Aaron said, nodding with his head. "I aint never heard that before in all my life."

Johnny turned to him, mouth gulping like a fish, his hand extended.

"I couldn't help it. He put his hands to me, and I couldn't help it. You think they know that? You think they know I didn't go in there lookin for that?" He looked out into the dark again. The feeling in the pit of his stomach similar to what he might encounter should he buy a house he thought was empty, only to find it chock-full of somebody's kinfolk living in the basement. Troublesome kinfolk, too. Ones who were prone to come and stand by the bed at night and stare down on him while he was sleeping. Kinfolk he'd spend eternity explaining.

"I didn't ask for a durn thing," he repeated, sitting down abruptly in the yard, just outside the light's reach, his hat tossed to the ground beside him.

Aaron, in order to avoid feeling foolish, sat down beside the man. He kept his hat to his knees, though, because it was his only good hat. His face was still hidden in dark. He turned to his friend.

"I aint a stupid man, John. I know what I look like. How many jobs I gone through since I been here?"

"A bunch."

"Folks always blame it on somethin other than my face and how it affects commerce, but I know better. They aint ever gonna be a thing I can do other than hope that field out there behind my house turns up enough green to see me through."

"What are you gittin at?"

"Sometimes we end up with what we aint asked for."

There was soft singing inside the crowded room.

"Blessed assurance Jesus is mine; oh what a foretaste of glory divine . . ."

Annie's large shadow moved past the window, her hands out in front as though she might be blind and feeling her way through the crowd. They both watched her gray-whale shape back itself away from the group and disappear.

Time passed between the two men.

Another muted song, then. A softer one.

"Just as I am without a plea, but that His blood was shed for me..."

Finally Johnny spoke. "You hear what that preacher said to her?" He looked at Aaron and then he looked away and picked at the pants crease ridging up on his left knee.

"Yeah. I heard what he said."

"You reckon that boy really is comin home? Comin back?"

Shapes and shadows elongated across the window while both men watched, hands around their knees.

"I'd hazard a guess," Aaron said finally, wishing for a cigarette.

"How'd that guess lean?"

"In the direction a one more bastard bein born in George County come next week."

Next to him Johnny Roper sighed and Aaron wondered at its origin: relief or sadness? Relief, he guessed, seeing how the man had worn his heart to his sleeve for eight and a half months and counting. "This religion thing's got me puzzled," Aaron said to change the subject.

"How so?"

"Where you reckon he come from?" Aaron said.

"Caint no man say where God comes from—" Johnny waved his hands impatiently in the air, wishing he'd stayed to his own house that night, never gone straying over looking for a miracle, wondering how he could accept a God who'd overshoot the distance by a good two inches.

"I aint talkin about God, John. I'm talkin about that one in there."

Johnny Roper looked to the light again. It was fully eight o'clock now and the two men sat inside the dark, shadows hunched together as if welded by night or disbelief, or possibly both. Looking to the window, Johnny judged Henry Prox to be standing next to the skinny preacher. He could see his round-head shape looking up and then down and then it grew still.

"Caint say. Texas, maybe. He's got the accent. Somebody, maybe it was Rosie, said he come from there."

"He come from over Tyler, Texas way."

They both jumped at the sound of Annie's voice.

"He et with us last night. That's how come me to know."

She stood backlit by the light, her great shape out to the front of her.

Both men came to their feet, fetching up hats and turning them nervously in their hands, just like before, but with good reason this time.

"I brung you some cake," she said. A glass plate was extended, two fat slices of pound cake stacked in its center.

"You ort to be settin," Johnny Roper said, looking around for something. Chair. Cinder brick. Bucket. Anything.

"I been settin too long, I'd say." Annie rubbed her back while she looked at the two of them with frank amazement.

"How come you both to leave. Seems now more than ever you'd want to be inside, listenin to what he says. Especially you, Mr. Roper." Her blond hair seemed golden and spun. Damp tendrils clung to her round ivory face. She was a plain girl whose plainness had been made special by the sparse population of the county, and she seemed to know this and take a measure of confidence from it. She stood taller and smoothed one hand over her stomach in a way that was not ashamed, while she peered down into the shorter man's eyes.

"I aint asked for a thing, Miss Annie. I swear I aint—"

"You got it, regardless." She studied him up and down and sideways and still judged him as way too short. And with a lean, now. "You don't eat this, I'm gonna."

With no stomach for it, Johnny Roper reached for the cake and ate it like hot bread, shoving it into his mouth as though starved. Nodding his head, he watched her with hurt-longing eyes.

Aaron saw the exchange and judged it for what it was: hopeless. In his opinion near-midget Johnny Roper was as doomed as a car-chasing dog.

"Mama's gettin herself baptized next Sunday. Down to the creek," Annie said, seeming pleased.

"What about you?" Aaron asked, his skepticism as broad as Lake Perry.

"I aint. I mean, I *caint* do that." She looked at them. "You heard him. You know I gotta stay round here, just in case he comes . . . I mean, for *when* he comes." She played with a corner piece of cake, picked at it with tiny mouse fingers, her head lowered in study of the plate. In Aaron's estimation she appeared to lose some of her tallness.

"He made a lot a promises, Annie. Didn't a one sound counterproductive to a baptizing. Besides, I'll be around to tell him where you're at. Should he come, that is."

Annie ignored him, turned to Johnny Roper instead. "You heard what he said, didn't you?" She looked at him with lips parted slightly. As if she needed to breathe in his answer, fill her lungs with it so that she might live and keep on living.

Aaron Class watched in disgust.

When both men fell silent, Annie frowned and stepped back to the porch and their hats slowed down inside their hands while they watched her bear up her weight and disappear into the dark by the side of the house. Once she was gone it was as if she had never been there at all. But for the crumbs of cake on Johnny Roper's mouth, there would be no proof of it.

"I reckon I could a told her I heard what he said. I guess I could a done that much for her," Johnny said, distressed. He brushed off his knees and headed for his house. His head was down as if his shoes held all the answers.

"Wouldn't a made no difference," Aaron said to nobody in particular. "No difference atall."

Later, when night was fully in and the nominal haze of the moon barely adequate to judge one's hand truly in front of one's face, Aaron sat in Rosie's busted rocking chair on the leaning side of her porch, and waited. One palm was up alongside his face, cradling his angular chin while he drummed his fingers along the crest of bone beneath his eye.

Rosie had never cared how he looked.

Didn't seem to bother Annie, either, at least when she was little. Henry Prox used the purple scarring to match a color once for a painting he was doing and Aaron was pleased to comply. Johnny Roper was the only one left who seemed distressed by it.

Aaron moved his hand and leaned back against the rocker to ease his shoulders while he watched Johnny Roper unload blackboards in the dark. Thinking while he watched: For Christsakes, I'd hate like hell to have that shit all over my yard. Swamped school's salvage, was what the man claimed. Desks, chairs. Warped things. Leaf River's flood damage scraped up and gathered together for impossible resale.

The prayer group had left. All moving away quietly and respectfully, sorrowful almost, as if meeting God face to face had been a funereal experience. Aaron had sat out in the dark smelling the fresh honeysuckle and listening to the closing prayer with a contemplative frown. The traveling preacher not only had the largest set of bullhorns he'd ever seen perched atop a car, he also had a quietness to him that was eerie. His quiet delivery made one strain to listen, and the very act of straining lent an importance to his words that seemed orchestrated somehow. Orchestrated by what, though? Aaron wondered. Necessity? And if it was necessary, why was it necessary? It was almost as if the man had read a book somewhere that pointed out the value of surreptitious behavior.

"Shit. Maybe he wrote the durn book his own self," Aaron said out loud, wondering why Rosie didn't bother to get the damn rocker fixed so folks could have a decent place to sit while eavesdropping.

"What book would that be, sir?"

Surprised twice by a voice inside the dark, Aaron stood to his feet. The broken rocker skidded a bit behind him.

"A book a answers, maybe. I got me a few questions."

He kept his face to the dark, where the man couldn't see his scars.

"Well, go ahead then. I think I'll sit, though, if you aint about to. I been standin a while."

They changed positions, Aaron moving to a spot near the front door and allowing the preacher his already warmed-up chair. The preacher glanced up once, seemed unconcerned by what he saw, and then he looked out again into the dark, rubbing at his bony knees with equally bony fingers. He seemed ill-adjusted to the damp.

"Night here creeps up on a body," he said. "Seems darker than most places out west. Woods full a tall trees, maybe."

"Don't seem different than any other place I seen," Aaron answered. He felt offended somehow for George County and its blatant insufficiencies.

"You said you had some questions."

"How come you to promise such a thing to that young girl in there?"

"What thing would that be, sir?"

"Tellin her that bastard she's about to drop aint gonna be one. That the sonofabitch who planted it is about to find his way back to her and make things right." Aaron paused to slow down his breathing. "You know exactly what I'm talkin on. I don't need to explain."

"Them was not my words, but His." The preacher folded his hands over his stomach and light fell to them as if they were anointed.

"Who are you talkin about?"

"The Lord God."

"How come you to know for certain you speak for him?"

"The Holy Ghost spoke, and I become the voice. You heard it, same as the others."

"What I heard was a bunch of gibberish ushering out the mouth of usually sane Johnny Roper."

"He spoke in the Holy Ghost tongues and I interpreted. It was not me, but the Lord." The preacher stretched his legs out and his knees popped.

"How come you know what this Holy Ghost was saying?" Aaron asked.

"You ever catch a big fish, sir?"

Aaron thought the question a stupid one. He was from Mississippi. Everybody he knew had caught more than their share of big ones. "Once or twice."

"You remember that feelin you got right before it hit the line? That tremblin feelin that come up through the pole?" The preacher's hands danced in the moonlight. Made ornate patterns in the night air.

"Maybe."

"Well, that's what I feel. All I do once I feel it in the pit of my stomach is open up my mouth and speak. It is an act of faith. Them was not my words, but His."

"Like some sort a radio receiver? Is that what you're sayin?"

The preacher shrugged his shoulders. "I got no cause to mislead nobody. Not you. Not the girl. Folks is very kind in these parts. They been good to me, a stranger in a strange land. I'd not hurt them for the world. But hope deferred makes the heart sick, sir. The Good Book says so. A man who would lead a people so obligin to such a place of desperation should be skinned first and shot second."

Aaron figured the man's discourse overly theatrical.

"So, you thought you'd say a few words to make her feel better. Seein how she's stuck here on this back road with a big belly. Maybe thought she needed somethin other than a wagged finger in her face for spreadin it for a damn fool sharecropper."

"Them was not my words, but His."

"What's hope got to do with a damn bit of it anyhow?"

"A body needs hope, sir. Hope deferred makes one ill. Especially one in that young girl's position."

"Well, mister, that may be true. But it seems to me that hope that's hightailed it outta here is better than a lie that's standin around. A lie can kill a body."

And with that Aaron walked down the steps and away from the man. The man was a busybody. A fixer-upper.

"Them was not my words, but His," the preacher called out and then fell silent.

Then God aint as smart as I thought He was, was Aaron's last thought as he headed for his house.

CHAPTER 19

"What you aimin to do with that crud?" Aaron said, irritated.

The desks were drying. All their tops shaping up warped and canted and tilted toward the sky, as though inside their very wood they knew what a man learned slipped sideways and disappeared as soon as it entered the ears. Johnny Roper scratched at his neck and watched Annie descend her front steps and head toward the back of her house. His heart hurt so bad with a large physical pain near its center, he felt shot through. He had to scratch his left tit as a pretense against it.

"Man over in Cumbest said he might buy a few," he said, guarding his voice.

"He ever buy anythin from you before?"

"Nope."

"What makes you think he might this time?"

But Johnny didn't bother to answer. He had listened to the preacher and had started to have faith. The man had laid hands to his head and whispered down into his hair and started him believing he just might not be the poor man he'd been last week. While he watched, Annie walked across the field behind Henry Prox's house, tiptoeing across furrows holding tiny green. She moved away until she was midway in the soybeans, standing still as though listening underneath a blazing hot ten o'clock sun.

"I count out four a them desks that are decent enough to sell. Four out a forty. What about them blackboards?" Aaron nodded to the group set against the fence.

"They aint ruint. Got a little water to the chalk trays but that's about it. I tell you what, I have never been one to think it before, but there is no denying the bounty of the Lord," Johnny Roper said. He couldn't look at Aaron when he said it, though, and even though it was important to give testimony to the goodness of God, the words make him feel weak and false. He looked to the side and then back at the warped desks, his face reddening while he flapped his shirt around his waist, looking for a breeze.

Aaron took into account the salvage, desks and boards and boxes holding pencils and chalk spread out all over the place, dead wet books. Bending, he picked up a small box that fell apart in his hands, the cardboard like loose skin on a small rabbit. White cylindrical tubes of chalk were all that remained.

"How long you been sellin salvage, John?"

"Too long."

"How much you make last year?"

"Not enough."

"Bounty seems a poor choice of words for such a meager existence don't it?"

Johnny looked at him and then at the preacher's car sitting down the hill, its grillwork pointed upward, covered with dust and the drying spew of dead insects. The man had held an all-night prayer vigil, a thing Johnny had entered into with the hope that his leg would be evened out; that God would fix him so that he could stand straight and without a lean. He'd dozed off in his chair around eleven o'clock and then jerked wide awake, a rope of slobber dripping off his chin, embarrassed as hell, his leg still two inches too long.

"I stayed up listenin for the end of all that vigilation," Aaron said. "Waited to hear the sound of all those shufflin feet finding their way home to decent lukewarm living. Finally fell asleep. All you folks sleep over? Wake up together spread out all over the floor?"

"There are treasures the eye caint see, Aaron."

Johnny Roper had climbed into the back of his truck and was moving around and restacking boxes. His voice sounded small to his ears. "Soon as you realize that, being poor don't seem so bad," he said.

"You grow any taller yet? You even out, or are you still walkin with a limp?"

Johnny Roper faced the dark and shut his eyes, thinking, I could say a hurtful thing, but I won't because the Lord wouldn't liken it. I could though, and be counted a man for it by other men who'd do the same, but I won't. He said instead:

"You tell me what's so wrong with seein things as positive? What's so wrong a thing as that? Blest are the poor in spirit for they shall see . . . For they shall see . . ." He couldn't remember the rest of it; what in hell it was a poor man might have the privilege of seeing, but he was sure it was good and worthwhile. "I never once ask God for a durn thing. He saw fitten, is all. He saw fit—"

"She aint ever gonna love you over it. Annie aint ever gone come down off that high horse of hers and settle for less than what aint there. You're bein dragged into this religion business for nothin, is all. Wearin out your knees settin bait for a gal already full up to the gullet." Aaron was leaning on the door frame of the truck. "And if the good God keeps growin out that same durn leg of yours, you gonna end up standin at a forty-five degree angle. No use for nobody except as a shelf bracket."

Johnny sat down on a not-too-soggy box and watched out the back of his truck as Aaron walked toward his own house, the man's hindquarters as stiff as his neck. Absentmindedly Johnny pulled at his pants leg. In the early morning hours, the leg was still two inches longer than the other and he walked with a true lean. As day wore on, it settled down and the loose-hipped feeling near his back pocket eased a little. A miracle from God ought to stay a miracle, in his opinion, and he wondered if the Creator might be having second thoughts about what he'd done for him. He sat there studying his foot, waiting for peace to settle in just like it had last night inside the ring of prayer.

The preacher said it's new wine in old wineskins, is all. That's how come it all to feel so strange. And for me not to worry, God werent done with me yet. And when I asked him how come, he said Why aint he done with you? 'Cause he's a God who finishes what he starts, is how come, and Annie seemed in agreement. She sat there in that ruby dress of hers, belly out like a stolen jewel.

Johnny Roper heard a sound and looked up, navigated its course. It was just Aaron, banging the door shut behind him for good measure. Sad. The man is sad, is all, he thought. That's the reason for the anger. Too late to join a party he was invited to, but refused. Too late to join in now that the party's in full motion and he's still wearing that same old riddled face a his. Didn't get his miracle. Didn't even have the good sense to ask for it. Well, you go inside then. You bang that door. You go on to your own world because this is not a bad thing. I never once asked the good Lord for nothing and he seen fittin is all and when the man put his hands to my head I saw the words like a glorious sunset spread on the side of her belly. I saw those words written with a godly hand and I will obey those words. I will be there inside her shadow waitin. 'Cause I have known the steadfast non-love Aaron aint ever heard of. I have known the non-bounty of the Lord for so long a time that waiting inside a shadow is as sweet a thing as havin. I will wait while she watches the rows and I will wait inside her shadow for her not-seein. I will wait for this thing and when she turns from the not-seein I will be there for I have newly known the bounty of the Lord. Even me. Even short Johnny Roper, once a sinner unknown by God, but now known. I will wait . . . and I will wait . . . and I will wait.

CHAPTER

It was early enough in the day, but already hot. Aaron Class stood with Henry Prox inside the fenced perimeter and eyed the dirt road, its idle surface, the spangled light falling down through the trees. Aaron glanced up and saw the corners of the brown ribbed field jutting out behind Henry's blue house. Ten acres he leased to a Negro intent on making a living at cotton. The black man had already come and gone, such was the heat. Aaron knew this and wondered how the noise of the tractor had managed to slip by him. He thought he noticed everything these days. Prayers. Songs. Whispers. Life. Yet a man's work-hard sweat had dripped to the ground with only the fresh-turned dirt to show for it and Aaron had missed it. The wind picked up a little, stirred among the gamboling limbs of the sycamore, charged the sun-patterned ground 'til it danced and danced. The wind brought in the smell of Henry's house, too, that curious blend of turpentine and linseed oil from those paintings of his, alongside the odor of fried-off bacon fat and greens. Pulling his handkerchief out of his pocket, Aaron fitted it across the brim of his hat 'til it touched the curl of an upper lip. Like it or not, Rosie's method of sun protection had become a habit, at least on bright days, and there seemed to be more and more of them of late.

"There's a fever here, Henry. A true fever." Aaron crossed his arms over his chest. The cloth fluttered at his words.

Henry studied the ruined face while he puzzled over Aaron's nonparticipation. A sour memory involving Mother Church, he figured.

"I'm cool as a cucumber, myself. Aint been took with a fever since I was sixteen years old and got tangled up in barb wire."

"Lie to yourself, then. I don't care."

Rosie Gentle had set up one of the water-sogged blackboards to the front of her house, out near the small white fence where the primrose ran. Aaron could see the message:

The fear of the Lord is the beginning of wisdom

Rosie's hand hadn't done the writing, though. It was the preacher's that'd done it, bright and early before even the full lot of chickens was up.

Aaron had watched him pilfer through Johnny Roper's front yard for the chalk, seen the man put his hand to one of those curled-up desktops as though he wanted to heal it, or wish it straight for education's sake; his fingers were sorrowful and full of pity and bent curving like a plowhook, but powerless. Aaron had watched these things out his kitchen window while he put the coffee on, and once it was brewed up and black, the message was there for all to see. The fear of the Lord . . .

Henry Prox was quiet, an air of amusement about him, as though whatever was going to happen next had been orchestrated for his own personal entertainment. He stood, his coveralls a blaze of random color, spots here and there hardened to a crust, others wet as fresh blood. There was a swatch of cerulean blue near the man's elbow and Aaron watched him rub at it as though it were a bruise.

The sound of a screen door then, and both men watched Rosie come out her front door lugging something resembling a suitcase. Brown-gold and squared-off, it seemed as wide as the woman's ass.

"I worked in a painted rock for the wife to fish off of," Henry said, reaching into his pocket for his smokes, tipping one out and then holding it to his eye as though checking its circumference. "I always said 'Hon, they aint no rocks that close to the water, 'specially one as big and rounded out as you got in mind. A rock that big would carry the bank down with it. End up along the bottom of the river, and not no where else.' But Lord, she wanted it, so what can a man do. I had no other course than to paint it." The man went to patting his pockets, looking for a match.

Somedays Aaron wondered if Henry realized the wife was dead. This was one of those days. He snapped open his lighter and lit Henry's cigarette for him.

Across the street, Rosie sat herself down in her busted rocker while Aaron and Henry smoked. After a moment or two, she opened up the suitcase-shaped thing and it made a crackling sound, as though it had never before been used proper. Which seemed appropriate to Aaron seeing how the woman had never once left the street for more than a two-hour stretch.

"She would a liked that rock," Aaron said.

"Yep, I reckon she would have. Should a painted it sooner, I guess. But I dawdled so, time got away from me. Time seemed a slow man back then."

"How's the river comin?" Aaron said the words automatically, not caring about the answer. Henry had been working on the damn thing for close to seven years. If he hadn't got it right by now he ought to put those brushes aside, because he never would.

"At first I figgered it to be the Leaf and then I changed my mind. The Leaf can turn ugly before a man knows it. But not this one. Not this river. You can come in and see it if you like. I'd not mind."

Henry's eyes were magnified behind his glasses, more liquid than true eyes should be.

"There's a fever here, Henry. Got no time to go swimmin in your river," Aaron said.

"Feels like pure-d fun to me. Seen more cars and trucks come through here than comes through Lucedale at rodeo time." He nodded to the baskets of produce on Rosie's front steps, those makeshift offerings presented by the poor and low on cash. "If that preacher fella don't want them sacks of tomaters and squash, we ort to open us up a co-op. Sell that shit and make us a buck or two."

"I aint believin this." Aaron pointed across the street to Rosie, who was sitting and reading an open suitcase. He could see now that the suitcase was actually a Bible, one large enough to shield a small family from the rain, spread open across her lap. Rosie licked a finger and turned a page; looked up and smiled like a child.

"Oh, that. One of them big-ass family Bibles, seems to me," Prox said. "Man come through years back and sold the wife one. Got a great big shiny picture of Jesus hangin on the cross on the cover. Eyes open and blink shut dependin on how the light moves across it. Got places inside for all the borned and dead. Paid fourteen dollars for the durn thing." Prox rubbed at his nose and left a streak of vermilion near his left nostril, as though a nose bleed were birthing. "Only got one entry in mine, thank the good blinkin Jesus." He smiled at Aaron.

Rosie was turning giant pages and moving her lips.

"This is crazy."

Henry Prox dropped his smoke and snuffed it out with his shoe. "She aint harmin nobody, Aaron. Just readin."

"But that's just it. She caint read. I know it. She brings me all her official-looking mail. She's pretendin to read is all."

"Not no more." Prox seemed smugly confident.

"What'd you say?"

"I said not no more. Man prayed over her last night. Lord, I was there until midnight, I guess. Tongue-talkers everwhere. People slain in the Holy Ghost—"

"Slain in the Holy Ghost?"

"That's what the preacher called it. And I tell you what, I think it's real. He'd pray over the folks and then put his hand to their head and they'd fall clean out their chairs and just lay there like dead fish. I'd not believe it of just anybody, since frauds are thick as thieves in these parts, but I knowed firsthand some a those struck down. One woman in particular from over at New Augusta. A woman I been tryin to go out with for two months now. A stubborn, prideful woman."

"A smart woman, I'd say." Aaron grinned.

"And there is no way in hell that one would play possum like that, unless it was real. I stared at her until I was ashamed a myself. Women were putting towels and tablecloths over their legs to keep their underwear from showing. I tell you what, I'd like that job. I could do that easy. Just stand there and wait for them to fall over while watchin out for their drawers. Do my Christian duty by keepin a woman from bein embarrassed. Just call me Brother Henry Prox: Panty Priest."

"What's this got to do with Rosie over there readin?"

"Well, yes, I was comin to that. Just hold your horses, Aaron Class. Anyhow, Rosie wanted to read and the preacher prayed over her and asked Christ Jesus to teach her the letters, to break open the alphabet for her. Seems He did it, too. Thank the good blinkin Jesus." Prox beamed. There'd not been this much fun on the street since Johnny Roper hit a cow late at night on his way back from Pascagoula.

"And you believe this?"

"She's over there readin, aint she?"

"She's pretendin is all."

"What's scuttled your butt, Aaron?"

"Not a thing. It's just everbody around here is acting like this fella's Santa Claus."

"What's so bad about Santa Claus? I like him, myself." Henry grinned at him. "What you ort to do is come on inside and see what I done. I got a blue mountain in my kitchen now. With snow atop. Come on inside and see." Henry pulled out his paint rag and rubbed at his face.

"I got such a good seat, I hate to move. I might just miss somethin."

Rosie had a pencil and seemed to be underlining places in the book, making notations in its margin.

"I say kick back and enjoy it. Quit your worryin. That preacher'll git his fill and leave," Henry said.

"I aint worried, it just seems weird. Johnny Roper thinks his leg grew out a full two inches. Rosie thinks she can read."

There was a quiet pause and the two of them appeared to be studying different subjects of interest. A tulip poplar. A pyramid of cinder bricks stacked near Aaron's front porch. The woman across the way reading a giant Bible. "Maybe Rosie needs to feel good about herself," Henry said.

Aaron snorted out his nose. "I doubt there's a book big enough for that."

Henry turned quiet and Aaron immediately wished he could call back the words, remembering the woman and the steadfast way she had about

her. "I don't know what's come over me. None a this is my business, anyhow," Aaron said as way of explanation.

"Maybe you're worryin about what's on the way."

"Maybe."

"Worryin aint gonna help, though. Found that out my own self."

Aaron watched him, relieved the man was still in touch with reality
and that he knew the wife was dead and buried on a hill in Agricola. "Seems
to me I've wasted good air talkin about this. And I brung it up. I guess I
can remedy that by gittin busy with somethin else."

Henry Prox watched him walk away. He had wanted some more conversation but had been tossed aside as easily as a skinny drunk out a bar.
But that was okay. He had his paint. One wall left and then he could swim
in it. Could float on his back through his hall and bedroom and back out to
the small living room. And once that was done, he just might do the floors.
Walk on water for a while. Just like the good blinking Jesus. He ran a
hand underneath his nose, surprised by emotion. The river. She'd lost her
yellow fly, the one he'd hand tied for her alongside such a river. The lure
he'd given her the day she'd found out she was barren as a gourd and
would never carry his seed. She'd stood up on the river's bank and cried
like a baby. I lost it, Prox! I lost it! she'd sobbed. Why, here it is, Sweet,
right here beside this rock. Here it is. Don't you cry now. Paint me this
rock one day, she'd begged while she wiped her nose, and by God, he
had. Glowing rocks in water all over the house. Beautiful moss-covered rocks
that looked real enough to touch, and best of all: over her bed was a rainbow
breaking from a cloud. She lay there dying of the cancer and watched the
bewitching paint whisper words of comfort down to her. Soft as dew, those
words rested in the corners of her eyes and along the tender folds of her
neck.

Prox watched his friend walking away from him and once his shadow
elongated, he pulled out a notepad and drew a few strong lines; turned a
page and drew a few more for memory's sake. The shade along the street
formed designs along the ground like a warm quilt. In the spring the pattern
seemed that of a wedding ring, ushering in hope along with the crops; in
the fall it set itself up like a log cabin and made a remark or two on the
coming harvest; and now here in the late, waning winter comes a little gal

with a blooming belly. Prox looked over at Rosie and her great big Bible and wondered if she'd noticed how the shade from the trees along the road seemed her grandchild's birth announcement. That this laid-down mosaic of diminished light seemed portentous and remarkable and absolutely preordained.

CHAPTER 21

He had no fondness for town, but climbed in his truck and headed there for two reasons. One, to pick up something owed to him, the other, to escape the all-day prayer meeting burning itself out down near Beachum's Corner. There was only so much of white folks' singing a body could stand.

"I'll be needin that hay mower I ordered," Marion Calhoun said, leaning carefully on his hands. The counter was rough-planked. Hateful. He had already picked a half-inch splinter out of his palm. While he waited, he took inventory of his surroundings: one or two cars passed outside stirring up the dust and clouding the windows; the screen door to the feed store was ripped open in a corner, letting in the flies; a plain-faced woman in coveralls was standing behind him measuring out loops of rope from off a metal spool. Out his side vision Marion watched her slip it off the roll and unreel it to the floor. There were three more piles coiled behind her.

"Shirley, you aint got a reason to be doing that," the store owner said.

"I got me a reason," she answered.

"Where's your daddy at?"

"He aint the reason."

"Hell, I know that, girl. That's not why I'm askin."

Jenkins rolled his eyes at Marion Calhoun. He had mouthed something a few seconds earlier that had gone right over Calhoun's head. Never could read the mind or lips of a white man, Marion thought to himself. But I sure as hell know crazy when I see it. He looked over his shoulder at this woman named Shirley while he counted out the wrinkled bills and placed them on the counter. He hadn't much land left to mow, but the rats were multiplying in the back plat and becoming a nuisance, and he'd grown tired of watching Hezekiah chase after them with his slingshot. Besides, a hay mower was a thing he'd always coveted for his tractor.

"Shirley, I need you to put them things back up, now. I aint got the help to clean up all your mess—"

"I'm doin you a favor, Mr. Jenkins. Just you wait. Seeds sealed up caint breathe..." And then she stopped and stood frozen as ice next to the galvanized buckets. Yellow loops snagged at her feet like dead snakes.

"Lord. Here we go again," Jenkins said, and rang up the sale while he hollered for his help.

"Aint no need to call nobody," Marion said, pocketing the receipt. "I can git it loaded my own self."

"I aint hollerin for you. I got me a truckload of trouble in here. That's how come I'm hollering. Aint nothing safe, I swear..." He whistled loud as a cattle rancher and two black faces appeared from up the hall like magic. Marion knew the young men. Curtis and Slough Peabody. Knew whose boys they were. Good boys, too. Not too bright, but still good boys. Out working to help their mama, he guessed.

"Git on down to Pure Oil and see if Jim's still there." Jenkins pointed with a covert finger to the woman named Shirley, who was tearing open seed packets of mustard greens and dumping them on top of the unreeled rope. Curtis and Slough disappeared the same way they had appeared: instantly.

I reckon they smart enough to know crazy when they see it, Marion thought.

"Lord have mercy," Jenkins said to the thin air.

"I know me a joke, Mr. Jenkins," said this Shirley.

"Well, you leave them seeds alone and I'll let you tell it."

Shirley picked up a handful of paper packets and ripped them to shreds. "There was this man that everybody knew was the town idiot. Folks knew it, but just 'cause a man's a idiot, don't mean he caint learn. So one day, he went into a store and said he wanted to learn how to clerk. Most folks felt sorry for him, so the boss said, okay, he'd show him how. 'You see this customer here? The secret to being a good clerk is to double the sale. You sit and watch what I do.' The customer wanted a shovel. Boss says, 'Seein how you're buying this nice new shovel, maybe you ought to buy yourself a wheelbarrow to put the dirt in', and the man saw the reason in it, and bought one. 'See, this is how you do it,' the man told the idiot. 'You try to sell something extra ever time you have a customer.' You listenin to the joke, Mr. Jenkins?"

"I'm listenin." Jenkins leaned on his hand while Marion Calhoun wondered where exactly his new equipment might be.

"Well, the next day the boss let the idiot run the counter. A woman come in and was looking around for something. 'Can I help you ma'am,' the idiot says. Well, she looked shy and all, and finally pointed to a box of Kotex behind the counter. The idiot handed it to her and then went up the back aisle and wheeled in a lawn mower. 'How come you bringing me a lawn mower? I didn't ask for one,' the woman says, looking at him real puzzled. The idiot picked up the Kotex box and says, 'The way I see it, if you caint fuck you might as well cut the grass.' " The woman named Shirley doubled over laughing; howled like a wolf with her head between her knees.

"Her daddy be here soon, I guess," Jenkins said with a sigh.

Not soon enough, Marion thought to himself.

"Did you like my joke, Mr. Jenkins?"

"I'd like it better if you'd leave off tearin up my things."

She turned and gave them both a blank stare. Coveralls aside, she seemed scarecrow skinny and ugly as a hound. Marion turned and leaned against the counter, waiting for the boys to return, and for Jenkins to get rid of the craziness in his Feed and Seed and point him, once for all, in the direction of what he'd already paid for.

"I know you," the female said to his back.

Marion looked at Jenkins and felt the hair stand up along the back of his neck. He could sense the woman moving up behind him, steady as a cat.

"I said I know you." He felt her breath; smelled its sour smell.

"I think the woman knows you," Jenkins said, bored with it.

"I be needin to git on home, Mr. Jenkins. Now, if you show me the way I'll go load it in the truck," Marion said.

"You loved that singin gal," the voice whispered.

Marion kept his gaze steady forward to the wall reading the weekly bulletin printed out by hand: *Hogs for Sale. $10. 45388. Party line. If the voice aint talkin hogs, the voice aint the one you want.*

"I said you loved that singin gal who taught that singin school over Lucedale way. The one who run off with the trucker. You sold your land to white trash just so's you could leave and be with her . . . with that singin gal—"

"Oh for Christsakes, leave the poor man alone." Jenkins rubbed his hand over his face, then drummed his fingers along the hateful counter.

"You got the mower out back? I be glad to go there and git it myself." Marion could feel her breathing against his shirt back. He remembered her holding a gardening spade and wondered if it was still in her hand.

"I got stuff out there ordered from all over. Plows. Disks. Manure spreaders. All kinds of stuff. Nobody knows that back room like them two boys and I aint one to learn a thing this late in life. Don't want nobody thinkin I cheated nere a man. Not even a Negro."

He's scared to be alone with her is what he don't want nobody thinkin, was Marion's thought.

Jenkins leaned toward Calhoun and whispered: "If I leave right now and turn my back on her, I'll come back and find my store burnin down around my ass. I worked ten long years for this place . . ."

Marion wasn't sure what it meant. Whether he should go around back, rummage through the shed and get the part himself, or wait, or let Jenkins go and get it while he kept the Shirley woman clear of the kerosene. He was at a loss.

"Give it five more minutes and I'll take her out myself," Jenkins said.

"Heard that white trash you live next to set up a rummage market.

'Cause of you, and 'cause of that gal. Lost the best part of the land, and a nigger ownin land in Mississippi aint a thing to lose easy," Shirley said.

"I sold my land, ma'am. I didn't lose a thing." Marion cracked his knuckles and tried to calm himself. And now here I am rentin out land all over the county just so's I can put in a crop, standin lost in a store with a crazy gal who's only got one worthwhile thing and that's a memory as fierce as a durn elephant's. Almost ten years, and it still lingerin and screamin out, and remindin folks, no matter—

"There's a scratchin post over in Lucedale. Out in front of the diner. A huge white scratchin post." Shirley scratched hard at her nose in illustration.

"We all know that, Shirley," Jenkins said, yawning wide.

"I guess what that gal needed scratchin she couldn't manage out in the street, or up to your place."

Slough and Curtis came in through the back hall, while a man as wide as a barn came in through the front.

"Daddy!" The woman threw herself into his arms and then started weeping uncontrollably, blubbering nonsense about seed and rope and the scratching post over in Lucedale.

"I owe you one," the big man told Jenkins while he half-carried, half-dragged his daughter out the front door. "Send me the bill for damages and I'll clear it. I'm good for it, same as always."

"No problem, Jim. No problem atall."

Fifteen minutes later, his haymower loaded to the truck bed, Marion Calhoun was driving home underneath a topaz sky. While folks were studying it from their workbench, or back feedlot, or out the kitchen window, and remarking on its strange palette, Marion Calhoun drove as one color-blind through the narrow back roads of Agricola. The sky was nothing to him. Nothing at all. The only thing of any consequence was that day ten years back when everything changed. Older now, and worn around the joints, he couldn't help but wonder if those personal damages rung up a decade back would ever be satisfied. He was smart enough to know they wouldn't. He was smart enough to know there was no such thing as justice in the world; there was just the wish for it.

He passed the county marker and turned, his hands doing their business of driving as if disconnected from his brain. Turn. Downshift to second. Accelerate. Shift again. Roll on down the road. It was 1955 and what she'd done was ten years behind him, but still it trailed like exhaust, or maybe a ghost.

But God, he loved her skin! Almost a decade, and he still loved it. A golden sky was spread out over his head but Marion didn't see it. He saw a decade back instead. The way he'd quit his tractor work early that day just so he could go and pick her up from the singing school down in Lucedale. I'll surprise her, he had thought. Show her the ring I just bought her with the money from the land I just sold to a moron. He had thrown open the wide doors to the barn and chugged inside on his tractor, leaving time and obligation and routine waiting outside in the sun, stunned by being pre-empted by a thing as precarious as love. Music had been riding on the wind; music from out the old radio down at Beachum's Store. The lyrics were muted, but the tune was a sweet one, some sort of a love song crooned by male voices.

"Nothin between thee and me but this hunk of precious land," he remembered saying while he climbed into his truck and set off down the road. All had been quiet then. The music strangled mid-verse when Beachum switched off the pumps and the lights, as well as the radio. Evening was fully settled in and breathing: an interminable rhythmic quiet broken only by the noise of the crickets. He wondered later if there had been a warning written somewhere inside the terrain, some hidden thing on the dark side of a pecan tree, or in the gravel shifting underneath his truck tires. He recalled the truck window being down and how he heard the distant sound of the river racing twenty acres back, how it carried with it a dark noise like that of steady thunder. He remembered how he ignored it and how he had lied to himself instead, convinced it was only the buoyant sound of his old, beating heart.

Dancers. This was what he remembered next.

"Why, aint this strange, their shadows seem just like dancers," he had said. His deep voice had echoed against the ravine wall before coming back to him. Above his head, the church seemed shoved into the side of a hill. A steep set of stairs accordioned out its rear like a fire escape. Below, a ravine spread out into an area fixed up with picnic tables and a springwater well.

A peaceful place. Folks called it Shiloh after that place in the Old Testament where folks went to rest. (Later he would remember that Shiloh had also been that bitter Civil War stage where grown men had their beating hearts shot clean out their chests.)

He had been half a mile away when he'd seen the lights switch off in the church and, as if his brain were disconnected from reason, or rather, connected to a truer reason than the one by which he was governed, he slowed the truck to a crawl and began to creep, as if he knew or was about to know the true face of something. With the truck lights off, he coasted the short distance. Heart pounding beneath his palm, he waited for her to come out the front door of the church like any good girl would do. Come on out now, and see who's here waiting. Me. Marion Calhoun. That man you love. Come on out now and be surprised at what I brung you. . . .

He waited for what felt like a century, the bill of sale on his land in one pocket, her ring in the other. When he reached in and touched the receipt it felt of dried leaves and dead bark. Cold things. Extinct things. The paper was clutched in his hand when he climbed out the window of his truck. He didn't open the door because the door made a god-awful noise, so he eased his ass out the window instead. And then he crept. And it was while he skulked along the shady pines, that he knew.

If I'd a walked bold, I would not have known. I'd a been a man walkin, lookin with safe regard for what I thought was mine, or soon to be mine. But I played at stealth and made flesh of the slink-word, and so I knew.

"Just like dancers—"

He had let the limb fall back in front of his face. If the two heard him, they paid it no mind. In that place called Shiloh their dancers' bodies moved and swayed as if blown by caressing wind, one shadow taller than the other. Bending. Lifting. Spreading themselves across the wooden picnic table. Fabric captured moonlight, threw illumination down her naked legs. Washed across those breasts he'd never seen, only dreamed about. She laughed then, and Marion felt shot-through. Not because of her elation or disregard of what he had assumed was a promise, but because he'd never heard the sound before. He'd heard her sing and talk and whisper, but never laugh. I could go now and forget this thing, he told himself. Pretend this is trivial. Go back home and wait and see if she shows up and what she might say to explain things.

I could do this and pretend none of this ever happened because I done sold the best of the land, the best of myself. I could do this thing, but I won't.

Marion turned at Beachum's Corner, saw the droopy revival tent and the folding chairs, noticed Susan-Blair was in attendance, her feet resting on sawdust same as all the others. And then he passed them, fed them his stirred-up dust. The years were behind him and still she raged like a tornado. The bill would never be paid because there had never been a service rendered. There had been expectation and hope and longing and love. Precarious entanglements that would shadow him forever.

CHAPTER 22

Aaron had done his own private propagation. Ginger lilies and blue phlox. Hedge bloomers and ramblers. Trumpet honeysuckle trained to a shape like that of setting sun. He looked to where it stood, freestanding as some careless god's lost discus, and reasoned he could plant a group of white rugosa roses across its base and give it the illusion of clouds drifting by. The one acre back plat in George County was fast on its way to becoming a miniature version of an English garden in spite of the cultivator's cynical nature. He sat beneath a wisteria-covered trellis on a stone bench Johnny Roper had dug up from somewhere, watching the butterflies. Egyptian star clusters pointed their yellow fingers to the sky while four monarchs balanced on a blazing row of justica. He blinked slowly, wanting nothing more than to reach out and tease one to his rough finger. Hard to believe I ever worked the boats for a livin, he thought, remembering the smell of the nets and the noise of the bars; the way even the most callous used to pine for his out-West stories. Them boys used to think I was really somethin, I guess. Off seein the world. Me bringin back maps of Oregon and California and spreadin them out across a table like I had somethin important to say. I bet they'd laugh their asses off now. One or two might even feel inclined to try and beat the sissy gardener out a me. He saw movement out the corner of his eye and realized he had company.

She was rubbing her hands on her apron as though she'd been cooking, those blue eyes of hers peering into his with a new missionary zeal he found alarming.

"You git done with your readin?" he said to her.

"I seen you and Henry watchin me."

"I swear Rosie, I seen a lot, but I aint never seen such a big Bible."

"It's been settin on my coffee table fer years—"

"Tell me true. You caint read a word of it can you?"

The woman sniffed and threw back her head a little. "I cooked enough for you should you want to come to supper. Henry's comin. So's Johnny. That's all I'm over here to say. The preacher tole me you had some questions fer him last night."

The little prick tattletale. "You wanna sit a while?"

"I just might."

She walked past the spillage of sweet william growing in matching urns and through a waving mass of Spanish moss Aaron had trained to a cypress.

He loved the moss. Those gray threadlike leaves. The way it had no roots.

"You got you some good shade in here."

"Good enough."

"You want to join us fer supper?"

He noticed her hair was yellowing, thanks to the artesian well water they all were subject to, and unless he was mistaken, she had lost a little weight in the last week or two. Hot weather, he figured, not to mention all that prayin. "Thanks, but no thanks."

"He aint that bad."

"I never said he was. I just got no need for it."

She hovered too much like a mother to suit him, and he shifted, looked the other way. "You see that over there?" he pointed to a gap inside a cluster of roses. "I lost La France to the black spot," he said. "Come out one day and seen a bush full of yellow leaves. Come out the next and seen black. Had to crawl around on my hands and knees just to make sure a single leaf didn't get away from me. Goddamn, I hated that." He sighed.

"You ort to watch your mouth, Aaron Class."

He just looked at her and let the quiet speak for itself. La France had been his first rose, considered by most authorities to be the first of the hybrids. It took him six months to get up the nerve to buy it from a gardener over in Hattiesburg. He figured it was worth a goddamn, or two.

"Did you get 'em all? All them leaves?" She picked up the edge of her apron and wiped her face. He could smell supper on her. Beans. Fried okra. Corn.

"All I could find. Black spot's a killer. Worse than aphids or rust or mildew," he said. "Them things you can deal with, but not the spot. The spot's a killer. Durn, I loved that rose."

Where the plant had been was now a dark circular space with dead interior. It would be three years before the ground would be safe for another plant.

He looked away and through the wisteria, toward the back field. The natural archway was bordered in larkspur and trumpet creepers and row after row of healthy floribundas. The hardy plants had watched their neighbor die and kept right on blooming and there seemed to be a heartless design to them now, an arrogance that had gone unnoticed.

"That Peace rose sure is nice," Rosie said studying it.

Aaron agreed. The pink was so white it almost wasn't pink, more true to the color of the female inner labia. He didn't want to, but he couldn't help but think of Annie, spread open in birth, and felt himself blush. "Come late summer, it'll be a sight." Aaron's fingers were linked around his knees. The woman wanted something of him, he just wasn't sure what it might be.

"I wish ye'd come on over to supper."

"I aint hungry, Rose."

"Annie seems to like the preacher."

"Him, or what he says?"

Rosie seemed to be considering it. "I aint sure. I guess it's the same either way."

"No, it aint the same. There's a difference."

"She's been inside cleanin and helpin me cook. She never took a interest in housekeepin before. I guess havin company's a good thing."

Aaron shook his head, bored with it. It was early summer and the goldenrod was turning lush. When he leaned back and squinted just a little it seemed he was witness to a field blazing gold as the sun. "How'd this guy find you, anyhow?"

"He says the Lord led him here."

"And you think it's true."

"We aint got nothin nobody would want. Aint nobody round here rich. At first I thought he was out to sell me somethin I aint got no need for. Like that fool who come through here with them encyclopedias years back. So far he aint mentioned it."

"He's gettin fed real good. Better'n he could git in town. Plus, it's free."

"I aint mindin it, Aaron."

He had thought she stood above the need for salvific hope or a fool's embellishments, and her compliance confused him, led him to wonder about her past. How many years had he lived there and never once questioned the presence of a daughter, or the woman, or how they came to be living on a dirt road in George County? Too many to start making inquiries now. He had seen the field hand. Seen him sniffing around where he shouldn't and had kept still on it. Annie was such a big, plain-faced girl, after all. A female with a lumbering Midwestern look to her. A face sheared of emotion by the hard wind of dirt-road limitations. Those wide-apart eyes. That pear-shaped body. He thought the boy was nothing but a tease. Just after a few laughs or a covert kiss. Idiot, he thought. I'm a bloomin idiot for not seein it comin.

"You think he's comin back?"

She was asking about the father of Annie's baby and Aaron knew it. "Nope."

"God told the preacher he was."

"He did, did he?"

"Don't you think God can speak to folks?"

"What I think don't matter." Aaron stretched out his legs. "Johnny'd marry her, you know."

Rosie looked at him as though he were crazed.

"Dear Lord, Aaron. Johnny's like her brother. Like family."

"All the more reason."

"Annie'd not have it."

Aaron looked at his watch. Let her have her bastard then. He didn't care. "Rosie, it's mostly dark already. You got company comin."

She seemed about to say something. Aaron watched her, saw various emotions flit across her face.

"I aint sure if I can read or not. I opened it up and seen them shapes and they seem to swim up and mean somethin. For all I know it could be fairy tales I'm rememberin."

Aaron cleared his throat, recalling how the woman had pursued him with good intentions. Chased him out of his isolation with the kindness of cloth. He should have been nicer.

"Okay. I'm leavin. I just wanted to talk a minute. See what you were thinkin about all this."

"Well. I'll tell you what I'm thinkin. I'm thinkin I'll be glad when he gits out a here and leaves us alone."

"How come you don't like him?"

He looked at her wide face, the tired lines creeping down from her eyes. It was a good question. One he couldn't quite answer. Whatever he was feeling, it roamed nameless inside his head. "I don't really know, Rosie."

"There's plenty a supper, should you change your mind."

And then she was gone, disappearing through a curtain of moss. "You could make a livin at growin things, Aaron Class. But I guess you already know that."

He heard the sound of tires on shale and watched the preacher's black car turn toward the west and begin to ease up the dirt road in their direction. He creeps along like a roach, Aaron thought. A hungry one. One about to get fed.

"This is such bullshit."

Across the way, the butterflies were trapped in some rude late evening wind. Fragile patches of color pressed and darted about the wide skirts of the trees before being lifted by a slight catch-pocket of air that swept them neatly into the low-limbed chambers of magnolias. They were helpless in the dark. Helpless.

Aaron watched them for a long minute and then he stood and walked into his house.

CHAPTER 23

Inside her crowded yellow living room Rosie was wailing, swabbing at her
face with a tear-soaked handkerchief while rivulets of salt water ran down
her cheeks. Her broad rear end was spread across two chairs on a front row,
a skinny woman wearing a loose gray sack of a dress jammed in on one side
of her and a skinny man in a sweat-odored shirt on the other. Johnny Roper
watched the trio, thinking Rosie had taken on the appearance of a backwoods
clan matriarch, or perhaps some poor county's obese Watermelon Queen, her
attendants picked up by the scruff of the neck and rescued from their job of
begging in the street. The man and woman were crying, too. Johnny could
see this from his spot next to the wall, where his shoulders were jammed
next to the shoulders of strangers and he could smell sweat and dirty feet
hiding inside week-worn socks and clothing that had been worn way too
many times. His included.

A march of some sort was kicking up complete with curious wooden
clacking sounds and he leaned down to see. Across the way Rosie's feet
were tapping on the floor, her worn-down black pumps pounding away in

some ancient morse code. Holy shit. This is it, he thought, mesmerized by
the jiggle of fat and the sound of wood being stamped upon. "Touch me,
Jesus! Touch me, Lord!" she cried, her legs jerking faster and faster, in a way
that was contagious. Johnny put out a tentative hand to his own knees and
judged them immune to it, and then he leaned forward and positioned his
hands behind Annie's back in case she started to fall. The night before bodies
had ended up all over the floor and he'd not have her tumble and hurt
herself, or the baby she was carrying. The couple from over in Cumbest
reached for each other and started to cry and then their knees began to move
as though jerked by a puppeteer's strings. Old Henry Prox leaned forward
in great anticipation, his discarded coat in his hands, a folded tablecloth on
his knees, and Johnny knew he was ready and waiting for the next victim
to fall out their chair and expose their undergarments. The contagious spir-
itualistic symphony of knockings and foot tappings and jerkings spread
slowly across the floor, infiltrated ankles, shins and knees, and then the room
exploded in a chorus of harmonious singing. Unrehearsed. Genuine. Terrific.

The preacher was silent inside this roomful of people—some strangers,
some friends—operating on a level reserved for heads-of-state, or politicians,
or over-the-hill ball players making the circuit at the county fair. Johnny
Roper, anticipating a call for testimonies, sat up straighter and tapped his heel
on the floor, testing it. The lift felt solid and true. He'd built up a false bottom
for his shoe because his leg had gone back to normal and he'd stopped walking
with a lean. And while he secretly wished he had asked for a warranty on his
miracle, he still felt obligated to consider it done. Why God took it back, he
didn't know. Maybe because he couldn't get Annie off his mind. Couldn't quit
letting his hand do what he wished her pussy would.

Johnny sat up with a start and nervously ran a palm down his Brillan-
tined hair. A sheen crowned the top of his head, down to his ears, for he
was slick with oil, having lost all sense of restraint in all sorts of areas—
grooming and masturbation foremost on the list. He was being stared at by
the preacher and he knew it. Come on, then. Call on me. I aint afraid to
talk. I can give it everthing I got. He straightened his back.

Annie was in front of him, Johnny's hands to either side of her. The
left one so close to the wide expanse of her pregnant belly he could feel the
heat wafting up off the cloth. When he leaned forward he could smell lilacs

and Ivory soap and the warm, tangy sweat embedded in her dress. It was
all he could do to keep from licking her neck.

The preacher watched him for a moment, seemed to be considering the
merits of letting him speak (Johnny had stood and walked around on his too-
long leg the night before and sent three women into a holy conniption fit,
and the preacher seemed pleased), and then he looked away. Hey. Come on
now. Don't do that. Let 'em think I still got that extra two inches, he thought.
But the man seemed tired. Worn out. That strain of melancholy deeper than
it'd been the night before. He held the Bible out in front of him and then
he pulled it to his chest and touched his chin down to its cover.

There was a slight shaking coming off Annie's shoulder and she began
to cry, rocking and singing a melody that had at its core a lullaby. Johnny
leaned forward and touched her shoulder, squeezed it in a man-clumsy grip
he felt all the way down to his privates. His eyes were shut in ecstasy when
she turned and shoved him so hard he would've fallen out his chair had he
not been pinned in by the two stinky bodies from Lucedale. Annie bent to
her belly again, sang to her stomach while Johnny looked around to see if
anyone had noticed the attack.

The man lifted his hand and held the Bible in the air, waved it a few
times over his head. "I caint talk," he whispered and the singing skidded to
a stop while his voice broke like glass inside the roomful of tears. "I aint got
the words," he said, and stood there sobbing.

Johnny studied his face and judged it real and felt his own eyes begin
to water. The man had a way of reaching deep down inside and pulling
some emotional string and Johnny liked it, surprised by how good sobbing
could feel to a full-grown man. The experience of having fear and pain and
love levered out the lower gut was worth paying good money for. He ran
a hand over his eyes and then wiped the wet on a trouser leg, before pulling
out his handkerchief and blowing his nose, finally.

Chairs were backed into chairs. Legs were sideways. Skin was touching
unfamiliar skin. Johnny looked up and saw people outside on the porch,
their wide-eyed faces pressed to the windows, their ears listening. He remembered the Bible story where the crowd grew so thick they lowered a crippled
man down through a hole in the ceiling just so Jesus could have a go at
healing him. Johnny looked up. Rosie's ceiling was solid, intact, with a fancy

knobby globe holding dead and drying flies inside it. He thought she just might want it to stay that way, too. Should he be commissioned, though, he bet he could figure out a way to ferry folks in through the windows. Hitch him a rope to the large sycamore tree out by the road and fix some sort a canvas sling for them to sit in while they rode the glory train to Christ. He made a quick list in his head: a hunderd feet a good rope, a pulley or two, maybe twenty yards a good canvas. Should he have the time, he'd like to fashion, out of consideration, a super-large size for women with asses the size of Rosie's. I could pick 'em up out by the tree, strap 'em in and then git Aaron to help me pull 'em along. A course I'll have to take down that door right over there. I bet there'd be a right smart amount a salvage from such a job as that. He sat back in his chair, wishing he had had the foresight to bring along an adding machine to do his figuring.

Mavis Crane, overcome by glory, hurled herself out of the chair and momentarily interrupted his calculations. Henry Prox spread a tablecloth over her legs and then sat back in his chair, his hand covering his eyes.

"Consider now the goodness of God," the preacher said. And most folks seemed to think that was a damn good idea. Not since the funeral of the Burkett twins had there been such a sea of round, wet faces. Heads were nodding; women were crying enough tears to fill a bucket; Annie shifted in her seat, put a pale, swollen hand around behind her, and Johnny knew her back was hurting. Hell, mine's killin me and I aint carryin a baby in my belly. He gave a quick fish-eyed look around, thought of climbing over the legs and the laps of strangers and making his way to the rear of the house and finding her a pillow in the back room, and then he discarded it. I doubt the Lord, nor nobody else would liken it too much should I go strollin into some female's private quarters in the middle of a prayer meeting.

The preacher was praying, or testifying, or whatever it was he did when he spoke for God. Johnny listened, his hands clasped around his knees, his eyes closing. The cadence was healing, soothing in a way that defied understanding. "Thus saith the Lord, I aint forgot ye . . ."

Good, thought Johnny. 'Cause this here gal in front a me is hurtin.

"—or how ye've stood strong. I have seen ye goin out and comin in, and I will keep thee safe."

Annie rolled forward, fell to one knee and buried her head on the back of a total stranger. Johnny sat back, stunned by the rejection.

"The Lord will give you a vision and it will carry you through the sufferin. Through these cold times. It will bear you up. You seen winters aint nobody here ever seen. I feel it freezin you. Freezin me. Lord, I feel it now!" The preacher's whole body began to jerk like a landed fish fetched up in unexpected death. A small drop of sweat from off the preacher's forehead flew across the room and landed on Johnny's lip. Afraid to wipe it off because it had come from holy lips, Johnny sat still as a starving frog, waiting on the Lord.

*   *   *

"I need to know!" Annie said.

She had never felt such desperation hinged on hopelessness. Not even in those early months when her monthly moon-time hid its face from her and she spent days and days trying every backwoods home remedy she'd ever heard of: swallowing pennies, drinking vinegar, cutting a splice off a maple sapling and burying it under a mossy rock. But desperation and fear were making a meal of her heart now, and if ever there was a time for knowing a thing, and speaking up in order to know, it was now.

"What are you needin to know?"

"If your words is true."

"They's not my words, but His." The preacher put his hand to her head as a parent might check a child for a low-grade fever, and smiled at her. She reached up and pulled his hands off her head and hooked her cold fingers around his skinny wrists, his answer not good enough. Not nearly good enough.

"I felt the first of it and he aint here yet."

Annie looked around for her mother, and licked her lips and tried to straighten her back because it was hurting. She saw Rosie inside the kitchen brewing coffee, oblivious to four hours now of a daughter's silent suffering.

"The Scribes and Pharisees asked for a sign, child. The good Lord said 'Blessed are ye who believe without seein.' " And then the preacher looked away.

Annie could feel the warmth of his hands and the way they tingled and she wondered why the preacher didn't heal her back pain. She felt another hard cramp and it stole the thought away.

"I feel it, and he aint here yet. I been looking. Everday. Just like you said, with faith."

"If it truly was faith believin, the boy would be here."

Annie tried to imagine a human being picked up from where he was and transported to another place on the earth, just because a person believed it so, and couldn't. "So the fault is mine?"

"The Word of God don't lie. If ye have faith as a mustard seed ye can move mountains."

"I don't *want* to move no mountain! I want him! Here! Now! Like you said he would be!"

"Believin faith sees the impossible and makes it happen, Annie."

"It *is* believin faith, as believin as I can git it to be!" She felt close to panic. This God was turning into a lizard before her very eyes. One able to change colors depending on what He was resting on. Rest on belief and God was good as gold and would make your leg grow out, or your teeth turn presentable, make a dead washing machine run; but settle down on something less, say unbelief, or fear, and He was as hard to pinpoint as a bent blade of grass in a ten-acre field. "I caint believe any more than I'm already doin." She began to cry, her eyes cast toward the door where beyond lived the dark.

"I am the Lord's servant. I am not the Lord." He peeled her hands off his arms, patiently, and then he patted her arm. "Go seek the Lord, Annie. Seek ye first the kingdom of God and His righteousness and the rest will be given to you."

The rest of what? she wondered.

She watched him walk away and survey the empty chairs with an air of satisfaction, as though he'd done well for himself and this God of his. Earlier, when she'd walked down the street to ease her cramps she'd seen his suitcase on the backseat of his car and realized the truth of her dilemma. Packed and ready to go, was what the preacher's suitcase said, and still there was no shadow headed her way from across the field, no matter how many times she stood out there looking.

"We must wait on the Lord," he said as he put his hat to his head, done with her, it seemed. While she watched he glanced at the front door.

"How long do I wait?" she asked him, one hand to her lower stomach.

The women were coming out of the kitchen. Annie could smell the lemon-scented soap and see the white hands and the shy looks of awe to their eyes. Standing up straight, the preacher turned and studied them, and then spoke in his hidden language, that guttural outpouring of syllables and clickings, quick and harsh. Almost angry, was how it sounded to her. And then he put a hand to her belly, and while his other hand was up in the air with fingers spread open and waving, he waited, his head thrown back to the ceiling while he translated his own words: "This child will be a *mighty* child, Annie—these are the *words* of the *Lord! Right here!* In this *very* house! A precious child *sittin* on the lap of its grandmother" (at this, Rosie, who had a blue-and-white striped dish towel in her hand, beamed and made a note to herself to get the durn busted rocker fixed). "Thus saith the *Lord God of Israel*, this precious child will *confound* the wise and do *mighty* works of *salvation* for the many. You must have faith and *believe* this thing because these are not—"

"I know. Not your words, but His," Annie whispered.

His words could have been carved in stone, such was the power behind them. Liquid and hot, they fell on the women, who shut their eyes and cried. The preacher acknowledged it with a bowed head. Annie did feel a stirring of something. Maybe hope. Maybe a contraction. Whatever it was, she felt soothed a little and she told herself that she would wait. For however long it took, she'd wait. Maybe this man was a liar wearing a dusty hat, but God had done things that she'd seen with her very own eyes. Made a leg grow out. Given her mother the words of understanding so she could read. God had done things and regardless of who wasn't walking toward her anytime soon, because of what she'd seen in days recent, she would wait.

CHAPTER 24

The white gal's stomach was flat.

Marion Calhoun sat his tractor and watched the girl go out to the watering trough in her backyard and fill a bucket. On slow feet she climbed those concrete steps. First one, then the other, then the other. She paused and took a breath on the last one and ran the back of a hand across her forehead before opening the back door and disappearing behind a dusty gray screen.

Three days now, and her stomach flatter each and every day.

"That gal dropped hers," Marion said.

He had a few more rows to go and then he could get on back to where he belonged. It was his second year of leasing land from the man in the blue house, just in order to put in a crop, and he hated it.

The boy walked beside the tractor, hitting at the muddy tires with a stick. Dirt would fall off in various shapes that seemed remarkable: a giraffe, a pistol, a shoe. He made a game of it while his neighbor worked.

"What'd she drop, Mayurn?" he said.

The white boy didn't seem to feel much need for bathwater. Marion saw a crust of dirt beads underneath his neck. Earlier in the day he'd found a tick behind the boy's ear, already burrowed in, near the size of an apple seed. Had to light a match and hold it to it, so the tick would pull out its blood-sucking head. Once done, he'd smashed it against the tractor's tire well leaving a big red swatch blazed against yellow that turned dark. God's truth, here I am plowin somebody else's land and baby-sittin somebody else's off-spring. But Hez werent too bad. In spite of stupid questions, and ticks, and dirt beads strung underneath his neck.

"What'd that lady drop, Mayurn? A chicken?" He put a hand over his blue eyes, shielding the sun. "I dropped a baby chick on its head once when I was little, and kilt it. Susan-Blair like to beat me silly over it."

"She didn't drop no chicken."

"What then?"

"Seems like she had her youngun. Aint heard no cryin, though. But her belly aint swole up no more. Gone flat now." And that was it. He might remove ticks and teach the boy about plowing, but there'd be no discussing the facts of life. Not from him.

He said, "Where's that water jug gone to?"

"It's right here. Hold up." Hezekiah tilted it to his mouth and drank deeply, then handed it up to the man who did the same.

"Shit. It's turned hot, aint it?"

"Amen."

"You got the religion, too?"

"Shit, no." Hezekiah scratched at his nose, then bent and picked up a dirt clod and hurled it at a bird. "Ma has, though. She quit the bottle a month back."

"Hell, Hez. That caint mean nothin but trouble."

"You're right there." A pair of hawks screamed out from some hidden height and Hez looked upward to the sky. "She had the pukes this mornin. I figure she'll be payin a visit to old Jack Daniels round noontime."

"How many rows we got left?" Marion said.

Hez looked up and down and sideways. "Seven."

"Git on home and git my feet to a tub. That's what I want."

"I aint sleepin out in the tent no more. Not since you pulled that tick off me."

"It's dead now."

"Wish'd I'd saved it and stuck it on Arena. I swear, I hate her guts."

The disfigured man who loved flowers was out walking in his garden, Marion could see his back while he bent and clipped and dug in the dirt. When the tractor made the turn to the final row, the man held up a hand in a good-natured wave, which Marion returned.

The ways of country people were strange. A white could shun a wave, but not a colored. A colored had to keep his wave short and his eyes down when he did it, though. A damn nuisance when folks waved at him. White folks, that is. Could live my whole life without seein the palm of a white hand, he figured. My whole damn life. Now, if he could just get the tractor to behave the five miles back to his place, he'd be there before dark and could soak his feet in a pan of hot water while he listened to his radio.

A short man, too short to be called normal, but not short enough to be called freak, had joined the man in the garden. While the sun beat down on the top of his head, Marion watched the beginning of an argument. Arms flailed about. The short man going so far as to stomp his feet in the dust. Marion couldn't hear what was said and he was glad. Enough nuisance in the world without being a party to more.

"Them two men don't look too happy. Seems like we're about to see a fistfight or something."

Marion neared the last of the last row. "Time to git from here, I reckon."

Done with plowing, Marion chugged homeward, Hezekiah riding on the back of the tractor. The dirt road a blessing. Not too many trucks to blow their horns at his slow progress. No white palms to greet him from any vehicle of any type. Once he passed the break of trees and the row of tiny houses, he could breathe easy. He turned to Hezekiah, "Hand me that jug a water again."

The boy unscrewed the lid and handed it over his shoulder and watched the man drink. "Next time we ort to bring us a beer or two," he said.

"You aint old enough yet."

"How old I gotta be to drink a beer?"

"Older than you are. I aint goin to jail over a Pabst."

"You think they'd haul you away over a thing like that?" Hez said.

"Boy, I think they just lookin for a reason to haul my black ass away."

They watched the approach of their road, tired and sweaty and ready for the night.

CHAPTER

"What in Christsakes are you talkin about?"

Aaron had work to do. No time for this happy horseshit.

"She's done gone and had the baby." Johnny Roper looked green around the gills, like he'd swallowed a whole bag of chewing tobacco.

"I be go to hell. Guess Rosie's in hog heaven right now. Maybe she'll fix that broken rocker so she can comfort a baby proper."

"It aint good."

"What aint good?"

"The baby."

"Another girl?"

"Nope. That aint it."

Aaron looked up, his spade in one hand, his knife in the other, impatient with this slow issue of news. "You gonna git to it, or make me guess?"

"The baby was a girl, born three days ago."

The night of the prayer meeting. The last time he'd seen the preacher.

The car had disappeared from off the street by the time he woke up and Aaron had breathed a huge sigh of relief, felt that surge of life rushing back into his legs and his shoulders and his heart. He stared at Johnny Roper, his mouth in a grim line while he waited.

"The baby's dead, Aaron. Dead as a knob."

Aaron didn't believe it.

"Three days ago."

"Three days?" Well, durn. No gardening work today, what with the funeral. Lord, he hated it. But maybe this was for the best. He'd found a fungus on a polyantha and it was wearing him out. "What time's the funeral?" he asked in a tired voice.

"They aint gonna be one."

Aaron looked at him, saw the greenish face, looked over at Rosie's house where her porch sat empty and realized there'd been no cars or visitors. Just that crazy message on the board.

He'd been up early, walking barefoot across the dew-covered grass, watching nervous morning birds flitting down out of the trees to peck along the ground when he'd seen it. Coffee cup in hand, he sat on his steps and watched the woman standing in front of the blackboard as though it might speak to her. With great hesitation she picked at the words, which surprised the hell out of Aaron. Either she had always been able to read and just lied about it, or God had broken open the alphabet for her. Either way was fine with him. The gift of reading and understanding words was a mighty gift, in his opinion. What she wrote gave him a chill, though.

And a little child shall leed them

"I swear to God, Johnny. You should a throwed them blackboards off the bridge."

Prox had one set up in his front yard. His message was reasonable, though. A warning about his river:

I am working on the floor so dont walk in without knockin
And i'm nearly bout deaf in my right ear so knock loud please

"What I should or should not a done with them chalkboards aint the issue no more. The baby's dead and they aint gonna be a funeral." Johnny hopped from one foot to the other. Aaron could see he'd let the cuff out in his pants leg to accommodate his healing. The bright whitewash ring testified to it. The sole of his shoe seemed thicker, for some strange reason.

"We could take up money for it, if that's the problem. I got forty-two dollars tucked away."

"That aint it."

"The hell is it then?"

"She aint wantin to put the baby to the ground."

Aaron stood there, stunned, all his words drying on his tongue. If not burial, what? Taxidermy? Cremation? This thought horrific. How could one burn up a baby, regardless of it being dead? Fire was so permanent; so obliterating of life's temporal proof. He rubbed at his forehead. Before he could open his mouth, Johnny Roper spoke.

"Annie's got the baby hid somewheres inside that house. Says Jesus is gonna raise it up because of what the preacher spoke concernin it. And if you're thinkin about talkin to her, don't bother. The onliest way she's talkin is on that blackboard of hers. I've been inside three times since Sunday and the two of 'em won't utter a word. Not a durn word."

"Oh, for God's sake."

"The preacher's disappeared. Beachum over at the corner store said he packed up his tent and left. Rosie come knockin the night of the prayer meetin. You know the one—"

"I know the one."

"Well, Rosie showed up about two in the mornin and wanted to know if I knew where the preacher had gone to and I said no 'cause God's truth I didn't even know the man had left. That's the last I heard her talk. That night when she come lookin for what werent here no more."

"How do you know the baby to be dead? Maybe it's just a quiet baby."

"Prox told me."

"Henry? How the hell'd he find out?"

"He seen Rosie out buryin somethin and walked over, nosy as ever."

"And she admitted it? That the baby was dead?"

"Prox said he asked and she wouldn't say a thing and then he read it in her face, and I believe him, Aaron. Rosie was buryin the afterbirth, he said."

"What'd Prox do, dig it up to see?"

Johnny looked away. "Caint say. But I would guess yes. Prox seemed firm on it being the afterbirth."

Aaron looked over at his neighbor's blue house. And now he's paintin his durn floor. Like there's nothing in the whole wide world to worry about. He threw his spade to the side of the house and watched it rebound into a stack of terra-cotta pots, breaking three of them.

"I don't know what to do." Johnny Roper was wringing his hands.

"First of all, you don't know for sure the baby's dead. Nobody's said a word about it. Just that message on the board. Not even Henry Prox has got the word firsthand. Maybe it's nothin."

"I know, for sure."

"How in the world do you know for sure?"

Johnny wouldn't look at him. Just kicked at the dirt, instead. "I looked in her winder last night and seen it."

"The dead baby?"

"No."

"What, then?"

"Annie was . . ." He couldn't say the words. It was just too shameful. Through a hedge he had peeped in and seen her standing in front of her mirror binding her large breasts. Milk with nowhere to go had soaked through the wrapping, and while she sobbed, he watched her undo the wrap and do it again, tighter this time, exposing engorged bluish tits the size of melons in the process. Though the girl had been standing inside a darkened room, suffering in grief, Johnny had a hardon the size of Kansas. "They aint no baby, Aaron. Annie's dryin herself up."

Aaron noticed the hedge runners were getting out of hand. Overhanging. The juniper ground cover was having a hard time of it, too, fighting for sunlight. Most of the time they didn't need it, but everything needed a little light, sooner or later. A little illumination. "You know this for a fact?"

"I know it."

"Well, I gotta hear the words for my own self, by God. I aint doing a thing unless I hear the words spoken in the air."

Aaron walked over to the busted terra-cotta and stared down at it. Without a backward glance he tossed the Buck knife he'd been using for pruning over his shoulder. It landed two inches from Johnny Roper's right foot. Johnny pushed at it with his shoe as if it were an upright snake and then, without taking his eyes off Aaron, who was moving away and crossing the street, he bent and picked it up and put it in his back pocket.

Aaron would not have thought it, but the color of Rosie's living room walls had gone unnoticed to him, even after all these years. An observant man who drank color down instantly (flowers, sky, grass, water), he sat on the couch and thought with surprise, Why, these walls are yellow. The durn walls yellow as an egg yolk, with glossy white trim round all the windows, too. Different from his place where the interior walls were panelled in pine and dull man-brown, grain going all one way, downward to the floor, which seemed to suit his nature. Rosie's place had cheeriness written all over it. The white-trimmed door led out to the spotless kitchen with black-and-white linoleum squares to the floor. Another to a hallway that broke off into two small, bright bedrooms. Cheery as a birthday card, he thought. The house lent itself to light, which made him cringe while he looked around for a sign of what was hidden. He sniffed the air and smelled the leftover odors of pork grease and biscuits.

"Where's the baby at, Annie?" he asked quietly, looking at her stomach, which was definitely flat.

Her mouth opened in a tiny *o*, and then sealed itself shut, her eyes settling on his purple scars and his hat that was still on his head. He couldn't really blame her there. The indoors wearing of it was considered rude, and he knew it. He also knew he'd grown attached to it for reasons that were obvious, necessary, so to speak. While he watched, her mouth curled upward ever so slightly and he realized she was laughing at him, daring him to take it off. Why, we got us a tug-o-war going here, he thought, alarmed at her nerve, and her cruelty. He surrendered, removing his hat and smoothing a hand over his thinning hair, while he stared back at her.

The two of them, Annie and Rosie, were standing there, hands crossing their bellies, Rosie's belly big as a whiskey barrel, Annie's small and empty now. A visual lesson involving fruition and loss, he supposed.

Aaron placed his hat beside him on the couch and then leaned back, his fingers linked together over his stomach. "Where's the baby at, Annie?" he asked again.

She didn't flinch or act scared or surprised. Just stared straight at him as though he were a boring salesman peddling a vacuum cleaner to a tent-dweller. She was awash with immune, untouchable politeness.

"Henry Prox says the baby is dead. Died three days ago. Is this true?" He cleared his throat. "We got to know where it's at, so it can be took care of."

Rosie looked away and up the hall and Aaron decided that must be where it was. He swallowed hard while he wondered if it was spread out on a bed or wrapped in a blanket.

There were footsteps out on the porch, and then a tentative knock. Annie moved to the front door and opened it, a smile widening her face. When Johnny Roper came limping in, he was more ashen than before, with eyes that pinballed all over the place: walls, floor, Rosie's checkered apron, the picture of Christ at the Last Supper. He looked everywhere but that one place where he most wanted to look: at Annie and her beaming smile, her large breasts.

"Come on in," Aaron said. "They aint talkin. Just like you said." He leaned forward and studied the spotless floor.

"I never said they werent talkin—"

"Oh, well damn me to hell for being such a moron. I sure did think that was what you told me." Aaron was done with politeness.

"What I said was that they was communicatin on them blackboards out there. That aint not talkin. It's just talkin in a different way. Aint that right, Miss Annie?"

Annie seemed dumbstruck, tired and polite, but still dumbstruck. A fly lit on her eyebrow and she waved it away with a slow hand.

"We got to do somethin here, Rosie. Got to go on with things. Take proper care. The way the Good Lord would want it," Aaron said.

"Aaron, now don't be so rough here. They tryin to believe and wait on God to finish what he started," Johnny said.

"And I'm tryin my dead-level best not to jump up and beat the shit out of you right this very minute," Aaron said, standing to his feet and poking a finger in Johnny Roper's chest. "You come runnin to me over this. You was the one so upset by it all."

Together in an act of synchronization Rosie and Annie moved until their bodies were touching. A human dam that blocked the bright hallway.

Aaron watched the two women, then reached for his hat. "So this is it? This is how it's gonna be? The two of you walkin around and pretendin everything is fine and dandy and the rest of us goin on like nothing in the world is wrong? Please, Rosie. Don't be so foolish. You aint like that."

The women looked out the window to the backside of the chalkboard.

Johnny walked over to Annie and put a hand on her shoulder and the girl leaned into him, put her head down near his neck and seemed to be whispering something. The room was so quiet Aaron could hear Rosie's stomach rumbling, so he knew Annie wasn't talking, just leaning and breathing and giving Johnny a hardon in the process.

After a moment or two, Johnny looked at Aaron. "They think they need to wait on the Lord, Aaron. I think that's what goin on here."

"I see you got the gift of interpretation now. I didn't hear no speakin in tongues, though."

Annie was peering at the men with stricken eyes. Her hands were up near her chest, at a place close to the heart. Johnny patted her on the arm, and she moved to the side, away from his touch, closer to her mother.

"The preacher said to wait . . ."

Aaron whirled on him, storming past the coffee table and the shelf holding bric-a-brac. Before he reached the door he turned and said, "Seems to me you been waitin for what aint there for a right long time now, Annie. Seems to me you'd be over this foolishness by now." Crumpling his hat to the size of an apple he walked out the front door and into the sunlight that stung like hell.

He could hear Johnny Roper's apologetic voice behind him and he wanted to shoot the man. Pull out a gun and shoot him for being such a fucking idiot, for daring to make a lame-sided apology on his account. Durn them to hell. And now what? What in holy hell was a person to do in this sort of situation? Call the law and get the police to them? The Department of Health? Or should one just mind his own business?

With that thought Aaron headed to his house where he could think.

*   *   *

He couldn't mind his own business, though. Aaron judged the hours and minutes and the ticking of seconds against measurements of decay, and he just couldn't leave it alone.

Henry Prox was sitting next to him, covered with paint. Brown paint with a touch of aqua green. The man had painted himself into a corner, literally, and was taking a break out on his porch. They both sat huddled, their arms folded across their chests, their breathing sychronized. Near a spot by their shoes, the bottlebrush grew lush and thick against porch siding that was rotting away.

"You sure it's dead?" Aaron said.

He still held to the hope that the child was just a sleepy, slow one.

"I mean, she didn't say one word to you. Roper says you just read it on her face. Says you come to this conclusion when Rosie was out buryin the . . . buryin her . . . doin whatever the fuck it was you caught her doin."

"You ever listen to a woman talk, Aaron?"

Aaron just stared at him while night filtered down around their heads. Shapes were disappearing into gray commonality, the only distinction the dance of the fireflies inside the dark of the trees.

Henry continued, "You might think you have, but you aint. You might a watched a woman move her lips on more than one occasion. But that aint quite the same as talkin, now is it?"

Prox pulled out his paint rag and rubbed at his face, smearing his complexion to the color of an autumn gourd.

"When the wife was dyin, she couldn't talk. Had that tube to her stomach so's she could eat, and that kept her goin for a while. Powdery pink stuff I mixed up three times a day for a full year. Well, but for the time I mashed up them butter beans and ran it straight through just 'cause I was so sick of that pink stuff and I was sure she was sick of it, too, but that's another story. No need to talk on a dyin woman's gas at this sad point." He straightened out his legs. "Anyhow, she got so weak she couldn't talk. Would just point her finger at the ceiling once in a while and try to smile. I'd sit and watch. Turn her head so she could see them hydrangeas she loved growing outside the window. Kept the fish tank clean so she could see the angelfish fight.

"I finally figured out the wife was talkin. With her eyes. All I had to do was stop long enough to listen. She told me wild stories you wouldn't believe. How she loved her Big Mama—that's what she called her mother— and her father. And how much she had got to missin them. Told me how sorry she was we'd never had no kids. She talked a blue streak in those last hard days without ever once openin up her mouth. That's what I mean about listenin to a woman."

"The hell does this have to do with Rosie?"

"I looked in her eyes and seen it. The movement of her hands give me the details, but it was the eyes that held the full of it. I knew it. Just knew it. And she knew that I knew it. When I reached out a hand to her she held my fingers just like the wife had. The baby's dead, Aaron. Dead as last season's watermelon. You can bet your left nut on it."

"How do you explain the failure to bury it, or call a preacher, or do anythin that makes a bit of sense? How in the world do you explain these things, Henry?"

"Look at that there message. The one on her board about how a little child shall lead them. Think about what that preacher said before he hit the road. All that talk about what this child was gonna do. How the child was gonna be special. Somebody who'd make a difference in the long run."

Yeah, one that got fucked into place by two fornicators out in the middle of a plowed-up field, Aaron thought to himself, feeling sick. The minutes were ticking away. Day five now. There was bound to be the expansion of gasses. He'd walked around Rosie's place earlier, gone as close as the low throng of camellias in search of freshly turned dirt, a small tamped mound, a pile of rotted leaves that would signal they'd come to their senses and done the burying. He'd found nothing.

Henry was studying his paint-clogged fingernails.

"First off," he said. "There was a lot a promises made about what this baby was gonna do. Last I heard, the dead caint do much more than just lay there and be dead." Henry seemed pleased with his evaluation. "That's how come they aint in a hurry to bury it."

"Henry, this has nothin to do with God."

"Maybe. Maybe not. I guess what it comes down to is whether or not a body believes God is real and able to speak to us personally."

"How so?"

"That preacher went and said the boy was comin back for her, and, what's worse, he said that God Himself told him this and it got Annie's blood up again when it should a stayed low-runnin. We're all country people here. Little or no education. So busy tryin to eke out a livin, most are too tired to do more than drop at the end of the day. And as meager as our life may be, at least it's our life. We build up our daily book of knowledge and rely on it and study it on occasion and along comes this man who stops us dead in our tracks and tells us we aint as smart as we think we are."

"How so?"

"Why, he speaks for God Almighty, Aaron Class. Who could argue with a boast like that? You think the average country woman is going to stop and say, 'Now wait a durn minute. That aint what I think God is sayin'?"

"So, you think it's all nonsense?"

"Hell no, it aint nonsense. I believe in God. But I believe God slung us out here, set things spinning the way they ort to based on nature, and then He just brushed his hands together and said, 'I think I'll just stand back and watch these folks live their lives as best they can.' That's the God I believe in."

"I don't believe in God," Aaron said.

"Well, I seen a few miracles, so I got no choice but believe."

"What? Johnny's growed-out leg?"

Henry snorted, "I'm smarter than that and you know it."

"What then?"

"I seen two women who have fought like cats for most of their life turn around and reconcile right in there in the middle of Rosie's living room. And these were hateful women. Women you'd not want to turn your back on or be left alone with. I seen a man locked in a fence-line war for over twenty years suddenly take and move his posts back inside his boundary more than he ort, just to give his neighbor his due. I seen a sharecropper who don't own a thing in this world give his last bag of corn to somebody in need. Them kinds a things. This is what I seen. Them is the real miracles."

Aaron looked at Henry in surprise.

"Some folks git so caught up in looking for the big things, they forget the small. That's what's happened here. Them two gals has forgot about being square with life. Knowing what's real, and what aint," he paused and rubbed one hand atop the other. "Now, look here. We got sense enough to know when a thing aint right. We live by these rules. It keeps things balanced out. We know the crops and the seasons and how to tune a motor or scrub a floor. The only thing we don't know about is what's waitin at the end of the line. And most of us don't give a rat's ass about that 'til we turn up with cancer, or our flesh and blood turns up with it, or we find we own a bad heart, or we scrape our hand on a fence and a case of gangrene springs up and eats the limbs away, bit by bit. Then we call a preacher in to make our peace with God."

"I don't remember you callin nobody."

"I learned a long time ago there aint no peace in this world except between the covers of my own bed. I didn't need the good blinkin Jesus to bless that union. I blessed it my ownself, thank you very much." There was quiet between them and a whippoorwill began to call, the mournful notes signaling the end of the day.

"Henry, we aint talking about a corn crop here."

"I know that. I aint even sure God figures into it atall. Maybe Annie don't care one way or the other if the child is Christ-like or not, or if somebody might benefit from somethin the child has to offer. I don't even think she really cares about the baby atall. She just wants that boy back so she can have a family and do right by herself. Maybe hold up her head when she goes over to Lucedale."

"She's a fool, then."

"Could be, but she's a determined fool and they're the most dangerous kind."

"She's gone crazy," Aaron said.

"Maybe. But even crazy folks can become attached to an idea."

"Well, whatever she is, what she's doin is against the law. There are laws somewhere regardin this."

"Laws." Prox sighed as one well accustomed to magistrations. "Yep, I guess they's always a bucket full a laws somewhere for a body to dip out of."

"And because we aint doin a thing about it, it makes us party to it. Which means there's going to be trouble, one way or the other. Bad trouble."

Prox shook his head in disbelief. "There's always trouble, Aaron. Some folks has more of it than others. But there's always trouble." At this point he stretched back on his porch and seemed near to falling asleep, his paint-smeared face peaceful as an angel's.

"I thought I could reason with you," Aaron said, looking at him with tired resignation.

"I thought I *was* being reasonable. Aint said word one yet that sounds unreasonable to me."

CHAPTER

Annie walked as one dream-hexed.
        Like a ghost, with weavings preternatural to normal female feet,
she wandered through the bramble bushes and low holly, her white gown
catching and shearing parts of itself away in ratted clots. Parts that come
tomorrow would resemble leftover gouts of cotton harvested out of season
and against the odds of temporal weather. She was outdoors and wandering
because she couldn't make her baby cry. But it was a stubborn baby, one
not yet learned to obey the voice, or breast, of its mother. Mother and breast
both being offered at various points of time: nightfall, early morning, midday
while the crows sat humorless on slack power lines. Her breasts were drying
up and dripping less now. Had only leaked through her shirt front once
today, and the realization was dawning on her that she should not have
bound herself so tightly. She should have worked her breasts instead, so
she'd have the milk the baby would need once it got over its stubbornness
and decided to eat.

If you don't cry soon, if you don't give up this muleishness, aint gonna be nothin left for you . . .

She had no doubt she would make the baby cry. She would find that missing secret that motivates breath and movement and temperature. Annie knew this because she'd found other things before. A missing cake pan gone for three years. A pack of misplaced buttons, mother-of-pearl ones. A face holding dark eyes that spoke to her heart and whispered she was loved. She'd found things. All she had to do was listen and wait and walk in the Lord. She couldn't do this indoors, though. Reality stomped on loud feet all around the kitchen. Pounded on the cabinets. Banged on the doors. All the room and air taken up by the obvious inside that place of black-and-white tiles and tin canisters and dotted-Swiss curtains. It had been a safe enough space for apple pies and dumplings until little over a week ago, but not anymore. The truth of the kitchen had driven her outdoors, condemned her to nightwandering inside a cool breeze that hid things.

Her ghostly weaving took her to the blackboard with its warped maple tray holding small fingers of chalk. The chalk had grown as familiar as white bread, or butter, or a plastic comb for her hair. And it was a strange thing, too, this advent of the chalk's friendliness; strange because a part of her had suddenly woken to a new awareness: the chalk had always been with her. Maybe since the beginning of time. Some symbiont part of her recognized this and knew that inside the white limestone cupped in her hand lived the unreasonableness of all creation. From its womb of the ocean, where all things, including chalk, birthed, to the womb of a somnolent female where birth seemed now a true failure, there seemed a familiar voice speaking. The writings had seemed mere parrot utterings of the long-gone preacher's until yesterday when the chalk had erupted from its cylindrical shape and taken on the form of flesh. It became her tongue. It spoke. It breathed. It cried inside the curl of a finger with those ancient keening whale songs. A cry she answered with upward positionings of her hand in front of the board. She would do anything to hush its howling, anything at all to make it be quiet. Hearing the scream building, she shut her eyes and felt her hand moving against black:

> If yall pray with me tonight at 6 this will be over.
> Will you?

She looked at the words and then stood back, mystified. It was not at all what she had intended to write.

"Chalk knows best, I reckon," she said to the primrose bramble. Taking the cloth of her nightgown up in one hand, she freed herself from entanglements and went back inside the house. She wanted some ice water from the fridge to drink, but went to the bathroom sink and drank from the faucet like a field hand. She had already given her fast-drying breast to her daughter not thirty minutes earlier, and regardless of the magnitude of the chalk's intelligence, its half-life radiated outdoors, on the blackboard, where scratched words gleamed like glittered glass in the moonlight. Inside she was just Annie, scared and alone, oblivious to its resurrective power.

*   *   *

The sky sure is blue up there, Rosie thought, looking out her living room window. And come tonight, I'll see the stars. She seemed comforted by this thought. That constellations still spun, in spite of things.

She had spent the early morning scrubbing as preparation for the prayer meeting come six o'clock that evening, and the house was as clean as she could ever remember it being. What furniture she had, had been polished with oil and the wicker wall butterflies as well as the velvet picture of Christ at the Last Supper had been taken down and dusted. The couch was comfortable, too, overstuffed and covered with her best quilt. Room enough for four people, should they want to sit and drink a cup of coffee, later, after they all got done praying. Maybe bounce the baby on their lap once they seen what the Lord had done. Rosie sat still, her heart pounding so hard she could feel it in her eyes. Reaching down, she pulled her leg up on the coffee table and wiggled her toes. She had tripped on the rug in the back bedroom and sprained something in her foot. Ankle, probably. All she needed was a little rest and everything would be fine. The Bible had been put away, hidden from sight and she hoped that God didn't mind. The question of reading still plagued her. Could she? Or couldn't she? What if the letters and meaning behind A Little Child Shall Leed Them had come from some hushed parental proverb whispered decades ago? What if she'd seen a picture of an angel hovering over two children on a bridge with the words printed underneath? She leaned her head back and tracked the mildewed ceiling and wondered over it.

The joist was canted, warped from poor carpentry, and the white expanse was no longer white, but gray-speckled, and seemed ready to drop down on her whatever it was that rested above the rafters. Her eyes moved. A bulb had burned out inside the ceiling fixture, its black blow-speck surrounded by brown husks of dead insects. The globe was knobbed glass, though. Pretty as a picture. She'd ordered it from the Sears Roebuck back in '38. While she watched, a fly lit upside down on the ceiling and fidgeted its way across the hump. Up the hill and then down again, crossing a terrain of plaster that was dirty and ill fitting.

Annie was somewhere in the house. Her silence more imposing than her presence. The girl was a large one. Always had been. Built from a blueprint Rosie felt responsible for. I seen it comin, too. The way them two would meet near dark out beyond the big magnolias. I should a knowed what would happen.

Annie's time had come suddenly, and without mercy, and in much the same way Rosie's had come eighteen years earlier. Being blessed with child-rearing hips was an endowment women kept to themselves and pretended they didn't have. Better to let the whole world see you as a fragile creature forced to labor long and hard (sixteen hours at least) before giving birth. What would folks think should they know how easy it was? That all you had to do was lie down on a bed, push three or four times, before spitting a baby out? Annie hurt, though. Rosie had to give her that. It aint gonna be forever, I kept telling her. Here now. Bite down on this. Six hours it took. Started right at the end of the prayer meeting. Annie stood in the hall, one hand clasped to her low belly, the other bracing her body as she leaned against the wall. The next minute she was huddled on the floor, her water breaking and soaking through the rag-tied rug.

Another fly had joined the one on the ceiling, the two of them nervously skittering across the expanse, working their way toward the small hallway. And then she saw another, and another and another. Five flies now. The screen door was shut and the window screens were intact and Rosie had no idea where they were coming from. Wherever it was, there seemed to be a vast supply of them. The ceiling was fairly sprinkled with them now. Fly-paper. That's what I need. A big square of it. And if that won't do, then I best find me a swatter.

Rosie heard the ticking of a clock from out in the kitchen, the drip of water out the faucet and envisioned the rust stain bleeding a new path down her sink. The black-and-white linoleum was clean. The dishrag was hanging on its hook. There were cookies in a jar and Annie was somewhere. Maybe sleeping in the back room? Getting ready for what was coming. Rosie looked around, puzzled over the quiet. It shouldn't ort to be like this, she reasoned. The preacher sat right over there, when he sat, that is. Annie perched in that chair in front of the window. I walked around and served coffee, proud as a peacock.

The men were circling the blackboard like cats on a stalk. She saw Johnny come out and rub his eyes and then she saw Henry Prox wipe his brushes on a rag. Aaron was there, too, his hat pulled low over his eyes, standing outside in the full sun in the center of the street where his shadow seemed to stretch a long distance behind him. The three of them were eyeing her yard as though craziness lived there. And maybe it did. Come six o'clock she guessed they'd all find out, once and for all.

"The hell is this?"

Aaron was talking to himself from a spot in the center of the road. He saw Johnny Roper out on his porch studying the new message and scratching at his head and, in Aaron's opinion, the man seemed shorter and smaller, humped-down around his shoulders and shrinking. Aaron looked away.

Henry Prox was already up and ready for work. Paintbrushes stood inside cans of turpentine against the fence, their wooden handles resembling the streamlined tails of rats. Aaron saw the man's front porch had taken on the appearance of a half-baked bachelor pad. Entertainment, food and sleeping arrangement, obvious. No trash can, though. His yard was strewn with debris, which seemed shocking and indicative of the letting down of one's standards of clean mediocrity.

Prox's huge wooden radio had been dragged out the door and a small shelf made of planks resting on bricks held potted meats and jars of jam and sardine tins. There was a sagging army cot underneath his window with a frumped pillow naked in its striped ticking, and next to it, a cooler held essential liquid. The space was cluttered as the man himself, and paint-strewn. Wooden palettes were arranged like proud oval shingles against the wall of the house. They caught the light and shimmered like scales off a gargantuan fish, smeared with hues shit-colored but good smelling.

"Paint still aint dry?" Aaron said, walking toward him.

"Nope. Guess there werent but one intended to walk on water." Prox bit into an apple and then tossed it aside to the yard while he reached for a Coca-Cola.

"You got a ringside seat, at least," Aaron said while he watched Johnny Roper, who seemed still undecided on things. The man would stand scratching at his head one minute and then squat on his steps like one constipated the next.

"There he goes. Durn fool never could make up his own mind about a thing." Henry fished a green bottle out of the cooler and offered it to Aaron.

Refusing, Aaron surveyed the man's front porch before looking over at Rosie's. "How much longer you reckon?"

"Caint say. The shaller end's dry enough but that'd only allow me access to the ironin board, and I aint ironed in ten or more years."

"Shit, Henry. I aint talkin about your floor. I mean how much longer before we do somethin about this corpse bein hid on our street?" It was easier to think of it as a corpse and not a baby.

Henry Prox shrugged and then looked at Annie's message of the night before. "I never been one to admit I was wrong, but maybe this thing aint gonna right itself without a little help."

"It's too late for help, Prox. We're in it now up to the eyebrows. Guilty as those two are."

"You reckon?"

"Christsakes. You been out here on the porch for days now. Had yourself a ringside seat for all this creepin around. Don't tell me you aint worried."

Henry Prox nodded.

"I'd be lyin if I said I werent a tad worried. I seen Annie out here last night, roamin around in her nightgown. Nearly bout scared the bejesus out a me. That gal walked clean up and down the street before she went and stood in front of that there board and wrote them words. A couple a nights back, Roper over there had a case of the nighttime walk-arounds. I tell you what, Aaron Class, you never can tell what you might see while sleepin out on a porch. Beats all I ever seen."

"And then some," Aaron said.

"Hell, I've knowed those two gals longer than you have and, for the life a me, I guess I thought they'd come to their senses before now."

"Well, they're not."

"I can see that."

"I'm callin the law. There's nothing else to do. Not a thing else in the world to do."

"Hold now, Aaron."

"The fuck for? They're crazy. They've gone over. Both of them think that dead baby's gonna up and open its eyes and start cryin if they just sit back and wait long enough. We need help here, Henry. Lots of it. We caint just stand around and do nothin. It aint proper."

"You may be right."

"Hell, yes, I'm right. I'm goin for the law."

Prox nodded to the board. "Will you consider one thing, first?"

"What's that?"

"Let's do what she's askin. Let's git all cleaned up and go over there at six this evening and do whatever it is she wants us to do. Make a show at prayin with her over it. And then, once she sees they aint nothin to come of it, we'll call somebody." He drank from his bottle. "Thataway nobody's got cause to get mad at nobody over it."

"We're way beyond worryin over feelings, Henry." But the suggestion seemed reasonable. There were about three hours stretching between now and six o'clock. Time enough to get ready for it. Or maybe work in his garden. Or maybe just sit inside his house and get drunk as a man can get.

"She needs a answer, I reckon," and with that Henry Prox climbed off his porch and made his way to his board. Looking around, then checking all his pockets, he pulled out the white chalk and worked at a response. Johnny Roper came out to the middle of the street to read what was there, and then as obedient as a well-trained dog, he went and wrote on his own board, leaning around in comparison to make sure his letters were the same size as Henry's.

Pulling out of his drive thirty minutes later, Aaron put a hand to his face and felt its heat.

"String me up 'cause I'm in it now," he said to no one. "In it up to the eyeballs."

I will

they all had written, and it was like a vow, or a pledge, or some other thing sworn to with eyes wide open.

There was a roadhouse across the county line where a pint bottle sat with Aaron Class's name on it. All he had to do was get there and part with a few greenbacks and then tilt the bottle up to his lips, and he could hardly wait for that moment. He had never been overly zealous where drinking was concerned, but thought that the current circumstances might be pointing him in that direction.

He reached over to the glove compartment of his truck and scrambled around for a pack of cigarettes. It was a foolish thought, but it seemed to his frame of mind that the dead baby might be riding in the back of his truck with him. Tucked down inside a spare tire, or maybe covered in a croker sack that provided safe keeping for tire jacks and random tools. It was all he could do to keep from stopping by the side of the dirt road and rummaging around the clutter in the truck bed and checking out the possibility of it. "The hell with this," he said to no one in particular, slamming shut the glove box, sitting back upright against the split cloth seat and cranking down the window to his truck, dangling his left hand out to catch the wind. The pack of Lucky Strikes bore one bent smoke and Aaron picked it out with his right hand while he steered with his knee. Once it was lit he inhaled deeply, feeling the burn of it down in his lungs. He stretched his right arm along the back of the seat and let his knee go about the business of driving. He liked how it made him feel: reckless, and like he didn't give a damn. Fate had him by the balls, it could run him off the road and kill him should it want to, or keep the knee steady and allow him to make it all the way to that pint bottle holding that whiskey he was already tasting.

His face stung, and he wished he'd brought his hat. It was the first time in over ten years that he'd traveled more than fifty feet without it. He leaned out the side of the truck and studied his reflection in the side mirror. "God, you sure are ugly," he said and he felt the hair on his arm stand upright, blown there by the wind. "Look like you got sent to hell and then kicked back out again. Too ugly even for them."

He quit talking, just leaned back and shut his eyes, seeing how long he could leave them closed without worrying over the road, or whether or not he was staying on it. He was proud of his knee and the good job it was doing. His foot eased up on the accelerator and he figured he was doing about twenty miles an hour. Plenty of time to get where he needed to get before heading back to the final prayer meeting on the street. Besides needing that drink, there was another reason for heading off into the countryside. He knew a deputy who was hot for a girl who worked the Rebel Gas Stop and this deputy had the habit of hanging out there and nursing a hardon all day long. Aaron intended to have a few words with him. Maybe see if he could arrange for an ambulance, or a hearse. And if neither of those were available, then maybe a dogcatcher with an empty cage or two.

There had been a subtle shift in nature and he felt it all over his body. The humidity had eased up and the breeze he felt blowing in through the window was cool, almost. The road was a quiet one. Dirt, like most of the roads that switched back throughout the county, huge plats of corn springing up on either side. He could smell the fertilizer and pesticide and once he thought he heard the low drone of a crop duster dropping its load. He opened one eye and peered out and saw that he was driving straight as could be. A gentle plume of dust trailed behind him and he watched it for a moment in his rearview mirror and then he shut his eyes again. I guess I could drive all the way to that whiskey bottle with my eyes shut the whole while, he reasoned, realizing his actions were strange, but not so strange as those activities he'd left stirring on a road where his home sat. And so he leaned back his head and steered with his knee. A few minutes passed and he felt his confidence in fate climb a few more inches up that totem pole. If I can make it all the way to the end of the road without breaking my neck, maybe things will be all right. He eased off the accelerator again, slowing to around fifteen miles an hour. He'd talk to the deputy, get him to make whatever phone calls were necessary, and then, come tomorrow, life would get back to normal. Just a few more miles and I'll have a little drink and then I'll head back and pray that prayer and git on with things. Aaron sighed, tired as all get out, his hands folded behind his head now, his eyes closed to the world.

"And look at my knee. Aint it doin a shitbang job?"

It was right about then that he ran up behind a yellow tractor and sent a Negro flying through the air.

If the sand had not caught the tires of the truck and sent it into a swerve there would have been hell to pay. As it was, the radiator was busted and the front grill of his Ford was smashed, but other than that, Aaron Class would live to tell the tale. He walked around his truck, inspecting damage. The tractor tires had stopped him cold and in an offhanded way he was grateful to them.

"I guess yeller aint a color you're familiar with," Marion Calhoun said, brushing off his knees, so angry he didn't care if the man pulled out a gun and killed him for his insolence. He supposed it was like being shot out of a cannon, the way he had flown through the air and landed in the dirt. Nothing was broken, except a tractor tire, issuing in a steady hiss.

"Hell, I had my eyes shut."

"I like to keep mine open when I drive," Marion said, his hands to his hips. This was one white man who wasn't going to get by with a simple wave.

Aaron looked around him, the steam of the radiator and the exhalation out the tire made it sound as though all the world might be in the act of deflation.

"I guess I've had my fill of seein things of late. It was pure foolish, I know. Here. What's the damage to your tractor?"

"Nothin I caint fix."

"You reckon it'll run?"

"Better 'n your truck."

Aaron looked around, saw nothing but tall waving stalks of corn. Over six foot, most of them were. For a fractured second he felt a sense of déjà vu, lost underwater again, seeing the piercing light of blue sky against emerald green. He turned and caught the colored man staring at him, and thought, Well hell, mister. What're you starin at? All I did was slam into the back of your perfectly good tractor while I was driving along with my eyes closed. And then he realized the Negro was studying his face, its purple scars, and Aaron wished for his hat.

"You got a chain in that truck?" Marion said.

"Yep. In the back there."

"I think I can hitch it and pull you on down the road before the air leaks out my tire. You gonna need a mechanic to git to that radiator. I reckon it'll have to be pulled."

Aaron tried to bump up the hood with the heel of his hand. It wouldn't budge. "Shit."

Marion wanted to ask a series of questions. The foremost being, How come you white folks can turn idiot at the drop of a hat and do such foolish things? Another was this, How come you white folks take your slowass time in accepting an offer for help? The third question would be, Where in hell did you get that face? He cleared his throat and looked up at the sun. It was nigh on four o'clock.

"It might just be the hose," Aaron said. He gave up working with the hood and went around the back toward the bed of the truck and stood there hesitantly, his hands in his pockets.

Come on now, Marion Calhoun thought. Get a move on. Because the man was just standing there, acting for all the world like he was scared of his own truck, or what was in it.

After a moment, Aaron climbed up and Marion heard the sound of a chain being dragged across the metal bed. "I knew I had one in here."

"You sit and steer and we just might make it."

"We can hope," Aaron said, calculating the hours, wondering how long it would take him to get it up and running again. Wondering if the work might stretch long enough to keep him away from what was waiting at home.

C H A P T E R 30

The three men met out in the center strip of the road and stared at Rosie's yellow house. It was ten minutes after six and the woman had already come to the screen door once and opened it and made motions with her hands for them to enter, but still they stood there. From a bird's-eye view they would have seemed simple farmers locked in the act of discernment concerning the seasons, or the lay of the land, or whether or not a certain cow was ready to calf.

Henry Prox put a hand to his chest and rubbed gently, his heart pounding at the familiar presence it seemed to recognize. He sensed Death, its Great Flapping Wings, its Final Quietus hovering in the space directly over his head. He glanced up and saw nothing but the low bead of clouds near the horizon. A red spray of evening sky so wide it seemed a fiery river set ablaze. He looked to Aaron and said, "Let's leave it where it is boys," for he was afraid and Aaron glanced at him and seemed in agreement. Rosie came to the door again and motioned with her hand and still the men stood there.

"All we got to do is pray," Johnny said, popping his fingers. "Just say a little prayer and then we'll call the law, or the doctor..."

Or maybe the dogcatcher, Aaron thought. His truck was parked out in front of his house, its nose smashed in. He had hoped it would die before he made his street, but the truck seemed guided by divine purpose: it chugged along smooth as could be until he made the road and then it stopped right outside Aaron's own gate.

"I don't see Annie nowhere," Aaron said. He pulled his hat low over his eyes, stunned by the sensation of insects crawling over his skin, or prying eyes peering down his neck. He reached around a hand and swatted the air. Nothing was there. But he felt it. Something.

Johnny Roper swallowed hard and glanced up toward the low limbs of the trees. He had thought he had seen something. A pair of infant eyes, perhaps. The same pair he had been avoiding for a week now. Every time his hand went to his crotch, he had had the feeling he was being watched. He saw a red sunset through the leaves, nothing more. He shrugged his shoulders, accepted what he was feeling as pure nervousness, nothing more.

"Well, come on then," Henry said, leading the way.

The sun dropped its final degree and connected their shadows while they walked across the yard and into the house where Rosie stood waiting, her arms folded across her broad stomach, four broom straws clutched in her hand.

CHAPTER
31

"If this aint your knife, how come you sat bolt upright when you seen
it?"

It was the next morning and Johnny Roper had spent a sleepless, hellish
night, and was weak over it, nauseated and trembly, scared nearly out of his
wits. He looked around and then gripped the arms of the wooden chair set
in the interrogation room, for the knife he was peering at was Aaron's, the
one Johnny had picked up from off the ground where it'd been tossed, and
then buried in night. Shit, he thought, studying it. So much depends upon
me figurin this out, he reasoned, shaking his head.

The police station in Hattiesburg smelled of a recent scrubbing with bleach.
The walls were squashed-bug green and the floor had packed valleys of dirt
along its floorboards. The dirt long mopped-over and then waxed into place,
so that whatever corruption it held was sealed safely beneath gold-colored
sediment.

He licked his lips, wondering how in the hell he'd landed in such dire
straits. His knees were knocking below the table and his bowels were talking

back to him. He'd not ever been in such a predicament. Not even that time he hit that cow coming home late at night from Pascagoula and started seeing visions of hamburger meat and easy free steaks splattered across his grill. He'd been scared for about a week over it, but not like this.

"I know whose it is, is all."

"Well, speak up then. You caint be helt in lockup for knowin a thing aint yours. Who belongs to this here huntin knife?"

The detective had hairs springing from his ears and nose, and his eyes were set into a great bulb of a head shaved close as a Marine's. He studied the small man sweating pools onto the table and thanked his lucky stars the case had dropped down atop his head. The elements so obscene and contrary to the usual culling-out of niggers from bar fights, and the occasional refer-eeism between thrashing, angry spouses, not to mention the off-duty repos-session of shiny automobiles from those Quarter blacks over in Petal who owned eyes bigger than their paper-thin wallets, that it seemed a true gift shat down from Heaven. This was choice. This was something that only come along once in a blue moon. The detective blew on his badge and shined it with a black coat sleeve, proud of his occupation.

"It aint a huntin knife. It's a prunin knife," Johnny said, wondering as soon as the words were out his mouth why Aaron Class had not had the good sense to use shears to level out his plants.

"No, it aint. See this serrated edge? It's a knife meant for killin, and that's exactly what it found itself doin."

"I don't know nothin about it."

The detective picked up a piece of paper and read from it.

"You called this in, it says here."

"Yessir, I did."

"That right there seems to set you in good light. Caint think right-off of a criminal who'd dare to pick up the phone and say, Look, come on over here I done killed somebody." He leaned forward and tapped the table. "That gal nearly 'bout got her head cut off, son. And this is the knife that done it. Now if you was man enough to get the law involved, I think you ought to be willin to talk a little bit about it," he said.

He unfolded a small Case pocketknife and began to pick at the square nails on his large meaty hand. The knife was a smaller version of the buck, but its miniature sharpened edge was sure to be a steady reminder.

Johnny Roper swallowed and heard the sound of it echo in his head, "The knife aint mine. Just belongs to somebody on the street," he said, wishing for all he was worth he'd never laid eyes on it.

The detective picked up the knife carefully, keeping the handkerchief around its handle while he studied the specks of dirt that were low on the shaft. Dark Mississippi mud blended with blood. As long as he'd lived, he'd not ever recalled seeing such a thing. "Do you know this somebody personally? Is he a friend, somebody you might feel obliged to cover up for?"

Johnny blinked while he studied the cigarettes in the center of the sweat-stained table. Pall Malls. *In Hoc Signo Vinces* was printed under the crest of a pawing lion, and he wondered at the language and why it was printed there.

His last cigarette had been around seven o'clock, the evening before, right after they'd come out of the kitchen and gone and stood on the porch to clear their heads. Aaron had shook one out for him. A Camel. Johnny's hands had been dancing so badly, he couldn't hold the lighter, and Aaron had finally lit it for him, and then they had both stood there, two idiot men trembling on the porch. Annie had never seen him smoke and he recalled how he had spent a few anxious moments looking around for her, wondering why she'd made such a big deal of inviting them to a prayer meeting and then not bothering to show up. Puzzled by it, then glad she'd been elsewhere and missed seeing the fiasco, he had smoked silently, alongside Aaron Class, the two of them struck dumb by what they had seen. *In Hoc Signo*. The words were calling him and he tapped his fingers along the wooden arms of the chair. He had thought at first to ask for one, and then cast that thought away. Cigarette consumption spelling out nervousness, an impression he was trying hard to squelch. He watched the pack instead, deciding that if offered one he would take it up casually and smoke slowly, thoughtfully, like a farmer looking at a boring feed bill.

The hairy detective seemed one thought ahead of him, for he reached out and shook one free and lit it up with the loudest Zippo Johnny Roper had ever heard. Roper jumped in his chair at the noise.

"He a friend or not?" the detective said.

"I'd call him a friend."

"What kind a friend? A good friend? Casual friend?"

"Just a neighbor friend." Johnny sat back in his chair and worked his neck for a few minutes because it was beginning to hurt and then he leaned forward again, looking for an ashtray. The empty table stretched as long as six feet and was barren and scarred with varnish peeling along its edges. Not an ashtray to be seen.

Johnny cupped his hand and caught the ash himself and watched it curl like a tiny penis in the center of his palm.

"See. Nobody on that street was ever really close," he offered. "I mean, we spoke and stuff like that. We was always polite enough, I guess, but there werent never any cause to get up-close friendly. Nobody fished much, or hunted. We was all too busy. Nearly everbody worked all the time at one thing or the other. Except for Henry Prox, but then I reckon he did his own hard work from inside that house of his."

"So this Henry Prox would a been there at the time of the incident?"

Johnny Roper swallowed hard. I say but one or two words as explanation and the whole street gets indicted, he thought. He looked at the thick-necked detective.

"You'd have to ask him about that, sir. It aint my job to say where everbody was that day. I just know about my own self is all."

And Annie. He sure knew about Annie. Watching her from beside a bush or behind a tree, or once, out-and-out creeping into her house to stand over her bed, leaning low and studying her white sleeping face. He knew about Annie. The smell of her. The things she wore in her hair. The soap she used. How many pairs of shoes she had. He didn't really care about the baby. Any fool knew a dead baby was a dead baby same as a dead cow or horse was a dead cow or horse. But he did care about her and what she believed was going to happen when they all joined up hands and prayed together, just like the chalkboard had asked them to. He wasn't nearly prepared for what he'd seen, though.

"I guess I'm as guilty as the rest of them," he said finally, dumping the ashes on the floor and running his hands down his pants leg, a damp smear of gray left as proof.

The detective said, "Now you *can* be helt for bein guilty," and then he heaved himself forward in his metal chair, face jutting tableward until it resembled that of a giant jowled bulldog leaning over a bowl of biscuits. He looked at the ash on the floor and said, "We got niggers who sweep these floors, boy. Don't you go dumpin ashes where they don't belong."

He folded his notebook to a fresh page, "And so you say you're as guilty as the rest."

"I'm guilty a knowin the baby was born dead and not telling the proper folks about it."

"Why'd you keep quiet on it?"

Johnny shut his eyes, "We thought there was gonna be a miracle." It sounded so stupid now. So ridiculous. He paused to catch his breath. "She was told the baby was gonna do special things—"

"Back to that old crap again."

The springing hairs out the man's ears and nose moved along with his pulse, vibrating like bedsprings. "So this preacher fella did it? Was it the preacher's big old Buck knife what ended up in that young gal?"

"No sir, it werent." Roper was trembling.

"And you aint sayin one way the other whose knife it was ended up in that girl's throat. Slit her from here to Picayune."

The detective eyed the man, who was going green around the gills. Well, good then. Maybe we'll get somewhere, he thought. They had been dancing inside a circular conversation that had its beginning and ending with the preacher for four solid hours.

"Seems hateful to me the way you're willing to sit here and watch me drag in each and ever one a them poor folks. Including that pitiful grievin mother out there. Seems downright sinful how you're bound and determined to keep your mouth shut and hog-tie this investigation. I'd never let my mother, God rest her sweet soul, get dragged in just to save my sorry ass." The detective sighed as one burdened. "I'd kill a man who'd drag in my dear sweet mama over a charge like this."

"Them folks is my friends, sir."

looks like dough, misshapen bacon-smelling dough...

Roper felt water rush up in his throat.

"They aint your friends."

"They are. I caint say more than what I know is true. I caint make up stuff." He swallowed it down, felt his throat tighten up, knew he was puke-bound.

"What if I was to tell you that one a them has already told somethin on you? Somethin that don't quite make you look like that Reverend Billy Graham feller."

The officer crossed his hands over his barrel chest and waited.

"Somebody in your bunch a friends aint weighted down with your qualms, it seems."

Johnny Roper blinked hard and looked down at his small hands and then up to a clock on the wall. Below the clock, squares of tile were losing their grout.

"There are things to tell, I reckon."

Things he'd done out in the open that he wished now he'd done in the dark.

Aaron had seen one thing, he was almost sure of it. Johnny had been hiding inside a boxwood and almost at the tail end of it when Aaron pulled up driving a truck that had been on the losing side of a collision. As soon as Johnny finished and zippered up, he knew he'd been caught at it.

"Folks said your leg growed itself out." The detective snapped the knife shut and put it away in his pocket.

"I never asked for a durn thing in my life," Johnny Roper whispered.

"I paid a dollar once to see a monkey fuck a football, but I aint never seen a leg growed out just by praying over it," the detective said while he leaned back in his chair and folded his heavy arms over his large stomach.

"I didn't pray over it," Johnny said.

"The preacher then."

"Yessir. The preacher."

"Did you pay this preacher for this service?"

"No sir. He singled me out. I aint never went and asked nobody for a durn thing in my life. He seen fitten is all."

so cold oh sweet jesus oh sweet jesus oh sweet jesus

"Who seen fitten?"

"The good Lord." Johnny Roper was caught in a shudder.

"Well how come you to think the good Lord singled you out for this special favor?"

"You'd have to ask Him, I reckon."

The detective leaned his head back and looked at the water-stained ceiling. There was a design near its center that had the look of Saturn and its rings. The rings stretched oblong with little impediment, permanently swirled and fixed into asbestos by last year's storm. The outside ring was the prettiest, almost gold.

The detective drummed his thick fingers across his stomach; he couldn't wait to get to the wife and fill her in on the nonsense. He'd come in and get himself a beer and take off his tie and holster his gun and then he'd sit on the edge of the bed in his undershirt and watch her get undressed. All the way down to that white slip of hers, and then after she'd brushed out her hair, and she began to rub her face with the lotion, that's when he'd tell it.

He cleared his throat and looked away from the ceiling and back at his suspect. The man was uncommonly short for one not in the circus.

"The way I see it not only do we have a homicide, we got trespass, according to that so-called friend of yours that's done spoke against you and what you was doin. And then we got harm directly caused by a *negligent* act and then we got harm caused by a *failure* to act and then we got all kinds a possibilities concerning obscenity laws. And if we run short a those we can sit right down and start all over again."

The detective shifted in his chair. "Failure to properly dispose of a body fits somewhere inside this mess, too. Coroner said it'd been dead ten days at least. No signs of strangulation." He picked up the piece of paper and then put it back down again.

Johnny Roper shut his eyes. The smell everywhere at once: his shirt, his shoes, up his nose. He was near choking.

"I never seen Annie and I never seen the dead baby . . . I mean, I seen it that final night . . . we all seen it, then. But we didn't know for sure until that moment that there even was a dead baby 'cause nobody was talkin to nobody about it." He clinched his hands together before continuing. "At least not out loud. They, I mean we, was talkin on them chalkboards, but not out loud with our mouths."

"How come you folks taken to spellin things out on a board?"

"I don't know."

"That aint good enough."

"I don't understand any of it," Johnny said, looking around the room. There was only one door in and one door out. The door had a window and it would take a man a lot taller than five foot to break through it to freedom. Freedom. Now aint that strange. I aint ever gonna be free again. I'm just foolin myself into thinkin I will.

"I guess we was all followin the preacher's lead," Johnny said. "He wrote on it first and then Rosie and Annie, and then Henry and me. Aaron was the last to do it." Johnny was watching the detective's face. It seemed the man was about to laugh. "I guess you needed to be there to appreciate it."

"I think I'll pass. That young gal was there and look what happened to her." He reached across the table and tapped another cigarette out of the pack and lit it up and handed it to Johnny. "But you look like a man drawed back to tell somethin. Why don't you just take a deep breath and lean back in your chair and tell me the whole damn story. See if you can make me appreciate it." He looked at his watch. Noticed sweat had formed rings around the short man's arms and a large square swath across his chest like a flag.

"We got the time. You and me both aint goin nowhere fast."

He got up and walked to a small cabinet against the far wall and fished out an amber ashtray, heavy and square, putting it in the center of the wide table.

"We caint have those clean-up niggers complainin about the work environment now, can we?" He pulled out a notepad and sat ready to take it all down.

Johnny Roper sat leaning forward, his mouth slightly opened, his eyes watching the fat man across the table. Through the magic of pulse, the fat man's face was drifting closer and closer, so large now, it seemed like the moon. Licking his lips, Johnny Roper pulled his thoughts together, tried to form some conjunctive point of communication that made it easy to understand. While his breath wheezed out of him in slow degrees he watched the face across the table, thinking,

the poets is right. the wantin of a thing is not enough. not nearly enough. the wantin grows and the belief in the wantin grows and the belief that you will have what you want grows until it is so large it fills up the sky. and then the body misbehaves because the wantin and the waitin is in the heart but the proof of it is below: lower; large as a sky. so large that to deny a sky is to deny breath and sweat and blood and still the wantin is there. but you put it off, for just a minute or maybe even two because the wantin is sweet, almost as sweet as the havin. and then you do it because the wantin has turned to a knife in the belly . . . and then . . . and then you want again and so you stand beside a bush or a tree or in some dark corner where caint even you see yourself and what you're doin and you think the sky is smaller now and the wantin is less than the sky, only the size of a tree now, maybe the size of a leaf which each and all knows you can live with, and so you breathe easy and calm until you see her face and her soft shoulders and her turned-down eyes and those bound-up breasts, and then you want again. and so you write I will even though you wont, because only I will will make the wantin go away and so you do. you walk up the steps into a house where already you can smell it and it is large as the sky and the wantin goes away without even havin to stand in the dark or out beside the house and you tell yourself that you should a come inside and smelled it sooner so the wantin would vanish. but it's too late now. all the rest are there. all with looks around their eyes that say it is dead, surely it is dead and even Christ the Savior who was able to raise hisself without benefit of prayer or refrigerator caint do a durn thing about this one. but still you want and the wantin is large and so you stand shoulder to shoulder and draw straws to see who will open the door to the fridge and you pray you wont draw the short straw even though everthing about you says you been drawin the short straw for all of your life. but you draw anyhow and sure enough the short one is in the palm of the hand and you go into the kitchen where bread used to bake and you stand there sick at heart thinkin of bacon and eggs and milk and you wonder what you will eat now seein how them things are forever gone from your menu. and the others crowd in with bony shoulders and shaky hands and they know now what incredulous means and horrific as well as true disgust and amazement. but the short

straw is in the palm and so you reach out and pull on that steel handle and
shut your eyes while you're doin it, same as you shut your eyes while you do the
other deed out beside the house or in some dark corner of a room, because they
are the same. and you see the rim of tin first like the leadin edge of a frozen
moon. galvanized. a thing to wash beans in, but not no more because there it is
all cold flesh and filled-out face with eyes cracked and glazed and blue-filmed over,
and you see or rather sense Rosie reachin past, pot holders on her hands because
of the cold and you shut your eyes same as you shut your eyes them other times
because to look at it is to see it as big as the sky and the sky is hopeless and
unending and mean in its permanence and so is this thing. and Rosie lifts it out
and it is stiff as wood and she cries and Aaron stands back and swears long
and hard and vicious and Prox says oh sweet Jesus oh sweet Jesus oh sweet
Jesus in a voice smaller and smaller. and Annie is nowhere. nowhere at all. and
when it comes your turn, for they have taken it out and passed it around like a
opened gift at a party and in the passing around of it all their fingers leave
imprints like those in swollen dough and when it comes your turn you reach, as
though reaching for the wantin, because this thing come from what you want.
and once you feel the coldness of it your ears stop workin as well as your heart
and you see the ground rise up to meet you and you pray for darkness and for
once in your short-straw-drawing life your prayer is answered and the floor hits
you in the face and the dead thing rolls like a log underneath the table

Johnny Roper threw his upper body across the table, his head butting
the edge of the amber ashtray, while he cried like a baby.

"I got nothin to say. Not now, not ever."

CHAPTER 32

"Y ou just sit tight and let me handle this. You aint gotta say a single
word—"

Henry Prox whispered this into Rosie Gentle's ear before he turned to
the other side and beamed a large smile at the prissy reporter from the
Hattiesburg American.

He had been engaged in a lively conversation with the man for close to
an hour while he sat waiting for his turn at bat inside the Hattiesburg police
station. He thought the reporter charitable and interesting but, decked out as
he was in a snappy bow tie and shiny black shoes, dressed too much like a
city boy to do anybody any good. Searching for an angle was what that one
was doing and Henry Prox knew it. The young man had a keen awareness
for art, though, having admitted that inside his very house a signed lithograph
by Norman Rockwell was hanging on his living room wall. Probably has
Louis the Whatever furniture inside his place, though, and tiny stuffed
velvet pillows with purple silk tassels dressing up his couch. Probably some

pear-shaped librarian lined up to be his girlfriend, too. But Prox hid these assumptions and turned to the man.

"I usually don't like them New Englanders, but I taken a likin to old Norm Rockwell. I sure do. I never had the gift for renderin the human face, though. Tried to once for a shrimper down in Gulfport. Wanted a picture of sweet Betty Grable done up on the side of his half-crap boat. Durn if I didn't work for most of a month just to have the thing end up lookin like some great Orca whale with tits out to kingdom come."

Prox held his hand out from his chest in a mimic of teats while he crossed his legs. His old eyes roamed the borders of the room, which could do with a fresh coat of paint. Blue would be nice. The bench he was sitting on was hard as a grave slab, sending his piles into a full assault he could feel clean up to his teeth, while next to him Rosie Gentle was crying into a shredded-up piece of tissue.

Defenselessness and grief were two of the most powerful things in the world, in his opinion. Made poets out of idiots and caused swords to spring to the hands of cowards. If ever the anger would set in, it would be better for her. He knew this. Knew, as well, that her great wall of sorrow would crumble in great smashing heaps once she got mad as hell over things. He fished into his back pocket and came out with something that used to be white and handed it to her. Without hesitation or shame he leaned to the side to ease his hemorrhoids.

"Here you go Miss Rosie. This'll do you better, I think."

He patted her fat leg but avoided looking at her. She took the handker-chief and undraped it and held it over her face, and Henry smelled the familiar odor of his paint drift across to him and judged it better than the Clorox smell of the police station, which reminded him of the job waiting back at her place.

Prox turned back to the reporter.

"Man said he was gonna pay me fifty bucks for the job, too. Fifty bucks just to paint a picture of a movie star on the side of a boat. We ended up in a skirmish over it. Said he werent shoppin for no ugly whale wearin a bathing suit. Not even if the boobs were good looking. Nearly 'bout come to blows. Finally managed to settle up and walk away with a ten-year-old cooler to keep my beer in. And we in a dry county at that." He sighed. "Life don't seem fair, does it?"

"No sir, I guess not. Now tell me this, Mr. Roper called the police around four o'clock this morning—"

"He called the Lucedale sheriff first. Let's git it right."

"The Lucedale department. And they notified us here in Forrest County," he looked down at his notebook, "around five."

"Seems you folks thought Lucedale couldn't handle it," Henry said.

"Yes. Well." He held his pencil in a well-manicured hand. "I wonder about those hours during the night. What might have been goin on before the phone call."

Henry shifted in his chair. Bastard, he thought. What the hell do you think was goin on? A bake-off? A tea party? Annie was dead and Rosie was screamin and Johnny was cryin and Aaron was cursin. And me? I was tryin my dead-level best to decide which fire to put out first. "What'd ya think was goin on?" Henry said.

The reporter shrugged. "I can't imagine."

"Try. It aint purty."

The reporter crossed his legs like a woman and wiggled his right foot in agitation and seemed at a loss as to how to continue.

"You seen Aaron Class? I been here most a three hours and aint seen hide nor hair of him. They got him locked up somewhere?" Henry Prox leaned out and looked up and down the hall, tried to block those weasel eyes from the woman next to him, which was hard, seeing how Rosie had more surplus to her than that whale he'd rendered on the side of the boat.

"I guess I could go check for you."

Prox patted the reporter's leg, left it there for a long second, watched the fellow blush.

"That'd be right kind of you. You go on and do that. He's my neighbor, you know. Seemed upset by the whole affair. Terribly upset."

The reporter looked up and saw that the one interrogation room was still occupied. Taking his notebook with him, he got up and made his way to the gal at the front desk. He leaned over and she looked up and the two engaged in low conversation.

Prox turned to Rosie, still avoiding her eyes.

"Aint he a little mincer. Look at them shoes. Don't you worry, neither. I aint gonna let him talk to you and I aint sayin a thing in the world I don't intend to. Don't you fret over it."

"They aint no reason to fret now."

"I know. I know. But we'll get out a this in spite of bein sick at heart. We'll get out a this and take care of things. I'll help you, too. There'll be talk for a while, but that's all it'll ever be: talk. And I'm good at talkin, just you wait."

The reporter came back to them, his notebook open.

"They're holding your friend in isolation. Suicide watch," he said.

"Suicide watch!"

"Yessir, that's what they said."

"What the Christ is a suicide watch?"

"They have to take special precautions there. Take away his belt and shoestrings and such. Things he might use to hurt himself."

"That one in there would never in a million years do hisself in. He's got that durn garden of his to tend to for one thing. Got good friends he thinks the world of, too." Henry felt personally offended by the concept.

"That's where he is."

Well, shit then. I guess they think they've found their man for sure. Henry Prox rolled his eyes, cursed himself while he scrunched up his shoulders and thought for a minute. "I see where this is headin and as far as I'm concerned you can head there without me. Fold up your little notebook and git on outta here, 'cause I aint sayin a word against him."

"How long you known the man?" The reporter's pencil was ready.

"Well, here we go," Henry said, disgusted.

"It's just a matter for the record Mr. Prox, nothing more. There might be a way we could clear up this mess. Get your friend out a isolation."

"You and your magic pencil gonna do that? I seen how that pencil works, so leave me alone. I aint talkin."

"They're speculating he loved the girl and she shunned him," the reporter whispered.

"That's outright bullshit."

"It seems a crime of passion—"

"You're here for a story. Don't care nothin about the truth. All you want is to spread something and make it even harder for the man to show his face in public," Henry said.

"He showed up back before the war," Rosie said, quietly, her fingers making a knot of the handkerchief, her voice so low the reporter had to lean around Henry to hear her. "Acted like he had somethin to hide, even then. Stayed in his house. Never went nowhere. Didn't want to talk to none of us."

The reporter was scribbling at a feverish pace.

"He come up from the coast. Lived down around Bay St. Louis way. Come in a hurry, too. Oncet or twice he mentioned fishin and how they run him off from it. His face got scarred for a reason and I bet folks aint forgot him down there, neither."

There was the sound of pages turning, and muttering and then the man rose to his feet and left through the brass-plated front doors as though shot out of a cannon. Henry sighed, tired, his eyes downward to his feet, wondering how many steps he had walked in his lifetime and if there were many left to go. "Now Rosie. You had no call to go and say what you did—"

"It was Aaron's knife what did it."

"Rosie, Annie was sad. Too sad to deal with it. She just couldn't face what was happenin anymore and so she . . ." he squirmed in his chair, struggled for the words, gave up on the idea of finding them. "She was sad, was all."

"My daughter wouldn't do that. Annie was murdered."

"Rosie, we was there most of the day. There werent no way somebody could sneak in and do something like that. A stranger would a been noticed."

"True. We'd a seen a stranger."

He leaned to the side and stared at her.

She was folding the handkerchief to a neat square and her jaw was set and she seemed suddenly strong with conviction.

Prox shook his head while he watched the glass window to the interrogation room. He could see the shadow of Johnny Roper's head bobbing every once in a while against a far wall. Even his shadow seems nervous, he thought in amazement, the carrying over of a man's mental condition into a shade oblong and variable, a new observation. Well, I'll be go to hell. Not only do we have to mind what our sorry body's doin, we got to look out for our durn shadow, too.

"I know Aaron Class and I aint ever gonna believe he had a hand in it," he said, rubbing his chest where it hurt. "I think we should hush about it and let folks smarter than us figure it out."

"Henry?" she said.

"What?"

"You reckon they'll wash her?"

Henry Prox shut his eyes, horrified. It was too hard a question for a tired old man to deal with.

"They took her away from me before I could clean her up. Do them undertakers wash the blood off? Do they go to that kind a trouble?"

He tried to imagine the sequence of events, washing, logically one of them. Trying for a calm, matter-of-fact voice, he answered, "I figure they would."

"They up and taken her from me. A mama would make sure a child was clean. I caint do that now and I'm so tired, Henry. Tired," she said. "Too tired to be sittin here like this. I got things to do ..." her voice trailed off.

He patted her leg again. Noticed the shadow on the far wall indicating Roper was still and bent as though listening, or praying.

A shadow at prayer. The cleaning of a corpse. Now aint these two strange thoughts?

"I know you're tired Rosie. I surely do know it," he said, his voice soft as a man his age could make it. "Lean your head on me if you need be. I aint mindin it. Not one little bit."

Rosie stared at the floor instead, the pattern hurting her head. All those tan squares reminding her of Annie's building blocks, the ones she'd cut up and sanded herself when the child was two years old. They had put her daughter inside a canvas bag and wrapped her up, like an old dirty suit. Her head pounded alongside these memories.

"I'm tired," she said. And she was. And it was an exhaustion to such an extreme, she felt blindsided by it.

"Amen to that."

"Too tired, Henry. Tired a breathin. Tired a talkin."

"Let's not talk then. Let's hush a while and be still. Go on now, lean your head."

This could go on forever, he realized. A litany of response upon response upon response.

He said, "I bet we'll have us a goodly season a rain this year. I bet we see things take a turn there. What with this warmish wind that keeps kickin up when it ought not to. Seems some type of indicator to the way things might be headin. I say a goodly season. We all had us some fair crops, didn't we?"

She was finding his voice soothing, and shut her eyes, and tried to nod her head in agreement. Her voice was gone. Flittered out some high window like a bird. Flittered safely away to that solitary place hurt things flitter to.

"Yes ma'am, we surely did. Hauled in some of the fattest tomaters I ever put to the mouth. Things is gonna change for us. Already changin, I think. Got my floor just about finished. Purtiest thing you ever seen. Got real-looking rocks over near the corner and the water, my God, the water seems to flow right across those old floorboards a mine. Did I ever tell you about the time the wife tried to clean them floors with gasoline? No? Well, she did. She surely did. Got it to her head about wax buildup and couldn't find no solvent nowhere. I was out, I reckon. Out doin some foolish thing I guess. Well, anyhow. The wife goes and gets that old gas can and works herself up to a pure-d sweat tryin to lug the durn thing up the steps..."

Henry Prox droned on, feeling the weight of Rosie's head touch down to his shoulder after a while. He kept on with his low murmuring: sensible syllables spent soft and easy out the mouth. While he spoke he patted the woman's mottled hand, his eyes straight ahead and unwavering on the shadows on the wall.

C H A P T E R 33

Now it was true Marion Calhoun was a smart man who'd had the non-luck to get cuckolded once, but he still had enough of the smart left to him to know a lynch boss never looks like a lynch boss in the beginning. In the beginning when he first climbs out of his car and makes his way up to the porch of a Negro man living almost alone on a dirt road, he can look like a sewing machine salesman or maybe a lineman for the county or maybe even a mule. The man in the dark suit looked mule-like in Marion Calhoun's opinion, what with his overly large ears and equine-shaped teeth, but the gleam in his eyes spelled simple human lynch boss plain as the nose on a face. The man sat leaning on the Calhoun porch rail, that by the very presence and placement of the narrow rear end seemed to set the true standard of ownership concerning the visit.

"You be Marion Ulysses Calhoun?"

The man was chewing on a toothpick, swinging one foot and acting bored, which Marion knew to be a lynch boss lie.

"Yessir."

The man pulled out a wallet and exposed a badge. "I reckon this ought to explain I'm here on official business."

He said it like two words: oh fishul.

Marion Calhoun was silent, waiting, watching the bowing of his porch rail underneath a white rear end, while he wished the man off of it, the weight of his torso distributed to his own two feet. Marion nodded his head.

"All right then. I'm here on account a what happened down the road there," the man pointed to the west. "County sheriff's office sent me out to check on a mild peculiarity. Seems somebody says you seen somethin three days ago that just might clear up a little mess we got happenin round here."

Across the way Hezekiah was digging a ditch. The boy had seen a movie showing the guts of a trench a group of prisoners had used to dig their way out of a German prisoner camp. Suddenly inspired, he had been working on the thing for close to a week. It seemed a disturbing fact to Marion that the prison camp was located on Susan-Blair's side of the property line, and freedom on Marion's. Hezekiah had worked his way across six feet and the thing had the look of a narrow grave, or a trough for a water line. The top of the boy's head had popped out when the county car drove up. A few seconds later a shovel was thrown to the side of a mound of dirt; a few seconds after that, the boy birthed himself out of the earth, his blond hair caked with it, as well as his hands. Marion saw the activity and held up a hand meaning for him to stay put right where he was at or else.

"You been listed as a possible witness in an investigation."

"Who drew up this list?"

The man looked at the piece of paper. "I think I just told you."

"No sir. You said somebody. Didn't say who they was."

"Aaron Class."

Marion thought of the man and how he'd shorted his tractor one good tire and wondered if the sorry son of a bitch had filed a suit against him for being in the way of his truck.

"He run into me. I was just mindin my own business."

"Well, we need you over to Hattiesburg to talk about it. Had to call in most everbody who ever knew the man. Seems you've had the bad luck to be added to the list."

"Mayurn?"

The boy stood on the bottom steps, his overalls black, his hair straight up on his head as if coated in lard. A shovel was in his hand and he bounced it off the step, scattering dirt.

"I thought you said your name to be Marion?" The man in the suit put his badge back in his pocket.

"That's my name."

"No it aint. It's Mayurn. Mayurn Calhoun." Hezekiah scratched at his nose.

"Hez, git on home. You aint got no business here."

Marion looked around for Susan-Blair. The yard was empty but for the usual ground clutter.

"What'd Mayurn do to bring out the law?"

"Now, how come you think I'm the law?" The sheriff grinned at the boy.

"You are, aint you?"

The man puffed up a little, put out his hands like pistols and fired away over the top of the dirty head. "You might say I am."

"What'd he do then?"

"We just want to talk to him a while."

"He don't like to talk."

"Is this your kid?" The man looked at Marion, who was shaking his head.

"Hez, git on now." Marion pointed to his neighbor's yard.

"He didn't buy me no beer. I asked him to, but he didn't."

"Hez."

"Beer?"

"He said he would oncet I was old enough. But I aint there yet."

The officer looked down at the boy and finally raised his rear off the porch rail.

"I aint talkin about beer here. You git on home and let me do my work."

He turned to Marion again.

"We're holdin somebody who says you can speak for him."

Hezekiah had moved up one step. "Susan-Blair says folks go to jail all the time for no reason. Specially niggers and whores."

"Caint we do somethin about him?"

"I been tryin for years now, and aint made no progress."

Marion looked at the county car, at the man with the hard lines down his nose, at the mean, no-nonsense lynch boss set of his shoulders.

Now, if this aint the ticket. This here man's gonna want me to get in that car of his and far as anybody knows I may or may not ever be seen again. Road runs both ways, both ways dangerous and to the river no matter what. Have to turn off to a main road to get near the city and by then I may or may not be Marion Calhoun no more.

He looked the man steady in the eyes and then he looked down at Hezekiah and winked.

"I need you to get on in the car and come up to Hattiesburg and talk with us about this," the man said.

"Hezekiah, where's your mama at?"

"Inside readin a magazine."

"Where'd Arena go to? Where's your sister?"

"Dunno."

"Well you run on home and look after your mama. She might need you to turn on a light or help watch your sister. Might even need you to help her git supper on." Marion reached into his pocket, his fingers around loose change. There wasn't much of it. "You git on now. I got to go somewhere."

"You comin back?"

Marion looked at the sheriff, or whatever he was; the flash of the badge had been lightning quick and indistinguishable.

The man said, "He'll be back. Don't you worry. Just got us a few questions, is all."

Marion looked at Hezekiah and smiled.

"Mayurn's a nigger, but he aint a bad nigger."

"Well that's good. That sure is good." The man walked down the steps and stood waiting in the center of the yard, his shadow long and rigid as a knife.

" 'Scuse me a minute." Marion turned and went inside his dark house for his hat and coat. Shrugging it on he saw the boy was still on the steps, worried. Taking Hezekiah firmly by the shoulders he shoved him in the direction of his house and said, "Git on home, boy. You got diggin to do. Them prisoners is countin on you."

Then Marion went to the car, opened the back door and climbed in, embarrassed by being carted up in front of Beachum's like a common criminal, but not knowing a thing in the world he could do about it.

The last thing he heard was Hez yelling out behind him, "I'll dig you out if they lock up your black ass, Mayurn! Don't you worry!"

"Well shit, what a mouth on that kid," the man said and Marion relaxed.

A lynch boss would have laughed or hooted and given a thumbs-up to the boy. No lynch boss here. Just a country errand boy bringing in a witness. To what, Marion had no idea. But at least he didn't seem to be the one in trouble.

"It says here you was on your tractor from twelve noon 'til late that evenin."

"Yessir, as best I recall."

"Workin on that leased-out land?" The detective was a different one from the last. This was the third one to question him, each more slovenly in appearance than the one previous.

"Yessir."

"You see anything strange goin on that day?"

"No sir. I was workin. Not payin attention to nothin but that."

"You ever see this girl?" The man slid a picture out of a manila folder and across the table. The girl peered up at him from out an old schoolhouse picture. Those plain, wide eyes. She was younger looking; thinner. But the same.

"I seen her out behind the house over a week ago. Maybe two weeks even."

Another picture was in a folder. A black-and-white one. A shard of gray was exposed. Marion could see something that looked like the tips of her fingers clutched around a pillow casing. The nails were clean and white, all but one. The nail of the little finger was broken off down to the quick. A horrible act seemed to be hiding behind manila. The preamble to it that broken nail, that broken finger, that frantic clutch of cloth. Marion began to tremble.

"She had her throat cut."

Two men in the back of the room cleared their throats. Marion could see their bodies hidden in the shadows. A clock was over their heads. A large clock with huge numbers. A clock for the nearly blind, or folks overly concerned with time. One man was smoking and drifts of it swirled and swirled. The man standing beside him gave a low, warning cough.

The white man turned around. "Shit. It's true aint it?"

There was somethin terrible here. And I got my black ass too close to it.

"Aaron Class says you seen him that day."

Marion was quiet, waiting. Let them do the business of explainin, he thought. I aint sayin a word.

"Says he ran up on you on your tractor."

"Yessir. We had a small accident. Out on the county road near old Sheffield's place."

"He hit you from behind."

"Werent really a hit. More like bumped me hard." Marion wondered why he felt defensive toward the man, seeing how he owed him a brand-new tractor tire and there hadn't been any ready offer to run out and buy him one.

"Did he seem distracted? Upset?"

"He hated he busted that radiator, was all."

"What happened then?"

"I towed him to my place and we worked on the truck for a while. Found out the radiator werent struck, just the hose leadin to it."

"How long?"

"For nearly 'bout two hours."

"What time did he leave?"

"I'm guessin round six o'clock. Maybe a little after."

"We don't need no guesswork here. I need somethin I can write down and swear to and tell my boss about."

"I aint got a watch, sir."

"Shit, you can read the sun, caint you? You a farmer. How many farmers you know caint read the time a day by what's in the sky?"

There was no answer to the question, nor a reason to attempt one. Marion Calhoun sat as still as he could while he watched the detective spread out sheets of paper on the table, arranging and then rearranging and finally folding up the topmost piece to a shape like that of an airplane. The black-and-white photograph got shuffled a bit, slid out a little. Marion could see the under plains of the girl's arms, now. The blue juncture of veins at the wrist. Speckled with something, though. Splatters round and angry dotted the creases of her skin and continued across the pillow casing. He looked at that larger triangle of gray. Seems her hair is wet. Is her hair wet? Jesus. Her hair is wet! Marion clasped his hands together under the table, dislocating his thumb with a loud pop.

"We're just about done here. Just need you to take a look at somebody and tell us if this is the fella who owns the truck." He slammed his notebook shut and stood, his chair slamming against the wall behind him. "Well, get up then and come with me. Let's get this thing over with."

*   *   *

The man inside the tiny room looked as though he'd already fallen victim to a lynch mob, one that had left him dead as a board, but still stubbornly blinking. His facial scars had been leeched to a shade between green and white and they stood out like thrown paint against the trunk of a tree. His neck was freshly pink, and finger-marked, too, as though he'd leaned on his hands in an effort at self-strangulation.

Marion looked around for a threat and couldn't find one. Just a room that was empty but for a slab and bare mattress and a neat stack of folded-up clothes. No sheets, or covering of any sort, just monotonous gray ticking that blended with the man's ass and made it appear as though ashen veins had bled out in both directions to the walls. Marion wondered what it might be that held the power to drive the blood-color from a face. A white face, at that. The man seemed to be sleeping, or perhaps napping half-up and sitting, as though what was to be had already been and he was just a shell. A lone locust shell stuck to the side of a tree waiting for a violent wind.

"Is he the one who bumped you that day?"

The man had a fresh bruise across his shoulder and he was sitting naked. His clothes were folded next to him and one hand was stuck inside a pocket and this seemed a pitiful thing. A terrible, pitiful thing. Marion frowned. The man's face was hideous and hard to look at, but he was the one. He was definitely the one.

"He's the one."

"And you both worked on that truck all that evenin?"

"Yessir."

"Well, you're done here, and so are we for that matter. Caint nobody be two places at once. Cept maybe a ghost and I aint ever met a ghost doin time. Leastways in Mississippi."

He turned to a group of men lounging in their chairs. "Caint say we'll be able to do a thing with this." He shuffled papers together. Fished a paper clip out of his pocket and began to pick his teeth. He continued, "Seein how this one here vouched for him and everthing. Seein how the coroner put the time a death at around—"

He paused, seemed to suddenly realize he was talking with somebody around who shouldn't be hearing things.

"Boy, I reckon you can git on back to wherever it is you come from."

When Marion Calhoun walked out the door, the bench was empty, the hall dimly lit and cold as a morgue. He followed the signs that led him out, not realizing he had been holding his breath the whole while.

There was never a mention of transport back to Agricola and Marion was glad of it. He managed to hitch a ride as far as Lucedale with a cargoless pig farmer traveling home in his empty truck. Marion rode in the back, smelling the awful smell of what spills out a terrified hog, and barely even noticed. He watched terrain fly by through the wooden slats of the truck, saw familiar nothingness that neither garnered nor discarded speculative thoughts. He tucked his cold hands in his armpits and looked up at the sky, a thing bigger than Marion Calhoun and all that he knew.

Never thought I'd be glad to see Susan-Blair or that messy Hezekiah, he reasoned while he watched a distant cloud. But I surely will. I surely will.

BOOK THREE

1961

...there is perhaps something in passion too, as well as in poverty and innocence, which cares for its own.

—WILLIAM FAULKNER

CHAPTER 34

Fairy Sheehand drove through the narrow streets of Lucedale in his bus with its pots swinging and sheets flapping out open windows like pennants. In spite of its awkward shape and size, the vehicle made sounds similar to a carnival ride, or maybe a circus van, or some preamble of entertainment on the way, and more than a few noticed and climbed down off their barber chairs and off the swivel stools in the drugstore to wander out and see. Once they realized it was just old turkey-neck Fairy Sheehand and that bus of his, they went back inside to whatever business of theirs had suffered momentary interruption. A group of local farmers, seeing how their business was to sit and watch, sat on the still-fresh iron benches and studied the man's slow, clanging progress.

The bus was not large, in fact it was small—but still large enough to take huge bites of curb with it each time it made the loop around the square before heading back. The group congregated on the iron benches had already had three ringside visits.

"Oh for Christsakes. Somebody ought to teach that one there how to drive," one farmer said.

"That aint good enough. Somebody ought to tell that one there that Henry Ford invented cars long enough ago to be reliable and not just a flash in the pan. If that aint enough, they ought to tell him there's such a thing as a good reliable truck. And if that still won't do, they might should say there's been mules around since Moses what know the difference between a curb and a street."

This particular farmer spit onto the fresh cement sideway the Ladies of the Eastern Star had procured for all four of the stores around the square. Thinking to himself, *Hell, it's the sixties now and things are changin in spite of me sittin here wishing they wouldn't.*

"Jim, Mavis aint gonna like you markin up her fresh sidewalk there."

"Mavis aint here that I can see."

But he climbed down and went and picked up a handful of sand from a fresh new flowerbed and rubbed at the stain; clumped it up till he could kick it aside to the brand-new curb gutter with his boot. He'd not done it if he had not been in good consensual standing with one particular Eastern Star lady he was not wedded to. One who'd sold forty-two pound cakes just so they could have those sidewalks men were prone to spit on. And the flowerbeds the dogs were prone to dig up and scatter. And the new wrought-iron light posts the crows took to decorating with gray-white droppings.

The wooden benches were gone. Had been for six months now. Carted away by Roper Salvage on a bright winter day and replaced by green iron benches that put circular creases in the skin of the back that even by day's end were still plain evidence for any inspecting wife to see and finger and carry-on about. *There's fields to be got to,* most would say. *Fields. And all you do is sit and gossip. You and your friends.*

"Where you reckon Fairy's goin to this time?"

"He aint got a mouth governer. He'll let us know."

Four of them were sitting there: Johnson, the cuckolded husband of the Eastern Star lady who'd sold those pound cakes; Jim, the one currently doing the cuckolding; J. P. McCreel, whose son had lost his life while between the legs of a female; and Julia Beauchamp, who had never had the stomach for entanglements, but sat wishing for the memory of one to occupy her mind.

She sat, elbows to knees, on a separate bench from the men while she watched her brother-in-law make a spectacle of himself in a doctored-up school bus. He'd painted the words Blue Goose down the side of it and she wondered why, seeing how there was nothing blue or goose-like about it. Her working jaw was the only sign of her irritation. The clinching and unclinching pressed a furrow up to her temple and then back down again. The muscle saying her hands and their placidity were liars.

J. P. McCreel was the only one of the group to notice. He looked at the watch on his brown, weathered arm and then back at the woman again and then toward the street where the bus had turned. She'll move toward Fairy and not the other way round, he thought. She'll wait, though. Wait 'til she's positive there aint no other way to get that moron brother-in-law of hers out a Lucedale.

Julia watched the street. Smelled the still-new concrete beneath her boots; moved her foot around and listened to its grit. She looked over at the statue and speculated that unless someone put their foot down and put it down quick, come March the Eastern Star ladies would have the town square looking like a Victorian dollhouse. A country intersection was a country intersection. No need to try and turn it to a town.

"Julia, seein how you're kin, maybe you ought to flag down that bus. Maybe offer him a token just so he'll pick you up and let you guide him wherever it is he's goin."

Jim said this, his eyes straying to her yellow shirt front and her sloping breasts while he spoke. In his opinion all she needed was tassels to look like a rodeo gal.

"I know where he's goin to," she said. She looked at J. P. McCreel when she spoke. "He's lookin for somebody."

J. P. nodded, his eyes to her eyes and not to her yellow shirt, his eyebrows cresting upward in a white arch that seemed to indicate he knew where Fairy was headed, too.

"Don't seem to be havin no luck findin who he's lookin for. Doin a fine job a mutilatin our brand-new sidewalks, though." Jim pulled out his knife and picked at his sawed-off nails. "We all know whose legs he needs to take a switch to and I don't see that gal nowhere around."

The men chuckled, except for J. P. McCreel, who kept his eyes on Julia.

"He'll get up the nerve to ask for help, eventually. I got time to wait even if you fellers don't," she said.

Julia crossed her legs. Swung her booted foot. Studied the ice-cream parlor look to the new light posts. There were even rumors flying that a black-and-white striped awning would soon be going up over the barber shop.

J. P. McCreel cleared his throat and said, "Fairy was out earlier. On that bike of his." They all looked at him, shocked the man had spoken.

The death of his son beneath a ton of gravel had built a barrier around their speech. They couldn't talk about what had died recently—cow or pig or even distant relative—because of what had died underneath a gravel pit down at his place. They couldn't talk about fucking (either their own personal wife or someone else's) because of the fucking that had been interrupted by the falling of a gravel mountain down at his place. Speech was thwarted by J.P.'s history, and the men had found this a burden. Now here he was, wearing a nice blue shirt, faded same as everybody else's, but ironed, which made it different from everybody else's, opening up his mouth and speaking. It was the first time he'd uttered a word in a great score of months.

"Lord God, J.P. I caint believe it," Johnson said. "I knew you'd take a interest in life again. I told the wife the other night in bed, just you wait, J.P.'s got what it takes to stay in the world of the living regardless of what fell on the head of his son."

Jim stopped his knife work, hearing the words "wife" and "bed" and remembering those Eastern Star legs that didn't belong to him (but that one might could say he was borrowing), up around his own neck out in that vacated house on Sweet River Road.

"I got bored with quiet, I guess." J.P. kept his eyes on Julia, the only one of the three he was interested in.

The bus disappeared around a corner and they all heard the crash of a garbage can.

"He aint gonna stop 'til he finds Arena," Julia said while she popped her knuckles.

Sharlene Headly had three cows about to throw their calves and Julia needed to be there, wanted to be there, and not just for the veterinarian fee, either. The woman was too quick with the winch, in Julia's estimation. She looked at her watch. A man's Bulova they all admired.

"I tell you what, boys. Anybody here got any news about Arena that might be relevant, I'll deal out shoein or wormin or whatever, for it. I aint got all day either." She leaned forward and all expected her to spit. She wiped at her boots instead, her fingers leaving clean paths across the fancy leather. "You all know what's goin on here. More than that poor fool in that bus does. He aint got a clue."

There was a silence that lasted almost a minute.

"He wants the man down on Autumn Road. Back a ways off the main highway. Got hisself a screened-in front porch and fancy flowerbed. House sits all by its lonesome." J. P. McCreel offered this up and again, they were all amazed.

Jim and the one whose wife he was poking looked at one another and then back at their boots again.

"Well there you go," Julia said, stunned at the pile of information he'd dished up easy as pie.

"'Course, I'm shy a farm animals that need tendin," J.P. said. "Don't have no cows that need shots neither. Got other things that need lookin at, though."

J.P. calmly watched her, his sky-blue eyes lighting up a little, while he grinned. And then he did a strange thing: he removed his hat and swept back his snow-white hair with one clean hand in a manner similar to that of a mayor or alderman, at least.

Johnson and Jim held their breath.

They'd seen Julia mad as all get out. Seen her shoot her truck just because it threw a rod. Seen her do a lot of things. And the man had verbally copped himself a feel in broad daylight. True, she might grant him some form of leniency seeing how his son had been killed in a humiliating way, but they didn't think so.

She stood up and the two men sat back and waited.

J.P. leaned forward easy and calm, his elbows to his blue-jeaned knees, his eyes brighter than any remembered seeing.

"Well J.P., seein how you got no need a large animal care, you got yourself a date. I reckon you already know my personal phone number. And if you don't, I guess you're a smart enough man to figure out how to find it. I'll be home by six." And then she went and stood in the center of the street and waited for Fairy to make his swing again. She didn't have to wait long. Two minutes, tops. But it was the quietest two minutes any of the farmers ever remembered sharing.

"The onliest thing I want to hear from you is where she's at."

Fairy was out of breath and sweating so profusely he'd soaked his shirt and it was a chilly day, too chilly for that much sweat.

Julia looked around the bus, amazed.

He'd taken out all of the seats but two and built himself a bed and chest of drawers out of knotted pine that looked halfway decent. Line was stretched across the back between two windows where he could hang out (or hang in) his washed-out laundry to dry. A pair of jeans was pinned by the hems and she couldn't help but think that to one traveling behind it would appear a man was standing on his head in the back of the bus.

"I know where this man lives—" She yelled this over the grinding gears. "I don't know that Arena's there, though. Susan wasn't too wordy on things. You want me to drive?" Her seat was set slightly behind him and she could see the back of his head and a large knob behind his ear, much like a swollen sting of a bee. His color was awful, too.

"I aint wantin a durn thing but that you sit there and keep your mouth shut," he said.

"How you gonna know where to go if I keep my mouth shut?" Asshole, she thought.

Fairy looked in the rearview mirror and glared while he wondered how much she had to pay for that yellow rodeo shirt of hers.

Julia studied him. "What's the matter with you, anyhow?"

"Nothin."

"You're mighty yellow for nothin."

"I aint sick."

"Well for somebody who aint sick, you sure look it. You got hepatitis or something like it. You may not feel sick, but you sure are."

She looked down at her feet and saw a citizen's band radio and thought, Well shit. Now who in hell's he been callin on one of those things? A portable radio was there, too. And a shoebox full of batteries.

"Shellfish can make you sick before you know it," she said while she shoved the batteries out of the way with her foot.

"Nothin wrong with me. I just aint been out much in the sun."

"Yellababy turned this color and look what happened to him."

"I don't need you to remind me a my son. This aint the same thing."

"But it sure is somethin." It was a statement. One he didn't intend to comment on, apparently. She looked down at the radio's black coily wire, and then back behind her and to the side where he had his canned goods stowed underneath the bed. Cans of pork and beans and tuna fish and boxes of crackers as well as pots and pans were covered in netting that swung its cargo with easy movements while the bus caught every pothole there was to catch. Julia was momentarily taken aback. She'd not thought him an organized man, or one who could design such a nautical compactness to the skeletal frame of an old school bus. This was a complete surprise what with the way he kept his yard; and then she reminded herself that it was Susan-Blair's yard, and not his.

"This bus is too noisy, Fairy. Let's go get my truck and I'll drive."

The clanging pots were giving her a headache.

He thought about it. Whoever this feller was, he'd hear the bus coming a mile away. A truck was better. But Julia doing the driving made him feel weak and stupid and like an old dry female who needed chauffeuring.

She seemed to read him. "I'll let you drive, then."

"Never thought I'd be relyin on you for assistance." Fairy wiped at his sweaty face with a trembling hand.

"Well, I never thought I'd be the one offerin it. Fairy, you really ought to see a doctor about your color."

"I tell you what Julia, soon as I take care of what's goin on here, I'll run myself right down to Singin River so they can take one look at me and charge me a arm and a leg I caint afford to lose before they tell me there aint nothing in the world wrong with me." He shifted gears. "I got business to tend to first. Arena's the only one. The only ..."

He hushed. Found he couldn't verbalize the thought.

She knew what he was about to say, and disagreed. In her opinion, Hezekiah was the only worthwhile one of the bunch.

"Hezekiah is a good boy," she said quietly while she looked out to the landscape jarring by, her fingers to the frame of the window, its upper half opened, its lower half cracked, while they rumbled past a forty-acre plat of pecan trees. Some ingenious somebody had planted peach trees in between the pecans and Julia wondered if the joining had been successful, if the fruit trees got enough light.

She said, "Hezekiah's never complained."

"It aint the same with boys. Boys will make their way. They caint help it. The world's set up for a man. Set spinning by God who just so happened to be a man."

Idiot, she thought, shaking her head.

"Girls need help seein how they aint got the inside track on things. On how men work hard to . . . how men might say things in order to—"

"Fuck," she said while she reached into her shirt pocket for a cigarette. "I think that's the word you're looking for."

He glared at her and she shrugged. "I always believed kids learn from what they see at home," she said.

"Well, I guess I aint been there to show her how to do things proper."

"Seems you been busy. Maybe Arena's smarter than you think. Maybe she's seen all this runnin around you been doing, or at least heard of it." Everybody else in town had.

"Silva loves me."

"Love is a stupid reason to discard my sister," Julia said while she smoked, believing love a fable somebody dreamed up out of boredom. Men were idiots. All of them. Well. Maybe not all of them. But most of them. There was a pause, then: "Susan-Blair's sick, Fairy. You need to be with her."

Fairy studied her, his eyes sunken but curious. "What're you talkin about? What kind a sick?"

"The kind a sick it aint easy to cure." How does one say, Look, I don't like you and I never have, and what you're doing with that ex-wife of yours, that Silva, is none of my business and don't even seem bad anymore after what I saw this morning with Susan-Blair sitting in the middle of a pile of shit that nobody in their right mind would ever want to buy; going on and on about Jesus hovering near the ceiling, spying on her; but regardless of that, regardless of how long it took you to get your life together, the one you left at home is trying her damnest to kill your baby? Maybe not in an obvious beat-the-shit-out-of-a-kid way, but it's there just the same. The bus rocked while she thought about it. "I think she's havin some kind a breakdown, or somethin," she said, finally.

"She had a headache, is all."

"She needs help with the youngest, and you know it."

Fairy was quiet for once, thinking about things he already knew. The smallness of his life. The importance of prioritizing. Yellababy was hard to look at nowadays. Growing so big, all of a sudden. Hezekiah was a help; a sure-enough help, and he didn't even seem to mind. *My life is so small now. A diorama. I can ignore this small child and put the thought of him away in a barn, or out in the woods, and no one will be the wiser. I can stand idly by and watch my teenaged son put on a pack and walk down a road—*

"Fairy! Get back on your side a the road!"

He had swerved across the center line, barely missing a hay truck.

"Holy shit! What's the matter with you?"

"I got distracted is all."

"I swear. You all need help." Or a bullet to the head.

"I got all the help I need. Silva loves me. She's more than ready to help." Fairy coughed loud and thick. "A goat would be a better mother than Susan-Blair, anyhow. And Silva aint no goat. But whatever happens between the two of us is none a your damn business."

"So, you're thinkin of an actual trade? Silva for Susan-Blair? Here at this stage of the game with me just tellin you how worried I am about my sister?"

Fairy was silent.

"Fuck it, then. Forget everthing I just said. Susan's got troubles, but then I guess everbody's got troubles. Even you."

"I always had sense enough to not bother folks with mine," Fairy said.

"Well, I tell you what, let's just write the Pope and see if he'll give you a medal for it." Julia watched out the side window as his lumbering bus passed the bridge that marked the beginning of her land. "Turn here," she said.

"I know where I'm goin."

"Well, turn then, and don't take half my culvert with you when you do it, either."

CHAPTER 35

It was getting on to five o'clock and while he knew he didn't have any obligatory reason to be, Marion Calhoun was worried. He stood in his doorway, looking down the dirt road thinking: I should at least be seeing some sign of him; should at least be seeing some small speck down by Beachum's that will grow larger and larger 'til it aint a speck no more, but Hezekiah and Yellababy. One with a story to tell—maybe about that gal that don't wear no underpants, not even on Sunday—the other sleepy and drooly-faced.

But there was nothing at all for the eye to see, just an ambient green spread of almostnight that filled the air and the tops of the trees and the fields and even the heart, with its in-betweenness. Not day. Not night. Just the best of both saved for one last face-off before relinquishing the keys.

Stop this, he told himself, alarmed by his line of reasoning, the way it was building to an equation of injury or at least drama. But he couldn't. Truth-told he felt a victim of it, a victim of time. Not time in the little sense, the inconsequential sense. But transparent, denigrating Time in capital letters;

the only thing in the whole universe that held the power to expose events long-over and chilling.

As far as he could recall he'd only felt this way twice previous. Once, while he stood atop a gravel pit, a rag tied over his mouth and nose, digging while J. P. McCreel stood waiting for the pile to trickle itself down low enough for the man to see with his own two eyes where his son was at.

The other time was when he was waiting for his truck to coast to a stop in front of a church set on a dark hill in Lucedale so he could see with his very own eyes what the woman he'd loved was up to.

And now, a third time, while the green spread of not-day not-night held its breath and waited inside tumescent silence. Which meant that Time, that great revealer of man's foolishness wasn't ready to open its mouth just yet. "It" had already happened. Marion was sure of this. He just had no idea what "it" was.

"But somethin sure has," he said while he watched the empty yard. "I just feel it." He stood on his porch inside the dark shade of the pecan tree, a part of him knowing that his dark skin blended into the wood neat as a weathered board.

The door opened to the Sheehand place across the way and Susan-Blair stepped out wearing a glitter dress that looked like Sunday. He could see her feet were bare and her hair a mess, but the dress was pale shimmery pink, tightly fitted at the top. Its full skirt was covered in what looked to be roses and it seemed to radiate with life. The top was too tight, though, and Marion could see it cut into her surplus and how she spilled over around the armholes and neckline.

The woman put one hand up to a post and leaned forward on her hand. She had not seen him, he was sure of it. In fact, she didn't seem to be seeing anything at all. Her eyes were directed toward the road, but the road held nothing, not even the vague promise of stirred-up dust.

She's gone crazy, was his thought, standin there like that, lookin but not seein, in that fancy dress. "And it aint even hers," he muttered and then he was quiet. Listening.

He could hear the dress rustle when she moved, though she barely moved, just leaned forward once or twice while her eyes stayed trained on a dirt road going nowhere; a road so still even the dust was speechless.

That sound again. Similar to the murmurs of autumn. Like dried-up leaves blowing around a statue.

Fed up with himself, he turned and went indoors. A few minutes later he was at his kitchen table, the shoebox and its contents sitting in front of him. A jeweler's receipt was in there. And a photograph of his mother taken the month before she died. Old newspapers crumbly and fragile were opened, their folds speckled with mouse shit. He thumped a piece away with his finger.

Death Being Investigated. Foul Play Suspected.

And there was Aaron Class's face, reproduced for the whole world to see. Maybe not the whole world, but the world that mattered the most.

"He'd be servin time but for hittin my tractor square in the ass," Marion said, reviewing the words, remarking to himself how life seemed carried on mean shoulders. "Take what a man's embarrassed over and shine a light to it," he said, his voice joining with the sounds of his water heater ticking and a cricket chirping and the refrigerator kicking on. Somewhere outside beyond the opened kitchen window a frog cried.

Down at the intersection Beachum switched off the lights at his corner store. Marion sat at the table, quietly smoking a cigarette. Viceroys. He picked the pack up and put it across the image of Aaron Class. Only his chin showed. He looked at the wall clock and decided he would give Hezekiah thirty more minutes to make a speck of himself down where the dirt roads crossed and then he'd crank up his truck and go looking. Not even stopping to realize that it would be the second time that day that he'd climbed into a vehicle and gone looking for a Sheehand.

Susan-Blair stood out on her porch in the woman's dress remembering the time she'd gone to a beauty parlor for a permanent wave. She'd only done it once because once had been enough seeing how she'd lost most of her hair. The woman who'd cost her most of her blond hair and whose dress she was wearing hadn't recognized her when she handed over the clothes: three wool suits, one of which was a Lili Ann original; a Mardi Gras ball dress with a dragon on its bodice; and the garden party dress with the shiny roses. Hadn't recognized her at all. She had lifted them off the backseat of a Pontiac, carried them briskly up the steps past two holy yokes and then handed them over. Because she said she was in a hurry, she'd put her signature—Lucille Walkee—to the consignment form while still outside, using the porch rail as a flat surface. And then she'd driven away in a car so big and shiny and freshly new, it hurt Susan-Blair's heart just to look at it. The consignment form was fastened to the dresses hanging on a rack in the crowded living room and she knew, in spite of the memory about losing most of her hair, that she had been the one who had pinned it there, and she felt proud.

Keeping up with things was important.

She'd paid three dollars and lost most of her hair to learn that lesson.

Susan-Blair looked over her shoulder through the opened door and saw the paper's square white ghost-shape standing out in the crowd. The paper was fastened with a straight pin to the wool Lili Ann, high up, near the pearl buttons.

A former tax man who had been a former insurance man had given her the hint.

The one about consignment forms and keeping up with things.

He had also been responsible for her losing her hair. But that came later. What was his name?

Robert Something had been printed on the business card. Underneath his name was a word she didn't understand: entrepreneur.

Susan-Blair had gone to him because she'd read a hand-printed advertisement up on the board at Beachum's, which should have been a warning in itself what with the store's weeviled flour and stale bread and dinted-up cans. Run Your Own Business in One Easy Lesson, the words promised. And in spite of the weevils and the staleness and the dints, she'd taken the piece of paper at face value because, as anyone living out on a dirt road knew, anything that promised a way to get off that dirt road sounded good. A dirt road person will believe anything, and Susan-Blair knew it. Believe it even while they spend the last penny left in the can. Believe it even while they know sure as their name that nobody but God can lift them off a stretch of land He Himself saw fit to put them on in the first place.

Because she still had hope, Susan-Blair wrote down the address and finally, along with her two toddlers, found his unmarked shop down on Front Street in Lucedale.

She had wasted a full hour, huffing and puffing while she looked for it, too. There was a card in the window of a narrow building that she'd walked past three times, all within plain view of the skinny man sitting behind a desk with a gooseneck lamp. Hezekiah had been riding on her hip while Arena clutched at her dress anchor-like, and for the man to have missed seeing them parade along the sidewalk, a country conglomerate of three, he would have needed the excuse of blindness.

Once inside, so grateful for a chair, even a hard one, she'd felt close to crying, she looked around the room and breathed in those smells of renovation. She smelled new wood and old plaster and dust, and A. B. Dick Mimeograph ink as well as another brown smell she couldn't quite identify. Yellow and green tile was on the floor and the walls still wore three leftover strips of peeling wallpaper, a beige wheat design that made her hungry.

Why, I've eaten enough bread to choke a pig, but never seen a wall decorated out of what it was made from. She felt encouraged, almost euphoric, at the visual illustration of cereal grass hanging in strips. A part of her feeling like she was sitting in a waiting room three-quarters full of the Bread of Opportunity.

The man handed her a form that she filled out with a number-two pencil.

Once done she looked down at her children, quiet for once, but not for long, snapped the pencil in half and handed a piece to each child. One would have the eraser and the other wouldn't. There would probably be a scuffle over it that Arena would win because she was bigger, but it would take them at least two minutes to start comparing the two parts and realize they were different. Two minutes of peace and quiet, which she desperately needed.

I would a give you another pencil, the man said, and Susan-Blair just stared, feeling stupid for breaking that pencil in two before thinking about it. Realizing that just because a wall used to be covered in pictures of wheat, it didn't mean she had become a partaker of the Bread of Practical Sense. She swallowed hard, embarrassed.

How much, she asked, finally.

For the pencil?

No sir, for the lesson.

Three dollars, he replied and so she'd paid her three dollars and was handed a packet of paper while her two toddlers scrambled along the floor like rats.

The top paper was a list of helpful hints concerning time management. All laughable seeing how she had two in shitty diapers who took up every spare minute of her day. But while she scanned the worthless list, the man, this Robert person, started talking about selling things on consignment; explaining the procedure.

While he kept his eyes on Hezekiah, who had crawled over to the wall where he was scribbling on a baseboard, the three-dollar business man, now short one long number-two pencil but suddenly the benefactor of two short nubby ones, which added to the one he held in his hand, equaled three in her book, said: Consign means to entrust. To entrust someone is a powerful thing, don't you think Mrs. Sheehand?

No, had been her answer, and he had looked momentarily startled and unsure of himself.

I messed up the order of his speech, she realized, pinching herself on the arm. He was sitting there waiting for a Yes and got himself a No instead. And then she shrugged, over it. As far as she could see, trust never put food on the table or changed a single one of her kids' dirtied-up diapers and there didn't seem to be a good enough reason for lying about it. She had sat up straight in her chair with the feeling that maybe all that was about to change, that maybe those remnants of wallpaper-wheat had meant something.

Arena was trying to climb up the front of his desk, making an awful racket of it with her shoes. Leaning over he handed her an obloid paper weight that was clear and heavy and held something locked inside that resembled a tiny bird's feather. She promptly banged it against the green-and-yellow floor, trying to get at what it held. Susan-Blair jerked it away from her, put it back on the man's desk and then pulled out a lipstick from her purse.

She'll smear for a while and then be done, Susan-Blair said.

The man, this Robert, seemed stunned to see a child run a clown mouth all the way up a face to the ear, but Susan-Blair had seen it all before and sat there quietly, her hands folded calmly in her lap, and waited.

Well, when you sell something on consignment, he said, eyes nervously darting around the room watching Hezekiah and pretending not to.

Well here—let me explain: on consignment means that the goods, in your case, used items that are still considered valuable, are delivered to you for sale, but remain the property of the original owner until sold.

You mean I aint got to stock my own store?

Arena took a bite out of the lipstick and then spit it to the floor.

Susan-Blair fished it up and foraged for a tissue. All she had in her purse was a plastic cowboy wallet (now minus three dollars) and a black comb. She held the lipstick in her palm for a minute and then bent down and slipped it into her shoe. It would be easier to clean her foot than the inside of her purse and as far as she could see this man who claimed to know how to run a business had failed to purchase a trash can.

That's the beauty of it, he said. Folks bring you their things and you display them. In your case, hang them up, or whatever you choose to do with them until they sell.

She was planning on wearing them, but she kept quiet on it, and listened to what he was saying while she stretched out a foot and herded Hez away from the door.

And then when they sell, you get a percentage of the profit.

He believed strongly in writing everything down.

She found this out one minute later and realized this was probably the reason he had been so shocked when she'd ruined his yellow number-two pencil.

It's 'cause folks need to write things down with a normal-sized pencil and now they caint because I broke his pencil in half and he won't have enough of them and he'll be too embarrassed to offer up those nubs.

She looked over at Hezekiah and then down at Arena, suddenly hating both of them for making her look like such an idiot.

You gotta get it down in writing, he said. I caint stress this enough. The last thing in the world you need is some type of disagreement over your stock. If you trust actualities to memory, you end up in the poorhouse.

She had wanted to laugh then, because she was already in the poorhouse. She held her peace and took a few notes and watched his eyes and the way they wouldn't look at her. It was strange, too, because he, this instructor, or rather this entrapanurial-something, found the baseboards and what her children were doing to them more fascinating than her face.

I've really lost it, she had thought, fighting the temptation to peel off her sweater and then her bra just to see if he'd notice.

She put a hand to her hair and realized it'd been years since she had tended to it. Years. And she'd always had such good, rich hair, thick and true blond, never needing bleach. She washed it regular enough, but she couldn't remember the last time she had actually sat down in a beauty shop and had someone else roll it up or trim off the dead ends. I need a perm, she decided right then and there. And not a cheap one from Agricola, either, where the only beauty shop operated one day a month from the inside of a barber shop. Maybe that Lucille Walkee Beauty Salon I passed while I was looking for this place.

I hope this was beneficial, he said even while she was thinking on her hair and wondering if she had enough money left in her plastic cowboy wallet to get what she wanted.

There was a quiet break then and she flashed back to what he had just finished saying. He still wasn't looking at her; he was watching her two children instead.

Yessir it was, she'd said, hopefully with the proper amount of sincerity in her voice.

Like a true gentleman, he held open the door to the shop and she gave it one last look. The stencils were still on his makeshift desk and she knew that this man, this instructor person, had big plans for this business about writing things down and keeping oneself out of the poorhouse. Big plans even though his shoes were run-down and his pants were worn at the knees and shiny.

She grabbed Arena up off the floor and wrangled for Hezekiah.

The collar to the man's white shirt was starched, but old and yellowing and even while she shook his hand—leaving a smear of red lipstick across his palm—she was thinking that all she'd ever known was threadbare cotton and men who wouldn't stay put and male eyes that wouldn't look at her.

And now here I go looking for a beauty shop in Lucedale just so I can get something done to my hair so this one here wearing worn-out shoes might notice me one day should our paths cross.

*   *   *

"At least he told me how to make a few dollars—"

This was more than the others had done. I lost most of my hair because of him, though. Mr. Robert Somebody didn't know it, and it wasn't like he held the rollers in his hand, but it was because of him and because I thought that maybe someday he might see me and stop long enough to ask if I'd learned anything that day I'd broken his pencil in half. And then I could say, Why yes! I learned a lot! I learned so much I don't even live on a dirt road anymore. I live in town now. And he would say, In town! Why that's wonderful! And I would say, Yes, over in New Augusta. And he would say, New Augusta? Why, I thought I knew everybody there was to know in New Augusta. And I would say, Did I say New Augusta? I meant Leakesville—

"And Lucille Walkee didn't even recognize me," Susan-Blair said, puzzled.

She looked out over her yard at the holy yoke leaning against a tree: THE EYES OF THE LORD ARE IN EVERY PLACE, BEHOLDING THE EVIL AND THE GOOD. POVERBS 15:3.

"Well I hope you saw that she ignored me, Lord. I hope you saw that while you were seein everthing else there was to see round here."

Pressing a hand to her hair she said, "Give me a perm that fried my head, charged me six dollars on top of that and didn't even have the nerve to say hello. Just dumped her clothes and left."

They were good clothes though. Some of the best she'd ever had the privilege of seeing. Susan-Blair couldn't deny that the woman had apparently been successful—at least financially—as a beautician. There was a stack of cotillion panties tucked away in a cleaner's bag, big-bloomered, white, size twelve. The woman who had stolen her hair handed them over like gold, probably thinking the whole while: here take these panties Mrs. Sheehand; I aint got the time to apologize over ruining your hair but I sure got the time to hand over my drawers. Sell them cheap, just shove 'em out the door. I'm sure there are poor white-trash people, maybe even niggers, who'd be willing to pay ten cents, or maybe a quarter for a pair a panties that once housed an ass that danced itself around a Mardi Gras ball—

She walked back inside and slammed the door and heard something fall over out on the porch. A storm is a storm, she thought, feeling its advent. And a storm is good and necessary for two reasons: wetting a too-dry land or ripping already-dead limbs from off the trees. A storm is necessary to settle things, she told herself while she jerked the consignment note off the dress it was pinned to and tore it into minute shreds the size of oatmeal. She dumped the debris into the overspilling trash can in the kitchen. Like king-sized dandruff it lay next to a smelly cluster of tuna-fish cans.

Just as suddenly, the storm passed while she made coffee, and she fretted over it.

What if the woman came back and demanded her merchandise?

Most didn't. Most assumed it never sold.

But what if this one was different?

What if she came back with the law, maybe drove up in one of those county sheriff cars, and wanted to see the note?

What if she knew, or guessed, that as soon as her Pontiac hit the dirt road out there, I pulled out the best of the lot and dressed myself in it?

She looked down at the pink dress.

"Oh Jesus, what if she knows this and is comin back this very minute?"

The coffee had perked and she was so preoccupied with worry that she burned herself while pouring a cup. In a rage (that storm again) she threw the whole pot to the wall where it crashed in metal pieces, leaving a huge steaming brown stain that matched an earlier stain from something else that had been thrown in the middle of a storm. Syrup, she remembered, Log Cabin maple syrup.

Scrambling for the trash can, she dumped its contents to the middle of the floor and picked through the garbage, ruining the roses on the dress. She found the soggy pieces of the note she'd torn already disappearing into un-recognizable glue. Huddled down with her back to the ceiling so Christ would at least have a hard time at spying, she put the pieces together, making a list of things she'd need. Tape. Lots of it. And then she would need to get a piece of waxed paper and put it to it and iron it flat just to make it presentable.

"Daddy called me in that time, too," she whispered so Jesus couldn't hear. "Whipped me good 'cause I tore up my test. Tore it to a million pieces."

Come here Susan-Blair and git your medicine, he'd said.

Come on in here. No mama, I aint needin you. I can tend to this one here by my ownself. Come on in here and git what you got comin. Shut that door too, sister. Shut it hard now. Pull em on down and lay cross that bed. Pull em down or sure as God I'll do it for you. If I told you once I told you a hunderd times. One who hates wisdom is like one who hath cast down many wounded. Yea, many strong men have been slain by her. Her house is the way to hell. Goin down and down and then down some more to the chambers of death.

Susan-Blair rocked back and forth in the middle of trash, remembering.

The day had been just like a lot of other days: a dead tree limb day that needed a good storm to settle things. Funny how Julia never seemed to accumulate against herself dead branches or decay, or any other thing that needed God's hand to help the body rid.

She held her stomach and rocked, ignoring Christ and what he was seeing, only worried about one thing now. Not her teenaged son and crippled baby, or her disappeared daughter, or her house on its way to hell. All Susan-Blair could think on was the shredded-up consignment note and what she was going to do about replacing it.

CHAPTER 36

There was a place where Arena Sheehand went to sit and think, that nobody in Agricola knew about. The wind whispered to her in this place while it touched the tops of the trees like a soft benevolent hand, those dogwoods and poplars and sycamores.

She dug in the sand with her bare feet inside this place, at once peaceful and serene, her eyes up to a patchwork of blue through the trees, and then over her shoulder toward his house with its gray shingles and wide screened porch that was behind her, set a good distance away from the trees that were just now budding up.

She was lost in thought. With pale blond hair resting on her shoulders, and her feet bare and her arms crossed around her knees there was a scholarly air to her. Her lower lip caught between her teeth, she watched the winking afternoon light play off his roof and the pump house and the small round barbeque grill set underneath a back window. She was envisioning doom, in one sense, thinking of her place and how she lived and his place and how he lived. "His place is not full enough of things," she said with a soft sigh. She'd seen what he had inside, partially, through the screen, and judged it puny. Behind those French doors, there it was: the good furniture, the Oriental rug, the flowery couch; the clean, almost empty living room.

"He aint got enough stuff. God's gonna come lookin for him for sure. I just know it," she whispered against her knees while her hands dug into the wet.

The water ran slower at the point of the creek where she sat waiting and thinking and building a birthday cake for herself out of dirt. Her dusty socks had been rinsed out and were drying on a smooth rock and she had bathed her legs, almost hypnotized by the movement of water. The way it was slow and sweet, with wide shallow borders the color of honey.

Across the way under an onyx swag of trees was the spot where the creek bank fell off to a depth of nearly twenty feet; the color changed there, turned a blackish-green that seemed so oily rich in hue, Arena felt faint, for it bespoke of organic matter: leeches and dark snails and musk glands and hearts. The water's cap swirled in both directions at once in confused whirlpools, which meant that far below the surface was a slick clay bank that would trap and hold while it killed. But before that, moving out at a sweet grade, was the softest, kindest, most golden water she'd ever seen. Baptismal water, was what she thought of when she looked at it and then she glanced up through the trees, startled, wondering suddenly if she'd ever gone under in the name of the Father, Son and Holy Spirit.

"I guess not," she thought, placing it in a category reserved for big things: that first period, that first bra. "It'd be almost like shavin your legs for the first time. I'd surely remember it."

And her voice filled the place, blended in with the salt-colored sand and the low swishing of tree limbs dipping into water before coming back to her. She put single pieces of pine straw on the top of her sand cake in place of candles while overhead, the leaves of the live oaks stirred and shimmered in the mid-afternoon breeze.

Pieces of their conversations and actions played constantly in the back of her mind. She'd said this. He'd said that. Even went so far as to call her his own sweet girl once. She had almost laughed, too. Had to bury her head in the surplus of his trousers to hide her grin. Such a fool. She wasn't a sweet girl. She never had been. Being unsweet was the only smart thing she'd ever done; the only thing that kept her safe.

Turning, she saw the tree break and the bright green beyond that indi-cated his lawn. He didn't know she knew about this place, or that it was so close—within earshot—of his house because he'd never once thought to ask her if she ever went somewhere special in order to think. He never stopped to ask her much of anything at all, now that she thought about it.

"I'd sure like to get that lighter a his before I leave here for good."

She had saved up forty dollars from their year of being together and Jackson, Mississippi, was on her mind. She could almost see herself in a white waitress uniform flipping a pork chop high in the air.

"I think he owes me that lighter, though."

She dug her toes in the sand and looked around, pleased.

She had found the spot on another day when she'd come for a visit (and a quick five dollars) and peeked through the screen and seen he had a guest. It wasn't that Arena minded the guest. She hadn't, except for the loss of the folded green Abe Lincoln. The visitor was older. Pretty enough in her own way, with all that black hair shot through with gray. So much gray, that nobody, not even Lady Clairol, her queenly self, could manage to hide it.

Tall and slim, the woman looked at the pear-shaped man and her eyes lit up just like in one of those movie magazines, and it was seeing that great shining look of love that made Arena forgive him, and her, for shorting her the five dollars. They were too Hollywood *not* to forgive. Arena stood there shivering in the cold, her eyes drinking in their waltz around the living room courtesy of a scratchy, but adequate, Frank Sinatra record on the phonograph. The man began to sing into the woman's hair while he danced her around, and Arena was glad that it was the woman and not her who was hearing the singing because his voice was thready and stupid-sounding and off-key. Then, like a durn fool, he changed the words and began to sing about a horse on television. S something. He even made a "high-ho!" sound when he did it, too, and the woman laughed up at him. Not a great big broad Hollywood laugh, but a quiet one, behind her hand, as though embarrassed.

They moved to a shiny mahogany piece of furniture where he took out a cigarette case and lit the woman's cigarette with a knobbed crystal lighter that was simply gorgeous. It sat in the palm of his hand like a giant jeweled plum, shoots of light everywhere at once: ceiling, across the pillows, even splashing the dog dish near the front door. Frank Sinatra sang on and on while outside in the cold, her nose pressed to the window screen, Arena stood shivering in the dark. It had been December and even though she'd worn a good corduroy coat she'd hid away before her ma could put it up for sale, her teeth clicked together in time with the music.

Now, eight weeks later, on a glorious, unusually warm February afternoon Arena leaned back on her hands and looked up through the trees to the sky.

Why caint I remember the woman's name? she thought. He said it often enough. What was it? Something that reminded Arena of jewelry for some reason, a reason that was probably important, but at the moment was gone from her. What's in a jewelry store, anyhow? Diamonds. Rubies. Gold—?

She sat up straight, remembering.

"No, not gold. That aint it. Silver, then. The woman's name was Silver. Just like the Lone Ranger's horse."

C H A P T E R

Cathy stood in the middle of Chalktown needing to pee so badly she felt as though her bladder would burst. She squeezed her legs together, thinking, I'm gonna piss these stupid shorts and never live it down. Next to her, Yellababy was screaming at such a heightened pitch she cringed and put one hand over her ear while she looked around for something to shove into his mouth. Cloth. Pinecone. Shoe. Anything. His cry was nasal and desperate and curiously blasting, much like the sound of a screaming duck. She looked over at Hez, who was trying to swing the pouch from off his shoulder.

"I gotta pee," she said.

"Do it then. I got my hands full."

"They aint no place to go."

"For God's sake, Cathy. Help me out here."

She moved to the little boy, put her arms around his torso and tried to lift him out. He wouldn't budge and screamed into her shirt. When he cried he slid into himself; pulled his hands to his chest like a turtle, the cloth of the backpack collecting near his privates.

"He aint cooperatin," she said.

The big woman with flour on her hands crawled forward on her hands and knees while Cathy and Hez took one step back.

"Whoa there," he said to her, holding up one hand, glancing toward the two men, one as short as a child, the other wearing a hat low over his face. Their eyes had connected for a brief moment and then the man seemed to remember himself and ducked his head, and all Hez could see was the top of a worn fedora. He had caught a glimpse of it, though. Godamighty, he sure had. A purple fungus seemed to have multiplied across the man's face, slick and congested. Hez wondered what that plague was named, if it might be contagious. Whatever it was, he and his gargoyle affects could stay right where they was at. Leave him be.

The fat woman seemed to want to speak. Her dirt-crusted hands would slap down on her legs one minute and then she would throw them up in the air the next, tears streaming down her lined face like rain. The short man went to her and began to help her to her feet and the endeavor took such a huge chunk of time, it seemed a comedy of sorts.

They seemed like a curse-struck group, these humans standing in the dust. We showed up and stirred 'em up, too, started somethin, Hez realized in alarm. Remembering that movie he'd seen where the spaceship set itself down in a domesticated city park and folks puzzled over it and kids ran forward to strike at it with sticks and the pretty blond woman wanted the scientist to give the strangers a chance and then the door opened up and the robot came walking out and decided to destoy the whole fuckin lot of them.

"We shouldn't ort to come here," Cathy said, trying to pull Yellababy's leg out of the pack.

"No shit, Sherlock."

"I'm about to pee myself." Cathy peered around, saw the chalkboards leaning against various supports: a tree, a fence, the porch of a house painted blue. The dirt road running in front of the houses seemed engineered by a clown; tire troughs meandered around the green humps of tossling hay grass and a person would have to be drunk to make sense of it. All the houses had tar-paper roofs that appeared to have melted, peppered about with vent pipes stuck up in bent angles. Next to the blue house stood a brownish-red house, and across the twisted road stood houses that were yellow and green. To assign them a true color required a stretch of the imagination for all the woodwork was faded and peeling, and it seemed as though a high value had been placed on the cultivation of weeds.

She looked at the house that was missing its door. It won't hurt to ask, she figured. Cupping her hands around her mouth she yelled in the direction of the kneeling fat lady, *"I need to use the bathroom!"*

"Holy cow!" Hez jumped like he'd been shot. "Are you insane! These folks aint deaf! They just don't talk!"

The short man began to giggle. A hand clapped over his mouth. His lower jaw jutted forward like a bulldog's and his pants looked like they had been worn for the last decade.

He's gonna drool any minute, Cathy figured, watching him. We are in crazy land, here. Surrounded by folks who will more than likely want to kill us and smear our blood all over their faces before they go back to whatever it was that they were doin before we showed up. It had happened before. Who was she to say it couldn't happen again?

The man who wouldn't show his face lifted a hand and pointed in the direction of the blue house. She looked. The place was debris-flooded. As though a rushing wall of trash had done its work, settled where it would, and then traveled on to someplace new.

"There?"

The hat nodded.

"You sure?"

The hat nodded again.

"What're you waitin for? A handwrit invitation?" Hez said this.

While the fat woman wobbled on her feet, the short man grabbed at the scarred man's arm and Hez wished he knew their names so he could stop thinking in terms of short and tall and scarred and fat.

"I'm goin," she said.

"Good. Go."

"I'm. Goin. In. There." Cathy was still speaking in a shout, her words parceled out as though issued to foreigners.

"Dear lord, you're an idiot."

"I want 'em to understand, is all. I aint gonna touch a thing."

He shrugged his right arm out through the sling and spun and caught his brother with the other. It was a move as fluid as that belonging to a football player. The fat lady opened her mouth, breathed out an audible "ahhhh."

"Shhh, now. Hush," Hez said, bouncing on his feet in an effort to comfort.

Yellababy howled.

Cathy, her hands over her ears, headed toward the blue house, where garbage blew in the wind and weeds scuttered along the walk. A man had died in this house. A dead man lay for days, right here in this house where I'm about to set my ass. A man turned stiff—

She slapped herself in the face. "Cut it out!" she hissed. "It's only a toilet."

Behind her she could hear the wailing, but she ignored it, afraid that if she turned to see what was happening, they would have shed their human disguises and turned to bloody vampires feasting on a pair of beating hearts.

*　*　*

They got no biznis in his house.
Prox wouldn't want it

Johnny Roper wrote the words and tapped on his board three times for emphasis. He looked across in anticipation and when Aaron kept still on it, he picked up his chalk and worked some more:

he aint dead but 2 years now, how come them to be in there?

Aaron stood watching the white words appear like magic in the heat. On some days the messages would seem like a song sung by kind strangers, worthy of notice. Not today. Today the chalk messages looked childish and offbeat. Aaron wrote:

How n hell should I know!

The chalk so small now it appeared as a dot inside the crease of his palm. Aaron looked over at Henry's. Heard the crying of the child from inside the four walls of the blue house. It was softer now and easier, like the little boy was plumb worn out over exercising his lungs. With a damp hand Aaron wiped away his message and stood listening, studying the dried-up grass at his feet. Blades of grass appeared as slender harbingers of events, if one but stopped to look. The rustle of the leaves in the trees percolated a huge container of knowledge if one would just stand still and listen. They had followed Rosie's lead and quit using their voices, just scribbled occasionally on those boards Johnny had salvaged from God knows where. It had seemed noble at first. Some type of fitting respect due the woman who had lost her only two kin in one swoop of death's hand. And then Aaron had grown comfortable doing it, allowed it to become attached to his daily living the way coffee becomes a necessary formula for starting the day. He wondered how it had burrowed in so, and then he shrugged the question away and looked to the west. Dark was coming on. Just a couple of hours now and the myriad shades of trees and humans would blend as one.

Turning, he left the chalkboard and went indoors. The cool musk of the place greeted him, welcomed him back into its cradle, and he took off his hat and slung it to a chair. A hat hung against the kitchen wall, near the back door. Another hat was placed on the floor near his bedroom window, in case there should be a fire. I live in a world full of hats, he thought. And aint that a pity.

He poured up a cup of cold coffee and reached for the last square of cornbread and bit into it. While he chewed he wondered how he had forgotten the world and its people. Those small screaming children. Aaron lifted the lid to the honey jar and dribbled a gold rope of it onto his bread and gazed dispassionately out the kitchen window. He saw the girl, a broom in her hand, begin to sweep the porch next door and he wondered what old Henry would think of this strange invasion. I wish I could talk to him, Aaron thought. Hear his voice again. What I wouldn't give to have him settin across from me, smellin of paint, ponderin the workins of the world. See if he'd explain it to me one more time.

Because the man had tried.

*   *   *

Years back, once the police realized they lacked the proper amount of evidence and Aaron had finally been released from police custody, Henry had been the one waiting to carry him home, his black Ford streaked from early afternoon rain. There were no words between them, just a thick silence that seemed attached to equally dense stretches of sere landscape. The crest of a hill, then. And to the north, too close to the road for comfort, sat the small white church with its large sprawl of a cemetery. Large sycamores shaded the whole region, the old dead, the freshly dead, the empty plots where dead were yet to be. Annie had been laid to rest there, in a far corner space set aside for the public poor, her baby placed in the casket with her, atop her stomach. The Methodist ladies shed a tear at this act of endearment. Henry said it had economy as its backbone. The mound of flowers was fading, the one standing floral spray, wilted, but visible from the car; Henry pointed it all out as they drove past; the information accentuating the span of quiet between them.

It seemed the empty fields had reproduced upon themselves, taken it to mind to multiply and expand their acreage. Aaron glanced once out the window of the car wondering how long they had been driving, for it seemed like hours. After what seem a decade, landmarks took on the façade of the familiar, and they were finally at home. Henry steered into his small driveway and shut off the engine. Aaron had stood in Henry's front yard, confused, hating the thought of going into his own dark house. Henry settled it, clasping Aaron by the arm and leading him up the steps to the blue house as though he were crippled, or felled by some near-lethal blow. Cold coffee was in a pot on the stove and Henry scuttled about, putting a fire under it, shrugging out of his coat, finally stopping to stare at Aaron, who was frozen in place in front of the window. The newspapers were there, stacked atop Henry's kitchen table. Cursing himself for being a fool, Henry had taken the topmost, the one with the biggest picture, and slid it under the rest, but had been too slow with it. Aaron had already seen what was there.

"Them bastards," Henry said. "Now you sit down and listen to me." Henry set a cup of lukewarm coffee in front of him and stirred in a teaspoon of sugar and the noise of spoon against cup sounded like the soft tinging of a silver bell. "Folks'll forgit about this, Aaron."

All Aaron was thinking was that they had taken his best hat. The one with the widest brim. Knocked it clean off my head when they put me in that police car.

"There werent even a grand jury called. They said she did it her own self and I believe it. If Annie was sad enough to keep that dead baby around, then she was surely sad enough to put a knife to her own throat. Here now. Drink this."

Aaron looked at him, felt an unfamiliar knot the size of Texas in his throat. There were questions he wanted to ask. The foremost being the whereabouts of his hat.

"Caint nobody come back at you with this. Nobody."

Aaron opened his mouth, but the words were trapped in some low wasteland. He looked out the window toward Rosie's instead.

Henry waited for a moment and then continued. "And don't you worry about her. Rosie's got her own grief. She aint mad. Not really. She don't fer a minute believe you was the one who done it. I think she knows now that Annie did it herself." Henry pushed his glasses up on his nose.

Who gives a shit, Aaron wanted to say. All I want is my hat.

They sat in the quiet evening, elbows leaning on the kitchen table. The soft ping of a spoon against a cup.

"I've tried my best to figure it out and it just beats the hell outta me evertime," Henry said. "They called us all in, you know. Not just you."

Aaron stared at him.

"I know what you're thinkin. Them bastards. The way they brung you in was rude."

Yeah, with my hands cuffed behind my back. In a car the reporters were keen on. Into a sea of flashin blue bulbs. I'd say that was more than a little rude.

"But I want you to understand somethin." Henry leaned forward in his chair. "This'll be over soon. Folks'll forgit. We're all friends here. They aint nobody blamin you."

The shadows had fallen across the room, hiding Aaron's face. Only Henry's was illuminated. There were large things that Aaron wanted to say, but the words had lost their merit. Outside, Johnny Roper poked along with a stick, doodled in the sand in a way that was grief-struck. Aaron was yet to see Rosie and he was glad. Having old Henry lead him by the hand like a child had been hard enough. Those fifty miles home, not a word between them.

Aaron watched the blue hydrangeas bobbing in the wind. Remembered how Rosie had chased him that time, lifted the hat off his head, issued him an invitation to be a part of life, such as it was. I guess it aint the same as before, he thought. Them days is over.

Henry cleared his throat and Aaron looked across at him. "I wish ye'd talk to me," he said. "I know this is a mighty hard blow and I reckon you got things bottled up inside that are nearly 'bout chokin you." Henry cocked his head and peered forward. The man seemed intent on discovering some secret embedded in the folds of the skin. "Talk to me, Aaron Class. Hell, scream if you want to. Lord knows you got enough reasons for it."

Aaron nodded, dazed. He opened his mouth and spoke his last words. "Where you reckon they put my hat," he said.

*　*　*

Yellababy was awake and appeared to be floating on his back down the river. With stiff spastic motions he positioned his arms above his head where pigmented clouds drifted atop plaster, and then he kicked his legs with futile, puppet movements that pounded irregular beats against the painted wooden water. Any minute he's gonna drown, Hezekiah thought, alarmed. He felt his throat lock up regardless of looking at wood and ceiling and out and out fakery.

Like some poor stranded turtle with belly cooking in the sun, his brother waved his arms and legs and screwed up his face and sent slobber down his chin, and then he did something Hezekiah had never seen him do before, something spectacular. He bucked up in one amazing feat that rolled him over to his stomach. Bowed again—a tiny boat, now, with rounded-out stomach—he rocked back and forth going *blaablablablaaa*. And then, miracles of all miracles, he opened his mouth and said *yeeel-laaa*.

"Holy shit, Hez. He said his name," Cathy said, so startled she dropped the broom she had been holding in her hand.

Hezekiah wanted to answer, but couldn't. The speaking of it would send it away, like so many other spoken words had sent things away. The wish for a bicycle. A Red Rider BB gun. A mother who didn't hit. He swallowed hard and listened, watching his brother rock and rock. Chin to floor, heels to the ceiling, then toes to the floor and chin up toward the light. It was too beautiful to see and Hez turned away, afraid it would disappear, silent for one of the first times in his life.

Cathy had worked hard at the dirt but the place was still a tomb in his opinion, since a man had died there, a dead man with a gift at paint. There must have been a shortage of money for canvas, though, seeing how he'd painted up every square inch of the place. Walls. Ceilings. Floors. Hez put his hands to his pockets, overcome. *There's the river and then there's The River.* He'd come in off a dirt road and walked straight into a dream. A place he'd seen only once, and been made speechless. Somehow this old dead painter had reached inside another's skull and pulled out a completed picture and it was too much. Too much.

The floor had been painted brownish-blue. With pebbles painted underneath water. Pebbles that looked authentic enough to pick up and toss or put in a slingshot and shoot. Painted rocks that looked too real to not be were scattered in different places, some the size of a hand, others as big as a cow. One rock in particular started on the floor and then climbed up the wall with a flatness to its surface that looked comfortable enough to sit on and fish; white water foamed and swirled along its base while small whiskered fish swam undisturbed among the water reeds, a look of confidence to them seeing how they'd never be within threat of hook, line or sinker. A yellow fishing lure was held fast by the root of a water oak. While he listened to his brother's new language Hez walked over and touched it, tried to pick it up before realizing that it, like everything else he was seeing, was the product of paint. The wall scenes were just as beautiful—all lush reed grass and cattails and huge water oaks that climbed up and across the ceiling. Another wall held cypress trees, hundreds of years old by the look of them. They retreated in well-behaved battalions along the pigmented waterway. Another wall: a savannah or marshland. Incredulously real. Cypress knees humped up wet around the mother trees in the foreground. Knees so real looking, Hez had almost mistaken one for a stool.

For a full minute he couldn't talk. And for a full minute after that he couldn't trust his mouth to say the right thing. He watched his brother's movements and the way he seemed to be swimming on top of water in this empty house nobody was living in. What if? he thought, a plan forming in his mind. It took some moments, too, the art of design a hard lesson to remember. Runnin water. Does it have it I wonder? And where might the fuse box be? Vagrants settled all over the world with little or no repercussions. Why not here in George County? Hez had been to visit reluctant relatives before; he knew the routine. You show up somewhere around noontime without a suitcase, maybe just a clean set a underwear stuck down in your pocket, and you hang around 'til dark and somebody offers you supper and you eat it and then they offer you a place to stay the night and you take it and once three or four days have passed, you're sitting out on the porch wondering whether or not to repaint the house. Relatives grew weary after two or three weeks, sometimes going so far as to pack up and leave themselves. All he saw around this place was a group that seemed too tired to move, much less order anyone off their road.

Hez looked out the door. The tall one with the messed-up face was sitting on his steps trying to still his shaking hands. Across the street, the old woman was sitting out on her porch, visibly trembling. "Seems to me they ought to call this place Shaketown, seeing how nobody caint hold their body parts still." But he said it low, like one would while standing among the dead in a cemetery, in an effort not to offend. He swallowed hard while behind him on the floor his brother blew bubbles of spit. The plan, like hope, was a scary thing to have.

Blue-gray shade stretched from Johnny Roper's porch all the way over to Henry Prox's steps in a long wobbly hammock shape that swayed in the wind. Night was directly behind him, just beyond the field now. Late day was closing shop. Four or fiveish, probably. He stood on his porch and looked through the opening into Henry's blue house across the way. Every now and again a form would move past and dependent on color and speed, it would be the boy or the girl. The child was floor-bound and helpless; no moving around for that one. Immobile as Annie's dead child, in Johnny Roper's opinion; all that was left for that crippled squatter was the formality of dying.

Stiff spastic child, he thought, his mouth fashioned in a hard line. Henry Prox had died of heart failure inside that very house and it seemed a sad thing that a trio of gypsies had elbowed in on his ghost.

That's what they had done, too.

The board outside Johnny's house testified to his worry. Inside of an hour he had written three things:

that aint there house
That AINT *there house!*
THAT AINT EVEN THERE HOUSE!

He felt like a small boy pissing in a hurricane.

Aaron refused to read the board.

Rosie was inside baking some sickening sweet thing.

The only one who saw the sin of it all was Johnny Roper.

He kicked at his porch post, imagining the child, the overly long shape of it, its too-large head, while he wondered how it got through life with little more to do than drool. At least Aaron Class had his roses to tend. Johnny looked across at the back of the man's yard. Saw the upstart of privit and mimosa. Wondered where the roses were. We are all in disrepair, he thought. All of us. Me the same as the others.

But least I aint no murderer, he thought with a small measure of satis-faction. At least I aint got the ghost of Annie Gentle whisperin in my ear. Oh, Annie. Jesus God, If I'd only told you. Warned you sooner. He watched Aaron walk out to the mailbox and peer inside and then walk back to his house. Johnny wished he had the guts to shoot him. No wonder the roses disappeared. No wonder atall.

He could almost hear the sounds of intelligent voices whispering in his ear. Git on with things, seemed to be their familiar chorus. Well, I caint, he thought. 'Cause there's the place it happened and here I am lookin at it. He surveyed the road, saw Rosie's busted rocking chair stationed on her porch, saw the wide expanse of garden behind Aaron Class's house and reminded himself of the day he had stood next to a flagstone path and delivered up the news that suddenly changed everything for all of them. A knife in the dirt. There it was. Aaron tossed it over his shoulder and it landed like a hot rock right beside my foot, stood upright in the ground, dangerous as a snake. All I had to do was leave it alone and walk back to my house and forget I ever seen it but I didn't. I had to pick it up and stare at it like it was some gift just dropped down from heaven before puttin it in my back pocket and walkin away.

It was not that Johnny Roper had not tried to get rid of it.

He had.

He'd gone so far as to dig at night while the rest of the street slept and then, once the digging was done, he'd put the knife down into the dark, wet, loamy hole, and then covered the whole business over with a pile of mulch that looked like it had been there for years. Prox, with a voice like an owl, had called out from his front porch, What in hell you diggin at night for Johnny? What you doing out there?

The durn fool thought it was funny.

Laughed his fat ass off over it.

I wish I'd asked him what he was out and about for; how come him to be wide awake at two in the mornin.

Johnny had forgotten that Prox had painted himself into a corner, or rather, onto the front porch where he was living temporarily out under the stars while he waited for his floor to dry.

I should a never picked up that knife Aaron throwed. I should a left it there where it was at, down in the dirt, and harmless.

But no, he had picked it up and buried it underneath some leaves, fully intending to find that troublemaking preacher and kill him with it. The problem was, by the time it came for the killing, he'd forgotten the location of the hole. He reasoned he'd been so nervous the night before when he'd heard Henry Prox call out that he'd plum forgot where he was.

The next morning he had paced off the distance from his back porch and counted out the steps, but when he finally found the pile of mulch and dug down deep, the knife wasn't there. At first he thought he had dreamed the whole knife-burying incident the same way a person will dream they've won a thousand dollars and wake up so complete in the dream they've already got their shopping list made up. Plagued by it, he had run to his back porch and rummaged through his laundry and found the jeans with the dirty knees and his boots by the washer, mud-caked, same as he remembered. He'd dug all right, he was sure of it. But some black-hearted bastard must have waited 'til he was done with the digging and dug right after him, helped himself to something that didn't belong to neither one of them: Aaron's rose-pruning Buck knife.

Johnny had dug four more holes the next night, not because he still wanted to kill the preacher, that blazing instant of anger had passed, but because he was beginning to question his sanity.

Playing back the events of the week helped.

At least to a degree.

He remembered how he'd gone over to Aaron's to tell him the baby was dead and how Aaron had been around back puttering in that garden of his. And Aaron had sworn at him once he heard the bad news and then tossed his spade into the wall where it bounced down and broke some pots. And then, right before Aaron walked away, he had taken his pruning knife and tossed it over his shoulder where it landed not two inches from Johnny Roper's newly grown-out leg.

I picked it up and brushed it off and put it in my back pocket. I just know I did.

Aaron's knife turned up, days later, buried in the neck of Annie Gentle.

Unable to settle it or make heads nor tails of it, Johnny tried to put it away and forget it but it was like a broken arm that grows back a knob along the break that each and every time you use it, stands as reminder. So, knobbed, but hazy on it, he lived with it, or at least tried to.

Then there was the day three years back that it began to act up again.

Ache almost.

He even went so far as to put his evaluations down to paper, which he later burned in his kitchen sink. He rinsed the ashes down, at peace finally, realizing it was crazy old Henry Prox who had done it.

It couldn't be nobody *but* Prox who had killed her. Aaron couldn't have done it seeing how he didn't have the knife that had done the slaying in his possession and seeing how he werent even around at the time of the death, but down the road, fixing his broke-down truck. Besides, only Henry Prox had seen Johnny digging that night and yelled out to him. It had to be Henry. Couldn't be nobody else.

Knowing this, Johnny had given the man a decent enough chance to repent of it. Prox was already sick to dying with the heart disease (a righteous punishment, in Johnny's opinion; more proof of guilt) and Johnny had watched his steps get slower and slower and counted down those days 'til Judgment Day. They all knew it was just a matter of time. Only they, like every other human being, thought the time they were thinking on was a little more in the future. All of them, except Johnny, who'd never known time to do but one thing: stab him in the back as regular as a heartbeat.

But I aint waitin on this, he had told himself one morning. A man's eternal destination depends on it.

With this in mind he headed over to talk to Henry Prox.

He found him stretched out in the middle of his river, propped up on a boat he'd converted to a couch, looking up at the ceiling as though angels were winking at him. There was no way Johnny could drag in the chalk-board, but he had a yellow legal pad that was just as good.

"Well come on in," Prox said, holding a glass of iced tea. " 'Scuse me for not gettin to my feet."

I know you done it, Johnny Roper had written; he extended the pad to Henry Prox, who read it quietly while Johnny put his hands deep in his pockets, nervous at the sight of so much make-believe wet and all those hunched-up cypress trees along the wall, as well as the fact that Henry Prox was the only one on the street who had kept on talking.

He slung back the pad, "Lord God I wish you'd cut out this happy crap and talk like a man!" He looked up at Roper, "What's this thing you're so sure I done?"

You kilt Annie, Roper wrote, moving closer so he could just show him what was written and he could answer in quick order.

"If you aint a day late and a dollar short with just about everthing your hand touches I don't know who is."

Johnny Roper scribbled again. *Then you admit it.*
"No. That's not what I'm sayin. All I'm admittin is how dog-stupid you are. My God, Johnny, you wait three years to come and flesh this thing out with me? What kind a coward are you, anyhow?"

I aint a cowart. You did it.

Prox shook his head, "And how'd you meet up with this sureness?"

This time it took a while: *You seen me dig that night and hollered at me and then once I was gone you come over and dug it up and sent that knife strait into her throat.*

He handed the pad to Prox, who took his own sweet time with it. Then, once he had folded over to a new page so Johnny would have more room, he said, "Well aint you somethin. Here I was all propped up ready to study my ceilin 'cause there aint a thing in the world I could think of better than a ceilin to study and you wander over tellin me somethin I aint got a clue of. Thank you, Johnny. Now I got somethin else to study beside that there watermark. Somethin a whole lot more interestin."

Johnny Roper wrote so hard he tore through paper: *You hollereed at me.* He held up the pad.

"I've hollered at everbody on the street at one time or the other. I don't even remember that night—"

You was on the porch!

Prox studied the man, the trembling terrier look to him; played back the years while he tried to remember an event that would have sent him sleeping outdoors at night. Then he recalled how he had wanted to walk on water like the good blinking Jesus.

"Oh, the floor."

Prox chuckled and then he looked at his watch, tapped it with a yellowing fingernail.

"And so three years later you come over to talk about it. Well I be go to hell."

You seen me bury it. You yelt at me over it! Roper's hand was cramped; knotted up to a claw.

"Well I guess so. How in the world did you end up with that Buck knife in the first place?" Prox struggled to sit up and was worn out with the effort.

That dont matter now what matters is that you dug it up and you kilt her with it

Prox read the message, then tossed the pad to the floor where it clattered. "Oh for Christsakes."

Johnny Roper picked it up and worked at it. Once he was done, he laid it to the man's stomach like a rose on a corpse and walked out the door. What he had written was this: *You need to repent before you die and go to hell—thats all Im over here to say*

Henry never did reply, or repent, as far as Johnny Roper could tell. The man died three weeks later, during the night, with remarkable ease for such a talented murderer.

Johnny Roper never understood any of it.

*   *   *

He watched Rosie drinking lemonade out on her front porch. The ice made music sounds when she tilted her glass and the sound seemed at once innocent and pure, in direct contrast to where it was ice came from.

Of course, the woman had a new icebox now, a different one. The old one had been hauled off to the dump and left there, and Johnny supposed it was fully rusted and strangled by kudzu these days, perhaps filled with other debris tossed out the back of a truck.

He and Henry Prox had seen to its removal while Rosie dealt with Annie's bedroom. Dragging the durn wooden bed out to the middle of the street by her own self, and then setting fire to it. Red and blue flames curled up the maple spools like giant candles. Blazing and burning like there was no tomorrow against a mattress stained red-brown. The sheets and spread had been taken as evidence and never made a reappearance as far as Johnny Roper knew. But the mattress was theirs to deal with. Those outraged coils glowing blue hot. The wood disappearing to char. All proof of itself disappearing but for those metal springs any fool could a told her wouldn't burn. They lay in the street for a week and got doused by rain and began to rust before he went out at midnight and dragged them away to the dump.

And as if that had not been enough . . .

There was a whole list of things to which Johnny Roper could say, As if that had not been enough.

As if dropping that dead baby and watching it roll like a log under the table had not been enough.

As if walking into Annie's bedroom and seeing that knife and where it was stuck had not been enough.

As if that humiliating trip to the police station over in Hattiesburg had not been enough.

As if the whole street, or what there was left of it, knowing he'd cried like a baby had not been enough.

After he'd come back from the dumping of those leftover angry bedsprings *as if that had not been enough* he'd seen the huge glaring pile of ashen gray sitting in the center of the street. Enough ash for four or five sturdy bed frames, or so it seemed. Cinereous furnace sludge that failed to disappear, but stood as a reminder of what had seeped down onto that wood before it had burned. Johnny worked most of the night dealing with it. Carting it behind the house to the very spot where Annie used to stand and look for a shadow: her own back field. Three trips it took, three trips of cautious walking because, like an idiot, he still had the lift attached to his shoe and he'd not had the presence of mind to realize that the only one he was trying to impress with a miracle was dead as dirt.

"I wish to God I'd killed that preacher when I had me a chance. I wish I'd not been so foolish to believe in the overwhelmin bounty of the Lord."

He was talking again, at least to himself, and the voice sounded flat and empty.

He watched the street. Saw the boy, the way he'd located a rake and was working at the yard as though he'd found a new vocation. And the girl with the ponytail, the way she'd come out to the porch and then go back inside to where that crippled up child was drooling. And Aaron, who was sitting in the deep shade of his house, but supervising it all, his butt stationed on his front steps. While Johnny watched, Aaron would make vague gestures with his hands toward Hezekiah; turning basic nigger yard work into a scientific experiment, apparently.

Johnny Roper sat down on his made-to-order shortened chair and stretched out his legs.

"Never asked a single person for a durn thing in all my life. Not a durn thing," he said out loud.

Rosie came out to the center of her yard and pulled her chalk out of an apron pocket:

I'm bakin a cake johnny, should you want some

With a stride like that of a proud circus elephant she lumbered up her steps.

Annie brung me a piece a cake once, he thought. Stood over there in that very yard and held out the plate and wondered why me and Aaron werent huddled next to God inside at the prayer meetin. I ate that cake, too. I surely did. I aint eatin yours Rosie. I'll pass on that. I aint wantin a durn thing no more. Least of all from you.

CHAPTER 39

Fairy eased up the long drive in Julia's truck and stopped it in the shade of a sassafras tree and took one long look at the man's place and wanted to puke. He felt the bile swimming up from the lower vestiges of his corrupted gut where an obscene heat seemed to be exploding. Steady now, he thought. I still got work to do and then you can have me, he said to himself, trying to quiet his breathing. The man's house sat far enough back from the road that high female screams would have gone unnoticed and that was what Fairy was imagining. High screams, not of pain, or disappointment, or outrage, but of that very thing he'd lived his whole life to hear, but hadn't: passion.

The yard had little to say about fornication, though, what with its manicured and neat lawns, hedge bricks and good-smelling mulch. A picture postcard welcoming all to good clean Christian living was how it presented itself. There was a chert drive that fed into a double carport where a real barbeque grill sat. The windows had metal scalloped awnings over them and (I'll be go to hell) the man even had himself a durn window air-conditioner. Fairy shook his head, thinking, No way this could be the house belonging to a man who would put his hands, more than once, inside those private crevices of a female. He wanted to scream. That he, Eulis Farris Sheehand, was forced to sit in his sister-in-law's truck and see the place was like being flogged by a choirboy in front of the barbershop.

"Okay, now," Julia said. "She may not even be here. The place looks empty." Julia looked at her watch. They had roamed the countryside, gone down far too many dirt roads before coming on this place. Autumn Road was as long as the season apparently, with offshoots that wound through East Jesus before finally meeting the highway again.

"It's a quiet house, Fairy. Real quiet." There was no sign of Arena.

"This is the place, though."

She looked at him and shrugged, studying the yard. "Maybe," she said. It had that exotic foreign look about it. A look sure to attract a girl who was intoxicated by small luxuries: fertilizer that came packaged in a bag instead of being scooped out of a pig yard; real concrete steps; screening against the bugs.

"What does this man do anyhow?"

"The hell do I know?" she said. "Susan-Blair seems to think he works for the school board. Caint be sure of it, though." Her truck rumbled and she could see that shimmery wave of heat coming up off the hood. Behind them a low wall of sumac and blackberry briars combined in a thick wall and she realized they were hemmed in and protected completely from prying eyes or nosy neighbors.

"If he works any kind a regular work, sissy office work or such, anything other than farmin, he'll be shut of the place by five at the latest," Fairy said, calculating the hours. "He could work as far away as Hattiesburg, which I doubt, and still be here inside the next hour."

"We don't need a confrontation here."

"Oh yes we do." He put his hand to his chest and felt the pounding. "I think a confrontation is exactly what we need. There's a whole list of things we ought to confront. One. How'd he ever come to meet my daughter in the first place. Two. What in hell he's been doin with her, now that they've met." He looked at Julia. "And three. How he's gonna feel once he gits his neck broke for raping a teenager. If you aint got the stomach for it, just loan me your truck."

"Do I look like a fool?"

She wanted to say that "rape" was the wrong word to use for such a victim as Arena, but she didn't. His face wouldn't let her. She said this instead: "Only a fool would loan you their truck."

"And I guess you aint a fool." He studied her thinking, Fact is she looks like she knows exactly what I'm plannin to do. He pulled into the drive and then reversed and headed out toward the road. The drive was nearly a half-mile long, dirt, headed in on either side by thick trees, almost invisible in his opinion.

"There's a crossroads where we can sit and wait. Soon as I see a car that looks halfway offishal, I'll pull in and check it out. Arena's hidin from me. I feel it. She knows this is your truck too, which would make her hide all the longer."

"Fairy, we don't even know if this is the place, or that she's there."

"Oh I know it. I know it sure as I know my own name."

*   *   *

Marion Calhoun drove his tractor into the barn, reached down and pulled the compression hook and allowed the machine to die. It shuddered in denial, same as it always did, but he knew it would be still finally; still as the dead but for the ticking and cooling of its diesel engine. While he listened to the sound, he collected himself against the night.

The barn was the same as it had always been.

The corner holding a stool.

The workbench holding cans of diesel and old batteries and spark plugs for his truck.

Leather harnesses hanging from the wall.

Evening was the best. It always had been. Dust motes drifted stunned inside the sweep of suspended air. Light filtered down, unaffected by the smells of hay and oil and mouse dung. The barn seemed a final memoriam of the day; the ending of it; offering last-minute clarity for oncoming night with its opaque shadows and blindness. He took one last look and pulled the door shut behind him with a heavy thud and headed to his truck to go and look for Hezekiah.

Susan-Blair had turned on the lights in her living room and what with the clothes hanging on rods, it appeared she was entertaining a party of fifty. He could hear the breathless spittled speech of a radio preacher thundering on about hell and damnation and he thought to himself, Now aint that a strange one to have at a party. Cranking his truck, the last he saw of his place that night was the silhouette of the woman in her doorway: frozen, inert, near-worthless.

A few minutes later he looked at his watch. Five-thirty. Marion tapped at it with a long brown finger and watched the minute hand sweep forward two paces. "I'm slow. Losing time somewhere," the sound of his own voice irritating him. He thought on it: how he'd lived alone for so long a time that the very sound of his own black voice had begun to make his skin crawl. Her voice sure hadn't. I guess I could listen to that one sing for the next ten thousand years and not grow sick of it—

And then he stopped. Reality slapping him in the face so hard he almost swerved off the road.

"Well I be damned," he said and began to laugh, soft at first and then harder and harder. "Well I be goddamn!"

He didn't miss her. In fact he was suddenly glad that all he had to do every single day was get on his tractor and go to work. That all he had to do was pour his sweat into the ground instead of onto a woman. His parts had reunited, was how it felt. Like those pieces of himself that had separated off from soundness and headed for ruination had suddenly come back home to roost. "Well I be go to hell—!"

Now he could think on that extra land of his he had to cut in for the cotton. That land Susan-Blair had agreed he could farm out. Marion could plan out his rows, now that he was done with that coffee-colored woman. Plan out his season and the planting and the slight variations his hand would employ while it steered the tractor. Where he'd swerve ever so slightly to get just the right move to it, just the right melody. A man could alter the very state of eternal ground by what he planted. And then once that seed is dropped, a man can sit back and watch the landscape change, day to day. To watch those rows disappear and drape over a small hill and then swim up to meet you again once you topped the breast of the mound was the museum of the farmer, the museum and the church as well as the marriage bed. It was all a man needed if that man were not too ambitious, or too romantic or—

The lights, even though they were flashing, had come up behind him unnoticed. By the time he saw those turning globes and heard the spiraling scream of the siren, it was almost too late. He had to swerve over into loose sand to avoid being struck by the black-and-white police car speeding up the county road.

CHAPTER 40

Hezekiah Sheehand found the ramshackle pump house out by the side of the dead man's place and bent to it, wondering how he had taken running water for granted these sixteen years. Tall weeds grew all around and Hez poked at them with a rake handle, leery of snakes. Seeing none, he went to the door and pulled and fell to his ass when the durn thing came off in his hands.

"Two bucks," a voice said.

Hez looked to the side and saw the man sitting in the shade, one hand leaning on the smooth surface of his steps. "What'd you say?"

"I figure you owe two bucks for breakin somethin that aint yours."

"Well shit then."

"Ye got to have the power on to make it work anyhow. And the power aint on," the man said, his voice feathery and hesitant, as though his mind was mistrustful of vowels and their placement.

The sun moved an infinitesimal increment and sent its light through the trees where it hit the man. It lit him up as though he were on stage, those rusty words delivered up in perfect timing.

Hez sat, his arms circling his knees, and peered inside the darkened room where the pump lived. The tank rose silver-jaundiced and old, speckles of green mildew topped it and it seemed more a cylindrical gnome than a tank for water storage. There were other things, too.

"What are all them paint cans for?"

"The man never throwed nothin away."

"If you don't mind me askin, who owns this house now?" Hezekiah said. If squatting was not an option maybe they would let him pay a small rent to stay there. He had fifteen dollars stowed away and not much chance of more coming in. But it was a start.

The man stood and looked around and then pulled his hat down lower on his face. It was an old habit that was hard to break, this affection for hats. He could see Johnny Roper standing, his back to a porch wall, watching him with killer eyes. With that in mind, Aaron pulled off his hat and set it on the topmost step, its brim covering the bronze crescent moon, but not the camel. He swept a hand through his thinning hair and took a step toward Hezekiah.

"I reckon we all own it," he said.

"How in the world can everbody own somethin?" Hez had been fighting with Arena over ownership of beat-up toys for as long as he could remember.

"Henry left it to all of us. Caint none of us sell it without getting the others' approval. We aint never agreed on much around here. Don't seem likely we will anytime soon."

Hezekiah stood to his feet and brushed off his pants and looked around. He had put Yellababy on the strange boat made into a couch and placed a couple of ratty pillows on the floor, should he fall. His brother was sleeping.

"Henry was a good man. I aint never regretted knowin him," Aaron said. "What made you think you could just walk inside and make yourself at home?"

Hezekiah looked at him. The man wasn't questioning in a hard way, just a curious way. "My brother was tired is all. And there werent no door on the place."

"How old are you?"

"You aint with the board a education are you?"

The man laughed and it had a rusty sound to it, but it was still a laugh. "Nope. I sure aint with them. Why?"

"Well, my nigger neighbor said the truant man come looking for me yesterday. I caint figure it out neither, 'cause I'm certain I got at least two days left..." He thought for a minute and then decided his plan to squat was dependent on trust. "My name's Hezekiah Sheehand and I'm sixteen."

"How old's that little one you was luggin around?"

"He's my brother and he's five."

Aaron looked across the street at Rosie and thought, Well I be damned. The woman was sitting patiently on her porch in that busted-up chair of hers, holding a cake on her lap. He moved one step forward, following the sun, which lit his scars to a blazing crimson.

Hez remembered himself and didn't step back, but he sure wanted to.

"Seems Rosie over there baked you two a cake."

"A cake?"

"Yep. She had a dream last night that she thinks was about you and your brother comin to see her."

"I don't believe in dreams," Hezekiah said. "I believe in nightmares, but not dreams."

"Yes, well," Aaron said. He believed in those, too. He looked over the fence at the yard. At all that splattered blue paint bathing the base of Henry's tree. "My name's Aaron. Aaron Class. I'll git my hose and help you prime that pump once we turn the breaker on. We'll work out how you're gonna pay for that pump house door later."

"I'd be much obliged, Aaron," Hez answered, hope raging through his heart like a river.

An hour later Hezekiah Sheehand stood, one hand on the low-riding chicken-wire fence, the other in his pocket. He felt swept up into the air with emotion, borne-up as one resting cautious inside strong arms that felt good, but couldn't yet be trusted. Like a weak bird, or an autumn leaf, or anything else that thinks it's not ready to let go but has no choice, he stood there and trembled. He looked up and down the street. Four houses. He could see his reflection frozen into the window of the one directly across from him. His hand was to the fence. His legs were spread. His head was lifted and he was beginning to harbor strange thoughts, foreign to his nature. Maybe darkness is not forever, was one of them. Maybe there's somethin out there that is bigger than darkness, was another. Maybe this place is like that, was the last. He ran a hand under his nose and wiped it on his pants and watched his reflection across the way do the same.

The short man across the street, the one named Johnny Roper, was hiding behind a living room curtain. The cloth would move every once in a while and Hezekiah's reflection would dance. Hezekiah watched the effort at spying and sighed. The other two had had an easier time of jumping over that broom: Rosie doing her part by pulling a Betty Crocker inside that kitchen of hers; Aaron sticking his nose into it when the door to the pump house had come off in Hezekiah's hand.

Cathy was gone on home. Her and her pretty ponytail and tacky green shorts. Before she'd gone, she and old fat Rosie, who seemed uncommonly interested in his brother, had bathed Yellababy. Hezekiah felt free to let them, knowing that if Cathy dared comment on the little boy's large privates, Rosie would shame her for it. They washed his hair with soap, powdered him and put him into fresh clothes that Rosie had pulled out of some box. Clothes that looked suspiciously like girl jeans and a shirt that had its buttons on the wrong side, but they were clean and dry and his for the time being. The diapers had been washed out (Cathy had done this) and were out on a line behind the house. Hezekiah knowing that Cathy had probably opened her mouth about Yellababy's dick at some point during bath time and the washing out of something shitty had been her punishment from Rosie.

Before she left she had walked up to him and touched him on the back and said, "How long you gonna stay here anyhow?"

He looked at her, at all those freckles, and that strong pretty neck and ponytail falling down.

"I don't know." He looked at the house next door to him where the man named Aaron lived, and wondered at the color of it: eggplant.

"Shit. I wish she'd go back to writin on that board of hers," Cathy said, rubbing her nose. "Talked a blue streak to me about what's proper. It aint proper wearing them shorts young lady. It aint proper starin at a naked little boy young lady. Swatted my hand once, even."

"She made you wash them shitty diapers, didn't she?"

"She aint so bad I guess." Cathy smiled and stuck her hands in the pockets of her shorts. "Wants to call him somethin other than Yellababy, though. Says he needs a real little boy name and not a slang." She raised her eyebrows. "She's in there rockin him. Or at least tryin to. The chair's busted so she's just usin her big old body. He's sleeping."

She paused and it felt like a long pause.

"I'd like to come back and see you. If that's okay," she said. She took her hands out of her pockets and pressed down on the fencing, making a boat-shape to it. "I know you got yourself a girlfriend and all. That aint what I'm tryin to be . . . I just meant that I'd like to come back sometime."

"Okay," he said. "I don't know if I'll be here. But if I am, I guess I'd like a visit." Hezekiah turned to her. "Teresa Beth don't even know she's my girlfriend. Besides, I'm almost sure she's Eyetalian." He took her hand off the fencing and held it, not as a sentimental mushy act, but to keep her from messing up the fence. "I want you to not git in trouble with that Uncle Jimmy of yours. I want you to do what you got to to keep that truant man away from you."

"You don't go to school."

"I went some. Not enough, I guess."

There was a silence then while they looked at the chalkboards, weathered and gray, barely black anymore.

"I'm goin now. Don't let Rosie take over, you hear? She's the kind that might."

"She'll be all right." He didn't add that anything would be better than what he'd seen.

"Well, good-bye then. I'm gonna walk straight this time, but I'd be willing to bet I could cut across that back field and cut my distance in half."

And she left, hair swinging, hands brushing up off her neck while she walked down the road. Right before she left the street she pulled her hair loose out of the ponytail and it swung down to her shoulders, so shiny it looked like gold.

"I'll see you around sometime!" she yelled, and then she was gone.

Hezekiah waved, saying to himself while he watched her shiny hair,

She aint no dummy. That one there knows exactly what she's doin. He grinned. And by God, they aint no way she'll not get kissed.

Wind picked up a little and scattered the leaves near his feet while his reflection traveled another inch or so down the window pane in the house across the street. The sun was behind him, elongating his shadow, eclipsing the chalkboard in front of the house. He heard steps behind him and turned and saw the old woman, Rosie, coming toward him, her yellow hair made even yellower by the sun, her lined fleshy face calm and peaceful. She swayed side to side on top of rubber flip-flops mismatched in color. Hez noticed her toenails were thick-crusty and just as yellow as her hair, but clean.

"Always used to love this time a day," she whispered. "It'd be right about now that Annie would be belly-achin about helpin me with supper."

Hezekiah didn't know who Annie was, but he knew that she had been important to the people on the road, so he just looked at Rosie and held his peace.

"That baby's got bad bruises," she said.

"It werent me who done it," he said in a small voice, grabbing the fence and squeezing the wire.

"Lord. I know that." She pulled out a hanky and blew her nose. "His arm's been broke once and set crooked. Burn marks healed over in places on his legs."

"Shut up," Hezekiah said, ashamed, his head down and his eyes shut.

"What kind a life you lived, Hez?"

He kept silent on it.

"You love that boy. I'm smart enough to see that for myself."

"Yes," he said.

"I aint gonna chase you off with a stick should you wanna stay a while."

"I got a nigger neighbor who'd miss me," Hezekiah said, somewhat confused on how she'd known he had considered staying put. "Mayurn aint got nobody to talk to except me."

"I reckon that's somethin to consider. Talk's important to some folks. Not as important as a broke arm. But still important."

"How come you to offer this anyhow? You don't even know me."

"I know that." She sighed and folded her arms across her big chest.

"Did Cathy tell you something about me?" He couldn't imagine what she might have said, seeing how she didn't know shit about him or anything else.

"That gal? Why, no." Rosie took the hanky out of her dress again and wound it around her finger. Her speech was a little louder than before; not quite the whisper it had started out being. "The baby's sleepin quiet, breathin good. I got him back there on the bed with pillows all around. There's a pot of limas to the stove, bubblin. Henry Prox may not have believed in much, but he believed in lima beans. Kept himself a stock of them. They need to cook for a couple a hours yet." She looked at him, at the bewilderment on his face. "Boy, the girl didn't say nere a word. You didn't neither."

"How then?"

"Caint say that I know how I know. I just know. I recognize certain things. I guess in any other part of the county this would seem a strange thing, but here—" and then she stopped and shrugged.

He seemed to know what she meant.

The five o'clock sun burst through the trees behind them, illuminating their reflections in Johnny Roper's windows. The brambled-up yard and the weed-riddled remains of grass brightening momentarily with the setting sun, which seemed a strange thing. He looked over at her message about the angels.

"Tell me about your angel dream," Hezekiah said, his voice stronger.

After a moment of preparatory silence, Rosie did.

CHAPTER

The sorry business (or maybe it was the lucky business) had fallen to the very same detective, and he could not believe it.

Big-necked and barrel-chested, wearing that same narrow necktie and white shirt that started each day clean but finally just gave up around noon-time and took its punishment same as all the other white shirts that ended up stained and yellow, he leaned back against the seat and buried one fat finger up to the knuckle, in his ear. Two weeks 'til retirement and he had been handed a top-notch story to go out on. He scratched long and hard and thought that digging in the ear was as good-feeling as scratching out one's balls at the end of the day.

"What'd the woman say?" he asked, wondering if he'd get home in time for dinner, hoping his wife had got herself out of the house long enough to buy him that pork chop he'd asked for.

"Which woman?" his partner asked.

"The one who called it in. How many gals are involved in it for Christsakes?"

"Three." The young, wide-eyed partner was driving and couldn't look at the list he'd written down in his notebook. "Caint say I know which one I was talkin to, though."

"Well what'd the one you *was* talkin to say? Think you can remember that?"

"Said some fool took a face off with a horse tool. A hoof rasp, to be exact."

"Hell, I thought I'd seen it all."

"Looks like you get to see a little bit more before you die."

The older one watched him swerve to avoid hitting a truck meandering its slow-ass self down the dirt road.

"You almost run that nigger down," he said, craning his fat neck to see.

"I asked you."

"You asked me what?"

"Not to."

"Oh, excuse me—*Neegro*." He gave a loud snort, looking over at the younger one. "It don't pay to have high ideals in Mississippi," he said. "Didn't realize you was such a libertine."

The younger one drove on in grim, tolerant silence.

Satisfied he'd made his point, working the other ear now with the other meaty finger, the older one continued. "Autumn Road runs along the river, I think. Just this side a Agricola you'll get to it. I come out this way once before. Dirt roads goin nowhere fast. Nearly had the bejesus scared out a me, too."

The younger one sighed, his signal that he'd heard the story a thousand times and didn't want to hear it again. The fatter, older one knew it too, but didn't give a rat's good ass. A story was a story. True, it werent *From Here to Eternity*, but it was still good. "After what I seen, I'd sure hoped not to be out this way again, I tell you." They never had solved Annie Gentle's murder. Oh, they pretended it was a suicide and wrote it off as such, but he had practiced on a watermelon, a cantaloupe, as well as a slab of Wisconsin cheese his sister had brought back from a trip north, and he knew there was no way in hell that gal put that knife to her own throat and cut. "Between that and the infant we found it was the worse thing I ever seen."

"Hmmm."

"You bet it was." He pulled out a cigar and lit it. Threw the match out the window. " 'Course this horse-rasp killin might just beat the dead baby in the fridge, though. Might just get rid of it once for all."

"We can hope."

"Yessiree, we sure can hope."

*   *   *

When Fairy had first turned the truck around and headed away from the man's house, Julia had relaxed and stretched out her legs along the floorboard of the truck and wished for a cigarette. She thought she knew his limitations and what he was going to do next, thought that now that he'd made that initial obligatory grasp toward the responsibilities of fatherhood he'd be willing to sit back and wait, maybe relax a little bit, maybe even reevaluate his position; realize that trying to stop his daughter from doing what she was doing would be like attempting to plug a leaking dam with a forefinger. Arena was doomed (or maybe "doomed" was the wrong word, destined then) to be female and because she was female and destined, this thing that she was doing was just the first of it, just an indicator. If Fairy really was foolish enough to want to stop her from climbing out windows or walking broadly out the front door, he would have to physically attach himself to her with something stronger than steel. Believing he'd come to this conclusion had been Julia's first mistake. Julia's second mistake happened when she climbed out of the truck and left him alone while she walked fifty feet to the corner store to buy herself a pack of those cigarettes she was wishing for. This gave him the minutes he'd needed to rummage through her farrier tools in the back of the truck and slip what he'd found underneath the truck seat.

"Holy Christ," Julia said. Police lights spun up and down the dirt road, lighting up the man's boxwoods in perverse Christmas colors.

She sat down exhausted on the front steps; the only place where there wasn't a pool of blood, and studied Silva. The woman wasn't as good-looking as Susan-Blair had been at one time, but she certainly looked a helluva lot smarter. Standing there in her neat black pants and white shirt, her gray-streaked hair pulled back from her face, her arms crossed over her chest, she leaned against the car she and the man had driven up in. She'd been the one to make the first phone call, Julia had to give her that much. She'd also been the one to comfort Fairy, of all things.

An ambulance was pulling up the long drive. Julia could see a new wave of red washing through the trees alongside the road, announcing it.

The body was out on the lawn, covered in a sheet; Arena stood inside the screen porch, shaking. Julia could hear her teeth chattering behind her. She didn't know where the girl's shoes were, and it was a pitiful sight: the way she was wearing those white socks dirty on their bottoms with stepped-in blood. Julia looked over the yard, the flash of ambulance and police red blending to chorus itself with a crimson sun. An outraged color, really: red. Nothing like it in the world. Out on freshly cut St. Augustine grass, Fairy squatted by the walkway, his hand coated in blood. Just saying over and over again, "Kilt me two birds with one stone. Well, I be go to hell. Kilt me two birds with one stone. Well I'll be go to hell."

Silva said, "Shut up Fairy," and then put her hand to his head and left it there, those long fingers of hers tender in their ministration in spite of the fact that the head she rested those fingers on belonged to the man who had just killed her fiancé.

"If you don't mind I need to go over it one more time."

At least this one was polite. The old fat one had been rude as hell.

"We were waitin..." (Julia wanted to kick herself—"waiting" sounded premeditative). "What I mean is, we were lookin for Arena, his daughter," she nodded with her head to Fairy, who was in handcuffs. Silva was standing quietly, sadly, to the side of the house, a look of stunned disbelief on her face. Julia continued, "Arena, that's the daughter's name, run off this mornin and her mother, my sister, that one there's wife, told me about it. Told him, too, I guess." She thought for a minute. "He wanted me to help find him. I mean her. Find her. His daughter."

Lord, witness one brutal murder and you turn into a blubberin idiot, was her thought. She pulled in a deep breath. "Anyhow, we heard she might be out this way."

"Who told you this?"

"Somebody."

"Who?"

She lowered her voice, "Look mister, everbody in town knew about Arena. Everbody knew it—"

"How do you know this?"

Julia summed him up: attentive, but wet behind the ears. "Just open up your eyes and look at her. My God! It don't take much to figure it out. You never lived in a small town before, have you? Never had to sit on a dirt road and count the cows for entertainment. I bet you even went to college." She lit her cigarette, her hand shaking. "Of course you went to college. Everbody goes to college these days, don't they?" He was watching her with puzzled eyes and she gave up her discourse. "Rumors, okay? Just look at her. What else is she goin to do with her time? Read a book?"

He turned and looked at the girl. She was standing next to her father now, her hands to the pocket of her dress. A dated dress, too. One that looked like it had belonged to his mother's era. Of indeterminate height, seeing how she was leaning, he guessed her to be possibly five foot seven with a full pouty look to her face. Blond hair pulled back. Good shape to her. But too heavy for him. He liked his women thin; thin and older.

"Yes. Well she seems awful young," he said. "And shoeless."

"Young or no, everbody was talkin about it. We just didn't have the name of the one . . . the name of the man who . . . the one who got—"

"Killed."

"Yes. Killed. Thank you." She tilted her head into her cigarette and waited a moment. "How the poor fool managed to be datin Fairy's ex-wife is still a mystery."

"Wait a minute," he said.

"You didn't know? This'll be a hot story for you for years. Your grand-kids will end up tellin this one."

"So," he looked at his notebook, "Silva Garand is Fairy Sheehand's ex-wife, as well as the victim's intended? She drove up and found the body?"

"No, she drove up before it was a body. He was still livin and breathin and lyin, too, I might add. At least he was lyin at first, as well as denyin and swearin by everything there was to swear to, that Fairy had the wrong man. And Silva, too. Silva was denying it all, same as him. The man wasn't even worried, that's how inconsequential the girl was to him. Wasn't even worried. The two of them just stood there actin like they didn't know heads nor tails about what Fairy was saying. And God's truth, maybe Silva didn't. It seemed that she didn't, at least for a few minutes there, and then she started staring and lookin at Fairy with her mouth opened up a little. Like maybe what he was sayin had a slight ring of truth to it. That was before it all started. There was still time then. Still time I tell you."

She hushed, and waited.

He continued, "Did the victim threaten Mr. Sheehand in any way?"

"No," she said. "Unless you count what Fairy was seein as the actual threat. The man was so tall, you see. So business-like and professional. Standing out on his yard next to Fairy, he seemed so composed and city."

"City?"

"Yes. City. A person or thing that's not 'country.' " Julia stared at him. "You aint from around here, are you?"

The man stood staring, puzzled, and Julia shrugged.

"Right in the middle of all his denials, right at the point where we were all starting to believe him, Arena comes walkin up out of the woods. From right over there." She pointed out the direction. "She'd been back by a creek, or something. Been there all afternoon, apparently. And boy, I tell you what, as soon as he saw her walkin up out of the woods, he went pale. Pale. That's when Silva started in. Knocked his sunglasses clean off his face for starters. Grabbed him by the tie and slapped him in the face, which brought Arena runnin up and howlin to his defense. Christ, you should a seen the girl. Running up in her sock feet from the woods. Yellin. Cryin. For a second or two I didn't know who was going to kill him, Fairy or Silva."

"Did you see Mr. Sheehand take the weapon to him? You sure it was him?"

She blinked her eyes. "It was him."

Julia looked down at her nails. Clean, but for dried-up blood and brain matter caught underneath.

"Fairy ducked down like maybe he was scratchin at a flea bite around his ankle, or worryin with a pants leg, somethin like that. When he came back up it was in his hand. My rasp. Stuck up under the truck seat the whole while, I guess. He took two steps until he was in front of the man and he drew it up over his head and brought it down hard. And the sound! Christ!" Julia rubbed her hands against her jeans. "Fairy hadn't the strength but for those two blows, but it was enough to break open his skull. The rest of what he'd done after those two blows hadn't taken strength, just insanity." Julia looked at her boots. "I saw him do it," she said in a whisper. "Lord, I've dehorned and castrated cows, put down a horse or two, but I never seen anythin like this." She looked up at the man who was finished with his note-taking. "I guess he's really done it this time. You'll have to take him away, won't you? I mean, there's no goin home and pickin up a set a clothes for this one, is there?"

There was silence between them, broken only by the chattering of Arena's teeth.

"I guess I need to go tell my sister," she said.

He put the notebook in his pocket and Julia was relieved. Huge gouts of flesh had been slung all over the yard and she was trying not to see them. The unattached nose had been found underneath the bed of the truck. That old, fat rude one had held it up in the air by a pen up a nostril and yelled out: "I'd say this one beat that dead baby in the fridge by a nose, wouldn't you?"

"Did the girl see this happen? Did Arena see the part that came afterward?"

"She's got eyes. She seen it."

"Well I sure hate that. A thing like this can scar a person . . . change them."

The girl was already in shock, obviously. Holding her hand stuck low to the dress pocket, she watched them with calm blue eyes that reminded him briefly of Sandra Dee's. She would look at Silva and then her father and then Julia over by the steps, finally, at the body covered in the sheet in the back of the ambulance. The man studied her—the very shape of her, clothing and all—and wondered where she'd gone to find an apple. The pocket of her dated dress was bulging with the size of it.

Julia looked across and studied her niece, caught a glimpse of something shiny and diamond-like in her pocket. She snorted through her nose in disbelief. Well I be damned. She stole that fuckin crystal lighter I seen in the living room! That's what she was doin inside the house while Silva was callin the police, and while her lover, minus most of his face, was bleedin to death out in the front yard. Stealin. Well, I'll be damned!

"I don't think you have to worry about her," Julia said to the detective. "I don't think there's much that's gonna change."

*　*　*

At the end of the dirt road, at the point where it split off into Autumn Road, Marion pulled up slow. Two police cars blocked the way, silent but for static bursts of radio talk, all their lights flashing, spinning out into the trees shards of indignant red and then blue and then red and then blue. A wobbly black man he recognized not by name, but by stiff-legged stance, made his way toward him. Once to the truck door he leaned in and said "You sholy don't wanna be goin down thataway, where them po-lease is. A smart man would turn right around and head in the other die-rection. You sholy don't want none of this . . ."

Marion, unfamiliar with the road and the people who lived on it, said, "How come?"

And the man told him.

CHAPTER 42

Johnny Roper stood before his bathroom mirror lathering up his face and thinking about things.

Annie's binding cloth was folded under his pillow where he could reach for it while he slept. The milk long gone. The yellowing stains pale proof of it. An old pair of shoes was on the walnut dresser, the sole of the right one two inches thicker than the sole of the left. He remembered how that two-inch height difference had made him feel like a man of importance for a few days at least. The preacher's handkerchief was next to the shoes, as well as a ribbon out of Annie's hair. He marveled at the procurement of these items and felt the need to pat himself on the back. The preacher had pressed the hanky to Annie's hand the night he left. Annie had laid it to her chair when she went back to her room. The ribbon had fallen out of her hair in the process. Johnny Roper had seen the opportunity and seized it, those years in the salvage business put to good use.

He finished shaving his face and rinsed the razor clean and put it in its case.

He saw the tableau when he walked into his bedroom to get the gun. The shoes. The hanky. A ribbon. A clotted paintbrush was there, too. Johnny had stolen it from out of Prox's kitchen once the man was buried. It was an apologetic type of thievery, though. A way to say he was sorry for having thought the man capable of murder. Johnny went to his bed and fetched out Annie's binding cloth and folded it gently and set it next to the other items. He wished he had a candle and that he still believed in worship. Had he those two elements within his possession, he would sing a song and strike a match and say a prayer or two. But devotion was gone from him. Like so many other things.

There was nothing of Rosie's on his altar save those things that had belonged to Annie. Rosie was there by proxy, so to speak, and Johnny could live with this. There was nothing of Aaron's there either, but this would soon be remedied. Johnny had a hankering for a faded wide-brimmed hat and he intended to have it. Aaron Class, sorry murderer that he was, would have no need of it after tonight, seeing how he was soon to lose his head.

Reaching under the bed, he felt the cold barrels of the gun and pulled it out. A gun could do the one thing a pair of shoes could not: make a short man feel bigger than he was. The box of red-cased shells was already on the bed and he dumped its contents, slid two shells into the chambers and two more into a shirt pocket, snapped the gun shut, the greasy click of it like music to his ears. He was not a man talented with weaponry, but felt that the long barrels of the shotgun put advantage on his side of the line. Tucking it under his arm, Johnny left the room without a backward glance. "I should a done this years ago," he said under his breath. "Should a seen to it sooner."

Aaron sat on his stone bench underneath a bough of wisteria and watched the sunset through the trees—that last play of red dropping down to earth in a color firelit and spectacular. The wind was up and building, sweeping loose debris around his legs, while he sat there wondering. Not about the too-warm season or the newest occupants to the street, but what that stretch of highway might look like out in Arizona. He had always hiked the minor roads because they seemed kinder and offered a wider expression of honesty, not to mention transportation. Truckers. Salesmen. The occasional hay farmer. The time he had left Yuma, he had drifted down to Somerton on the back of a flatbed pickup littered with ropes, and then traveled on to San Luis in a plush Cadillac the size of Brazil. A cowboy looking for a rodeo spoke highly of the Colorado River, the way it fed into the Gulf of California, how it was a site every living man should witness, and Aaron wished he had seen it. The wind brushed against the open map he held on his lap and he put down a hand to it, his finger resting on Flagstaff.

The red had gone now, the sky deepening to the color of the African violets, that deep purple hue that really wasn't purple, that bluish tint that really wasn't blue. The sky was a color somewhere in-between and transient, so temporal in nature, it defied naming. Aaron looked up into the heart of the trees and tried to figure mileage. That long traveling bone in his leg was beginning to itch and for the first time in over twenty years, he felt the need to scratch.

He could walk the Gulf Coast route. Maybe stop in on that bar in Bay St. Louis and see if anybody there might remember the boy who fell off a boat and lived to tell about it. And if nobody could, he'd not hold it against them. Time passes and people forget. It was this very thing that he was betting on. He could hang out a while and then go on to Baton Rouge and Lake Charles and Galveston. Once he had his fill of that, he'd head on over to San Antonio and then cut north meandering his way to Fort Stockton and Van Horn and El Paso. There was a fine Mexican eatery in Las Cruces he'd like to stop in on before heading west to Wilcox and Tucson...

"Well, now. Look at you," a voice said.

Aaron glanced up and saw the evening sun glinting off the twin barrels of a shotgun. Johnny Roper stood on the flagstone path hoisting a weapon that was nigh as long as the man was tall.

"Looks like ye're planning a trip," he said.

Aaron kept his hand on the map and eyed the make and model and judged it deadly, at least in the hands of a fool, and that was what he was seeing, a pure-d fool. "That's a mighty big toy you got there, John," he said.

"Oh, she's big all right. But she aint no toy." Johnny leaned down and wiped his sweaty face on the sleeve of his shirt. Once this was done he took one step forward and stopped, his feet next to the concrete urn. He nodded to Aaron and the spread open map, "Where you think ye're goin?"

"I aint goin nowhere. I'm just thinking about where I been, is all."

"Thinkin."

"That's what I said."

"Must be a lot a that goin around. I been doin some myself."

Aaron studied the man, trying to determine if he'd waited all these years to fall victim to drink. "Must be a hard thought for ye to be draggin out that gun." He could barely make his voice work. Not due to fear, but lack of use.

"Oh, it's a hard thought all right. I aint denyin that."

"You never was one to deny much a anythin. Not even the bounty a the lord."

"What'd you say?" The gun wobbled in the dusky light.

"I was rememberin somethin you said years back, is all. When that preacher come around."

"You can shut up about that."

"How come?"

" 'Cause I aint on trial here. You are."

"I aint on trial."

"You been on trial for years, you just too foolish to know it." Johnny leaned forward and peered at Aaron's face and swallowed hard. Holy God. The mass of scar tissue over the man's forehead was drooping over an eye. Another mass was sliding down his face, dripping off a chin. It seemed his face was melting.

"In your mind, maybe."

"Annie never was any good with a knife. Did you know that?"

"Whad'a'ya mean?"

"Think about it. That gal couldn't cut a tomater to save her life. And you want me to believe she cut her own throat? You done it, Aaron. Time to be a man and own up to it." Johnny's arms began to shake and he put his foot up on the urn and propped an elbow to his knee. "Now answer me this. Is there any reason on God's green earth I ort not kill you over it?"

"Hell, yes."

"What would that be?"

" 'Cause I didn't do it." Aaron stood to his feet and the wind picked up the map and plastered it across a rose bush.

"You hold still."

Aaron held up his hands, palms outward. "I aint movin, Johnny. Just standin."

"Well you keep it that way." He shifted on his feet, his hands slippery on the stock. "Now tell me."

"Tell you what?"

"Whether I should kill you or not. Course, I already got the answer to that and she's wearing twin loads and wantin to talk real bad. I'll give you a first go at it, though."

Aaron glanced over and saw a hump of dark wet dirt and thought, Well shit. I done wasted my time puttin out bulbs I'll not ever see sprout. He looked at Johnny, registered the wildness to his eyes as genuine and felt the first brush of fear. The night sweep was in and the trees were hardly trees anymore, just tall blurred shapes disappearing into black. The dirt road in front seemed a dark ribbon uncoiling until erased from the horizon.

"I thought for a long time that Henry done it. Now aint that a stupid thing? I should a knowed that poor fool didn't have it in him. But you sure do."

"John, you need to calm down a little."

"Calm down? Oh, I'm calm all right. It's this here gun that's growed nervous."

"You're wrong about this."

"Whad'a'ya think I am? Brainless? Of course you did it. You just thought time would pass and we'd git on with things and forget all about her. Even her mother over there's forgot."

"Rosie aint forgot."

"Oh, I think she has. Let one crippled child show up on the street and the woman turns her back on her own flesh and blood. I aint a idiot. I seen that cake she baked. Christ. You people make me sick."

"I didn't do it."

"Yes you did."

"Think about it. After we prayed that night, after you got all upset over droppin the baby on the floor, I was the one who walked back to Annie's bedroom and found her dead. What kind a killer would lead the way to his victim?"

"I don't know. Maybe you're a lot smarter than I give you credit for bein. Maybe you knew leadin us to her would make you look less guilty."

"You're wrong about this."

The worn map of Arizona broke free of the rose bush and flew off into the night and before he could stop himself, Aaron turned to see where it might have landed.

"What're you lookin at?"

"Just my map. It blowed away."

"Your map! You're worried over a map? Here's what I think a that." Johnny pulled the trigger. The flare from the muzzle of the gun lit up Johnny's face to the color of an October mum and Aaron fell to the ground, his mouth filling with dirt, while all around him latticework shattered and rained down. In the middle of all this, a child began to cry.

"Well, hell. I missed you. Got the map, though."

A hole had been blown through the trellis, and wisteria vines dangled about, shredded and ripped. Aaron rolled to his back and looked up at the skating clouds. More than one floated across the moon.

"Johnny, I didn't kill her," he said.

"If you didn't, who did?"

"I got my own idea."

"Well, why don't you share it with me before you die."

Aaron leaned his head up and looked at him. From a flat-on-the-back position, Johnny Roper actually appeared tall. "I think you did it and it's somethin you caint live with. Hell, maybe you don't even remember doin it."

"I ort to kill you right now for sayin such a lie! It was your knife what done it."

"I throwed that knife away. I never thought about it 'til they hauled me in. Now cut this out." Aaron began to crawl up on his knees.

"Hold it right there. This gun's beggin to shoot your legs off one at a time. It's all I can do to hold her back."

Aaron sat back on his haunches and studied his garden. "You know how hard it is to get a rose to stay alive here?" He climbed to his feet, brushed his hands off on his pants. Keep talking, he thought to himself. Just keep talking 'til you come up with a plan. "All this land used to be under-water and we're still payin' for it."

"I don't give a shit."

"I know you don't. I do, though. Caint say why I do, but I do. You plant a rose too close to a shrub or a tree and it'll die. You plant a rose in the wrong spot and miscalculate the passage of the sun, and it'll die. You put one down where the land don't drain, and it'll die."

"Maybe some things just don't want to live," Johnny said, moving until he stood directly in front of Aaron. "Where's your hat?"

Aaron looked at the man, sure he was crazed.

"You always wear one. Where's it at?"

"In there." Aaron nodded at his house.

Johnny stepped back a pace and tripped on a pot and the gun exploded, blowing Aaron's honeysuckled sun to smitherines. The child began to scream in earnest.

"Jesus, Johnny! Are you insane?"

"Not no more."

Johnny scrambled in his shirt pocket, brought out two more shells and reloaded. He was tired of playing, tired of everything, now that he thought on it.

A light came on across the street and they both heard the sound of Rosie's screen door opening and then banging shut.

"She don't need this," Aaron said. "Dammit, she don't need this. Not now."

"Don't you dare tell me what she don't need."

The curious sound a floor makes when kneeled upon sounded and both men turned to look.

"My brother learned his name today," the boy said quietly out the window of Henry Prox's house. "He's retarded and don't know much. But today he learned his name. He was sleepin real good, for a while there."

The clouds separated and Aaron could see the shape of the boy's head and the moonlight catching on the bridge of a nose and on those folded hands resting on the windowsill. From a spot farther back came the angry screaming of a frightened child.

"Billy Reuben stole his brains three days after he was born, but this afternoon he got some a them back. I just about give up on it, too." Hez disappeared from the window and they both heard the squeak of bed springs. When he showed back up again, there were two heads there, and the crying was closer but muffled against Hezekiah's shoulder.

"Christ," Aaron said quietly, spitting to the ground. "I think there's enough damaged goods around here. Don't you?" He looked at Johnny Roper when he said it.

Johnny was silent, his face a picture of torment. "Well shit then," Johnny said.

Aaron walked over to Johnny and gently removed the gun from his hand. There was no resistance. They stood there in the dark, two tired men who seemed undecided about the next course of action. "Go to bed, Hez. Go on to sleep," Aaron said.

"I was nearly 'bout there, 'til one a you decided to kill that garden. It's a shame too. Seein how my brother just learned to talk and all."

Rosie appeared in the alleyway between the two houses, stepping over pots and fighting her way through a veil of Spanish moss. Fed up with it, she reached up and tore it from the tree and seemed for a moment to want to strangle it in her bare hands. She threw the parasite to the ground and stood there, her hands on her hips. "Hezekiah?" she said.

"Yes ma'am?"

"You lay down on that bed and shush that baby."

"He don't shush easy."

"Then you better git started."

The two head shapes disappeared from Henry Prox's bedroom window. "Johnny?"

"Huh?"

"You never knew her and what she had in her heart. You remember this the next time you feel the urge to kill in her behalf," Rosie said.

"But—"

"I mean it." Rosie looked over at Aaron and there didn't seem to be a whole lot to say to that one so she peered up at the stars, the origin of her dream. *There they were right up there. Those angels who were spinning in circles over loblolly pine. The smaller one crippled, barely able to complete an orb. He had cried long and loud over his inabilities while the older angel led him in. "He needs cleanin, ma'am," the oldest had said. And Rosie had done this and smoothed down his gown. And there inside her kitchen with its black-and-white tiled floor, they had pardoned her....*

Two stars blinked out in quick succession and she sucked in a breath and put a hand over her large bosom. "I aint got the heart to lose again, boys," she said. "And if either of you taken it to mind to mess up this street again, then loan me that gun. I'll put you to the ground this very second."

And with that she turned and walked away while the two men watched.

CHAPTER 43

Now Marion Calhoun knew this much for sure: while God was rumored to have an excellent memory, even those with the best of memories can slip up every once in a while, and so, for formality's sake, he felt inclined to offer up a reminder.

He removed his hat from his head and put it to his lap while he drove through the dark and fashioned a prayer.

"I hope you aint insulted I'm remindin you a somethin that happened almost sixteen years back. A eye blink to you. A damn lifetime to me. You remember that time I stood out in the backest part a that backest field and shook my fist up at you? Well Lord God you a righteous judge and I aint denying it for a minute. I sold my land to a pure-d fool just so I could have a woman. And I blamed you for it instead of my own sorry self. But I tell you this much: if you will help me tell Hezekiah what up and took holt a his family, I will formally apologize. I will make it public, too. I will go one step farther than anybody in this region has ever gone. I will stand square in the center of Lucedale, next to that scratchin post everbody knows about and I will say this thing out loud. Me, Marion Calhoun, who knows he's a smart man in spite of doin stupid things. I will do this. But you got to help me first. You got to give me the words—no, you got to do one better'n that. You got to figure out a way to keep those two boys safe now that Fairy's bound to be gone for good. You make this thing okay and I will say I'm sorry. But if you aint got it in you to do it for me, if you got the bigger side of the universe to say howdy to, then all I got to say is you can go straight to hell along with the rest of us poor sons a bitches. Amen."

Marion Calhoun put his hat to his head and drove on, his black arm resting easy out the window of the truck. One more mile to go and he would be in Chalktown. Good thing, too, what with the way the dark had won. Again. Night was here and there werent a thing nobody could do about it, neither. Daylight gone. Et clean up.

"Just like the rest of us poor sons a bitches."

"I reckon the proper thing to do would be to check on her," Hezekiah said, his legs crossed at the ankles, rocking while supporting the weight of his brother on one heel.

Yellababy was draped over him, limp as a rag, immune to it.

Marion looked at those two sets of blue eyes and looked away, the porch light overly harsh against their skin.

They are both the same, he thought to himself. Both sweet and simple-stupid. One's just bigger is all.

"I think your ma aint the issue no more," Marion said. "They got your daddy over to the Hattiesburg lockup. He'll get a trial and then we'll know where things stand."

"He's gone for good, I just know it. You caint scrape a man's face off and not get put somewhere mighty fast. They might even fry his ass if he's not careful."

"Caint say. But, yes. They might do that." Marion looked away and across the yard.

"How come him to do it, Mayurn?" Hezekiah rocked, patient as summer. Yellababy's eyes would find the porch light; lose it; find it again; lose it.

Marion looked at him and shrugged. "Who knows why anybody does anything. I reckon you'll have to ask him."

"And Susan-Blair don't know yet?"

"Oh, I figure she knows. It happened two hours back. I guess everbody clean up to Collins knows by now. When I come to the crossroads, the police cars was headed back your way. I guess a whole passel of reporters werent too far behind, neither."

"Lord." Yellababy was reaching for his chin with a jerky hand attached to a stiff arm, fingers dodging around in the light like a drunk July fly.

"I aint never seen him do that before," Marion said.

"He's done a couple of things today he aint ever done before. It don't change the mess we're both in, though. Him learnin a new trick sure aint gonna change that."

Marion looked behind him into the house and saw the painted river flowing. He tried to remember the look of the man who had lived there. Henry Prox had leased out the land to him. More than once, too, but as far back as he stretched, Marion couldn't remember the man's eyes, or the turn of the mouth. "How come you to camp out tonight here in this place?"

"They said I could. Said I could stay for good should I want to. That is, if I keep the place up and work the field around back. And, oh yeah, go back to school."

"How come them to offer this thing?"

"I aint got a clue. But it's startin to sound like a good idea."

"Who'd watch your brother?"

"That one over there on that porch. That's Rosie. She's just itchin to get her hands on him. Bad as a durn fly the way she's hovered all day long."

Marion looked across the street and saw the woman sitting patiently in a chair on the porch; another one, a man, stood out on the porch of the house next to hers, smoking in the dark; foggy trails of gray drifting up and out before catching in the wind.

"This is a strange street, Mayurn." Hez wondered if he should mention how there was an assault on a garden with a shotgun forty-five minutes earlier, and decided he'd best keep his mouth shut. "A strange street."

"I guess."

"But where I come from is strange too."

Marion crossed his dark arms over his chest while he remembered how many rows there were to the land behind the blue house. What the profit had been, and there'd been a good amount of it, even after paying off the lease. Added to the parcel behind Susan-Blair's it just might mean a sizeable crop if cotton prices held and the country didn't go too crazy what with a Catholic president in place. He reached over and guided Yellababy's hand to Hezekiah's chin and listened to the five-year-old coo. "Maybe stayin here for a while aint so bad."

"That's what I was thinkin." Hez rocked his brother for a few minutes and then picked up Yellababy's long legs and laid them across Marion's knees like cordwood. "I bet she don't even miss us."

"You gonna miss her?"

"Probably not. Yellababy sure won't. I guess that's what's important. As long as she don't get the law to me and make me go back." Hez sighed like an old man. "Shit. It's been a long day. Caint believe it was just this morning I was standin there shootin the shit with you over by your fence."

Marion patted his shoulder and lifted Yellababy's legs off his knees so he could stand. "I'm tired, Hez."

"Me, too."

Marion watched the two adults across the road. When he stood to his feet, the woman stood up right along with him, her arms crossed over her broad stomach. "I'll check on things tonight and drive back over here to-morrow. Once I make a stop by the Lucedale scratchin post, that is." He shook his head, not cursing God this time, but his own silly vow. "Should Susan-Blair want to know about you, I'll explain it."

"She won't want to know."

"She might. You never can tell."

"Don't go dumb on me, Mayurn." He shook his brother. "I got all the dumb I can deal with."

Marion climbed into his truck and headed down the dirt street. In his rearview mirror he watched Hezekiah pick up his brother and stand on the porch for a second before going inside. The porch light went out and Marion put his hat to his head, done with Sheehand business, at least for the night.

He was already seeing that seven-foot scratching post in front of the Lucedale diner, as well as the one or two tourists who wandered off the pike once or twice a year, curious over it. He was already seeing himself standing in front of it while those tourists in rubber sandals pulled out their Brownie cameras and snapped pictures of his face to share with the folks back in Illinois or maybe Indiana. Marion snorted through his nose, "Well King Jesus, I guess you not only hold a grudge like nobody's business, but seems to me you love a good joke, same as everbody else."

CHAPTER 45

Rosie sang to the boy while she rocked, looking across Henry's yard, which was clipped and clean now, its chaos dealt with. It seemed a yard similar to everybody else's, now, plain and unobtrusive and sleepy in the heat. Prox's old living room with its iridescent river walls had a bed in its corner, a small bed with metal bars on its side and a crank at its foot that would elevate its head. Johnny Roper had salvaged it out of a hospital wing and set it up for them. Two of Rosie's quilts were spread in the other corner: a crawl palette for the boy. The river was still beautiful, but there was the flotsam of reality now standing in its corner and spread out on its floor. Aaron Class had finally fixed the old rocker for her and moved it over to Hezekiah's front porch and Rosie found herself able to sit outside with the child, rocking and thinking and rocking and thinking. The chair moved and creaked under her weight, groaning at the improvement.

"Them is Annie's wooden blocks out there on the ground," Rosie said while she kissed his sweet-smelling head. "I know you caint play with them yet, but you'll learn."

Yellababy went *blablablablaaayeelaa*, and reached for her chin. Rosie smiled while she worked his hands, those frozen atrophied muscles and tendons resistant, but beginning to melt.

The day was too warm for June. A day when fieldwork had to be done before noon because of the heat. Like hot breath, wind brushed against Rosie's face while she rocked and listened to the sound of crickets and cicadas: their hot white noise started low and then washed up in a scream before it ebbed back out again, in tune with the Mississippi heat.

Aaron had reworked Henry's yard and grass was growing again: dark green St. Augustine, sprigged and spreading. The same could not be said for his own place, though. That palatial back garden of his was wild with overgrowth and in need of pruning, and he'd never bothered to repair those areas damaged by the gun. The man had just let things go. "I'm givin it its head," he'd said before clamping down his mouth on the explanation. Rosie had seen him with those maps in his hands and knew this was the reason. It was only a matter of time before he left them. She looked across to her place.

In basic ways it was the same but for the missing chalkboards. Rosie's had been the first to go. Aaron Class had followed her example inside a week, not with acceptance, but resignation. Johnny Roper's was the last, a clear indicator of his stubbornness. The baby bed he'd salvaged from the hospital wing and then deposited in Hezekiah's living room had been his kiss of peace. His board came down that same afternoon. Rosie sighed. Happy in spite of the noisy summer heat.

Cathy was swinging on the tire swing Aaron had put up in the large oak. She would pull on the rope and stick her legs out and sail across the yard like a plane. Her deep purple obloid shadow stretching and warping across the two houses.

Rosie smiled, remarking to herself how the girl seemed a lot like Annie. Acted like Annie had acted during a brief season before womanhood tapped her on the shoulder.

As she swung on the tire swing, her head thrown back, her shirtail dragging in the dirt, the girl's ponytail harvested the light and gleamed like gold.

Summer was full in and the gnats never wearied of bothering Yellababy's eyes. Rosie's fingers moved constantly, fanning his face with a paper fan. "Cathy, take them some lemonade," she said. "I made it up fresh and it's sitting on my kitchen counter. You know where the jars are at." Rosie nodded with her head toward the back field. "They been out there since six this morning."

"Yes ma'am," Cathy said, hopping off and heading across the road. Rosie smiled while she studied the girl's long, tan legs. She'd need some talking to, come the next few months about how short them shorts were getting. As well as a few words about them cropped midriff blouses creeping up to her boob-line. Rosie knew the signs. She'd lived through it all before. Yellababy stirred and she looked down into clear blue eyes and thought she saw forgiveness and acceptance, wide-open as the sun.

The tractor was running back toward the far plat where the giant magnolias stood side by side with the pecans. There would be a summer season of high fragrance while autumn nuts grew inside a shelled womb. She smiled while she listened to the sound of farming. The Negro was a good man, a hard worker, a man who brought balance to Hezekiah, a boy who'd grown up wild as Prox's painted-up river. Yellababy found her chin and her fat fingers held his other hand, working his stiff wrist while the constant drone of the tractor sounded across from her.

"You're a sweet angel," she told him while she rocked and fanned away the gnats. "And I thank you again for forgivin me—"

Cathy came out the door with a bang, two huge Mason jars full of lemonade in her hands. She wiped her face with a shoulder while she tramped across the field in her shorts and tennis shoes. Rosie watched her disappear to a shape the size of a thimble.

"Annie stopped talkin first, you know," Rosie said to Yellababy. "Didn't talk none past that first day, not even when I went to the bedroom and shook her hard and tried to make her listen. I be durn if I didn't try. There she was, layin there with leaky breasts. I was talkin to her night and day, too. The others didn't know it. They thought I'd shut up just like her, but who in their right mind could shut up with so much goin on that needed talkin about? Lord, I couldn't keep quiet. I told her, too. Told her it was foolish and said how we needed to git on with things. But she'd not have it. Just laid there with it. Swollen and horrible. Most horrible thing I ever seen. Her layin there trying to feed it. Give it to me, I says. But she wouldn't. I didn't mean it though. Just meant to scare her with it. To make her see reason. To see how she was usin them words of the preacher even though she didn't no more believe them than I did. I just meant to scare her. Lordy, but she wouldn't have it. And Johnny, silly man, I guess he thought werent but him and Prox who was havin trouble sleepin. That me, the mother of one and grandmother of the other, could lay down her head and sleep at night. That only a man would be curious about what another man was doin out wanderin around in the middle of the dark.

"But I found it, I tell you. I surely did. Found it the very night he buried it. But I didn't mean to use it, I swear it. Just meant to scare her a little and make her see reason. But she wouldn't do it." Rosie stroked Yel-lababy's head, noticed that his eyes were watching her, wide open and fear-less, the reflection of clouds skating across his irises.

"I didn't mean to do it though. Just wanted some rest is all. Just wanted to git on with things. Just meant to scare her. But Annie aint never scared easy. Not even when she was little. So I took it and put it to her throat and said, This thing has got to end, child. I'm your mama and I love you but this thing is an abomination in the eyes of the Lord. But she still wouldn't listen. Just heaved herself up and into it and then I tripped on the durn hooked rug and fell and it slid over, slicing. I didn't mean to, though. Just meant to scare her with it."

Cathy was tramping back across the field, the Mason jars empty. Rosie knew she'd swing on the tire swing a few more minutes and then she'd watch and wait for the boy to come out of the field and then once he'd walked her to the end of the road, she'd head on home. Rosie sighed, almost sleepy in the heat. The girl was sweet, in spite of showing too much leg. Rosie heard the flat sound of a tractor horn and looked up and waved. The Negro was driving the tractor while Hez walked along at his side, a hoe in his hand. Their shapes larger now, their faces almost readable. The harmony almost as breathable as the sweet breath off a magnolia.

"I thank you for forgivin me," Rosie said while she rocked the child, sleeping now, the clouds, as well as the confession, hidden behind his eyelids.

"Because I surely didn't mean to kill her. I meant to scare her is all. I surely never meant nobody no harm."

CHAPTER 46

Susan-Blair sat outside on the splintered steps and waited for her sister. It was the fourth week of her clearance sale and even though she lived on a dirt road in the middle of nowhere, business was good, thanks to the murder trial. Fairy's old bus was full of the half-priced items. She'd painted over an old holy yoke with the words "Fire Sale" and propped it on the hood and half the county had come to see, even some folks from as far away as Jackson. A man had drifted up from New Orleans and photographed the bus and then sent the picture in to the newspaper. Woman Holds Pre-Electrocution Sale, was what he put underneath it in the way of caption and she supposed some thought it witty or comical. Whatever they thought was of no concern to her because the words translated to cold, hard cash. The very next day she was flooded with visitors and even though the verdict was not yet in, everybody wanted a piece of her, or him, or if not the two of them, then at least that thing that had happened. She sold out by noon. The box of broken hula girls being the last to go. Susan-Blair spent most of the night loading the bus again but with more expensive things this time.

She looked around, pleased. All the shoes were out on the picnic table in front of the house, sizes tied together by their laces, or taped together with bands of brown freezer tape. A table holding not-so-bent cookware and odd pieces of glassware was set next to the table of shoes and it seemed to her frame of mind that she just about had the bases covered, as far as life's necessities were concerned. The pricier things were still inside where she'd not have to move them or cover them up with plastic at the end of the day.

She heard a noise and turned, saw the brown dust cloud down at Beachum's and knew it was Julia. It would just be the two of them. Or the three, if you counted Christ. The colored man next door had left early, as usual, before the geese had even stirred. The noise of his tractor waking her up, reminding her instantly of Jesus, who neither slumbered nor slept, who was up already and staring at her from the watermarked ceiling.

"Now you leave me alone. I've had enough of you already," she told him. Seeing his eyes blink in sad confusion before he went back to his staring full-time. "You mind your business and I'll mind mine," she said, tired of fighting.

The truck pulled up with a sweep of loose gravel and Susan-Blair looked at her watch. Nine o'clock. The first wave of buyers had already come and gone. In by seven-thirty. Done by eight. There would be a second wave at ten, which meant that by noon she'd be done with customers until four-thirty or five. People shopped around their crops and she knew it, and wondered if that three-dollar business man from over in Lucedale had ever done a survey on the habits of the rural poor. "They see their husbands off and then they come with their cheap purses and piddle around and poke through things. And then, right before lunchtime, that second wave comes and hurries through before their men come in out of the field...."

"Who you talkin to Susie?" Julia stood there in a faded-blue work shirt, her boots regular and plain. Those highly decorated ones put away somewhere. Susan-Blair wondered for a split second if she might be interested in selling them.

"Nobody. Just myself, I guess."

She moved over so her sister could sit beside her and for a minute there was nothing between them, just silence. Oh, she'll open up that mouth of hers and ruin it. I just know it. Too much goin on here not to burp up a comment or two. Susan-Blair caught the fabric of her dress between her fingers and rubbed while she waited, soothed momentarily.

"Seems like Fairy's bus has come to good use," Julia said, staring at it. She saw the piled-high clutter while she remembered the man's nautical Spartanism that had felt so clean and economical.

"Seems like." Susan-Blair had made thirty dollars off it the first day. "I told Hezekiah he could have it, but he didn't want it. Said it would crowd that street he lives on."

"Hez," Julia said, shaking her head.

"I think parkin it right there in the shade and fillin it up was a stroke of genius, myself."

"You do, do you?"

"Yes ma'am I do. Christ don't seem to mind it a bit, either."

Susan-Blair stretched out her legs and Julia saw she was wearing white patent-leather heels. She needed to take a razor to her legs, though. Spiky hairs crowded her ankles. Julia looked away, embarrassed for her and more than a little scared that her sister was communicating daily with a long-dead Jewish rabbi.

The geese wandered up. Avoided the two women, though, headed instead to their new roost spot under the bus. Once there they peeped out from behind the wide tires, their necks snaking together like the writhing hair of Medusa.

"J.P. don't believe in Jesus, or God," Julia said.

"Who?"

"J. P. McCreel. You know who I'm talkin 'bout, don't you? Runs the gravel pit. He lost his son underneath that gravel pile." Julia's voice was soft and cautious.

"I remember that. Hez talked about it for a month. The nigger next door helped to dig them out, if I remember correctly."

"Yes. Well, J. P. don't believe in God."

"He's got a dead son, though. Seems to me God won that hand of poker."

Julia looked at her sister's dress: a box-necked sailor-type affair. There was a brown stain on its square linen collar.

"J. P. loves Emerson. Loves the idea of transcendentalism." There was a pause. "That's a form of philosophy that—"

"Julia, you're givin me a headache. I don't want to talk about a man who will die unredeemed. And I know you think you're in love, but you better give some thought to your eternal destiny. Love aint worth throwin that away. No ma'am, it aint." Susan-Blair looked around. She had a couple of hours to herself before the next flood of visitors came through and there were things she needed to tend to. Primarily hike the price on some of her merchandise. The Japanese lamps with the pagoda shades wore tags that were too low and she knew it now. Not optimistic enough. What she had was too valuable, even for dirt road people. Time to start thinkin like I'm not from around here. Time to start thinkin like maybe I'm from Jackson. Even Christ seemed to agree with her.

"I was just wonderin if you wanted to read some a his books. Or maybe come over for supper and visit with us." J. P. was surprisingly adept at getting to the root of a problem.

"No."

"Susie—"

"Look, Julia. I know you think I'm crazy. That I'm just one step away from bein stuck inside one of those institution places, but I'm not."

"Most people don't believe that Jesus is hangin around watchin their every move—"

"Who's to say what a person believes. Or should believe. Or should not believe." Susan-Blair turned to her and stared, "Am I hurtin anybody?"

Not now, Julia wanted to say. Not now that the boys are away from here and you can't get your hands on that younger one. Julia put her hands around her knees and studied the yard. It was a good thing too, that Arena was away in beauty school up in Jackson. Free the house and life of children and clutter, who knew what might happen?

"Do you know what I feel like, Julia?" Susan-Blair was still watching her, her eyes strong and not darting around for once.

"What?"

"I feel like a closet. I always have. A durn closet full a somebody else's coats. Coats put there by people who went on to someplace else, some other thing."

"A closet," Julia said.

"That's right. A closet. Daddy left his coat there inside me. Ma left hers. That preacher come through and pulled off his—"

"A closet."

"That's what I said. A cluttered closet. And you know what the worst thing is?"

"I'm afraid to guess."

"There's not one single thing hangin in it that belongs to me."

Julia looked at her sister and reasoned it twisted, but true; an evaluation that J. P. would probably consider fitting. What people believe is put there early on, and she knew this. Put there long before they can judge for themselves the truth of a thing. As hard to get rid of as fingerprints. Looking away, Julia noticed that the geese were sleeping under the bus, their heads stuck beneath their wings as though embarrassed.

*   *   *

The four of them were sitting there in the middle of a Saturday afternoon, not thinking about change, but how to avoid thinking on change, seeing how the town was crammed full of it. The green wrought iron cut into their backsides and drove their thoughts to ice cream, or maybe crochet, what with the new dressed-up feminine look to the square. There were even three or four pigeons trucked in from Mobile, some swore, that scavenged for hulls at noontime and shit on the new sidewalk from their lamp post perch. The Ladies of the Eastern Star were setting up their sidewalk bake sale next to the new wrought-iron fence caging an outraged statue of General Lee, his shoulders pigeon shat and decorated in white. To raise money for a fountain, was what the women claimed. White paper tablecloths pinioned by pound cakes were raging war with the wind, flapping like sails.

"Damnedest thing I ever seen, I tell you that much," Johnson said, noticing Julia's boots were different ones. Those fancy Hollywood, or maybe East Texas, two-tones gone for the time being. Plain brown scuffed leather was on her feet these days, mud-covered with worn-down heels indicating hard work. She'd given up those rodeo shirts, too. Wore plain faded chambray now. Not exactly the same as everybody else's. Just the same as J. P. McCreel's. Next to him, Jim sat, spitting with more accuracy these days. The wooden flower boxes were as stained as the wooden gallery used to be and it was somewhat of a comfort.

Johnson continued: "That nigger stood right over there by that scratchin post and apologized to God almighty. Me and the wife sittin inside havin ourselves a slice a apple pie, mindin our own business." Johnson didn't bother adding that his wife had had herself a conversion as a result of the nigger's heaven-bound appeasement. That she had sat there listening through the open window, that bite of pie still to her mouth, before jumping suddenly to her feet like one shot and rushing to the car where she sat and wept. Johnson didn't bother adding this since it wasn't cow- or horse- or death-related. Unless, of course, you count the death of his peace and quiet and consistent backsliding, since those things had surely died, and not at the hand of a farrier tool either. He looked quickly at Julia. And then he looked away and across at the women setting up shop, fighting with the wind.

Jim was there, sitting next to the man who was married to the woman whose legs he had borrowed, the one who'd taken back those legs to herself and given them to her rightful husband seeing how she had recently found Jesus. "Durn town looks like a ice cream parlor," he said irritably, watching the women.

"We're still country, though," Johnson said. "Caint milk a dead cow no matter how hard you squeeze. They can doll it up for all it's worth, it won't change the fact that we're still country."

"We aint gonna be for long if the durn women have their way with it. No offense, Julia."

"None taken." She leaned her elbows to her knees and watched J. P. McCreel, the two of them blushing simultaneously when their eyes made contact. Jim noticed and swore under his breath, remembering how he used to blush, too. And how those blushing days were over now that Johnson's wife had unwrapped those legs from around his head and embraced Jesus Christ, instead. Well, shit then.

"What's a nigger got to apologize to God for?" Jim asked, put-out and cranky.

"Who knows? Why'nt you go ask him," J. P. said matter of factly while he winked at Julia.

Jim just stared at the women, who were losing their battle with the wind.

"All I heard him do was tell God he was sorry," Johnson said, looking at his watch, remembering that tomorrow was the Sabbath and instead of watching a baseball game on his black-and-white Philco he'd be down to the Baptist Church watching a man sweat and pace and shout about hell.

"Well, speakin of what's sorry, how's Parchman Prison treatin your brother-in-law?" Jim directed the question to Julia.

"He's dyin. Won't be long now," she said while she wiped her hands on her jeans.

"Save the state a Mississippi some money at least. Maybe even git back some change," Jim snickered.

"Speakin of change, and I aint talkin money here, Jim, somebody told me things had changed for you. One thing in particular. Folks say you got yourself a brand-new routine. One that don't include a noonday trip down Sweet River Road." Julia didn't smile, just made her lips slash a little while J. P. McCreel snorted through his nose.

Jim stammered for a new direction. "Damn sorry to hear about Fairy, Julia. I meant no offense."

"Why, none taken, Jim," Julia said.

Johnson, who had the feeling he'd missed out on something, fished back over the conversation and found it blameless. Poor luck then. And a failure to concentrate, as his wife liked to point out to him over supper. "Somebody ort to go and tell them gals this aint Memphis, just Lucedale," he said. "And if that aint good enough, then somebody ort to tell them there aint a thing a man hates more than ruffles on underpants. They don't never end up anywhere but on the floor no how."

Julia and J. P. McCreel howled while Jim looked uncomfortable. "I think you should hush before one a them hears you," he said. There hadn't been a new one yet, but he never could tell when another Eastern Star lady might show a keen interest in the slow tide of his flirtation.

They moved on to crop prices then, and Julia leaned forward slightly, her hands between her legs, with the appearance of listening. J. P knew she wasn't, that she was really somewhere else in her mind, probably with her sister. The men talked cotton and corn and soybeans, with one or two speculations concerning Kennedy and the Cold War, which raised his eyebrows. He'd not thought either one of those hayseed mud clumpers capable of an awareness that escaped the natural boundary of the Leaf River. Bored with it, he watched Julia.

The rearward view is the best, but not the cheapest, he realized. Remembering the encumbrance of family and their devious ability to sidetrack his intentions. First Fairy, of course. Then the boys moving into that house down the road; Hezekiah setting up what came pretty durn close to resembling a co-op. Then Arena runnin away up to Jackson. Then finally, poor Susan-Blair, who grew crazier every day. Enough nuisance to last a lifetime, he figured, and then he smiled, glad of it. Time was on the downside of his gravel heap now and the rearward view was the best in his opinion. Enough of the past to talk with her about for at least the next twenty years. And come next weekend I'll drive her up to Parchman so she can keep the death watch. Fairy would not live another month and everybody in the near south knew it. But I'll drive her anyhow, just so she can see for herself. Just so she can tell him about those boys of his and give him some measure of peace.

A woman out in the square howled when the wind took a cake and sacrificed it to the ground. Jim stood up, stretched long and hard. "I caint sit here and watch them wrestle with it. I hate what they're doin, but a gentleman has his duty, I reckon." He headed for the square, his hat mashed down to his head.

"It aint duty he's thinkin on," Julia said and J. P. McCreel nodded his head.

The street was quiet then. The awning over the barbershop flapped in the breeze while the two men and one woman sat on wrought-iron benches wondering if the season would be kind, and still, and cooperative for once.

CHAPTER

Parchman would be a terrible place to live, but it was as good a place to die as any other, Fairy decided.

The Negroes took to it. The whites never did. Some ran (and were caught); some sliced through the Achilles tendon and hobbled themselves (and still had to work); some staged mass strikes that didn't do a durn thing but git them beat and stood atop barrels underneath a blazing hot Mississippi sun (most went insane).

Hand a white man a hoe and watch his face, he liked to tell Julia when she visited. Just watch what happens to his face once he realizes the truth of the Civil War.

Fairy, you've gone to philosophyin, Julia would say.

Well, you don't know what's it like, he would say right back to her. You aint got a clue what bein near death does to a man. This is a fine place to die, he told her. As good a place as any other.

Because they left him alone.

Not just because he had removed a man's face with a hoof rasp, either.

That was surely bad enough and more than a few commented on it and acted like they wanted to steer clear of him on account of it, but he knew his crime wasn't the primary reason trustees and gunmen alike let him be. They left him alone because he was a man who was dying and a man who was dying was like the dropped and broken mirror of a bride on her wedding day, or the burning cross out in the yard of a liberal city councilman. A man dying would likely take his secrets with him, as well as the secrets of others. Who could predict the influence of a dying man on the Great Judge? So they stayed away from him, and Fairy was glad.

Exempt from working the fields since he could barely put on his shoes without help, he got to push the magazine cart around instead. The squeaking, off-balanced wheels announced the small, stoop-shouldered man in prison stripes. A man the color of a late autumn squash with a ballooning torso that made one wonder if he'd swallowed a watermelon whole. The prison stripes rode over his belly like pavement up a hill and the warden, who considered himself the father of the place and therefore the sole namer of his children, called him Yellahill Fairy because of it. And while Fairy pushed the cart he marveled at the sound of it and how it had the ring of a child's story to it, and how he'd managed his life so far outside the margin of a child's innocence, he had landed in a spot as far from a child's story as a man could be. He was not without his comforts though. The pushing of the magazine cart was just one of them.

The weekend previous when she'd come up bearing pictures of the boys, Julia had told him she'd hired out a second lawyer. One who was doing busywork based on the inhuman treatment of a desperately ill man, and at first Fairy was alarmed; distressed even. But then he settled and took one more long look at the reality of his station and realized he'd not live long enough to hear word of it landing on some judge's desk.

He was dying and he was glad of it because if he had to spend the rest of his natural life inside such a place as Parchman being called Yellahill Fairy he would surely go mad. So he pushed his cart and counted his days and kept his mind on trivialities. Time was not one of them. Time was constant as a river and beyond his thoughts.

He'd wake each morning surprised he was still to the cot, smelling his shoes, which were set to the side of his bed. And then he'd rise and wait for roll call and he'd answer and then wait for his breakfast: a biscuit and a dollop of honey. Once done, while the largest majority of the inmates were out to the fields, he'd be shuffling to the library, ready to begin his rounds.

Most in isolation wanted the *Saturday Evening Post* with its Rockwell pictures to the front and he tried to oblige.

Those waiting for their turn in the Hot Seat wanted *Life* magazine, which Fairy found amusing.

Two or three always wanted a world atlas, and he knew they were dreaming of escape.

Only one person wanted the Bible.

That one, a tall man as skinny as Fairy, would always reach through the bars for the brown King James and then say, Much obliged.

When reading time was done, Fairy would make his second pass and King James would go on the pile and that would be the end of it. At least this was the way it had happened in the past.

"Much obliged," the man said.

"No problem," Fairy said and moved on, tired, counting the minutes until he could go to the infirmary and get his pills and, once that was done, get off his feet. There would come a time he'd go to the infirmary and not ever leave and he knew it: his own personal Get Out of Jail Free card clutched in his hand. He held this card to his chest, his heart pounding while he felt such a genuine truckload of pity and fear for all the others, he came close to crying. Day in and day out he watched them shuffle off, an anonymous herd of failure, all those black-and-white striped uniforms corralled between the bosses, unwinding nine-foot cotton sacks behind them like row after row of failed parachutes.

"The Revelation is missin," the man called out behind him.

Fairy turned back, saw that bony wrist dangling out between the bars, the brown cardboard King James extended.

Moving to the other end of the cart in avoidance of turning it, he headed back, passing two cells of sleeping inmates, one with the mumps, the other with a butchered scrotum.

Fairy had heard about the preacher. Knew the guards thought he was a nutcase. The man appeared disease and injury-free and Fairy figured he had been put to a cell for not shutting up his great big mouth when told to.

"The Revelation is missin out'n it."

"That so?"

"The whole of the scriptures is what I'm wantin. Not one jot nor tittle should be removed from it, accordin to God."

Fairy waited, staring at the man between the bars.

There was a strange glimmer of familiarity to his nose, the sheer drop-off of it. It sat on his face like a ski jump or maybe a tan banana. He was sure he had seen it before. And the man's eyes were wide and blue, somewhat faded now, and creased at their corners, but the way they were thickly lashed reminded Fairy of somebody he'd seen at some point in his life.

"I'd be much obliged to you if you'd check for anothern."

Fairy sighed and fumbled at the cart and moved the *Posts* and *Readers Digests* and *National Geographics* around. Finally, under a worn-out copy of *Huckleberry Finn*, he found another one. A Gideon loaner. The back cover was missing, but all the pages seemed intact.

"Here you go."

"Much obliged."

"How 'bout you make sure you got the durn book you want so I don't have to turn around again," Fairy said. "My pills are waitin."

And that infirmary bed where they would draw his blood and count whatever teeny-weeny things they had to count in order to give him a tally of time left. Yesterday the orderly said maybe a month. The day before the mean one had said six months while he grinned.

Both were wrong. Fairy knew by feeling the hard lump of a thing that used to be his liver he would be handing over his Get Out of Jail Free card in little more than two weeks.

"What kind a pills you takin?"

The man was patiently holding the Gideon book to his chest. His long fingers cupping its edges like he really believed it was precious.

"My cancer pills." Fairy leaned on the cart. Tired. Worn slap out at only ten in the morning.

"There's a scripture verse inside this here Bible that says 'I know thy works: behold I have set before thee an open door and no man can shut it for thou hast a little strength and hast kept my word and hast not denied my name.' Revelation chapter three, verse eight."

"If you knew the durn Revelation book, how come you to make me turn around and bring you anothern?"

"Because His ways is not my ways."

"Well, He aint got the cancer. Last I heard."

The man was silent and peaceful as a frog on a water plant.

"Folks say you're a preacher," Fairy said, finally.

"Yessir. I got the call when I was but six years old."

Fairy stood watching him, glancing once or twice to the cell where he had a cross hanging on the wall. Not a cross with a corpse on it like the Catholics used, but a bare and empty cross, stark and hard with a look of cattle brand to it. "You want somethin else a me, or can I go?" The man looked to be about his age. Forty-five. But healthy, and therefore doomed.

"What kind a cancer you got?"

"Ever kind there is, I imagine." Fairy thought the man's eyes were the mirror image of his youngest boy's. Of all his offsprings, only Yellababy's eyes were wide apart and cornflower blue.

"What they doin for you?"

"Nothin much. Give me a dose of the radiation. That was it."

"If I told you the good Lord wanted me to pray over you, would you allow it?"

"It depends. What you in here for?"

"Murder."

"Who was it you murdered?"

The man paused and looked to his feet before looking up. "Myself, mostly."

"Then I reckon I'd allow it."

The man made a gathering motion with his hand and because the place was empty of guards, and the two other prisoners were asleep, Fairy obeyed. It was easier to let the crazies do what they wanted with you than to fight, he figured. Argumenting always being hardset against his nature. Even before the cancer.

"Rabbbasataaeeleonolabassa," the man prayed, one hand clasped around

Fairy's frail one, the other hand up in the air, the Bible missing its back held high. The foreign-sounding syllables continued for a good two minutes. Fairy tried to pick apart phrases and place them to some localized region and failed at it. And then before he could jerk away, the man opened his eyes and proclaimed his own interpretation:

"For the Lord God Amighty has seen your sufferin and been made to cry over it. Even as the Christ wept over Lazarus, the Lord God Amighty weeps for you. I will *heal* him then, He told the angels, for My eyes cast to and fro across the earth seekin my children who are sufferin. I will *heal* him of his infirmity and make him whole again and he will walk out that Lazarus cave of cancer and proclaim my glory to all the world—!"

"No sir. I aint wantin any of it. Take it back," Fairy tried to yank free of the man and couldn't.

The man looked at him. Removing his hand from off Fairy's arm, he pulled the Bible to his chest again and stood tall as a steeple.

Rubbing at his wrist, a wrist strangely warm, Fairy felt a sneaky sidling heat begin to move through his shoulder where it spread upward to his neck. I got a lump there, he remembered. I got a big lump behind my ear and should I put my hand to it and feel it gone, I will scream like a struck-down woman. He could feel his heart pounding in his throat.

"You are healed," the preacher said with calm assurance.

"No sir. I aint interested. I only got me a few more days. Besides, I have to believe in a thing for it to happen and they aint no way I believe."

"That aint true."

"How come it aint true?" Fairy's voice ended on a high pitch.

"How could dead Lazarus believe?" the man asked.

And Fairy stumbled at the man's sound reasoning; knew that should he reach up and feel for that knot behind his ear, it would be gone. Panicked, he stammered, then yelled: "That was Christ doin them miracles! You aint him!" Heat was moving down his chest in a wave of betrayal.

"Whatsoever you ask in My name believin, you shall have. Greater works than these shall you do. Christ said that to his disciples before he got took up to heaven from the Mount of Transfigeration. You are healed mister. Now thank the good Lord." The man started to turn away, toward his cot.

"How come it don't matter what I want?" His liver felt hot. Heated up with a fire poke or some type of heavenly blowtorch. Cooking me a new one, apparently. Burning up my Get Out of Jail Free Card in the process. "How come what I just said don't matter! That don't seem right—!"

"'Cause them is not my words, but His," the preacher said, folding his hands together at the waist, light falling to them as though they were anointed.

ACKNOWLEDGMENTS

There are several individuals who were essential to the writing of *Chalktown*. I continue to be in their debt, and consider this indebtedness a great joy. Wendy Weil, my wonderful agent and friend, for her enthusiasm and sound advice, as well as her uncanny ability to understand my part of the South. Martha Levin, my publisher, who embraced this novel wholeheartedly and with great confidence. Sally Arteseros, my editor, who kept me steered toward center and whose guidance and generous advice significantly improved *Chalktown*'s final appearance. I would like to thank David M. Oshinsky for his remarkable book *"Worse Than Slavery": Parchman Farm and the Ordeal of Jim Crow Justice*. Bob and Mary Gerhardt, you talked me through the business of farming and climate and large-animal care with marvelous patience and good humor. Your friendship is one of my most cherished ideals. Emily Forland, who began this journey for me with her persistent belief in my words. Daughters Kristin, Spring, and Shiloh, who were waiting at the end of each writing day, and never grumbled over that shut office door, or that unreturned phone call. Thank you, from a mother's heart. My friend Traci deLorges for sitting up nights reading on my behalf, and for spending those hours on the phone assuaging nameless fears. My parents, Richard and Patricia Braswell, you gave me, perhaps, the greatest of all gifts: the freedom to be myself. And finally, my husband, Ray, for taking my writing seriously before I did, and for still believing.

Melinda Haynes grew up in Hattiesburg, Mississippi. A painter for most of her life, she now writes full-time from her home in Mobile, Alabama, where she lives with her husband, Ray.